The Viridian Dream
What Blooms After the Storm, Book One
Leah Frog

Copyright © 2024 by Leah Frog

All rights reserved.

No part of this publication may be reproduced, distributed, or transmitted in any form or by any means, including photocopying, recording, or other electronic or mechanical methods, without the prior written permission of the publisher, except as permitted by U.S. copyright law. For permission requests, contact Leah Frog at www.leahfrog.com.

The story, all names, characters, and incidents portrayed in this production are fictitious. No identification with actual persons (living or deceased), places, buildings, and products is intended or should be inferred.

Book Cover by Leah Frog

Illustrations by Leah Frog, Aiole Sauce

First serialized on www.leahfrog.com, 2024

To those of us who struggle to fit in, who yearn to authentically be who we are without judgment, and who long to find others like us. I see you.

Contents

A Note About Triggering Topics   VII
Map of the Reprised Shores   VIII
1. The Life Walker   1
2. The Cursed Baby   16
3. The Message   31
4. Rowan Spicer   43
5. Routines   56
6. Petrichor   74
7. The Nova   89
8. The Taste of Blackberries   101
9. No Good Choices   114
10. Conflictions   126
11. The Viridian Curse   143
12. Friends with the Sky   156
13. Quality Time   167
14. Speculations   180
15. The Right Choice   194
16. Who Deserves Kindness   207

17.	Nova, the Friend	218
18.	Unwitting Betrayal	233
19.	The Tempest	250
20.	The Last Viridian	267
21.	Answers	284
22.	Duplicity	298
23.	To a Better Tomorrow	312
Epilogue		329
Acknowledgements		335
About the Author		336
Content Warnings		337

A Note About Triggering Topics

This story contains the following potentially triggering topics:

- War
- Death
- Famine/hunger
- Violence/injury
- Graphic descriptions of gore or decomposition
- PTSD
- Depression/panic attacks
- Bullying/abuse

For those who wish to be aware of which chapters contain what, refer to the Content Warnings section at the end of the book for a list of chapters and their sensitive topics.

The Reprised Shores

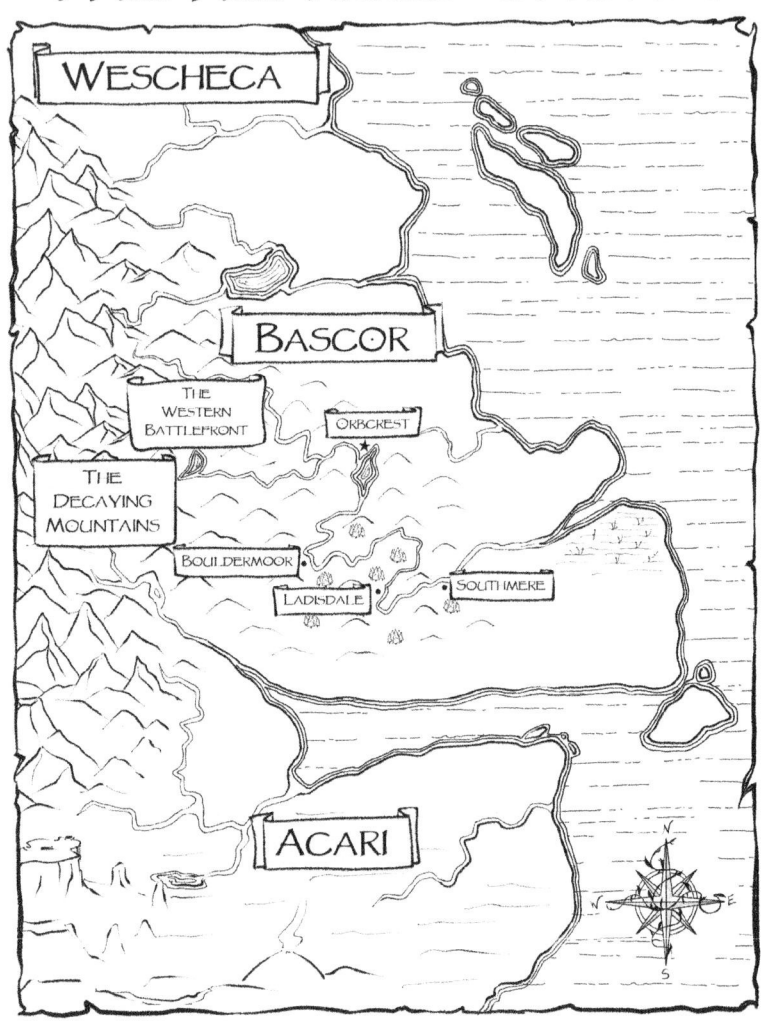

Chapter 1

The Life Walker

The sound of footsteps moving through leaves and underbrush felt far too loud, like the uncomfortable whispers of gossipers upon entering the room. Each crack of a twig was an accusation, and each rustle of grass was comparable to judgmental eyes from corners of the forest.

Sorrel Spicer clenched her jaw, pushing a branch out of the way as she moved through the rich woods nestled in the rolling hills of southern Bascor. Leaves grabbed her dress as she moved, twigs tugging at the periwinkle cotton as if to tell her to slow down, to stop. Instead, she made a frustrated noise, bunching the end of her skirt in one hand so she could move unhindered.

The trees provided some shelter from the late afternoon sun, but no reprieve came from the humidity in the air. It clung to her skin, uncomfortable and unwanted, making her curly, auburn hair stick to her neck. Sorrel only half noticed, far too focused on things more important than the unpleasant heat of late summer. She knew her father was waiting for her to come home, but she wasn't *ready* to come home yet.

And yet...all she wanted was to *be* home. She wanted the touch of mossy stones under her feet. She wanted the smell of herbs drying from the rafters and of potions brewing over the hearth. She wanted the taste and comfort of *home,* of the apple trees and the wild mint that grew around the cottage.

She wanted to hug her father and tell him how much it hurt. She wanted him to hug her back and tell her she would be okay. Tears burned her eyes, salty as her sweat, and she angrily wiped her freckled face with the end of her skirt, removing as much of both as she could.

Sorrel had tried so *hard*. She had tried, and tried, and *tried.* For twelve months, she had given it her all, and what did she have to show for it?

A ruined marriage, a hopeless future, and her heart broken.

She didn't stop the tears this time, letting them blur her vision as they swept away her anger, allowing hopelessness to seep in. The one thing she wanted most she couldn't have, and now she felt like nothing would be right again.

Eventually, the woods parted and Sorrel found herself at the edge of a small glade with a bubbling brook. She came to a stop, her breath labored from a combination of her emotions and the heavy air, rather than the walk itself.

She wasn't sure how far away from the path she had veered, but it was a fleeting thought as she tried to place exactly where she was. The brook should have been the same one that fed into the river behind her family's house, but the clearing itself was unfamiliar.

For starters, the trees were all covered in flowering vines that hung down like a great curtain around the glade. Thick, plush moss carpeted the ground around the stream, and butterflies danced across the wildflowers poking up from the earth. It was beautiful, but the way everything was organized felt almost... deliberate.

Brow furrowed, Sorrel stepped into the glade, looking around as she let her fingers drag over the flaky bark of a birch tree. Overhead, birds chirped and chittered loudly, and across the brook, a rabbit spooked and darted off into the underbrush. The scent of flowers was strong, mixing with the humidity in the air and clinging to her like a layer of sweat.

Never in her seventeen years of life had she seen anything like this in these hills, and the exotic view scattered many of her spiraling thoughts.

The view also made her completely miss for the first few seconds that she was not alone.

When Sorrel realized, she froze, eyes falling to the man across the glade. He sat with his back against a tree, one leg drawn up and a hand resting on the back of a deer tucked into the moss beside him. While the deer was as still as could be, the man himself regarded Sorrel with no small amount of scrutiny, his fingers lightly petting the creature beside him.

He was... *striking* in appearance, with long, wavy hair that draped over his shoulders and pooled in his lap. It was loose and dark, dotted with small flowers without a pattern. His viridian eyes looked almost like they glowed under the dappled sunlight, brilliant enough that she could see them from across the clearing.

He wore unusual clothes in shades of green, loose and thin. His shirt was open in the front, showing off a collection of necklaces made of wooden beads and dried seeds. Strangely, he was barefoot, toes curling into the moss at his feet. And most unusual of all, perhaps, was the birthmark on the inside of his forearm. Sorrel's eyes fell on it as he petted the deer, and honestly, it looked like burl wood painted on his skin.

He seemed unbothered by her sudden intrusion, although he tilted his head to regard her curiously. The movement snapped her out of her daze, and she swallowed, realizing she was alone in the woods with a strange man staring at her *intently*. Nervously, she took a step back, blindly reaching for the tree behind her.

"Ah, watch for the—"

She tripped, shrieking as she fell back onto the forest floor. The sound sent birds scattering, and the deer beside the man scrambled to its feet and took off, leaving them more alone than before. She winced, looking down at the root that had caught against her heel before her eyes flicked back up to the man. He hummed thoughtfully, gaze still on her.

"How curious," he started carefully, tapping a finger against his chin. "You announced your presence so loudly, and yet now that I have perceived you, you seem frightened. Do you want attention, or do you not?"

"What?" The word left her mouth before she fully processed what he said, but even after his words caught up with her, the question remained the same.

He gestured around him. "It is as I said. You stomp through the woods with emotions even the trees can feel. You wanted your feelings known, and the forest heard you well. However, the moment you realized your company was more than trees, you closed up, like a moonflower touched by morning dew."

He chuckled, tapping a finger to his bottom lip thoughtfully. "I find it so funny how so many treat the forest as if it does not listen."

Sorrel pushed herself to her feet, bracing her hand against the tree as she pursed her lips. "I didn't think someone would be out here. I'm sorry for disturbing you. I–I'll be taking my leave now."

"How does one take a leave?" he asked sincerely, giving her a confused look. "I do not understand. Please explain."

Sorrel stared at him, brow furrowing. Truth be told, he spoke strangely with an accent she couldn't place. While he seemed articulate, the formality and choice of words made it feel as though this was not his native language or that he came from aristocracy. Honestly, she wasn't sure which, but most people of influence didn't sit in forest glades barefoot and petting deer.

They probably also understood the phrase 'taking my leave.'

Despite herself, Sorrel replied, "It means to say 'goodbye.'"

He tilted his head again in a manner very animal-like. It was disarming, in a way, because his words and mannerisms carried almost a childlike curiosity, especially with the way he furrowed his brow like she had told him something asinine.

"Well," he replied, shaking his head, "I do not understand why you would not simply say 'goodbye', but I suppose it does not matter. Do you truly wish to make such a grandiose entrance, then immediately announce your departure?"

"I don't understand," Sorrel replied, huffing. She was tired and miserable, and she came out here to be *alone* with her feelings, not have some stranger prod at them. "I didn't think anyone would *be* out here."

"Why not?" He glanced around, eyes skimming over the flowering canopy draping around them. "Is it not a good place to be?"

Sorrel exhaled harshly out her nose, frustration seeping in to mingle with every other emotion simmering inside her. She could have directed it at him, given how he prodded at her already thin patience. However, she swallowed those feelings, letting them sit in her gut instead.

Truthfully, as much as she wanted to admit it was because she tried to be a kind and gracious person, the reality was that she understood the potential danger she was in. She was alone in the woods with a man who didn't act quite *right*, and she was far enough from the road to know no one would hear her scream.

And yet, instead of walling off completely or letting fear overtake her, her face simply contorted into one of emotional anguish as tears once again gathered in her eyes.

"I just wanted to be alone so no one could see me cry," she replied sadly, leaning against the tree beside her. She looked away from him, staring forlornly at everything and nothing at once.

"I do not understand the privacy of such a matter, but perhaps that is a shortcoming of what I am. Would it make those heavy emotions of yours go away if you hide your crying?"

The question was... strange, and Sorrel slowly looked up at him, giving it thought. "It... no. It doesn't make things better. But people seeing me in such a state would make it worse."

"They do not sound like good people then," he said thoughtfully, reaching up to touch the ends of a wisteria cluster hanging above his head as if admiring its beauty. "I do not understand what good it does to surround oneself with people who you must hide from."

He paused, blinking, then chuckled. "And yet, here I am, hiding myself in a similar way. What is the word used for this? 'Irony', yes?"

"And what do you have to hide from?" Sorrel found herself asking, although she felt a touch embarrassed by the accusation in her tone.

He smiled slightly, but it wasn't a happy smile. "Many things. People are unkind, as we both know. They make rash decisions and unfair judgments without regard to those they may harm, especially now with the undead army pressing against your borders."

Sorrel shuddered at the mention of the undead coming from the west and the reminder of how they were slowly encroaching upon Bascor's territory under the command of the dragons. Once upon a time, the Bascori people worshiped dragons as gods. That time had long since passed. Not wanting to dwell on it, she returned her attention to his explanation.

"And walking these lands used to be of no consequence to me, but now it poses great risk. My brethren are persecuted by someone I once considered a brother. His followers chase us every time we leave the safety of our home."

"Then why do you leave?" Sorrel asked quietly, turning to face him. As much as she wanted to sit, the ground was damp and uninviting, and standing made her feel like she had some control here. So she remained standing.

"I have a job to do," he said firmly, "and I must do it no matter the cost."

Sorrel fell silent, unsure of what to say to that. He seemed unwilling to give details, and she wasn't going to press, but it made her feel... small.

Of course, that wasn't a hard feat, given so many things felt monumental when compared to her personal troubles.

"I think that is enough about my plight, for talking about it shall not mend it," the man said after a moment, tucking a lock of hair behind his ear. Idly, Sorrel noted he had wooden earrings with flowers dangling from the lobes. "I would like to know what makes your emotions so loud but also makes you need to hide them from prying eyes."

Sorrel shrunk in on herself, her own reality being drawn back from where it had been lurking. She pursed her lips, brows pinching together as she wrapped her arms around herself, not from cold, but from discomfort.

She wanted to be alone. She wanted to cry in the solitude of the forest, to drown in her misery and anguish without the background of hushed whispers and prying eyes. She wanted to pretend, for just a few minutes, that she was a child once again, and that she was allowed to have big feelings and fall apart without repercussions.

Something in her gave, and Sorrel sighed, running a hand through her sweat-damp hair. It clung to her fingers as if trying to comfort her, but really, she only found it a nuisance.

"I... am barren."

The three words sounded so *loud*, like booming thunder in the still of the night. She bit back a sob, speaking a truth that she knew intimately but did not want to acknowledge.

"I have been trying for a year." Slowly, she sank back down to the ground, damp soil forgotten and fingers fisting into the fabric of her skirts. "I saw healers. I tried every concoction I knew how to make. Nothing worked. I would have kept trying, but my husband did not want a wife who could not produce children. Our marriage has been annulled at his request."

Sorrel swallowed, staring down at the water tumbling over the stones of the brook. "I suppose love is conditional for some. I didn't think of myself as so disposable, and yet I see that the love he had for me had a price, one of which I couldn't meet."

She smiled bitterly, tears clinging to her eyelashes. "Right now I can't even be angry at my former husband because I have also lost love for myself. I dreamed of motherhood, of raising children. I wanted a house full of giggles and laughter, to grow old and see my children's children come into the world. And I know now that is not meant to be."

She took in a shuddered breath, the sound stuttering over the noise of the bubbling stream. "The healers told me that perhaps the fates had chosen to spare me from raising a child during a war with the dragons, but I cannot accept that. What do the fates know? What does anyone know? Now I have this hole in my heart that can never be filled!"

She pressed her hands to her lips, eyes squeezing closed as the tears left searing streaks down her cheeks. Now that the words had been uttered aloud, she couldn't stop the emotions from tumbling out. They spilled out of her like a torrential downpour, filling the glade between them.

It only got worse as she realized that she had just spilled such personal information to a stranger—a *man*—who certainly could not understand her plight. Men did not have these problems, nor did they care unless it involved their own families. And yet, she had just laid out her most intimate secrets to some strange man in the woods who spoke like he wasn't even *human*.

That realization, new and sudden, invaded and interrupted her despair because it was both utterly ridiculous and, yet... She couldn't shake the feeling that it had some *truth* to it.

The Reprised Shores had many things, from great dragons that wielded powerful magic to Salamander people who lived in the caves in the south. There were even the Otherkin, tricksters that disguised themselves as humans. And while Sorrel had never met anything otherworldly before, she understood that they existed and that they could be anywhere.

Her crying slowed from sobs to hiccups as she tried to balance her anguish with her growing apprehension. Wiping her face, Sorrel opened her eyes, only to yelp at finding the man was now crouched in front of her, hands on his knees, and his hair draped over his shoulders like a wavy silk cape.

Instinctively, she leaned back, fear gripping her as she realized there was *nothing* she could do.

"I see," he said quietly, brows pinching together as he studied her like he could see *through* her. It made her skin crawl, but she could only really feel how her heart was pounding in her chest. "Those emotions are quite justified. Your mind and your body are not in harmony. That is sad, and I am sorry. However, I think I can help you."

She choked out a noise of surprise, coughing and hitting her chest with a fist. It took her a moment before she replied, "What is *that* supposed to mean?"

He hummed thoughtfully, expression smoothing over into something mild, if not serene. "I can give you a child if that is your wish. My magic makes it so."

Sorrel's mouth fell open, her fear replaced by incredulity as he regarded her like he had simply requested she join him for tea instead of propositioning her.

"Your— What, are you a healer? Are you—" She stopped, sucking in a breath through her teeth as her eyes flashed angrily. "Is this a *joke* to you?"

He blinked owlishly at her, looking taken aback at the heat in her tone. "It is not a joke. Did I say something funny?"

"I have gone to *countless* healers who failed! I have taken tinctures that did nothing and elixirs that only made me ill! Why should I believe a random man in the woods can succeed where all of that failed?"

He smiled slightly in the face of her anger. "Because my magic is life itself. Human healers cannot compare."

She narrowed her eyes at him, disbelief rampant on her features. "Oh? What are you, then?"

She realized as she said it that she had dared him to reveal himself. Perhaps he was an eccentric magus, although she had never heard of the arcane being able to cure infertility. But really, she suspected he was tricking her, and she wanted him to prove her *wrong*.

The man before her inclined his head, regarding her critically, as if assessing her. With a deep inhale, viridian fire erupted from his eyes, painting his face and hair in a brilliant emerald sheen. The tree above them shivered, its bounty of leaves doubling and flower blossoms sprouting like it was the beginning of spring and not late summer. Small petals of pale pink fluttered down, landing in her hair and lap, like a delicate snowfall.

Flowers erupted at their feet in pale colors and low to the forest floor, tickling her ankles where she sat. Their scent filled the air, cloyingly sweet in the summer heat, and their sudden appearance sucked the moisture out of the soil, turning the unpleasant muddy ground into something far more inviting, almost like sitting in a sunny field instead of deep in a forest thicket.

And finally, he lifted a hand and stretched out a finger, smiling as a finch flew down from the trees to land on it, tweeting softly like he posed no threat.

Sorrel sucked in a surprised breath, staring at him, and despite the fact nothing else changed in his appearance, she suddenly felt like he was much, *much* larger than he appeared.

"I am Osier the Life Walker," he said, his voice now carrying a thrum of magic that made goosebumps erupt across her skin, "and there is not another living creature who knows life better than me."

Sorrel swallowed nervously, recognizing that whatever stood before her was definitely not a human man, despite his appearance. Even if she wasn't a magus, she knew enough to realize this was the kind of magic that humans couldn't touch.

No human could bend life the way he just did, but no *human* could give her a child.

Here he was, dangling hope in front of her, and despite her absolute terror that she was about to make a mistake, Sorrel foolishly and recklessly took that bait.

"You can give me a child? A baby of my own?" No matter how much her voice quivered, it couldn't hide the desperate *hope*.

He nodded slowly and held out his hand. She stared at his palm, smooth and fair like he had never seen a day of labor in his life.

She wanted a baby. Consequences be damned.

She placed her hand in his, then gasped as he pulled her close and into an embrace. He wrapped his arms around her, tucking her head under his chin as his hair fell around her like a wavy curtain. The silk of his clothes dragged smoothly against her skin like no fabric she had ever touched.

She waited, expecting more to follow. For him to lay her on her back, or tell her to undress. Instead, a ring of brilliant green fire erupted around them, making her shriek in surprise. It gave off no heat, and the flames that engulfed her felt soothing, like a warm bath after a long work day. It left a taste on her tongue like spring flowers and sun-ripened berries, soft and sweet.

They stayed like that, wrapped in a fire that didn't burn and him holding her like her husband never had. And even if she understood there was no *love* here, she had to wonder if this was what love was *supposed* to feel like. To be held without judgment, softly, and with kindness. These were things she didn't recall having with her marriage, but she supposed that was why few talked about marriage and love going hand in hand.

And when he pulled away and she found her belly round with life and a crown of flowers decorating her hair, she realized that, no, this wasn't what love felt like, but she didn't *care*.

She was pregnant. *She was pregnant.*

She pressed a hand to her stomach in disbelief, feeling the taut skin through her dress, stretched to hold the life that now existed in her once barren womb. It took her forever to find her voice in the mixture of jumbled thoughts running through her head. When she did, it was hardly eloquent. "You really... You really gave me a child."

He nodded again, expression mild like he hadn't just performed a miracle. "It is as I said. No one knows life better than me."

Sorrel shook her head, trembling hands still holding her stomach. Finally, she looked at him, and asked, "Is there a cost? What do you want in return?"

He smiled at her, baring his teeth in a way that felt animalistic. "Love him and protect him, for he will be special. That is my request."

Special...

Sorrel swallowed at the potential implications of such a statement, feeling every muscle in her body tense as anxiety blossomed inside of her, settling in right next to her unborn child. She opened her mouth to speak, but he turned his head sharply as if sensing something in the distance. His nostrils flared, eyes glowing a soft, enchanting green, and his face contorted into one of trepidation. Whatever had his attention was *frightening*.

"I must leave now." He stood smoothly, eyes still trained on whatever was in the distance. "Do not speak of meeting me today or what has transpired. I shall return soon, then we may speak again."

The unspoken 'it is not safe' hung in the air between them as loud as the pounding in her heart.

Without another word, Osier the Life Walker fled, leaving behind a trail of footprints filled with dandelions and leaving Sorrel alone in the glade.

An hour later, Sorrel stood at the bottom of the flagstone stairs that led to the cottage she grew up in. The steps had recently been cleared of moss, and the flowers on the bank behind them looked on fire in the setting sun.

The thick ivy that always clung to the stone walls had been trimmed back, and the waterwheel moved as slowly as always, squeaking and groaning as water poured over it into the basin that led down to the river.

Smoke curled up from the chimney, bringing with it the scent of bread, and Sorrel felt her eyes water as she took in everything that was her home. But as much as she felt relief, she also still felt trepidation.

By now, she realized the gravity of what she had done. She had what she wanted, but at what *cost?*

She wondered as she glanced down at her belly, how she was supposed to keep quiet on such a thing. He wanted her to tell no one, but who would believe her anyway? A barren woman with an annulled marriage now months heavy with a child? And... was whatever growing inside of her even human?

She swallowed thickly, thinking back to what was said. *"Love him and protect him, for he will be special."*

She didn't know what 'special' meant, and that frightened her.

Sorrel sighed uneasily and ascended the steps, painfully aware of her foolishness and fearing how she would pay for it. For now, she would just avoid town and... well, there was no hiding this from her father.

It was as she reached the top of the stairs and looked out at the sun setting over the hilly fields that a brilliant green light erupted across the sky. It painted the sunset in shades of viridian and gold before falling to coat everything in soft, glittering mist.

She could tell by the way it tasted on her tongue and brushed against her skin that it was Osier's magic, and she had to wonder what he had done.

But later, when flowers wilted and crops failed, and Osier had not returned, Sorrel wondered less what he had *done*, and more what had been done to *him*.

Something had happened.

By the time she was ready to give birth less than two months later, all of the Reprised Shores had fallen into gray, from coast to coast. The harvests began to fail, livestock starving soon after, and the natural flora in the forests beyond slowly wilted. Very little bloomed and nothing thrived, and everyone began to suffer.

They called it the Great Wither, but Sorrel silently called it the death of the Life Walker.

Chapter 2
The Cursed Baby

Archmagus Avelore Amantius had seen a great many things in his one hundred and eighty-seven years of life, and he could confidently say he was done with *all of it.* Every damn species had problems, and those problems had snowballed into *bigger* problems, and now the problems wouldn't leave him alone. He lamented his youth, when magic was a mystical thing that humans could barely wield, undead armies didn't exist, and dragons abided by their prescribed order.

Alas, much had changed in the last century and a half, and now the world was in literal shambles.

He scowled at nothing in particular, pale eyes doing a broad sweep from underneath the hood of his cloak, scrutinizing the hills on either side of him. It was late in the day, with the setting sun casting dark shadows on the rocky, barren hills. It'd been several years since Avelore had been in southern Bascor, but his memory still served him well.

He could remember the way the land was covered in flowering shrubs and hardy grasses. Small groves of trees would cluster in the valleys, and livestock would graze the hillsides. And along the roads would have been shrines dedicated to the dragons, keepers of the Reprised Shores. Now, none of that remained.

The shrines had long been destroyed, most completely gone or reduced to piles of rubble, save a few. That, of course, happened some time ago, when the world thought the dragons turned on them.

His eyes fell on one such shrine by the crossroads as he passed. Although the statue was in three pieces, enough detail remained for him to recognize the clubbed tail and winged forelimbs. Given how many quarries and mines were in the region, it was no surprise the shrine was in the visage of a Bronze dragon, the keepers of the earth. They would have been sighted the most, once upon a time. And given how many of the Bronze clan had been turned, it was no surprise the shrine was destroyed, either.

Avelore sighed, looking away to scan the scenery, which was even more depressing. The patchy grass that should have been a luscious green appeared more like a faded sage. Hardly any flowers were in bloom despite it being the cusp of autumn, and the leaves on the trees were thinner than they should be, hanging sadly like they knew the cause for their dismal appearance. And to think this area was faring better than the rest of the land.

He *tsked* softly, aged fingers tightening on the gnarled wood of his walking staff. It wasn't just the poor state of the flora, but also the near absence of the fauna. Nary a birdsong could be heard and there was a considerable lack of insects. Rumors had it that wildlife attacks had also increased, primarily inland, as hungry predators struggled to find their usual game. The most common story was wolves and cougars targeting children and livestock. Avelore pursed his thin lips together, the action making the age lines on his face more pronounced.

The Great Wither, they called it. It was a suitable name, really, though the human race certainly didn't understand it. Their grasp on magic outside of the arcane was fairly shaky, given how elusive most dragons were, even before the war. All they knew was that two months ago, everything started fading like the very life was sapped out of the land. Some thought it was the dragons' doing but for malicious reasons. None understood it was the death of a clan.

Everyone saw the sky light up in green that fateful evening two months ago, but few knew what it meant. The display of Viridian magic that could be seen all across the Reprised Shores made it loud and clear that Osier the Life Walker, the last of the Viridian clan, had died.

But, at the very least... It meant Osier had *died*. He had not been turned, and while things were not ever going to be the same again, they could have been arguably worse.

Nature was suffering but not dead. Truthfully, Avelore was surprised by this. The entire Viridian clan was gone, and yet... their magic still lingered in the world, stagnant like a pool of still water. There was now nothing to move it forward, but that it still existed would have to be good enough.

Of course, he had to hope that humans wouldn't drive themselves mad in panic. Already, the looming promise of food shortages had sent many people spiraling. Trade had dwindled and market prices were rising to exorbitant levels. People with power were hoarding what they could, and small towns and villages were beginning to struggle.

Some countries had devolved into civil unrest, fighting amongst themselves for supplies. There wasn't much that could be done to stop it though, because each country was also dealing with the invading undead army. That was probably also the biggest reason countries weren't fighting each other right now.

Despite this, some areas were faring better than others. The coastlines were far less affected by the Great Wither, as sea life was thriving.

Viridian magic did not lord over the waters, and with the Cerulean clan retaining healthy numbers, fishing and other foods from the sea were sustainable. Truthfully, the Cerulean clan shouldn't have segregated from the other clans to live in the sea, but it worked. For now.

But the real, strange exception to the Great Wither was the hills of southern Bascor. Here, things were not quite as bleak. Here, the occasional flower bloomed and the stray insect buzzed. Fields still carried modest crops, and wildlife could still be found if one knew where to look. It was like the Viridian magic was still moving, albeit at a crawl.

This exception was one that Avelore did not quite have answers for, and this was why he had been slowly making his way from town to town to try to piece together why Viridian magic had not gone fully stagnant here.

He had some theories. For one, the origin of the green explosion came from this general direction. These hills were where Osier died. Likely the sheer amount of magic he released had seeped into the land and was still lingering in the wake of his death.

But that wouldn't have explained why every expecting mother in southern Bascor had her pregnancy expedited. Rumors traveled across the land that women were having healthy, full-term babies months early. Certainly, the Viridian clan were life-bringers in every sense of the word, but why would Osier's magic manifest like this? This was not passive Viridian magic. This was purposeful, and something had happened before Osier died to make him do this. A part of Avelore wondered if this phenomenon was also what led to Osier's downfall.

The first three towns Avelore passed through didn't give him much in the way of answers. None of the infants were born premature or abnormal, and the women soon to give birth looked healthy and hadn't encountered anything unusual. Their bellies simply... *grew* on the day of the green explosion.

Now, Avelore found himself entering the next town, Ladisdale. It was much like the others in size and presence. The town was built on a hill, with its towers and buildings jutting up like rocky outcrops. It had the usual public service buildings and in recent years erected a defensive wall as the presence of undead increased. And like the other towns, it had also faded in vibrance, its rooftop gardens faded, and surrounding orchards wilted.

Avelore approached the gates, dressed in a concealing cloak of dark indigo and nondescript robes in shades of gray. The guards paid him little mind, not that he expected anything else. They were trained to look out for shambling wights and approaching dragons, not magi. Not that he was a threat, but he couldn't say that for every arcane user out there.

By now, Avelore knew the best approach was to go up to the healer houses and find out if any new or expecting mothers had interesting stories to tell. With this phenomenon of expedited pregnancies, women were not birthing at home, which made his task easier. Of course, getting people to talk was still a challenge, as not many women wanted to open up to strange, old men of unidentifiable origins and a lack of bedside manner.

Fortunately, he'd only been run out of one town so far.

With a weary sigh, he approached Ladisdale's small hospital, climbing up the wide, stone steps that led inside. It was quite tiny, but considering the town had one at all was impressive. Normally only the big cities of Bascor had them, but the closest major city was a considerable distance away.

It was just as he stepped inside and looked around that a nurse rushed in through the hall, her face void of color and her eyes dilated in panic.

"It's a curse! The baby is cursed!"

Panic broke out as patients and medical staff both scrambled, while Avelore pursed his lips. Another cursed child? Before the Great Wither, this was nearly unheard of, but now it seemed that more than one idiot thought the best way to counter the various supply shortages was to just curse the next generation from being given a chance.

Fools, all of them, though admittedly, he hadn't expected to see it here where things were still affected by Osier's magic—

His eyes fell to the nurse who had made the declaration and he felt every vein in his body freeze at seeing what she was pulling off of her.

Mushrooms. *Growing on her clothes.*

Growth.

Adrenaline coursed through him as he pushed his way through the crowd, trying to find out which room and what kind of curse. However, no one was willing to move out of the way, and after only managing to push past one or two people in the crowded foyer, Avelore snarled out an expletive and snapped his staff against the floor.

A brilliant flash of golden light cut through the mob's panic, forcing everyone to turn and look at him as he pushed his hood off of his head. The fabric fell to show his wizened features, from his bald head to his long, white beard. And most importantly, the ornate diadem he normally kept hidden, proof that he was recognized across the Reprised Shores as an archmagus.

Which, of course, he was; he was one of the founders of the Arcane Academy over a century ago, not that they would know his face. The important part was that they recognized *what* he was, not *who* he was.

"Enough!"

His voice boomed across the room, enforced by his magic, and everyone around him came to a startled stop. With a tone far less demanding, he nodded towards the nurse. "Show me the child."

She shook her head, pulling fungus off of her clothes, then snapped a shaky hand down the hall. "Third room on the right. I'm not going back in there until that baby is gone."

"Harsh response for being attacked by mushrooms," Avelore replied dryly. "Very well. Step aside and let me pass."

Despite his age, he moved swiftly, fueled by the promise of what the 'curse' really was. Could it be? Could Osier really have—

He stepped into the room, and his eyes blew open wide at the scene before him. Mushrooms crawled up the walls, and thorny vines had wrapped around the cart of medical supplies, digging at the floor around it.

The woman on the bed in the middle of the room looked as pale as the nurse, sweat on her brow and eyes dilated. In her arms was a swaddled form that she cradled protectively against her chest as she rocked back and forth like she was a step away from hysterics. She seemed to not care that there were mushrooms on her robe or that a hairy root had wrapped around her leg. No, her attention was on her new baby, her expression both fearful and uncertain.

Her eyes flitted up to Avelore and he saw that fear switch to protection. "Don't you get near my child! He's not cursed!"

Avelore exhaled slowly and carefully, then stepped inside, hugging the wall. With the hook end of his staff, he pulled the door closed, out of the way of prying eyes who'd not yet been scared off by the promise of a 'curse.'

Oh, but this wasn't a curse. If Avelore's suspicions were correct, this was *hope*.

Making a broad sweep of his staff, he pulled magic in from around him, pops of golden light forming like soap bubbles in the air as golden lines raced down the length of his staff. With a soft *'ting,'* that magic spread out, creating a barrier that lined the walls of the room, trapping them both inside.

The woman pulled back, drawing her knees up, and she gave him a fierce look that promised she would fight if he tried anything. He admired that, truly, but he was the best ally she had right now.

"This is not to trap us in, but to keep everyone else out," he explained, moving his staff back into both hands as he placed the tip firmly on the ground. "No one needs to hear what I'm about to say except you, and no one except me should hear how you respond."

"My baby is not cursed," the woman repeated in a heated hiss, though Avelore suspected she was trying to convince herself, judging by the fear in her eyes.

Avelore nodded, brows lifting high on his head. "Yes, I know. I'd rather say your baby is quite special. But do *you* know that?"

She went still, and while the defensive posture didn't change, the look in her eyes did. "What do you know?"

Ah. So she did know something.

Avelore pursed his lips, fingers drumming against the lacquered wood of his staff. Each tap caused the golden lines etched into the wood to pulse softly. "Let me guess: your baby has some questionable features, including a mark on its arm?"

Her eyes widened, which was all the proof he needed, but he waited patiently nonetheless. After a moment, she gave him a terse nod and carefully pulled back the fabric her infant was swaddled in.

There, in the blankets, was a tiny little thing, red-faced and sleeping. It looked mostly like a human infant but with a head full of green curls and two small, wooden knobs sticking out of its crown. And there, on its tiny, chubby arm, was a wooden spiral, like the knot of an old tree. The mark glowed a soft, enchanting viridian as the growth continued to sprawl around them and push against the edges of Avelore's barrier.

For the first time in what felt like ages, Avelore found himself smiling. "Osier, you damned idiot."

At the uttering of his name, the woman snapped her head up, round eyes focused on Avelore. "You— you know him?"

Avelore blinked in surprise. "He told you his name? That's surprising."

"I mean... he gave me— He's my child's... father..." the woman replied, fumbling over her words.

"I know what I said," Avelore replied wryly. "Osier was a great many things, but being well-versed in social norms was not one of them."

"He— he said my baby would be special, but..." the woman trailed off, wincing slightly as the roots around her leg tightened. "Is— is this really a curse? What have I given birth to?"

Avelore sighed sympathetically. This woman had no idea what Osier was, and now she feared she had been given a cursed child. And yet... she still protectively held onto the infant, hopeful that she was wrong. He could work with that.

"May I approach?" Avelore asked, nodding towards her. "We should calm the magic before it hurts you or your baby."

"Don't hurt him," the woman whispered, looking up at him with pleading eyes. "Please don't hurt my child."

"I have no intentions of causing him harm," Avelore replied, lifting a hand as he focused his magic. Golden ribbons scattered out from him, zipping towards the baby and wrapping around the mark on its arm. The moment the golden light covered green, the roots and vines loosened, and the growth around them ceased.

"Now, Miss..."

There was a beat where the woman didn't immediately answer, eyes still on the golden light as if double-checking to ensure her baby was unharmed. Then, she blinked and shook her head. "S-Sorrel. Sorrel Spicer."

"Miss Spicer," Avelore paused until she looked up at him, "your baby is not cursed, this I can assure you. Your baby is a gift. But I am afraid we need to let the town believe your baby is cursed."

Miss Spicer snapped her head up, mouth opening to protest, but Avelore cracked the end of his staff against the floor sharply, preemptively cutting her off. "The green explosion two months ago was Osier's death, Miss Spicer. And for a being as powerful as Osier to die, it means someone equally as powerful killed him. That same someone will also come for your child."

The young mother froze, color draining from her face. "W-what?"

Avelore sighed. "I see Osier gave his name but not much else. Do you know what he was?"

"N-no... he— he said he was being hunted, and he gave me his name and a title... 'the Life Walker'. He showed me how he could just make nature bend to his will. I just... I wanted a baby." She bit down on her lip, her expression indicating she was trying not to cry. "It's all I wanted, and he said that he could give me that when everything else failed."

Well, that explains how she got herself into this mess, Avelore thought wryly. "Well, he certainly did. You are now the mother of a very special child, and that makes you both a target."

"I don't understand," Miss Spicer said fearfully, with a voice pitifully small. "What makes him special? Does he have Osier's magic?"

Avelore shook his head. "The more you know before I can ensure your safety, the more dangerous it is for you. There are people who can use magic to force you to speak, and I daresay you're not trained to handle attacks of the arcane, no?"

Her mouth fell open, clearly horrified at the idea of someone using magic on her in such a way. "N-no, I'm not a magus. I, um, I'm an apothecary. I studied potions."

"Admirable, but very few elixirs out there will aid you right now. So instead, we must keep you in the dark, and we must hide the truth about your baby. Only temporarily, until I can come back with those who can protect you."

Miss Spicer bowed her head, tears sliding down her cheeks. "I don't want anything to happen to my baby. My Rowan."

"Nor do I, Miss. Your child is the best news I've seen in two months, if not longer. Now I know why Osier's magic is riddled all throughout southern Bascor, pushing expecting mothers to term. He was trying to expedite... Rowan's birth."

Best not to call the baby Osier's heir until he could tell her everything.

Miss Spicer grimaced, frustration and emotional pain showing on her features. "Why didn't he tell me any of this? ...Why didn't I ask? I was so *stupid*."

"Well, if I can be blunt," Avelore said as he began to fish in his pockets for the materials for a binding spell, "you probably *should* have asked, but we can also blame him for being both reckless and lacking forethought. I could argue that was the nature of what he was, but that doesn't change the results."

Honestly, it was impressive that the Viridian clan lasted this long with that kind of thinking, though Avelore couldn't fault them, or any of the clans, for acting to their prescribed order. After all, if the one hadn't deviated, none of this would be happening right now.

A half-sob broke him out of his thoughts and preparations, and he looked up to see Miss Spicer squeezing her eyes shut as she rocked her baby against her chest. She was holding the infant so tightly that he worried she might smother him.

Avelore sighed. "For what it's worth, Miss Spicer, Osier wasn't trying to trick you, not in his mind. It wasn't in his nature, and had he not perished, he would have come back. He was, for all his faults by our standards, incredibly kind and loyal, just not in the ways we're accustomed to. Unfortunately, he still left you with a mess."

She nodded, eyes still squeezed closed and jaw clenched. "I'm scared."

"That's a healthy and reasonable emotion to have right now," Avelore said sympathetically. "But you need to keep a tight grip on that fear because your life and your baby's life depends on it. Now, here is what I'm going to do…"

He stepped up, holding a strip of inscribed cloth in his hands. "I'm going to wrap this around your baby's arm and bind it with a very powerful spell. It will not hurt him, but it will seal off his magic. He will look like a normal baby after I do this."

He paused, measuring out a length of the cloth and snipping it with his fingers. It sliced neatly like his hands were shears. "This cloth acts as a second skin, so it's fine to get wet or dirty. Only a very powerful spell can remove it or damage it anyway."

"And it won't hurt him," Miss Spicer confirmed, eyeing the fabric with every bit of concern a terrified mother should have. "You promise?"

"I swear my life on it," Avelore replied firmly.

She nodded slowly, exhaling a shaky breath. "I don't know if I can trust you, but… I feel like I have no choice. Who even are you?"

Well, at least she learned her lesson this time.

"Ideally, I shouldn't tell you. My name carries weight and knowing it is a risk."

She wilted at that, and Avelore held up a hand, offering a thin smile. "However, to keep denying you every truth is cruel, given how things have turned out. And perhaps… knowing my name will help us build some… tentative trust."

He paused, meeting her gaze, and as he spoke, he let his magic carry forth, promising what he uttered was truth. "I am Avelore Amantius, Archmagus of the highest order, and founder of the Arcane Academy."

Her eyes widened, recognition on her features. Before she could say anything, he continued, "Do not utter my name to anyone, Miss Spicer, especially in relation to Osier."

He paused, pursing his lips as he debated on what to say. Truthfully, taking her with him would be most ideal, if he thought he could keep her safe. But the truth was... he couldn't. The moment he sent a signal to the Silver clan, he would paint a target on his back for those lurking in the shadows. And while he was confident he could protect himself, he wasn't confident he could protect himself, a mother, and her newborn child.

But she didn't need to know all of that. "Now, once this is done, I will go seek the help of those who can get you to safety, because, unfortunately, the safest place for you is one I can't reach. When I return, and I promise you, I will return, I will come bearing answers and allies."

Carefully, he took the baby's arm and wrapped the fabric around it. "Until then, pretend I have bound your baby's 'curse' and let him be as 'normal' as can be. And tell not a soul about his origins, or that you know the name Osier the Life Walker."

He stopped, looking up into Miss Spicer's terrified face as his hands and the fabric erupted into brilliant golden light.

"Rowan Spicer *must live.*"

He never came back.

As Sorrel held her newborn baby, now with auburn hair and no horns, she heard a new commotion outside, unusual for the night. Fear gripped her, knowing she and her baby were in danger and not knowing what was going on. Her father, who arrived right after the archmagus left just hours earlier, went out to investigate.

Each minute he was gone made her skin crawl, and she nervously kept her eyes on the door. The vines and mushrooms were no longer present, and the nurse seemed to not remember the details of what spooked her, but Sorrel still understood the gravity of her situation.

Maybe Avelore Amantius had already returned and that was the commotion. Maybe he would finally give her answers on exactly what was—

The door opened, and her father stepped in, expression disturbed. Quietly, he closed the door behind him. "The man who bound Rowan's curse..."

Sorrel's face lit up. "He's back?"

Zebb Spicer shook his head. "No... he's, uh, he's dead, Sorrel."

She froze, her breath leaving her in one fell swoop. "W-what?"

Zebb pursed his lips, giving her an unsettled look. "The night patrol between Ladisdale and Southmere saw an explosion of magic and went to investigate. They arrived to see a ball of silver fire take to the skies, and... they found a body. The... patrol recognized him as the archmagus from earlier."

Sorrel felt everything in her go numb. "He's... he's dead?"

First Osier, dead by the hand of someone powerful, and now Avelore... by something that used silver fire? What kind of being could kill an archmagus? Another archmagus? A dragon? But more importantly... *why?*

Her eyes fell to her baby, and to the spell cloth wrapped around his arm that made him appear normal. She realized the 'why' was in her arms, and she felt her entire world turn bleak.

"Tell not a soul..."

"Sorrel," her father pleaded, "what is going on? Who was that man? What's this 'curse' the nurse said he sealed? Was he the baby's father? Is this all related? Why won't you talk to me?"

"I have a normal baby boy," Sorrel whispered frightfully, giving her father a scared, but determined look, "and that is *all* he is. Because if I don't have a normal baby boy, someone else will die."

Chapter 3
The Message

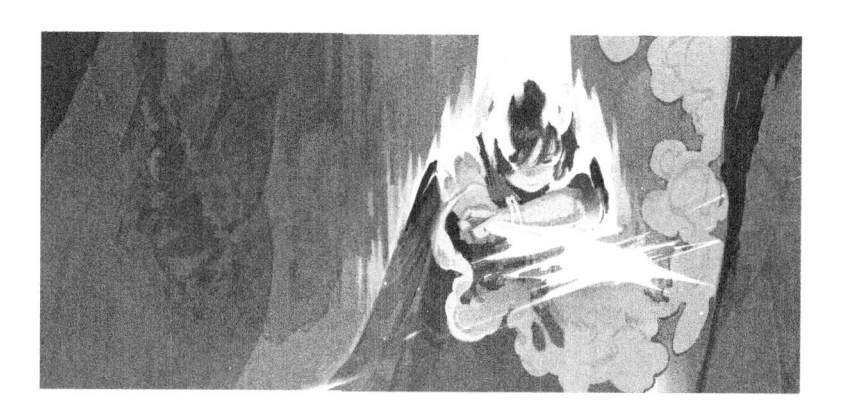

The western border of Bascor had been a battlefront for longer than Nova's eighteen years alive. The towns that once lined this edge of the country were now either military outposts or abandoned ruins, and nothing in between.

The smell of decay and death lingered deep in the earth and reached the skies, and not even the rains could wash away the scent. From her vantage point on the mountains behind the battlefield, it filled her nostrils with the stench of rotting flesh. At this point in her life, she was used to it.

Ash filtered through the air, coming from the corpses burning on the great pyres that lit up the battleground below. Humans had quickly learned that leaving their dead behind simply gave the enemy more soldiers.

Nova the Tempest *intimately* understood what it was like to fight and kill those who wore the faces of your allies but no longer remembered who you were. She wished it on no one, not even those who thought of her kind as the enemy.

She supposed she could not blame them, for the lich had done very well to deceive them, just as he had deceived her kind so long ago. Although she did not witness it, the evidence still lingered in destroyed archives and scorched buildings. Her home had once been a haven, full of history and beauty, and now all that remained were mostly damaged, barren halls and fragmented pieces of her culture.

Nova curled her lip in displeasure from under the shelter of her hooded cloak, scrutinizing the battleground from her place high up on a mountain ledge. The sound of war reached her ears over the harsh winds coming down from the mountains, and the crisp cold those winds brought was a welcome reprieve from the putrid smell of the undead army.

The sight before her was horrific. Between the Great Wither and the foul magic salting the earth, nothing grew here. Trees were nothing more than blackened burial markers, and the earth was devoid of grass. Stone ruins were covered in soot and bloodstains, and many buildings that once served as homes were nothing more than crumbled stone not even fit for shelter. It was all a bleak backdrop to the war itself, where the death toll continued to rise as the soldiers struggled to keep the undead held back.

Everything before her was the lich's fault. The undead army was his creation, crawling out of the Decaying Mountains to push against the borders of the surrounding countries. To what end, Nova was unsure. She suspected the attacks on humankind were more a means to an end, rather than the lich's real goal. After all, human bodies were how the undead army stayed strong in numbers.

The Great Wither, now in its seventeenth year, was also his doing, caused by killing the last of the Viridian clan. She was too young to remember what the world was like back then, only in her first year of life, but salvaged paintings back home still showed a world of color, and the surviving stories from her elders told of a world once full of life. Now, everything was gray when it had once been green, and only little pockets of growth remained.

Most of those pockets were found in the southern parts of this country where the Life Walker died. It made some sense, given he channeled a great amount of magic on the day of his death, although Nova was not sure how it still lingered without a Viridian dragon to move it. No one knew why Osier did that, but the evidence was there in early human births and traces of green. None of her clan found answers in their past excursions to the area, but surely he had a reason.

Nova also wondered if that reason was what led the lich to him. Whatever happened that day was a mystery, but it certainly changed all of the Reprised Shores in a way that could never be turned back.

Movement caught her attention, and she shifted her gaze to the overcast sky as the clouds parted from the beat of great wings. Moments later the familiar form of a dragon descended from the heavens, casting shadows over the trenches. The daylight reflected off of its mottled scales of gray and violet, highlighting its shape for all to see.

Most dragons, when in their true forms, had the same basic anatomy. They were four-legged, with long tails and great wings coming out of their backs. They had reptilian heads with horns, and thick scales to protect their hides. But each type of dragon, each *clan,* had specific features unique to them. One glance at the delicate, petal-like wings and the long, twisted horns, and Nova knew the dragon before her was from the Amethyst clan. Or had been, when she was alive.

Nova growled softly, the sound drowned by the howl of the wind around her. That was also the lich's doing. So many things made wrong by his hand, and Nova looked forward to ending his undead reign. She could only imagine the impact that would have on this world as well when the very creature responsible for the fall of the dragons and the forced evolution of humanity would return to his place among the ancestors. She was made to right his wrongs, and she would do so with *impunity*.

Alas, he went into hiding shortly after killing the Life Walker, and now he made others do his bidding, granting them power and ordering them from deep within the Decaying Mountains. That was fine. Nova would whittle down the enemy numbers, slowly reclaiming what was stolen, until he was forced to come for her, and then she would end him.

She returned her attention to the dragon in the skies, rearing back to attack the soldiers below. She was great in size, with the spread of her wings billowing like spectral pieces of silk. Nova recalled how other clans described the Amethyst clan's wings as 'butterfly-like,' although admittedly Nova had never seen a butterfly before.

Once upon a time, this dragon's scales would have been a glittering violet, and her mane a silky lavender. Now, her scales were damaged and jagged with pieces missing from her flanks. Instead of violet, they were mostly ashen gray with faint traces of color. Her curly horns had almost blackened, the tips crumbled away, and her pale mane now resembled the faded grasses of the Great Wither.

Undeath had sullied her appearance, and she was nothing more than a shell of her former self. But Nova still knew her name: Somnambula the Dream Keeper, former elder of the Amethyst clan.

With her under the lich's command, humanity had lost access to the inspiration born from dreams, and what remained were mostly dreamless sleep and haunting nightmares. That ended today.

Although Somnambula had been trapped for years, she had only been sighted in the last few months. Nova had been tracking her for many weeks, but the Amethyst dragon remained elusive, hiding in enemy territory until recently. This was her third direct attack on humans, and it would also be her last. With her death, her magic would be released to its rightful place, and the Reprised Shores would be better for it.

With a great roar, the Dream Keeper attacked, blowing Amethyst fire down on the trenches below her. Plumes of purple smoke pooled through the valley, wrapping around the panicked soldiers as they scrambled for cover.

The scent of her magic reached Nova from afar, twisted in a way that Amethyst magic should not be. She grimaced, crouching down as she waited, her heavy storm-colored cloak whipping around her. The magic woven through the fabric made its cloudy pattern swirl like a hurricane itself, like it was a prelude to what was to come.

Each billow of her cloak revealed glimpses of the warrior underneath, highlighting the broad build of someone made for battle, with taut muscle trapped under pale skin. The winds made the jagged layers of her dress flutter around her thighs, giving the monochrome fabric the illusion it was also made from the skies.

Silver eyes narrowed under the shelter of her hood, watching Somnambula's fire rain down on the soldiers. Amethyst fire did not burn, but its flames and smoke were not designed to. Instead, the attack sent soldiers collapsing on the battlefront, instantly dragging them into the world of dreams. The undead remained unaffected, for Amethyst magic, of inspiration, senses, and dreams, only affected the living.

It was a terribly discriminate attack and a powerful one, but it also left Somnambula momentarily unguarded in its wake. As the purple smoke spread thin and the flames died, Nova the Tempest sucked in a deep breath. The clouds overhead responded to her silent command, shifting from dismal gray to violent and stormy, like the beginnings of a hurricane. The winds roared, wet and angry, making the great pyres flutter in fear.

From beneath the hood of her cloak, Silver fire erupted from her eyes, and the skies opened up, firing down a volley of lances made of razor-sharp ice. They pierced Somnambula's wings, sending her crashing to the ground below and pinning her against the battle-sullied soil, away from any soldiers trapped in slumber.

Wrapping herself in silver flames, Nova dove off of the ledge, racing down the side of the mountain like a bolt of lightning toward the battleground. She dashed towards her target, electricity discharging off of her body and silver-flamed footprints burning in her wake.

Her fire worked well as a disguise to humans, for heavy use of her magic always made her true form show through. The soldiers far enough from the Amethyst magic to avoid falling asleep turned their attention towards her, and when they recognized the silver of her fire, they began to shout and cheer.

"It's a Dragon Knight! A Dragon Knight is here!"

The name 'Dragon Knight' was a strange choice, for it almost gave the illusion that humans understood what she was. They did not, though. They did not at all.

To them, she was a human using stolen dragon magic, because humans were still learning their new limits with magic now that they had broad access to the arcane. To them, she was a battle magus who slayed the dragons that humanity believed had turned on them.

To them, she was salvation, and perhaps, in a way, that one was somewhat true. She saved humans. She fought alongside them. She did not think she fought *for* them, though. She had too much bitterness for that, and it was not her purpose anyway.

After all, she was not a human champion destined to save humanity. She was the union of dragon magic and human skill. She was a half-dragon, a *prodigy* designed to free the dragons trapped in undeath, to end the reign of the lich, and they were none the wiser as they cheered for her to cut down her own kind.

"Kill the dragon!"

"Cut off its head!"

THE MESSAGE

Nova clenched her jaw, doing her best to drown out the words that the winds carried to her ears. They did not *know*. They did not *understand*. Their fear and anger were *justifiable*.

It did not make their words hurt any less.

She snarled as she channeled her frustrations into her magic and barreled straight for her target. Upon seeing her approach, Somnambula ripped herself away from the ice pinning her down, black ichor and violet smoke oozing from her tattered wings as undead eyes met Nova's across the expanse of the battlefield.

As she prepared to deliver Somnambula's second death, Nova once again found herself wondering if fallen dragons felt pain. She did not know the answer, and she wondered if she ever would.

Somnambula sucked in a deep breath, her glowing blue eyes focused on Nova as she gathered her magic once again, but the latter was faster. As violet flames licked out from the dragon's mouth, the Tempest shot over the trenches, Silver magic swirling around her like a blizzard. She drew her weapon, a bladeless hilt that suddenly came to life as a screaming sword of lightning in her hands.

With a shout, Nova descended, diving under her opponent's attack and stabbing up, impaling her sword deep into Somnambula's heart. Electricity arced out in all directions, ripping the fallen dragon apart from inside and exploding the Dream Keeper into a plume of beautiful, shimmering Amethyst smoke, vibrant and *right* once more.

The fresh scent of beautiful dreams and restful sleep hit Nova full force as the restored Amethyst magic escaped its entrapped form, dissipating back into the greater pool of magic it came from. It clung to her briefly, wrapping around her almost like an embrace as Somnambula sang softly in her mind.

"Thank you, child of the skies. I shall watch you paint the sunsets in your dreams."

Nova bowed her head sadly, whispering an apology that carried on the winds as the magic waved its goodbye. "May you rest now, in the world of dreams where you belong."

From behind barriers and shelters, Bascori soldiers cheered, and the sound brought her back to reality. With a deep breath, Nova the Tempest turned, doing her best to ignore the praise for killing a dragon. They did not understand, but she wished they did. She did not want to do this, but she had no *choice*.

The scent of rotting flesh doubled, clawing at her senses, and Nova whirled, eyes locking onto the crowds of undead charging towards her, drawn in by the smell of what she was.

Historically, the undead were drawn only to blood and sweat, seeking out humans to kill and add to their numbers. However, as the Silver clan made themselves known to the enemy, the undead army's attraction shifted, focusing less on the scent of the living and more on magical residue. Especially dragon magic.

It was not lost on her that the shift in behavior also came with a change in the strength of the undead, moving away from flimsy corpses that fell to a single swing of a blade to fortified monsters that continued to fight even after dismemberment. Still not a challenge for her, but it did not bode well for most of humanity.

Nova snarled, spinning in an arc as she expelled wind like a tornado, sending wights flying back from her. She attacked as they tumbled, her sword now a blade of silvery ice as she cut through the reanimated corpses, moving like the very wind she commanded. Even as the bodies fell, her magic continued, ice freezing them solid.

Nova could feel the lingering traces of Amethyst magic clinging to her, *inspiring* her, and with an upward leap, she called the skies to answer her command. Lightning rained down in rapid-fire bolts, striking at patches of undead soldiers, shattering the frozen ones, and electrocuting the others until all that remained were smoldering piles of twitching corpses and frozen chunks of rotten flesh.

She landed in a burst of cold wind with snow flurries and swirling fog shrouding her form. All around her, soldiers cheered, many having woken from their slumber. They cried their support for the Dragon Knight, the killer of dragons and guardian of humans. She was neither, but the lie was not one she would easily escape.

Without a word, Nova the Tempest left the battlefield in a swirl of mist and silver flames, her work momentarily concluded and bitterness on her tongue. The weather followed her, clouds weeping silently in the wake of Somnambula's second death.

May the world dream well tonight.

As evening fell, Nova returned to the far side of Bascor's western mountains and to the mountain cave where she had hidden her travel bag. A decaying pine forest wrapped around the base of the mountain below. She stopped to stare out at the tops of the dead trees before her.

Before the Great Wither, Nova understood that these trees were called 'evergreens', but that was certainly not true now. Under the rising moon, they looked rather like spikes sticking out of a pit, in her opinion. Other forests still had some life in them, but this one not so much.

She huffed through her nose, reaching up to push the hood of her cloak off of her head to reveal a pale, round face and upturned eyes. The cool wind ran its fingers through her black hair almost lovingly, tousling her messy bangs. She felt a drop of water hit her cheek moments later. Nova closed her eyes, welcoming the oncoming storm that was not of her own doing.

One by one, cold raindrops landed on her exposed skin. As they began to fall in clusters, Nova tilted her head back, inviting more. Rain kissed her cheeks and traced along her jaw, bringing with it a comfort that so few could understand.

Humans needed to eat. Dragons needed to recharge in their element. Nova the Tempest, a half-dragon, needed both.

She stayed there under the wind and rainfall of the night storm, letting the ambient magic of the skies saturate her form. She could have returned her appearance to normal, she supposed, but it was simply safer to appear as a human in human territory. And so she would remain as she was, with her long, midnight black hair a little less glossy, her eyes a false, icy blue, and her appearance otherwise that of a young woman.

Alas, her skin was still far too pale for the region, but her camouflaging magic had limitations. Fortunately, she rarely entered human towns, and when she did, most of them assumed she was from the northern regions of the Reprised Shores, where humans saw little sunlight. She was not going to correct them, not when it let them believe she was human.

Nova pursed her lips, a growl from her stomach reminding her of the other need she had to address. Tonight, her dinner was cured fish and seaweed, as it was most every night, for the oceans still teemed with life in the wake of the Great Wither. The Cerulean clan's numbers were strong, as reaching dragons that lived in the seas was difficult.

She ate her meal by the cave's edge, allowing the rain and wind to recharge her as the food filled her stomach. Once finished, she tucked herself deeper into the cave, using her cloak, enchanted with the heat of summer, for warmth. She could not sleep exposed to the elements, as much as she wished she could.

With a deep sigh, Nova settled into sleep, eyelids already heavy and mind prepared for what awaited her: the recurring dream that haunted her every night. It was relentless and unchanging, as it had been for years, and tonight would be the same.

In a change of scenery, she appeared atop a great mountain that stretched high into the sky, sticking out of a sea of darkness. Her form was human because she fell asleep as a human, and her heavy cloak draped around her like a storm in the night.

Shadowy tendrils reached for her from below, never touching, but echoing whispers that they would take everything from her. She responded as she did every night by setting herself on *fire*, silver light shining brightly over the abyss in defiance.

And like every night, her brilliance cut through the darkness. It shined across the sea of shadows, illuminating a figure standing at the edge of a wooded shore on the other side. The figure was always too far away to identify, but she could feel the way it called for her to close the distance. However, she could never leave her mountain...

...until tonight.

The dark sky flashed once in brilliant Amethyst, and the dream *changed*. Nova sucked in a breath, eyes wide as she felt a hint of the Dream Keeper's presence. Was it lingering from before...?

Her gaze snapped down to the abyssal sea as a path of silver fog rose up from it, forming a bridge between her and the distant shore. For the first time in years, the dream was *different*. Now she had confirmation that this was not a normal dream. This was a message, and maybe now she could finally receive it.

Without hesitation, Nova stepped out onto the bridge of mist, Silver fire dancing on her skin as the black sky above glowed faintly like embers of a purple fire. Tendrils of shadow clawed at her, but she was the *Tempest*, and the light of her fire burned away every attempt to touch her. She marched towards the distant shore, eyes set on her destination, guided by the traces of Somnambula's magic disguised as her own.

With each step forward, the shadows ahead bled away, showing her an island of lush green trees like she had never seen. Tall flowers and rich grass waved at her from the rocky shore, and colorful birds sang wordless songs from the canopy. But most importantly, as she reached the end of her path and stepped foot onto the island, the one waiting for her became clear.

The dragon before her appeared in his hybrid form, with wavy green hair that fell to his knees, draping over his body like a cape. He wore robes made of Viridian dragon silk, with long sleeves that reached his fingertips. Great horns in the shape of tree branches sprawled out of his head, heavy with long curtains of purple flowers that Nova had never seen.

His wings were folded behind him, covered in rich foliage and tiny lavender blossoms, and the light of her fire bounced off of his glossy, leaf-shaped scales. His tail lay curled at his feet, appearing not unlike a thick vine laden with clumps of plush moss. And spiraling out from his feet were colorful flowers and delicate ferns, curling in intricate patterns around them.

Nova sucked in a breath through her teeth, realizing just who stood before her, for only one answer made sense.

Osier the Life Walker nodded slowly, then lifted a clawed hand towards her.

"Seek what I left behind in the lands where I died. Protect my legacy."

His words echoed in her dream, and with sad eyes, the visage of the Viridian elder melted away in green fire, leaving Nova the Tempest standing alone on the island.

Chapter 4
Rowan Spicer

Every night, Rowan Spicer had the same dream. He stood in swirling darkness, like thick, black smoke that obscured his vision. Vague, distant shapes broke through the undulating void, hinting at a world beyond what he could see.

Despite that, he couldn't escape the darkness around him. No matter how much he ran or where he turned, it never receded. Slowly, it would close in with spindly fingers and shadowy tendrils, wrapping around him with whispered promises that it could end the cycle if he let it. It coached it like a comfort, but Rowan knew it was a threat.

And like every night, someone watched him from within the darkness. Most of this person was shrouded in shadow except for a pair of glowing viridian eyes that illuminated his face. He was a fair man with delicate features, and he watched with a sad expression like he didn't want the shadows to move in. But he never made a move to stop them.

Rowan reached out as the darkness wrapped around him, feeling it slide up around his face like deep water that would drown him. He prepared himself for that moment of suffocation that always woke him up.

Instead, light tore through the darkness like beams of sunlight through a cloudy day, and the dream *changed.*

The shadows scampered, and Rowan found himself crouched in the middle of a sunny, cliffside field full of tall grasses, vibrant and green like he had never seen. Lightning danced across the sky overhead, brimming with power. It sent a rumble of thunder that embraced him in all directions as if such a thing could be comforting.

But most fascinating of all was the being that now stood before him.

Gone was the sad man with green eyes, and in his place stood a figure wrapped in silver fire, shining like polished metal in the midday sun. They had no identifying features and they said nothing, holding out a flaming hand for him to take. Hesitantly, Rowan reached out to take the hand, and just before their fingers touched, he woke up.

Rowan opened his eyes, finding himself staring up at the ceiling of the bedroom, his heart pounding and sweat clinging to his skin. The pale sunlight coming in through the window indicated it was morning, and he could hear sounds coming from the kitchen as someone, likely his mother, prepared breakfast.

He sighed, wiping back his bangs from his forehead. They were damp from sweat, something he dreaded having to deal with, so he pushed it aside for a minute to focus on what was more pressing in his mind: his dream.

The dream had never changed. It had haunted him for years, as long as he could remember, but it had always been exactly the same. So why did it change now? Did it mean something? Was it about his curse?

His eyes fell to his right forearm and the skin-tight spell cloth wrapped around it. The inky characters were still as black as ever like they had been written only yesterday, and the magic always thrummed against his skin.

It was as much a part of him as any other body part, but that didn't mean Rowan liked it. After all, it represented something wrong with him. It was a reminder that he was cursed; he had been marked at birth, and he didn't know who did it or why.

Pushing himself up into a seated position, he inspected his arm, fingers sliding over the pale fabric that contrasted his tanned, freckled skin. No one else seemed to know either. Or perhaps it was more accurate to say most people didn't know, and the one person who did wasn't talking.

Brown eyes narrowed slightly in thought as Rowan pursed his lips. He suspected his mother knew more about his curse than she claimed. After all, curses were targeted, so someone had to have done this on purpose. Plus, she always had this pained look any time he brought it up, and he'd seen her crying too many times to count. But, no matter what, she wouldn't talk about it.

It was upsetting, because this thing was a mark on his life, and he had no idea why. Some people were wary of him. Some straight-up hated him. He hadn't done anything, but he felt like he was predestined to be disliked by society as a whole, and that was unfair. He wanted to understand why. He deserved at least that.

His mother wasn't a great liar, but she was stubborn, at least on this. She never budged, no matter how much he begged or pleaded. She denied knowing anything and begged him to stop asking questions and just keep his head down.

And that was the other part of the problem. She treated him like he was fragile, dangerous, or both. Part of him wondered if she feared his curse, or maybe she feared people would hurt him because he had one.

That idea wasn't too far-fetched, given a handful of people did bully him, but that wasn't justification to beg him to not leave the house.

She didn't even want him wandering the woods by himself, and that made no sense in context with his curse. She argued it was because there were undead out in the world, but that had always been the case since before he was born. Everyone else went about their lives with reasonable precautions, so why shouldn't he?

Something had her terrified, and he just didn't know if that something was a real threat, *him,* or all made up in her head.

Rowan huffed, shaking his head. He was almost seventeen. He was an adult as far as Bascori culture went, but it had been a constant uphill battle to get his mother to give him *any* autonomy. Truthfully, it took his grandfather yelling at her for her to finally let Rowan start walking to school on his own when he turned twelve.

He remembered that fight as clear as day, because his grandfather said, "You can't keep him on a tether for the rest of his life because of what happened."

His mother had shut that conversation down immediately, but afterward, Rowan got that tiny piece of freedom. He still didn't know 'what happened,' and he gave up on the hope that he someday would, but that was her fault, not his. He was doing his best to not think everything was her fault, but she wasn't doing a great job of convincing him of that.

His mind went back to his dream. When he first started having them, he told his mother, and she made him promise to never tell anyone about them. Eventually, when he told her he was having the same dream every night, she lost the color in her face and said he needed to pretend they didn't exist. Eventually, he realized *she* wanted to pretend they didn't exist, but damned if he knew why.

Part of him felt like he should tell her that the dream had changed. The rest of him loudly insisted that would not end well, and he'd be in a bad mood the rest of the day. He wished he understood what was going on in her head. It felt like she was the one trapped in a recurring nightmare, and she thought everyone else was trapped with her.

Rowan pulled himself out of his thoughts, knowing he needed to stop brooding and get ready for the day. With that reminder, he lifted his head to the mirror across the tiny room. It hung on the wall, dusty and in need of care, but it still served its purpose, reflecting a view of someone he struggled to like, who sat on a bed made of woven river reeds in a room mostly void of furnishings.

His hair was in utter disarray, auburn curls messy from the night of sleep, and his ponytail was half undone, causing part of his hair to hang over his shoulder. Big brown eyes stared back at him, too round and boyish for being almost seventeen. His freckled cheeks were tanned from spending time outside. His mother called them 'sun-kissed', but he felt that was a bit too poetic for someone like himself.

To him, 'sun-kissed' was a word to describe some dashing adventurer or worldly traveler. It wasn't reserved to describe a young, gangly man covered in freckles, with untamable hair and very short stature.

He shook his head, pulling out of bed to get ready for the day. As much as he dreaded it, he needed to comb his hair and get it somewhat manageable before he started work. But as he stood in front of the mirror and carefully picked through the ends of his shoulder-blade-length hair, he found himself wishing he could stomach cutting it off.

He tried once, or more accurately, his mom did. He came home from school one day when he was eight, his hair a tangled mess after being pushed around by other kids. Boys weren't supposed to have long hair, they said, but she had let him grow it out since it made him happy. When she wasn't able to easily get the tangles out, she cut it short, and Rowan was *miserable*. He turned the mirror away and told his mom to never cut his hair again.

The day he was able to finally put it back into a tiny ponytail felt like utter relief in a way he couldn't begin to describe. It hurt to untangle it every morning, and it was certainly frayed and damaged, but it hurt in a different way to have it cut short, and that pain felt deeper. He had no idea why.

All he knew was that despite his hair being messy and hard to work with, it felt... really important to him. He just wished more than one other person understood that.

When Rowan finally finished detangling his hair, he fixed his ponytail and left his room to wash up. His mother was in the kitchen, back to him as she tended the hearth, and the smell of cooking fish told Rowan what he was going to have for breakfast. He could have guessed that anyway, honestly.

His mother didn't notice him enter the room, and Rowan didn't quite feel ready to navigate a conversation with her, so he stayed quiet, tiptoeing around her toward the front door. He noted his grandfather was nowhere to be found, but that wasn't unusual, as he always went out right at dawn to forage for supplies. Usually, though, he woke Rowan up to come with him, and Rowan was a bit put out that he didn't today.

Sure enough, as Rowan stood out by the water wheel and rinsed off, his grandfather came walking up out of the woods, moving at a leisurely pace. Much like Rowan, he had quite the tan, albeit his skin was far more weathered from his years alive and his freckles were sparse. And much like Rowan, his dark auburn hair was pulled back at the nape of his neck, although it was thinner with blended gray.

When Rowan cried over his hair being cut, his grandfather stopped trimming his own hair, not that Rowan immediately noticed. When he finally did notice it, he asked why. Grandpa Zebb didn't look up from his work, but he smiled and said, "Because it makes me look more dashing."

It took Rowan a couple of years to understand what he actually meant, and Rowan remembered crying when he finally did. It was the first time he cried for a reason other than being upset.

The memory made Rowan smile fondly, watching as his grandfather approached, a walking stick in one hand and a basket with a small harvest in the other. The basket, like everything else of the last seventeen years, was made of river reeds because the only plants in decent abundance these days were those that grew in water.

Rowan found it both fascinating and strange that life inside bodies of water did so well, but everything else was on the brink of death. Some said dragons had cursed the world as part of their attack on humanity, and Rowan found that hypothesis ...interesting.

He was no scholar, but he had read a *lot* of books. The library in town was still available to the public, with enchantments keeping the books preserved. Most of the country's institutions had managed to preserve their texts, given that literacy and education were one of Bascor's prides. And many of those publicly available books had been written by magi of the Arcane Academy. They were researchers whose entire lives were spent studying the arcane, and the magic that *wasn't* arcane.

According to them, the rise of magi only came within the last century and a half, but the world was full of magic that had existed for eons before that. That magic was far different than arcane, with distinguishing properties and effects. Humans couldn't interact with those kinds of magic, but some other species could.

And allegedly, dragons could *create* that magic. So for life only on land to wither away over the last seventeen years, many blamed the dragons. Like the undead army, this was another way to try and destroy humanity. No one knew why the dragons turned hostile over the last century, but the most popular opinions were that it was due to either fear or jealousy. Humanity's use of magic was on the rise, and the dragons were trying to stop it.

It made sense, but that also begged the question: what happened a hundred and fifty years ago that allowed humanity to wield magic? None of the books he read had answers, but many asked the same question. Truthfully, if he had a chance to go to an academy, he'd love to research the history of magic.

Unfortunately, he was cursed, and he'd learned that barred him from entering most higher institutions. They feared the presence of arcane magic in those settings would set off the curse, or at least, that was the official reason. Rowan suspected a bit of prejudice was at play there, too. Of course, there were still the non-magical institutes, but not many of those remained, and getting noticed was hard. It made him sad because he felt like he could excel in that kind of setting if given the chance.

"Morning, bean," Grandpa Zebb said as he made his way up the flagstone steps. "How's the water this morning?"

"Cold," Rowan said wryly, flashing his grandfather a look as he wiped his hands on his pants. "As always."

Grandpa Zebb chuckled, coming to a stop beside him on the stone terrace. "Wouldn't be so bad if the summer hadn't left early. Didn't even stay for dinner."

Rowan hummed thoughtfully, looking out at the hills around them. "Yeah, it got cold fast. Normally doesn't for a few more weeks. Do you think we'll have another long winter?"

Grandpa Zebb wrinkled his nose in disapproval. "I hope not. The house doesn't keep heat well anymore. We'll freeze our arses off if we have something like that again. You almost lost your toes last time."

"I was seven," Rowan replied, lifting a brow. "I'm a little bigger now, and we can move the beds beside the hearth if we need to."

Grandpa Zebb huffed in amusement. "Still no meat on ya, though that goes for everyone these days. But, we'll eat well tonight. Have a look-see at what I got. Pretty bountiful for a Wither harvest, I'd say."

Rowan peered into the basket, skimming the contents. "Oh! You found some chicken mushrooms! And blackberries!"

"Sure did," Grandpa Zebb said proudly, a grin on his face. "We can have a break from fish tonight. But keep looking." He nodded to the basket.

At his request, Rowan moved the mushrooms aside. There were a scant few herbs, a small bundle of wild rice, and potion reagents as well, but his brows lifted at the cluster of pale mushrooms with blue warts. "Oh, wow! Are those mature bubble caps?"

"Good eye," Grandpa Zebb praised. "First time I've seen them in about two years. Do you remember what they do?"

"They're for counter-potions. As long as you have just a drop of the original potion, you can combine this as a powder with a base potion and create an elixir that cancels out the original effect," Rowan replied easily. "But I don't remember what the limits are on that. I think two grams is the target amount, and it needs to be dried out and ground?"

"No one remembers shit like that unless you use it regularly. It's why we have notebooks," Grandpa Zebb chuckled. "But good job. C'mon, follow me inside and I'll show you how the warts glow in the dark. It's why I like to forage right before sunrise! Easy to see them!"

Rowan pouted, following his grandfather inside. "Next time, wake me up so I can go with you!"

"I tried today, but you were dead asleep!" Grandpa Zebb laughed as he put the basket on the table. "Didn't even stir when I shook your shoulder, so I figured I'd leave ya be!"

Rowan blinked at that. He wasn't normally a heavy sleeper. Was that because of the dream? "Oh...that's weird."

But at least it meant Grandpa Zebb hadn't tried to leave him behind. That knowledge made him feel a little better.

"Sometimes we're just getting that good sleep." Grandpa Zebb shrugged and began to sort his foraged items, separating foodstuffs from potion ingredients.

Rowan's mom looked over from where she was pulling the skillet off the hearth. Her auburn hair was pulled back into a low bun, although a few wavy wisps hung loose around her chin. She wore her usual faded blue apron dress, along with a weariness on her face that never went away. If she noticed Rowan had snuck out without saying anything, she didn't comment on it, although her eyes lingered on him briefly before looking at his grandfather. "Welcome back. Anything of use?"

"Bubble caps," Grandpa Zebb said proudly, grinning from ear to ear. "Also found a nice patch of fire root. And some blackberries, but not enough to make a pie."

"I think we'd need more than berries to make a pie," Rowan's mom said softly as she prepared three servings of cooked river trout and a meager side of wild rice, "but the bubble caps and fire root are good news. The Athenaeum will be interested in the bubble caps for their studies, and we're getting more orders for warming draughts with the temperature drop. We might be able to meet demand."

The Athenaeum she spoke of was the Opus Athenaeum, the local magic center owned by the Arcane Academy. It served both as an institute for higher learning and as an administrative office for the work of magi. It also housed the library Rowan spent so much time at.

"They'd better pay us out the ears for the caps," Grandpa Zebb said sourly. "Not keen on giving these up just for one of them to waste it on a counter for a damn satiety elixir."

As they talked, Rowan flicked his gaze to the open doorway leading into the workshop. It used to be a grinding room, once upon a time, but that was before his grandfather bought the house some thirty years ago. Now the water wheel didn't power anything, and the stone walls were filled with shelves of vials and containers, although many of those were empty.

Despite the Great Wither making many reagents scarce, his family was well respected in their craft and made enough income to do a little better than just 'survive'. Sure, they ate mostly fish and didn't own anything fancy, but the roof didn't leak and magic kept the hearth lit in place of kindling.

In fact, they probably ate better than most people given their foraging skills, and the potion lessons his mother gave at the Opus Athenaeum were often paid back with free enchantments. Rowan's family actually had linen clothes from before the Great Wither and potion recipe books, because they had been preserved by the magi at the Athenaeum.

And honestly, his family's reputation probably made his own life easier as a 'cursed' man. He had heard enough stories to know how most people with curses ended up: ousted or dead. No one had ever tried to kill him, and most of what he dealt with in town was usually unkind remarks or unpleasant behaviors. Although admittedly, sometimes it was worse.

It was as he finished his breakfast that his mother started to fill the delivery basket with the day's potion orders. Rowan watched her, mentally going through his head what each order was and for whom. When she finished, she turned to him. "Today's orders are ready. I have a couple of hours before I need to start on the next set of brews, so I can go with you. Let me just clean up the kitchen."

Rowan shook his head as he moved past her to put away his dishes. "I don't think we both need to go. There aren't many deliveries today at all, really, and they're all to the same side of town, so I'll probably be done early. I still plan to stop by the library, but I'll probably be back by mid-afternoon. Then I can help you with whatever else is needed here."

He caught the frown on his mother's face before she could hide it. "Are you sure? I mean, there's been an increase in wight sightings around the neighboring towns. It's not safe—"

"Mom, I don't think you're scary enough to drive off the undead," Rowan said lightly, doing his best to stay lighthearted amid her usual tactics. "And I can probably run faster than you if they do appear."

He could tell she really didn't like that, but by this point, she needed better arguments for why he should let her chaperone him. And she seemed to know it, too, because her shoulders dropped in defeat.

"Well... all right then. Just be careful. Keep an eye out for wights, and make sure you keep to the busier streets, and don't talk to—"

"Sorrel," Grandpa Zebb interrupted, not looking up from where he was sorting through his foraged findings. "He's sixteen."

"Yes, I know, but—"

"*Sorrel.*" Grandpa Zebb turned, this time, looking at her over his shoulder. He said nothing else, but he didn't need to. This was almost as routine as breakfast.

His mother inhaled through her nose, working her jaw as her gaze flitted between Rowan and his grandfather. Rowan gave her an awkward smile and took the basket out of her hands, securing the strap over his shoulders. "It's fine, Mom. I do this every day."

"That doesn't mean it's safe," she whispered.

He wanted to argue it would never be 'safe.' He wanted to remind her the country had been at war with dragons and undead for longer than either of them had been born, and that people had to learn to live with that, including her. Instead, Rowan said nothing, holding the basket steady with a hand so he could slide on his sandals, because he knew pointing out the truth would not have the effect he wanted. "I'll be back this afternoon, and I can help you with any remaining brews."

With that, he kissed her cheek, waved to his grandfather, and left for town.

Chapter 5
Routines

Ladisdale was nothing impressive in Rowan's opinion, but he admittedly only knew of 'impressive' through old books that he read in the local library. 'Impressive' was the capital city of Orbcrest, spilling over one of the tallest hills of the region with its numerous spires and sprawling colonnades.

At its peak, it would have been covered in immaculate gardens, and even the stone walls lining the perimeter would have had manicured trees growing from the tops. The city squares held beautiful sculptures and murals, and it was said the city itself was once built upon the inspiration of muses with violet eyes.

From what he understood now, the trees had all died and their wood cut down for use. The gardens were barren of life, and no new buildings had been made due to a lack of supplies and available labor. The population had declined over the years due to starvation and high infant mortality, and many houses within the city sat derelict and in ruin.

Like everywhere else, art slowed to a crawl, and people no longer felt inspired. At best, the Arcane Academy was using magic to preserve the art and architecture of the city, much like they did for textiles and furniture. Rowan still wanted to see the capital in person, one day. The stories from his grandfather and the faded pictures in old books only fueled his curiosity.

In contrast to the capital, Ladisdale was far more subdued. Like most towns and cities in Bascor, it was built entirely on top of a tall hill, but it was still much smaller than the capital. Dirt roads wove up the hillside to reach the gates, cutting between the terraced fields that once held abundant crops and orchards. Now they were mostly barren, save a handful of meager vegetables and a few sickly trees.

The stone wall around the perimeter had been erected about twenty years ago in response to the increasing presence and threat of the undead army. It was functional, lacking flourish, with metal gates that could be pulled down to ward off incoming attacks. The only buildings that had spires or towers were ones like the Ladisdale Town Hall, the Opus Athenaeum, and the town's defensive wall. Although guard towers hardly counted, in Rowan's opinion.

The square in the center wasn't used for much anymore, though Rowan understood that before the Great Wither, it was a rather busy marketplace. His grandfather would tell stories of going up there to sell potions when Rowan's mother was a child. Sometimes they would trade for other wares, and sometimes they would take currency payment.

He supposed that part wasn't much different. The Spicer family still accepted trades for their potions, as long as the wares were things they could use, but they only accepted the local currency, Bascori shells, now. It was too hard to exchange foreign coins these days.

Rowan shifted out of his thoughts as he walked up to the first house and rapped the heavy knocker against the door. The absence of dread as he started his day was solely because the Tanners were one of the few families that didn't treat him like a stain on society.

He wasn't so certain that it was because of his own merits, though. After all, his grandfather once told him that the Tanners lost their grandson during the early days of the Great Wither. Rowan suspected that was a factor, given he was supposedly about the same age. Still, it meant they were respectful, and that was a rarity for him. He did sometimes feel a touch guilty about it, though. Like he was taking advantage of their loss. But there wasn't really anything he could do about that.

The tanner's wife was home and she smiled weakly at him as he delivered the numbing elixir that helped with her chronic hand pain. She once told him their potions were the reason she could still help her husband with his work.

"Thank you, young Spicer," she said quietly as she dropped the scalloped-shape coins into his palm. "Might I request another one for next week?"

Rowan nodded, offering her a polite smile as he pocketed the coin in his satchel. Neither spoke of the fact that this version of the potion only lasted about two days. Even with switching to tanning fish skin during the Great Wither, the business wasn't profitable enough for the Tanners to order more frequently or request a more potent variation. "Of course! I'll come by again this time next week. Do you have the previous potion's vial? I'll give you back five shells for it."

"Oh, yes, of course. Let me grab it." She quickly retrieved it, passing it over to him as he secured it in his delivery basket. He had gotten most of his routine customers used to returning the empty vials, offering a discount for doing so. "Here you are."

"Thank you, Mistress Tanner. I'll see you next week, and please take care."

She bade him farewell, and Rowan moved on to the next house, squaring his shoulders. Unlike the Tanner family who were amicable towards him, the Carpenter family was... definitely not. To be fair, they were generally unpleasant people, bitter that the Great Wither had forced them to find other work to sustain them, but they were especially unpleasant towards him.

Rowan inhaled deeply, preparing himself as he rapped his knuckles on the door. It was in dire need of replacing, the wood starting to rot, and the knocker had long since fallen off. Or maybe it had been taken down because Rowan wasn't entirely sure the door wouldn't splinter from it. Either way, it was clear they couldn't afford the enchantment that kept the wood preserved. It was sad, but Rowan felt his sympathy was pretty limited when they treated him like a blight on humanity for just existing.

Mister Carpenter opened the door, his expression sour, like he already knew who was on the other side. Or maybe he was just like that. Rowan honestly wasn't sure which, and he wasn't about to ask. Instead, he forced a tight-lipped smile and pulled out a potion from his basket. "Good morning, Mister Carpenter. Here is your order: a potion of insomnolence. It lasts three nights if you drink it all at once, and—"

"Just hand me the vial," Mister Carpenter snapped, holding out his hand. "Don't need a lecture from you on how to drink a potion."

Rowan pursed his lips, not quite meeting his gaze. "S-sure. Payment, please."

There was a beat of silence, before Mister Carpenter exhaled through his nose, face contorting into disdain. "Right. What was it? Fifty shells?"

"Ninety, sir." Rowan made a point of making eye contact this time, knowing how this was about to go.

Mister Carpenter scowled. "That's not what Zebb told me when I ordered it. He said fifty."

Rowan pressed his tongue against his teeth, debating on what to do. It wasn't lost on him how Mister Carpenter referred to his grandfather by first name, despite the families not being close. However, Rowan was quite familiar with people lying to him about alleged discounts, bargains, or even falsified complaints about his family's products, all to cut a deal.

The first few times it happened, Rowan floundered on what to do, being younger, inexperienced, and scared to assert himself out of fear of repercussion. He often gave in, panicked, or said the wrong things, resulting in his family taking a hit in earnings or his grandfather having to smooth things out.

Now, though, this was a game he was considerably skilled at, probably more so than the man before him. So instead of arguing, he pitched his face into something confused. "Oh, he must have forgotten to tell me. Well, since I can't approve any discounts myself, I'll need to go talk to him. I can be back by this afternoon around four, or I can come by early tomorrow morning. Do you have a preference?"

Mister Carpenter frowned. "I know what he told me, boy."

Rowan smiled apologetically, ignoring the way his heart was racing as he put the elixir back into his basket. "I'm sorry, but I don't have the authority to accept discounted payment without his direct approval. You're welcome to talk to him or my mother about it."

"Fine," Mister Carpenter snapped, pulling out his coin purse and fishing for the money. "I need it now, so ninety it is, you thieving shit. I'll be talking to Zebb about this."

Rowan flinched slightly as the older man slapped the money into his palm with enough force for it to sting. He glanced down to make sure he'd been given ninety and not fifty shells, thumb sliding over the four bigger twenty-shell coins and the one smaller ten-shell. Nodding, he pocketed the money and held out the potion once again.

"I'll talk with my grandfather when I get home, and if I made an error, I'll come back to refund the excess tomorrow. Will you be home?"

His response was the potion yanked out of his hand, followed by the door slammed in his face. The force sent a couple of wood chips falling to the ground. Rowan exhaled harshly through his nose, quickly leaving the premises and absconding off to an alleyway where he could have a moment to himself. Leaning back against a stone wall, he ran a hand through his hair, pushing his bangs from his face as he worked on calming himself down.

Even if he knew what to say and how to navigate those encounters, it always made him internally panic. He felt like he couldn't breathe, and his heart would pound like he'd run across the town. It made his skin crawl, and he had to force down memories of other bad encounters where things didn't go so well.

He sighed, closing his eyes and tilting his head back until it thunked against the cold stone. Slowly, he forced himself to untense, taking in long, steadying breaths, practicing what he'd read in books. Eventually, the urge to run home and hide went away, leaving him feeling drained in a way that wasn't physical. This was just part of life, though. So with a grimace, he pushed off the wall and continued with the rest of his deliveries.

The remaining orders were about what Rowan expected. General disdain or derisiveness, but nothing he hadn't experienced before. Some insults, and a lot of callousness, but nothing physically violent. No busted lips, no rough shoves, and no threats upon his person for existing in the same space. It wasn't like that constantly, but it happened enough that Rowan was always wary of it, and it was why he always needed to calm down after a confrontation.

Despite that, he still usually hid the details from his mother and grandfather when he could. He didn't need to give his mother any more reason to deny him freedom. And when he couldn't hide the evidence of bruises or cuts, he would spend the next day or two fighting back against being forced to stay home.

It was probably ironic that he kept fighting to keep coming back to this place full of hostility but being home and trapped was a different *kind* of pain and one he hated more. Besides, not *everyone* in Ladisdale hated him. Just... most people.

But now all he had left were the handful of potions to be delivered to neighboring towns. That knowledge lifted his spirits because that meant the only interactions he had left today were things he knew would be positive. With that thought, he changed directions and headed for the courier office, feeling the tension between his shoulders lessen the moment his destination came into view.

'On Bascori Wings' was a small business that cropped up after the national postal service fell apart during the Great Wither. It serviced the south side of the country, managing deliveries between the towns and surviving hamlets. Half of what they delivered were parcels, and the rest were verbal messages with the aid of magic since paper and parchment were hard to come by.

Rowan stepped inside the small office, eyes falling on the person counting unwrapped parcels on shelves. Cengor Tasker was a tall man, a few years older than Rowan, with short brown hair and somewhat fair skin for the region. A pair of spectacles sat on his nose, and he was otherwise dressed in a tunic and pants of what was probably fish leather.

He turned at hearing Rowan enter, and his face lit up into a bright smile. "Oh! Hey Rowan! You're early today. Got something for me?"

Rowan smiled, putting three potions on the counter. "Hey Cengor! I've got three for Southmere today. All to the same house."

Cengor hummed, walking up to a large chalkboard and scribbling details with a piece of chalk. "Three potions. Southmere... recipient's name?"

"Alwin Graves."

"Ah, the magus there? Should have guessed. Who else would order three at once?" Cengor chuckled, the noise almost drowned out by the taps of his chalk against the board as he wrote the details. "Great. I also have your payment from the last shipment's recipients. Want me to subtract the delivery fees from that?"

"Yes please; that would be great," Rowan replied, watching as Cengor nodded and disappeared into a back room. He returned a moment later with several coins in his hand. "Three hundred and ten, with eighty subtracted for shipping, so two hundred and thirty remain. Does this sound right for you?"

Rowan flicked his eyes up as he did the math in his head. "Yeah, I think that's right. Thanks for that."

Cengor nodded, passing the coin over before moving the potions to a secure place on one of the shelves. "Of course. Is that your last delivery for the day? You got here pretty early."

"Yeah, my route was kind of linear today, and not as many to deliver as normal," Rowan admitted as he pocketed the coin and adjusted his basket that now only contained empty vials. "Some weeks are like that, though. It just gives me more time in the library before I go home."

"You and that library," Cengor said with fond amusement, shaking his head. "I swear you're a scholar in the making if only they'd let you in."

"That'd be nice," Rowan admitted softly, looking whimsically out the door at the Athenaeum across the square. He didn't bother to correct Cengor that he didn't really go there as much to read these days, but that was only because he'd already read every book publicly available. "Doubt that will ever happen."

He heard Cengor sigh behind him. "Probably not. But if you had the opportunity to learn magic, would you take it?"

"Oh, definitely," Rowan said without thinking, looking back at Cengor. He paused, before clarifying, "I mean, I think so? I never looked into it much once I was told I couldn't because of"—he nodded towards his arm—"this."

Cengor nodded in understanding, expression thoughtful. "You know, I got a lot of contacts since we use magic to deliver messages. Want me to see if I can find out anything? I can't promise it would be much, but we might have some connections with the institutes not administered by the Arcane Academy."

Rowan looked up at him, blinking owlishly. "You'd do that?"

He winced internally at the mildly affronted look Cengor gave him in return. "Of course! Why wouldn't I? Honestly, I feel kinda daft for not thinking to ask earlier. I'll see what I can find out for you, but give me time. News only travels as fast as Bascori Wings, and unfortunately, our wings are metaphors attached to human messengers."

Cengor chuckled at his own joke, and Rowan felt himself grinning despite it. "Wow... thanks. I really appreciate that."

Cengor smiled, waving a hand at him. "Sure, sure. Now, shouldn't you run off to your library rendezvous?"

Rowan rolled his eyes, a smile still on his face. "Probably. Any interesting news before I go?"

Cengor's eyes brightened as he adjusted his glasses. "Oh, yes! How could I forget? One of my couriers came back this morning saying he saw a Dragon Knight. It's all they're talking about!"

Rowan's mouth fell open in surprise. "Wait, really? Are you serious?"

Cengor nodded, leaning against the counter. "Very serious. Just out in Bouldermoor. He said a wave of undead charged the town and the Dragon Knight appeared and slew them all before they could even cross the bridge."

Rowan's eyes went wide. "Wow! But I thought Dragon Knights were only ever seen in the war zone. Why would one come out this way?"

Cengor shrugged, looking amused. "I don't know. Change of scenery? Even hardened warriors using stolen dragon magic deserve a break once in a while, right?"

"I mean... yeah, I guess. I wonder what they look like," Rowan said thoughtfully. Like most, he only knew of the words 'Dragon Knight' in relation to the war, how magical warriors sometimes showed up to help fight off the dragons and undead with great feats of magic. Some argued they were the only humans who had successfully used magic that wasn't arcane. Others argued they weren't human at all.

Of course, if that was the case, no one knew *what* they were. Human-shaped and fighting dragons, so definitely not dragons themselves. Maybe Otherkin, except those were supposed to be creatures that took on human disguises to hide themselves, not draw attention. They weren't thought to be very powerful, either.

Cengor's response pulled Rowan out of his thoughts.

"Silvery, I hear," he said dismissively with a half wave of his hand. At Rowan's flat look, he chuckled. "Look, you know about as much as I do. They show up with obfuscating magic that hides their appearances, slay the enemy, and then disappear. Maybe if they show up here, we can see how true that is."

"Right..." Rowan replied slowly. "If they show up."

"Nothing special about Ladisdale," Cengor said by way of agreement. "Anyway. We should have the potions in Southmere in two days, so stop by in about four or five days to collect the payment. And I'll let you know if I hear anything about magical career paths."

"Sure, sounds good. And...thanks, Cengor. I'll see you later."

"See you later, Rowan. Watch out for the Dragon Knights, will ya?"

Rowan shook his head, smiling as Cengor laughed behind him and walked into the back room. He was a strange kind of man with an odd sense of humor, but he was always really jovial and never seemed to pay much attention to Rowan's 'cursed' status. Rowan appreciated that but had never quite verbalized it. He wasn't sure how, exactly. What did one say? 'Thanks for not judging me for something I was born with?' Or even, 'Thanks for being my friend?'

At least, he thought of Cengor as a friend. He wasn't entirely sure what qualified, given how he was somewhat estranged from society as a whole. He only ever talked to Cengor when he was making deliveries, and it's not like they interacted outside of a work capacity, but a lot of their conversations weren't around work so that counted, right?

He pondered on that as he crossed the street, walking up to the Opus Athenaeum where the local magi were stationed, all two of them. They also had a few apprentices, from what Rowan understood, although they weren't yet doing magic work unsupervised. However, his destination was specifically the one part of the Athenaeum opened to the public, and also his favorite place: the library.

Rowan stepped inside, eyes adjusting from the bright outdoors to the lower ambient light of magically lit lamps. The library had a bit of a musty scent since all the books were old, but Rowan found it rather peaceful. Likely, it was because he considered this place sort of a haven. He used to come here every day after school to read, and few people bothered him here.

At first, he would visit with his mother since she walked him to and from school. She would let him stay for an hour or two, then take him home since books could no longer be loaned out. Then, as he got older and was finally allowed to go to school by himself, he stayed longer, reading until the library closed each day.

Now, he didn't come to the library just to read. He'd already gone through every book available to the public, and no new books were really coming into circulation due to the lack of paper. And while he often came by to reread some of his favorite books, Rowan found other reasons to spend his afternoons here.

The 'reason' was sitting by the window overlooking the street, in front of a small table with an empty chair across from him. He was a broad-shouldered man with an eye patch over his left eye and a handsome face just barely touched by time. His beard was well-trimmed, with some silver threading through the black, the same as his hair.

He wore a dark green half cape over his right shoulder that concealed what Rowan knew to be an arm amputated just before the wrist. His uniform was black with gold accents, with a golden leaf pinned to his left breast. It was the insignia for the rank of Major in the Bascori army. His remaining hand had a golden ring on it with an engraved four-point star that he once told Rowan meant 'loyalty.'

On the table was a tiled wooden board that had seen a lot of use, with one set of light-colored game pieces in a cross in the center, and four groups of four dark pieces on each side. It was the traditional setup for a board game called tablut.

The man, who Rowan knew as Silas Baldry, nodded his head in greeting, gesturing to the empty chair across from him. "Ah, Rowan. You're early! Come sit."

"And yet you're already here. Do you just wait for me to get here every day?" Rowan asked teasingly, putting down his delivery basket and taking a seat across from Silas.

Silas smiled, the action making the crow's feet at the corners of his eyes deepen. "Maybe I'm early today, too."

"Sure, okay," Rowan laughed, brushing his hair back out of his face as he eyed the table. "We can play an extra round today, then. Do you want to play attackers or defenders?"

"Hmm, I defended last time, so let's switch." Silas reclined back in his chair, folding his arms across his chest as best he could. "Your start, for both game and conversation."

"No pressure," Rowan said with a grin, considering his move. He never expected to find himself playing a strategy game with a military major, and yet... that's exactly what he had been doing for almost three years.

He remembered the day Silas approached, helping him get a book off of a higher shelf when he saw Rowan couldn't reach it. Rowan was utterly embarrassed by being seen trying to balance on his tiptoes, but Silas hadn't said anything about it as he plucked the book that Rowan's fingers were barely touching.

Silas did pause, however, lifting a brow at the title. "An Introduction to Wartime Strategies?"

Rowan rubbed his arm, glancing at the floor nervously. "Was just curious about it..."

"Are you going to enlist in the guard?"

"N-no, sir. I'm... probably not fit for it, and... I don't think they'd allow me anyway, a-and my mother definitely wouldn't let me."

Silas's eyes fell to Rowan's arm, noting the binding there. "Ah. You're the Spicer boy."

"Yeah, um, Rowan, sir. A-and you're Major Baldry, right?"

"That's a bit formal for someone who doesn't report to me. Silas'll do." Silas held out the book for Rowan to take. "Do you like board games, Rowan?"

Rowan looked up, staring at Silas with wide eyes as he hesitantly took the offered book. "Me?"

Silas lifted a brow, the one not covered by an eyepatch. "I do believe you just told me your name is Rowan."

Rowan flushed, red staining his freckled cheeks as he clutched the book to his chest. "Um. I don't know. I've never played any, sir."

Silas regarded him critically, and truthfully, Rowan didn't know what he saw then, but he nodded and said, "All right. Let me teach you one, then."

And that's what he did. Almost every day after school, Rowan found himself in the library playing with Silas. Then, he graduated and continued to come to the library on days he delivered potions. Silas was usually there waiting, except for the days he had work obligations, and the two would play games and talk about the things Silas was well versed in: war, strategy, and combat.

Truthfully, it was the best part of Rowan's day, and he found himself smiling as he made the first move. "Well, I'll start with a question: what's happening on the western battlefield?"

Silas chuckled, moving his first piece. "Should have expected you to turn it around on me. Clever."

Rowan hid a grin and scrunched up his shoulders. "You have more interesting stories than me."

Silas arched a brow at that, watching as Rowan made his next move. "Interesting, maybe, but grim. The undead have taken more ground in their fight against our northern Weschecan neighbors, and things are equally concerning down in Acari. Bascor is currently in a deadlock, but I'm not sure how long that will last."

He paused, drumming the fingers of his left and only hand on the table before moving one of his pieces. "I also predict things will get worse soon."

Rowan looked up, making eye contact with Silas. "Did something happen?"

Silas nodded, expression pensive. "It's subtle, but if I'm reading between the lines correctly, yes. In the past, this war was troublesome because of sheer numbers. The undead army is relentless, and the dragons seem to have no limit in how many they can make as long as there are bodies, and war creates a lot of bodies."

He sighed, pursing his lips. "When we started burning corpses on the battlefield, that gave us an advantage, or I should say, it reduced *their* advantage. The enemy's numbers slowed, and that helped us keep up. But then the undead seemed to get tougher. The numbers no longer mattered, because now a single wight has the strength of three."

Rowan pursed his lips, moving one of his pieces. "You said 'it's subtle', so you're talking about something besides the undead growing stronger."

Silas's lips quirked up briefly. "Good. You're paying attention. The undead aren't just tougher. They move more strategically now. The smaller attacks on villages appear random, but they're timed between shift rotations for guards or after a dragon has been sighted elsewhere and people are distracted."

Silas paused long enough to make his move, capturing one of Rowan's pieces, before continuing. "The enemy also appears to be analyzing our defenses and striking at our weaknesses. Dragons haven't been known to do that in the past. They fight with raw power, not strategic thinking."

He stopped there, waiting for Rowan to make his move. Rowan stared at the board, then lifted his gaze to Silas's face. "So something's changed their actions."

Silas nodded slowly, staying quiet. Rowan understood that meant he should continue. He went silent for a minute, considering the board and what Silas told him. Then he carefully slid one of his pieces to a new location and sat back.

"Let's see... attacking between shift rotations or when people are distracted, and aiming for known weaknesses. Do you think the magic used to create undead is allowing them to be autonomous?"

"Not quite. If they were autonomous, they would be far less organized," Silas pointed out, leaning forward and moving another piece.

Rowan pursed his lips, eyes following Silas's movements. "They're being controlled."

"Yes, but that's not new. They've always been controlled." Silas pinned Rowan with a look.

Rowan stared back before his brows lifted. "Oh, wait... It's not dragons now, is it? Oh! You think humans are controlling them?"

Silas inclined his head in approval. "There you go. Yes, I do, and not just any humans. I think they have magi, maybe even archmagi, and that's how the undead are stronger. Fortified by magic."

"I can't imagine how people would side with the dragons willingly," Rowan said softly, moving one of his pieces to capture one of Silas's.

"It does leave one wondering," Silas agreed, considering his next move, "but at least the Dragon Knights are helping us keep even footing. I just wish we didn't have to rely on an uncertain ally that we know almost nothing about."

Rowan exhaled, the words 'Dragon Knight' reminding him of his conversation with Cengor. Then he sat up straight, realizing something said back then that was important.

Silvery.

He looked up at Silas as the other finished his move, then furrowed his brow. "Hey, Silas... have you ever seen a Dragon Knight?"

Silas blinked, considering the change in topic. "I have, yes. A few times from afar, but once close enough I could feel the discharge from their magic on my skin. Why?"

Rowan bit his lip, eyes falling to the board as his vision went slightly out of focus. He'd never told Silas about his dream, and his mother's voice echoed in his head, warning him to never tell anyone about it. Despite that... Rowan's skin was crawling with questions he didn't have answers to. It burned uncomfortably, and finally, he sighed, looking up at the officer who was the closest thing Rowan had to a father figure. "Can I... tell you a secret?"

Silas smiled slightly. "As long as it's not that you're the commander of the undead army. I'd have to turn you in and be disappointed that I'd have to find someone else to play games with me."

The joke cut through some of Rowan's anxiety, making a tiny smile form on his lips. "I don't think you have to worry about that. I can't even consistently beat you at tablut."

Silas lifted a brow, saying nothing, and Rowan took a deep breath, looking around to make sure no one else was in the library. "I... have had a recurring dream since I was little. I've had it every night, and it's always been the same. I dream I'm in darkness and that a man with glowing green eyes watches me. The darkness closes in, and then I wake up."

Silas nodded slowly, and Rowan continued, despite how quickly his heart was pounding. "Last night the dream changed for the first time. The man with green eyes was replaced by a person in silver fire. They chased away the shadows and reached out to me, but I woke up before I could touch them."

Rowan exhaled shakily, moving one of his pieces quickly and without much thought. "Then today, Cengor from 'On Bascori Wings' tells me that a Dragon Knight was seen in Bouldermoor, and he said they're always silvery. I wonder if... I'm dreaming about a Dragon Knight, and if so... why?"

Silas stroked his beard thoughtfully, and Rowan felt slightly relieved that he was at least taking the topic seriously and not looking at him like he was making it up.

Finally, Silas said, "'Silvery' was probably a bit of an ambiguous description to fixate on, however, I can confirm that Dragon Knights appear as beings covered in silver fire. Your dream... does sound similar."

He sighed, then added, "Although I'm not sure if it's a good thing or a bad thing that you're dreaming about them."

"Why?" Rowan asked, watching as Silas leaned forward and captured the piece he just moved recklessly.

Silas pursed his lips, leaning back in his chair. "Most people think they're human, but I've seen that magic. Humans don't wield that kind of magic, Rowan. It makes me uneasy. They fight our enemies, but I'm not entirely sure they're our allies. If I were you, I'd not go around telling people you're dreaming about a Dragon Knight, especially with that curse on your arm. You have enough bad luck as it is."

Rowan sighed, moving his king out of the castle. His excitement over the Dragon Knight was now dampened by Silas's caution, not that he blamed Silas. It made sense. He just... didn't like it. "Yeah... you're probably right. Can I ask... what does their magic look like?"

"Like they command the very skies themselves." Silas pursed his lips, eyeing the board, then trapped Rowan's king between one of his pieces and the castle. "And that's the match."

Rowan blinked at the board, before he sighed, shoulders slumping. "I wasn't paying attention..."

Silas chuckled, moving to reset the board. "Sometimes losses can be victories, too, Rowan. Shall we go again?"

Chapter 6

Petrichor

"Rowan, up here. I see some reeds."

At the sound of his grandfather's voice, Rowan looked up from where he was crouched by a rotting stump, inspecting the bits of lichen and fungus growing on it. Or rather, half-inspecting, half-lost in thought.

It had been two days since his dream changed, and each night it now ended with the Dragon Knight, because he *knew* that's what it was, reaching for him. He still didn't know what it meant, but it was all he could think about. Was the Dragon Knight a bad sign or a good one? He wanted it to be good, but Silas's caution sat in the back of his mind. What if it was somehow related to his curse?

"Be right there," he called, sheathing his gathering knife and walking up the hill's crest to stand beside his grandfather. The hills surrounding them looked dry despite the recent rain due to the pale color of the grass. Rocks jutted up out of the soil, providing some contrast to the otherwise monotone appearance of the land. Below them, the river wound through the valley, swollen and churning from the rain the night before.

Grandpa Zebb pointed out to an area where the river bank was generally flat and muddy, and the cluster of river reeds growing in it. "Looks like there might be some wild rice there, too."

Rowan looked around. The heavy rain last night had saturated the ground, and the hillside was not only steep but now slippery. "Want to trade, then? The rotting stump back there has some fruiting lichen on it, and I can probably get down the hill easier."

Grandpa Zebb considered the offer before nodding his head. "All right, but be careful, bean. That current doesn't look scary from here but I guarantee it'll sweep you away if you fall in."

Rowan nodded back and tucked his foraging basket against his hip before making his way down the hill. It was definitely slippery, and he caught himself from falling a couple of times. His feet sank into the mud more than once, and by the time he reached the bank, his fish leather shoes were muddied and wet.

He grimaced, wiping the toes of his shoes on the grass, and grateful he had switched out his usual sandals for his winter shoes. They weren't too insulating, but they were waterproof, and that's what counted right now. After all, the early cold wasn't so bad as long as he remained dry.

He looked back behind him and gave a thumbs up to his grandfather who waved and walked off towards the stump Rowan had been inspecting, leaving him to tend to the reeds. Hopping over to them, Rowan took stock of what was growing and could safely be harvested. He knew it was important to not take everything, so he selected a few of the more mature stalks to harvest, putting them in his basket. He did the same for the wild rice, leaving behind enough that they could propagate.

He stood up to see if there were any more clusters further up when he heard a wheeze from across the river. Eyes wide, he looked up to see a human form shambling towards him. Its arms swung with each uncoordinated step, and Rowan felt his skin crawl as he realized it was undead.

Despite the width of the river, Rowan could see how it looked emaciated and pallid, with a sunken face and cloudy eyes. Its mouth hung open, showing off a dark tongue and chipped teeth. Parts of the flesh had rotted at the joints, revealing the white of bone underneath, wrapped in congealed black.

He swallowed, nervously taking a step back. The undead twitched, its head looking in his direction. It made a raspy, inhuman sound, fingers flexing as it ambled towards him. Its movements were shaky and jerky like it was a puppet to a novice puppeteer. It stumbled, falling and tumbling down the rest of the hillside, landing in the mud by the bank.

Rowan's mouth fell open as he watched it struggle to get up in the mud. He had seen undead attacks from afar. They were fast, coordinated creatures, moving with ferocity and intent to kill. This... wasn't that at all. Why?

"Hey, bean! How's the harvest looking—*shit!*"

Rowan jumped, looking up to see his Grandpa Zebb standing atop the hill. "Get back! Get up here immediately!"

"It can't run though!" Rowan replied, gesturing to it. "Look at it!"

The wight was now shakily on its feet, slowly ambling towards the water, wheezing with each step. Despite the echoing shouts of his grandfather, it stayed focused on him, probably because he was closer.

"Rowan, *get up here!*"

"I got an idea; stay up there!" Rowan replied, hopping over his basket and moving further downstream. The wight's head followed his movements but lingered in place like it wasn't sure what to do. Rowan pursed his lips, eyes flicking around his surroundings. Quickly, he picked up several river stones and began to throw them at the wight. It turned towards him, its jaw waving in a way that signaled its skin was the only thing holding it in place, but then it took a step towards Rowan.

Rowan continued to kite it forward, pitching stones that sometimes hit it or hit the mud near it. Behind him, the sound of water became louder, indicating he was approaching the segment of the river where the rapids began. The wight followed, shambling along with its swinging arms and gaping mouth, and Rowan finally positioned himself behind some rapids and sharp rocks, throwing stones to keep its focus. Realizing he could no longer hear the noises it made, he chanced a quick look around to make sure no other undead were sneaking up behind him.

Seeing none, he turned back and began shouting, "Come on! Come for me! I'm right here!"

Up on the hilltop, his grandfather continued to scream at him, "Rowan, what are you doing?! Are you crazy?! Get back up here!"

Rowan waved at him to hush, keeping his eyes trained on the undead as he continued to keep its attention. Finally, it took a step forward into the river, plunging deep into the elevated waters. It flailed, the current knocking it off balance, and Rowan watched with delight as it was swept away downstream.

His elation turned into a high-pitched screech when he felt something grab his arm, and suddenly he found himself face-to-face with Grandpa Zebb, who was red-faced and furious. "What in the Shores were you doing?! You could have been *killed!*"

Rowan winced under the vice grip on his arm, prying himself loose. "But I wasn't in danger! Didn't you see how it was acting? It was so slow! It's nothing like the ones that attack town!"

Rowan craned his neck, looking over his shoulder to see it thrashing in the river as the water carried it around the bend. "I think that means someone has to be nearby to control it and give it orders! If someone can figure out who's controlling the army, they could easily shut it down by taking them out!"

Zebb snarled out a string of expletives, running a hand over his mouth. "Just because you play board games with Baldry doesn't make you a military strategist, Rowan! Stop putting yourself in danger like that just to test some half-brewed theories!"

Rowan flinched, expression darkening as he curled in on himself and took a step back. "You know, sometimes I think you're on my side, then other times you sound just like Mom."

Grandpa Zebb sighed in frustration. "Rowan—"

"I'm going to get the reeds," Rowan interrupted, his voice quivering as he looked away to hide how his eyes were watering. "Unless getting close to the river's too dangerous now, too."

"*Rowan.*"

He stomped off back through the mud, wiping away the tears that burned his eyes and battling emotions he could barely begin to describe. What he wouldn't give for someone who understood him.

The moment they got back home, Rowan changed shoes and left the house, stating he was going into town. He ignored his grandfather's protests and his mother's questions, exiting with a slam of the door.

Maybe he was being childish, but he was just so sick of everything! His family treated him like he was a fragile child who couldn't do anything, and the rest of the world treated him like an abomination. Where were more people like Silas or Cengor, or even Mistress Tanner, who saw him as a person? Who didn't look at him in disdain or pity?

He had so much stacked up against him. This stupid curse defined his life before he even had a choice, and everything else just slotted in neatly around it. He was too small and mild-mannered to be a soldier, and he couldn't go to the academy because of his curse. Maybe he could go to a non-magical institute, but he'd have to get noticed first, and while his potion-making skills were good, he was stuck at an apprentice level because the Athenaeum wouldn't let him test for his professional status.

And truthfully... he didn't even know if any of that was what he wanted. In fact, he probably didn't want to even be in the military, but he wanted a choice. He sighed, realizing that's really what it was. He wanted freedom, and he felt like he had none. He knew he should be lucky he was even alive and allowed into town with the curse on his arm, but was it really so selfish to want more?

It wasn't, right?

Feeling no better than when he left the house, Rowan looked up as he realized he was approaching the town's gates. He hadn't even noticed he'd made it to the farms outside of town because he was so lost in his thoughts.

He glanced around, looking at the near-barren fields that had a measly set of crops. In the distance, he could see the guards walking across the top of the walls and watching from the towers. In addition to defending from undead attacks, part of the guard's job was to make sure people didn't try to steal food. Even if there wasn't much growing here, it was still more than what most people had, so the temptation was there.

He kept to the middle of the road, knowing not to stray too close to the fences surrounding the fields, lest he get yelled at by the guards. The workers out in the fields paid him no mind, and neither did the other people on the road.

The sudden, loud wail of sirens made him jump, eyes blowing open wide as he recognized the warning coming from the town's towers. People scrambled at the sound, dropping what they were doing to rush for the town gates. Shouts erupted, signaling what approached.

"Undead! It's undead!"

"Get inside, hurry!"

Rowan twisted, eyes wide at seeing the mob of wights rushing up the road. Unlike the one by the river earlier, these moved swiftly and in unison. Fear bubbled up inside of him as he sprinted for the gates further up the hill. If he didn't hurry, the guards would close them before he could get inside, and then he'd really be in—

The world suddenly became *silver* as a thick fog rolled in through the hills, covering the fields and pressing up against the town walls. It poured over him, brushing against his skin in a way that left tingles like it was alive with magic. It smelled enticing, reminding him of the scent of the earth after the first rain, and for a brief moment, his dream flashed before his eyes, and he saw a silvery hand reaching for him. He sucked in a breath, eyes wide as he turned to look behind him, just as the sound of crackling energy reached his ears.

Brilliant light cut through the fog as a being wrapped in silver fire streaked across the hilly fields, looking exactly like the one in his dreams. His mouth fell open as the Dragon Knight leaped up into the air and struck down, landing in the middle of the oncoming undead with a thunderous boom.

The impact sent the fog swirling away momentarily, giving Rowan a clear view of the silvery Dragon Knight whirling in the center of the mob of undead, lightning spinning around them like an electrical whirlwind. The magic in the air was palpable, making the hairs on his arms stand on end and putting a strange taste in the back of his mouth.

A sudden arm around his waist yanked him off of the ground. Rowan yelped, panicking as he began to struggle against his unknown adversary.

"You're going to get trapped out here if you keep gawking!" Silas's voice shouted in his ear as he hauled Rowan towards the town with his good arm.

"But it's a—"

"Dragon Knight, I know! And you're still standing out in the open!" Silas didn't slow down, jogging past the gates as they started sliding down with a loud rattle. Despite it all, Rowan couldn't pull his eyes away from arcs of lightning shooting out over the swirling fog, his breath coming out in wisps as the temperature in the area dropped significantly.

The gates closed with a loud crash that rang in his ears. Silas put him down, and Rowan stood still, staring through the metal grates as the fog dissipated, showing a scattered pile of corpses on the road, covered in a frosty rime. The Dragon Knight was gone.

Behind him, Silas sighed, the sound snapping Rowan out of his thoughts. He swallowed, nervously looking back to see the much larger man frowning at him with no small measure of exasperation. "Wise men don't stand out in the open, Rowan."

Rowan winced, dropping his gaze to the ground between them. Earlier, he felt indignant with his grandfather's admonishing, but this time he knew Silas was right. Pressing a hand to his arm, he stumbled to find his words. "I know... I started to run, but... they looked just like my *dream*, Silas."

"And I told you to remain *cautious*," Silas said quietly but pointedly, putting his hand on Rowan's shoulder, "We can talk about this in private later. I need to go find out if anyone got hurt or is still trapped outside. Until then, stay out of trouble, and don't tell anyone about your dream, okay?"

Rowan nodded nervously, rubbing his hand over his arm as Silas took his leave, giving orders to the nearby guards as he walked off. On one hand, Rowan felt foolish for what he did, but on the other hand, he was brimming with a nervous energy that he was doing his best to contain.

That was a Dragon Knight! And they looked just like the one in his dreams! It couldn't be a coincidence that his dreams changed at the same time a Dragon Knight started appearing in the area. But what did it mean? Silas was worried it was bad, but... could it really be bad when they just took apart those undead? Could it really be bad when they chased away the shadows in his dream? He didn't want to believe it.

He began walking up the street, knowing he had nothing better to do for now. While he didn't normally get caught in town during the sporadic undead attacks, he still knew the protocol pretty well. For the next hour or two, the gates would stay closed as the guards confirmed the threat was over. For some, this was routine, and they would already be returning to their jobs. For others, anxiety prevailed and they would hide in their homes and fear the worst. But for Rowan, all he could think about was the Dragon Knight and his dream.

He stayed lost in his thoughts as he wove up the inclined streets towards the town square at the top of the hill. He kept to his preferred route, both out of habit and because he knew it well enough to escape if anyone gave him a hard time. While it seemed less likely that he would be bothered right now, Rowan wasn't foolish enough to take chances.

When he reached the edge of the square, he found a fair number of people mingling about, talking about the attack. Some were fretting over the guard's ability to keep them safe, others trying to distract themselves by talking about anything else. The rest were spreading the word about the mysterious fog and the silvery warrior who appeared outside the gates. The word 'Dragon Knight' was thrown out a couple of times as people piecemealed the story together.

Although the crowd made Rowan slightly uncomfortable, he knew by now that being in public was ultimately safer than being alone and out of sight. Most people didn't like to make a scene in public, which lowered his chances of being harassed. And he figured people would be too distracted by the Dragon Knight rumors to pay him much attention anyway.

The anxiety and excitement in the air was palpable, although Rowan really only cared about the Dragon Knight sightings. He stayed quiet and out of the way, trying to overhear various conversations without drawing attention to himself. Did anyone else see anything he didn't?

Overall, that answer was 'no.' In fact, he seemed to have the best view of that entire ordeal, having been outside past the gates and not fleeing as he should have. He wagered Silas would lecture him later, but he didn't regret stopping to watch. Even if he knew his choice of actions had been absolutely foolish.

Absconding away from the crowd so he could hear himself think, Rowan took to the edge of the square to go over his facts and the recounts he heard from others. Nothing stood out from what anyone had seen. Like his dream, the Dragon Knight was covered in silver fire, leaving them unidentifiable, and like Silas said, it was like they could control the weather with how that fog rolled in. It was definitely not arcane magic, but was it really stolen dragon magic?

He paused, thinking back to the way that scent filled his nose. There was a word for that smell, one he read in one of the old science books. Petrichor. That was it.

"Hey look, it's Spicer."

Rowan felt his skin crawl at the sound of his name, head snapping up as he looked over his shoulder. His hope of being left alone during all of this chaos quickly died as he realized just who had said his name.

Tilbert Brewer was an unpleasant man, in Rowan's experience. Born a few years before the Great Wither, he stood taller than most people of Rowan's generation, his growth not much affected by the lack of nutrition. Tilbert also let that go to his head.

He was notorious for his aggressive behavior, acting much like a territorial dog without any training. Or at least, that's what Grandpa Zebb described him as. Rowan hadn't seen many dogs in his life.

Still, Tilbert was bad news because Rowan was easy to pick on. Not only was he the target demographic: a small, younger man affected by the Great Wither, he was also not the most-liked person in town, so very few people would stand up for him. And Rowan didn't see any of the few who would.

He swallowed, standing up straight as he noted Tilbert wasn't alone. Some other men were with him, including Mister Carpenter's youngest son, Wulmar. Wulmar Carpenter was Rowan's age but got lucky with his taller height. Much like his father, Wulmar didn't care for Rowan, but he normally wouldn't go out of his way to bother him unless he had 'buddies.'

The other two, Rowan recognized but didn't remember their names, and right now that detail was *really* irrelevant. He frowned, eyes flicking over his surroundings. Cengor's office was closed, if the flipped sign was any indicator, and the library wasn't safe unless Silas was there. And he couldn't run home because the gates were closed. He had to hope they were here just to be gross with their words, and not anything else.

"Hi Brewer," Rowan said quietly, knowing by now that not greeting him was far worse.

Tilbert didn't acknowledge the greeting, turning his head to the other men with him. "You know, I was wondering why a plague of wights would charge the town like that, and wouldn't you know, I saw Major Baldry dragging Spicer in through the gate."

One of the other men laughed derisively, "Spicer attracts undead on top of everything else wrong with him. Damn, why do they let you into town, man?"

"I don't attract undead," Rowan said, squaring his shoulders. "They're controlled by someone. That's why they move like that."

"Did you hear that, boys? Spicer thinks someone's out there *controlling* them," Tilbert chortled, pressing a hand to his stomach. "Bet you think someone's controlling the dragons, too."

"I doubt dragons, but maybe Spicer was out there commanding the wights with his curse," Wulmar replied with an ugly grin.

"I don't *control* undead, either," Rowan said between clenched teeth, balling his fists. Getting frustrated wasn't going to help; he needed to stay calm.

"Hey, look, he's getting mad," Tilber said with humor in his voice that was more cruel than anything else. "What're you going to do about it, Spicer? Raise some corpses to do your bidding?"

"How do you summon them?" One of the other men asked, lightly shoving Rowan's shoulder. "Do you have a ritual? You use a potion?"

"Oh, that's what the long hair's for!" Wulmar exclaimed, eyes wide in mock surprise. "He's gotta sacrifice some hair for the spell. That's why it always looks like shit!"

"Is that it? So if we cut it all off, the undead go away?" Tilbert joked, walking up behind Rowan. Rowan froze as he felt Tilbert grab onto his ponytail in a tight grip, pulling his head back. "Not only would we get rid of this eyesore, we'd get rid of the undead. We'd be heroes, eh?"

"Please let go," Rowan gasped, wincing as Tilbert forced his head back.

"Sure. Let me just get my knife here, and we'll cut it loose and save the world," Tilbert replied mockingly, and Rowan panicked as he realized Tilbert was serious.

"Let go!" he cried out, reaching behind to pry Tilbert's hand off of his hair. "This isn't funny!"

"If you don't hold still, I might cut off a finger—*hey!*"

Suddenly, the pressure on his head was gone. Rowan gasped, whirling around and holding the back of his head with both hands. His fingers slid over his tangled curls, finding them still there, but he froze, eyes going wide at the sight before him. Tilbert was down on his knees, his arm twisted behind him while the knife fell from his fingers, clattering loudly on the flagstone.

However, the really shocking part of the scene was the person holding his arm. Rowan stared, slack-jawed at the woman standing behind Tilbert, keeping his arm pinned with little effort. She was taller than Rowan, with broad shoulders, and wore a heavy, plain, dark gray cloak with silver details. It draped around her in a stark contrast to her pale skin. Ice blue eyes narrowed under wispy, black bangs, and her face was contorted into one of cold rage as she twisted Tilbert's arm a little further.

"Let go of me!" Tilbert snarled, doing his best to look behind him and see who had him. Rowan didn't miss the alarm and confusion that flashed on Tilbert's face when he realized the person was a woman.

"Be lucky I do not snap your arm, for it is quite tempting," she said quietly in a strange accent, eyes flashing dangerously. "It is clear you do not know how to use it anyway with how you hold that blade. If you wish to save it, tell me why you would violate his hair like that."

Rowan blinked several times, questioning if he heard her correctly. She was defending him because of his hair? Was he dreaming?

"Fuck, why do you care, bitch? Let me go!" Tilbert snapped, voice tense with what Rowan assumed was pain, given how he twisted his body to try to alleviate the pressure on his shoulder. It looked uncomfortable, but Rowan certainly wasn't going to stop her. What could he do, anyway?

She scowled, eyes flicking up to him. Rowan stiffened as she gave him an appraising glance from head to toe. "Why did you let them? It was clear you did not want it."

Rowan blinked, stuttering. "W-what? How could I have stopped them?"

She seemed confused by his response, tilting her head in a way that drew Rowan's attention to the many silver earrings decorating her ears, and how the ones in her ear lobes looked like claws. "Are you not a magus? You have arcane magic all over you."

"N-no," Rowan replied awkwardly, trying to figure out how she came to such a conclusion. "I'm not—"

"He's *cursed,*" Wulmar spat, pointing in Rowan's general direction. "You're attacking the wrong man. Who even are you—"

"You do not have the privilege of knowing my name," the woman said contemptuously, letting go of Tilbert's arm as she shoved him forward with her foot. "You attack an unarmed man for something someone else inflicted upon him and pretend that vindicates you for your actions. Begone."

Tilbert scrambled to his feet, and Rowan sucked a breath through his teeth as he realized he'd grabbed his knife in the process. "You're going to regret that, bitch. It's four-on-one because Spicer can't fight."

"He does not need to," she replied dismissively, dusting off her cloak. "You are as challenging as walking through a morning mist."

Tilbert spat an ugly curse and charged at her in response, and Wulmar came at her from the other side with his fists drawn. Rowan expected her to duck or move out of the way, but he didn't expect her to simply stop both attacks head-on. He stared in dumbfounded awe as she caught Tilbert's knife hand and yanked him forward, using his own momentum to send him toppling.

She then snapped her leg out as Wulmar reached her, kicking him in his gut. He doubled over, gasping, and Rowan's eyes were drawn to the flash of white from the action. He blinked, realizing she was wearing a very short dress in jagged layers under her cloak, and he was staring at her bare leg.

Her very muscular bare leg.

Too shocked to be embarrassed at seeing so much skin, he watched as she grabbed the next man coming at her and threw him over her shoulder and onto the ground without any effort. He wheezed on impact, and that sound seemed to signal to the last man that they were sorely outmatched. He skidded to a stop, turned around, and ran.

She curled her lip in displeasure as she watched him flee, but Rowan felt his heart drop into his stomach as he saw the man stop in front of a soldier and start pointing in their direction. The soldier looked over at them, noting three men groaning on the ground, and Rowan just knew this wasn't going to end well.

He turned, looking at his mysterious savior, and made a split decision. "Come with me!"

Without waiting for a reply, he grabbed her by the wrist and pulled her along a side street. It was only as he rounded the corner that he realized that she let him grab her when she could have easily thrown him like she did everyone else. He felt like he was incredibly lucky to be still on his feet.

Chapter 7
The Nova

Rowan didn't stop until they were some distance away from the square on one of the quieter streets that had mostly abandoned homes. The buildings belonged primarily to people who hadn't survived the food shortages of the Great Wither or to soldiers who died at war. They had long since been gutted for their wood and textiles, leaving behind stone structures not fit for living in. He panted softly, not from the sprint so much as his panic, fingers letting go of the woman's wrist as he turned to look at her.

She wasn't winded at all, regarding him curiously, which was a nice change from the terrifying expression she had earlier as she pinned Tilbert in a death grip. Now that he could study her, he saw her eyes were a pale shade of blue, and coupled with her very light complexion, he had to assume she was from Wescheca, despite her black hair.

He had never met anyone from up north, but he knew they were supposed to have fair features due to the limited sunlight. And given she had an accent he couldn't place and spoke in a slightly stilted manner, it made sense that was where she was from.

Of course, her attire didn't match what he knew of Weschecan clothes. While certainly, animal furs were a thing of the past, her cloak didn't look anything like what he saw in old books, in style or material, and he was pretty sure Weschecan women didn't wear dresses that short.

Wasn't she cold?

He swallowed, noting she was taller than him by a head. That wasn't uncommon, but the way her cloak was padded made her appear much larger than him like she had the broad shoulders of a mason worker. That was ridiculous, of course.

But then again... she really had taken out four, well *three*, men her size without any flourish or breaking a sweat. She was quick and efficient about it, and while Rowan may not have been trained in combat, he knew some of the moves she used required raw, brute strength.

He shook his head, realizing he was just staring at her instead of providing an explanation after dragging her across town to an empty street. "S-sorry, I didn't want you to get in trouble for helping me out."

She hummed, glancing back the way they came, expression slightly pensive. "I do not know the customs of this land. How is what I did an offense?"

Ah, so definitely not from Bascor. Weschecan was probably right, then.

"It's... complicated," Rowan replied, fidgeting slightly because explaining this wasn't a great look for Bascori culture. "Although they started things, technically it would have been the word of four against two, and you're not from here and I'm not well-liked."

"I see. How spineless. They should have stood their ground and taken their defeat with dignity instead of shamefully attempting to manipulate it." She wrinkled her nose with disdain. It looked kind of cute, so much that Rowan awkwardly cleared his throat and glanced to the side because she wasn't trying to be cute, he was pretty sure.

He saw her gaze drop to his cursed arm out of the corner of his eye, and he resisted the urge to hide it behind his back.

"Regardless... This is a curse, yes? You are fortunate, then, to have it bound."

Rowan sighed, pressing his hand over the seal, feeling the magic thrum under his fingers. "Yeah, I just don't *feel* fortunate. Everyone holds it against me. Well, not everyone, but a lot of people do, and it gives me a lot of trouble, like what you saw back there."

"They fear what they do not know, and exerting control is a way to hide that fear. It does not excuse it, however." She nodded to him, almost in a way he could interpret as solidarity.

He pursed his lips, but before he could reply she stepped in a little closer, eyes falling to the spell cloth. He pulled back just a little, looking at her in surprise. "It is curious, though. A lot of magic was used to bind that curse. Much more than I have ever seen."

"You can... see it?"

She hesitated, eyes flicking to his face, and he could tell she wasn't quite sure what to say. After several seconds of silence hanging between them, she looked away and admitted, "I cannot see it, but I know it is there."

It was clear whatever actual explanation she had she didn't want to give, and Rowan wasn't about to press, especially not after she had gone out of her way to help him. So he smiled and said, "That's really neat. I can't really see anything, but it does sorta hum against my skin, so I always know it's there. I just couldn't tell it was a lot because I have nothing to compare it to."

She looked back at him, brows lifting slightly like she was surprised he didn't press the issue. After a moment, she schooled her expression into something more neutral and nodded. "I do not think I have felt so much magic on a... person before, so that is why I thought you were a magus. Whoever did it was very powerful. It is impressive."

Rowan winced. As much as it sounded like a compliment, it really wasn't. It was a statement of fact but with dark undertones. "Yeah, that's not a good thing, though. It means it's a bad curse."

The woman tilted her head, and honestly, Rowan felt like her gaze could pierce right through him. She had an intensity about her that he wasn't used to. It was a bit intimidating, not that he felt like she was trying to be threatening. It just seemed to be the way she was. But it sure did make him feel small.

"That is true," she said slowly, thoughtfully. "For that much magic to linger, that is a powerful curse. But do you not think it possible that someone felt you were worthy enough to expend that much magic to save you?"

"Or that was the only way to save the whole town," Rowan countered, pinning her with a look. "I've thought about this a *lot*. There's no guarantee whatever magus did this did it to save me. It could have been a curse that would have continued after my death, or even had some strange requirements where binding was the only option no matter what."

He twisted his hands together, glancing around. "I mean, from what I've read about curses, it's more likely that this was the only option. ...Instead of, well, me being worth ...saving."

He didn't mean to sound so defeated as he said that, but saying it stung. Because it was true. Whoever the mysterious magus was who bound his curse at birth didn't do it because Rowan himself meant anything. He did it because people would die otherwise. That was the kind of world they lived in, and Rowan understood that.

It still hurt, though. And his expression must have mirrored that because the Weschecan woman frowned, face turning pensive. "I see."

"S-sorry," Rowan said, waving a hand as he felt his face heat up. "Didn't mean to, uh, just ramble on like that."

"It is of no consequence," she replied, seeming unbothered. "Though, truly, you do not know, then? Of the magus who did this?"

"I don't," Rowan replied quietly. "I wish I did, though. It's hard to accept not being liked for something that's not my fault. I feel kind of trapped because of it like my life's been chosen for me, and none of it's good. It'd... be nice if I got a chance to be me. Or even find out who 'me' is. I feel like no one really lets me do that."

She gave him a sharp look at that, like what he said struck a chord in her. He blinked at her, and they held a beat of silence between them before she replied, "That I can understand."

He offered her a fleeting smile, tucking a lock of hair behind his ear. "Yeah?"

She nodded, and he thought he saw a ghost of a smile on her lips.

"That's nice to hear. Well, I mean, not nice, because you shouldn't have to deal with it, too, but I mean, it's nice that you understand, and, uh..." He took in a deep breath, realizing he was rambling once again. "Anyway... Thank you."

He paused, eyes going wide. "Oh! And thank you for earlier! You didn't have to help me back there, but you did. I really appreciate it."

Her brows lifted in disbelief. "They should not have touched your hair like that. It is gravely disrespectful, and now it is in need of care after what they did."

"W-what?" Rowan blinked, running a hand over his messy ponytail before he realized what she meant. "Oh! Oh, no. It kinda... always looks like this, because of the texture and curls and stuff. I try to keep it brushed, but it tangles so easily. And, well, I just don't like to cut it, so I just... deal with it."

She frowned, brows pinching together in a way that seemed puzzled. Rowan swallowed, glancing away. "Um, anyway... My name's Rowan. Rowan Spicer. May I have yours?"

She blinked several times, confusion passing over her face. "Why do you wish to take my name?"

Rowan's mouth fell open, pink blossoming across his face. "W-what?! No! I'm not! I just— I'm asking what to call you!"

"Oh. I am the—" she paused, catching herself on her words, before awkwardly finishing, "Nova."

"'The Nova'?" Rowan repeated, lifting a brow at her. He didn't think Weschecan people addressed themselves like this, but he wasn't going to pretend he was an expert, either. All the books he had read on the culture were at least 17 years old. A lot could change.

A faint pink touched her cheeks as she quickly clarified, "It is just Nova."

"Okay, it's nice to meet you, Nova," Rowan said, hoping the rote formality would help move past this moment of, in his opinion, extreme awkwardness. "What brings you to Ladisdale? Are you from Wescheca?"

She didn't immediately answer, instead pursing her lips and glancing away like she was debating on how to reply. It was another cute expression, drawing his attention to the way her eyes were upturned slightly and the round shape of her face. It made him smile slightly as he watched her debate on her answer.

Finally, she said, "Yes... that is where I am from. I am here because I am curious why this area suffers less from the Great Wither. It is not like this... in Wescheca."

"You and everyone else," Rowan said with a soft laugh. He mentally noted that she didn't speak very confidently, like someone who was fumbling through what to say. It may have just been that she wasn't used to speaking the Bascori dialect of Common Tongue. As far as he could recall, Wescheca's dialect wasn't supposed to be very different, but there were a few secluded areas that still primarily spoke Old Weschecan. Maybe she was from there? It would definitely explain her accent.

Well, that was fine. He could drive the conversation. And it gave him a chance to talk to someone from another culture! He never got to do that!

Excited at the opportunity, he continued, "So you're just exploring the whole region?—*Oh!* Did you see the Dragon Knight outside? I bet that must have been scary for you to just get here and have to deal with an undead attack!"

"Ah..." Nova replied hesitantly. "It was... interesting, yes, but I did not see much, for I was inside the town. I heard the gates come down. It is good your town has gates. Not all do, I do not think. Though, I notice they are slow to open them again. Do they fear another attack?"

Rowan blinked a few times, again noting the way she spoke as if very carefully considering her words. Honestly, it almost felt like she was lying, but what could she be lying about? Was he making her uncomfortable? He hoped not.

With a soft hum, he considered her question and glanced towards the gate where the Dragon Knight killed the undead. "Oh, this is standard procedure. They want to make sure the undead are all... uh, dead again? Once the guards conclude the surrounding area is secure, they'll reopen the gates."

She opened her mouth, her brow furrowed like she was about to point out something contrary. However, she paused like she was second-guessing herself, then finally said, "...I see. It is good to remain cautious, then."

Rowan lifted a brow at her but decided to not comment on her behavior. Instead, he sighed wistfully, glancing towards the closest gate. "Yeah, but I hope they lift the gates soon. I'm sure my mother is panicking right now. The sirens can be heard from my house."

"You do not live in this town?" Nova asked curiously. Her brows lifted slightly, but her expression was otherwise mild.

"Oh, no. My family lives out by the river, actually." Rowan turned towards the general direction of his home and pointed. "That way."

Nova turned her head to see where he pointed. She was silent for a moment, her expression thoughtful. "That is an interesting direction, yes. I am curious about it. Shall we leave, then?"

Rowan gave her a confused look as she turned back to him. "I mean, we can't. They're not going to lift the gates for us. We'll have to wait."

That was also... a weird thing for her to say. What was interesting about the woods he lived in, and why did she say 'we?' Did she want to follow him home? Or just have him show her the road to the woods? His mother's warnings echoed in his head, reminding him to not talk to anyone strange. He shoved the thought aside. Sure, she was strange, but she had helped him.

And besides, it's not like they were leaving right now. Or so he thought.

"They do not need to lift the gates. Come with me." Without waiting for confirmation, she walked off down the street at a steady pace that implied she had a destination. Rowan blinked, questioning just what she had in mind, before hurrying after her.

She led him down a couple of streets before coming to the town wall that faced the direction of his house. Rowan came to a stop beside her, eyes falling to the stairs that led up to the walkway and guard towers. He turned to her, staring in alarm. "You're joking, right?"

"I have said nothing, so how could I make a joke?" Nova replied, and the earnest tone in her voice made Rowan realize that she really meant that.

"No, I mean..." He trailed off, looking back up at the guard towers that most certainly weren't empty. "There's no stairs on the other side, and it's a huge drop to the ground. And the moment we get up there, they'd see us and probably arrest us. I don't want to spend the night in jail."

She scoffed, reaching up to pull at the braided silver cord that held her cloak closed. Rowan swallowed, paying actual attention to the color for the first time. It was just an accessory, but so few people had nice clothes anymore, and silver no less. But that was... a silly idea, and just because he'd never seen her before today when the Dragon Knight appeared, didn't mean...

His trail of thought died as she dragged her cloak off of her shoulders. The cloak did not have padding. She really was that muscular. And that was a *lot* of skin.

He swallowed again, tongue feeling thick in his mouth as his eyes swept over her form. She wore a sleeveless dress made of some glossy, dark material, and the skirt hung in layers of jagged triangles at mid-thigh, with some pieces a pale, cloudy silver instead of stormy gray. She wore a braided silver rope tied around her waist, and silver bangles around her wrists, and the presence of *silver* was frying his brain like a river trout on a skillet.

She had a dark gray satchel hanging over one shoulder, also made of the same material, and the only thing normal about her attire was her running sandals. Nova turned, eyeing the top of the wall, and Rowan made a choking sound at realizing her dress was open at the back, baring her shoulder blades. He had never read about this in books about Wescheca!

His eyes were then drawn to the gentle sway of her hair a moment later. He blinked, noting the length and how it stopped at her knees. It was midnight black, cinched together in three sections with silver ties, and part of him immediately became envious at how nice and well-kempt it looked. Oh, how he wished his own hair was like that...

He snapped out of his thoughts when she turned and walked up to him, cloak in hand, and he went stock still as she swept the fabric over him and wrapped it around his shoulders. It dwarfed him, but more importantly, it was *warm*, like he was sitting under the midday summer sun.

He stood there, stunned in silence as Nova secured the tie and pulled the hood over his head. "Hm, yes. This shall do."

And then she turned around, dropping down onto one knee. "Climb onto my back."

"I— *What?*" Rowan squeaked, feeling his face burn in embarrassment. "Y-you want me to..."

He trailed off as she spared him a slightly annoyed look over her shoulder. "Do you wish for me to carry you some other way? My understanding is that the other ways are more embarrassing for men, but if you have a preference it makes no difference to me."

Rowan pressed his hands to his cheeks, feeling how hot they were against his cooler fingers. "I..."

He fumbled, mind furiously trying to figure out what to say. Finally, he dropped his hands from his face, exhaling shakily. "I can't believe I'm doing this."

With that, he swallowed the cotton in his mouth and walked up behind her, wrapping his arms around her neck and ignoring the fact that half of her back was bare. He had only ever ridden on his grandfather's back when he was much younger, and *never* had he been this close to a woman who wasn't his mother. What if someone saw them? What if she thought he smelled bad, or he touched her wrong, or—

His brain came to a crashing halt when the faint scent of petrichor filled his nose. She stood up before he could really process what that meant, and the action of his feet leaving the ground made him suck in a breath through his teeth. She shifted his weight, securing his legs on either side of her. It was clear she was strong, if her physique wasn't clue enough, because she moved like he weighed nothing.

"You are tense. Do you think I will drop you, Rowan Spicer?" she asked, amused.

"I, um... I..." Rowan swallowed his attempted sentence, his tongue currently on strike. She smelled like the *Dragon Knight's magic.* It was faint, but it was there. Did that mean she was...?

He swallowed again, mouth suddenly dry. He pressed his face against his bicep as he clung to her, now completely shocked and unsure of what to say or do.

"What is it?" Nova asked, and the proximity of her voice made him stiffen. "You are frightened."

Furiously, he tried to think of what to say, not wanting to just blurt out what was on his mind, especially not with her holding him. Finally, he settled on the easiest, obvious thing and said, "...We're going to get in trouble."

His voice was muffled against his arm, but she heard him anyway.

"They cannot see your face, and they do not know who I am, so no, I do not think so," Nova replied calmly.

"But there's no escape once we're up—" He sucked in a breath as she tensed then bolted, dashing up the narrow stone stairs that reached the top of the wall. She was fast, and before Rowan could even process what was going on, she reached the top and leaped off the edge.

He bit back a yelp, squeezing his eyes closed and clutching her neck, waiting for a terrible impact. Instead, there was a light thump that jostled him against Nova's back, then Nova was sprinting down the sloping hillside towards the road.

Rowan opened his eyes wide and looked behind him, staring at the wall she had jumped down from and staring *harder* at the wisps of fog around the guard towers that weren't there before and were now fading away. His heart pounded, his mind a jumble of thoughts he didn't know how to properly untangle as he realized what that meant:

She was the Dragon Knight!

Chapter 8
The Taste of Blackberries

Nova the Tempest was confused.

Until now, the human settlements she visited in this southern Bascor had not given her anything meaningful. They all held the same stale Viridian magic, active by technicality, but barely moving, and with no indicator of a source. No one had explanations as to why the hills were more alive than the rest of the Reprised Shores.

Additionally, the small swaths of undead, while not a challenge, were more than what she expected to see away from the battlefields. Locals indicated undead attacks were not rare, and even stray wights could be found wandering the hills, but truly, Nova was not certain why the lich would send them this far inland in such small amounts.

Was it to acquire more corpses? She did not think so, but what else could it be?

Along with the undead, her nose picked up many traces of human arcane magic, but most of the time those went back to normal human magi who did not want to talk to her. She supposed when she looked only *human* she was not deemed worthy to talk to by anyone who felt they had esteem. Then again, perhaps that was fair, as she did not normally want to talk to humans, either.

The rest of the arcane she smelled was tied to the undead. It was pungent, but it began to fade once she cut them down. This was interesting because the magic was *human* and not from the lich, which implied he now had humans under his command.

And because of the way the lingering Viridian magic permeated the area, it was hard to pick up the scent of dragons. While she did not expect there to be much, given how few remain and the caution they must take, it was always good to know where they were in proximity. After all, it was dangerous for them to be on the Reprised Shores fulfilling their roles.

But these were not the reasons she was confused. This all was within her expectations and aligned with the stories of others who had inspected the area in the past.

She was confused by the little human perched on her back.

When she got to Ladisdale, she smelled the magic on him before she smelled the approaching undead. It was only that she saw the undead first that she moved in to slay them, and by then, he had hidden within the town.

It took no effort to find him afterward, as that magic was like a great signal fire in the night. She followed him at a distance, curious about the magic clinging to him. There was nothing really strange about the magic besides its strength. It was arcane, but not dragon arcane, decidedly human, and *powerful*. Truly, she had never come across a human with so much magic on him, so he must have been an archmagus.

But he looked so small. And unsure. And young. And unhealthy. These were not the things that she ascribed to powerful humans. Where were his magus robes and diadem? Where was his pride and confidence? They were all missing, and she found herself staring in confusion as other humans approached him to antagonize him.

She waited to see if he would retaliate, but when they grabbed his hair and he cried out, she could not simply watch anymore. It was the first time she felt such righteous fury on behalf of a human, although she understood part of it was because of what hair represented to her kind.

And it was fascinating, because he clearly felt strongly about his hair, but it was in such poor condition, even for a human. Most human hair lacked the gloss and shine of dragons or half-dragons. Even her glamor had to dull her appearance so that she could blend in. But his hair not only lacked shine, it looked damaged and dry, like the withered grass outside of Southern Bascor.

It must have been so painful to brush, and she wondered why he did not simply cut it, for humans did not often care about hair in the same way. And yet, she could tell it was important to him, despite its state.

How unusual.

The cowardly men called him 'cursed', but Nova did not immediately realize that was the reason for the magic on him. But once she was close enough, she realized how that pungent magic was coming from the spell cloth wrapped around his arm. She had to wonder just what kind of curse required that much magic.

It was fascinating, but it also explained why he seemed so timid. Perhaps the curse was also why his hair was unhealthy, too. And when he explained how the bound curse made him feel trapped and hopeless, Nova found herself resonating far more than she wanted.

Her plight was *different*. She was a champion created to fight, to save what remained of the dragons, and to free those taken into undeath. She was the Tempest, and a 'Dragon Knight,' and it was all she was allowed to be. She was glorified for performing a duty she did not want by a race that would hate her if they knew what she was.

He was not the same, not at all, and yet... she still understood. People judged him for something outside of his control, and his life was shaped around this curse. She never expected to feel camaraderie with a human, and yet, here she was.

She snapped out of her thoughts as the hilly fields blended away into withered forest, and she came to a stop on the empty road shaded by sickly trees. Rowan Spicer clung to her as tight as she suspected his little arms were capable of. For some reason, she found it amusing.

"This should be good now," she commented, letting go of his legs to allow him to slide down. She felt his grip on her neck loosen before it disappeared completely, and she turned around to look at him.

Truly, even with such scraggly hair, Rowan Spicer was an interesting little thing, with those big eyes and the way he pulled in on himself as if scared to take up space. He stared at her in wonder, like he was seeing her without her disguise. She knew that was not the case, and yet she found herself checking her shoulder to make sure her scales were not there.

He must have been awed by her strength, now that she thought about it. Perhaps it was too much to jump from the top of the wall? It was not very high, in her opinion, but come to think of it, she had never seen a human make a jump like that. She would have to be more careful, she supposed. That was fine. She doubted he had figured out what she was. Her disguise was pretty good.

She looked back at him, noting how he clutched her cloak to him. Ah, he *was* quite small. Likely the cloak felt nice against the chill in the air. She still did not know why it was cooler than usual for this time of year. Certainly, it had to be one of her clan, although she had not picked up any strong traces of Silver in the air. It might have been simply a natural shift, but she doubted it.

It was not a pressing issue compared to finding what Osier the Life Walker left behind. Her dream had come back the same every night since it changed, with him guiding her to seek his legacy. Perhaps it was not her duty, but she could not help but feel it was equally as important. Perhaps even more. She only wished the dream was more... clear.

When she realized they were both standing there looking at each other, she snorted softly and held out her hand for him to give her back her cloak. He glanced at it, then looked back up at her in a manner she could only describe as innocent and confused.

She lifted a brow, trying not to show her amusement. "I only lent you my cloak to hide your face. It is not yours to keep."

He blinked, and then his face turned quite an interesting shade of red as he stammered out an apology and fumbled with the ties. "O-oh! S-sorry. I wasn't— Here!"

She snorted again, taking the cloak as he passed it back to her and wrapping it back over her shoulders. "You are a strange man, Rowan Spicer."

"I–I am?" He rubbed his arms like he missed the heat, and truly, she did not blame him.

In response to his question, Nova hummed thoughtfully as she secured the tie of her cloak. "Yes, I think so. Most of who I interact with carry themselves in ways that belie who they are. You, however, do not seem to hide your emotions very well, although I cannot tell if it is a choice or simply a skill you do not possess."

"I..." He trailed off, nervously playing with a lock of his hair. "Um, well, I'm not always like this, I don't think. I mean, I guess... I'm trying to be better about it. My grandfather says being able to field your emotions makes it harder for others to use them against you."

"I do not understand," Nova admitted. "How can one 'use' your emotions? They are yours, no? Is it a type of magic?"

To her, controlling her emotions meant better control over magic. It meant being able to focus on her duties and her battles. She did not know how one could use her emotions, and now she was very curious.

He was silent for a moment, looking at her with a pensive frown as he shrunk in on himself. "Well… it's a type of manipulation. If people know what you're feeling, they can say or do things to make those feelings worse, and then you make bad decisions or act poorly."

She tilted her head, and before she could ask for details, he added, "F-for example, um, if there's something that makes you angry, and someone else knows it, they could continue to do the thing that makes you angry. Maybe they make you so angry that you attack them, but you can't think clearly, so it gives them the advantage because you're sloppy."

Nova's brows lifted. She understood keeping a level head in battle, but she never considered someone purposely trying to affect her emotions so she would make mistakes. Fortunately, most of what she fought were undead, and they would not be capable of doing such things.

It was not lost on her that perhaps her battle prowess was limited because of the opponents she fought. Would she fare well if her enemy were humans and this is how they fought? These were things she would give thought to later but for now… "I see. I thank you for explaining it to me."

"S-sure," he replied softly. "A-anyway… this is the forest you were curious about. As you can see, there's nothing really special here. It's like everywhere else in southern Bascor, at least, from what I understand."

Nova hummed, lifting her nose. Old Viridian magic touched her senses, tasting slightly of Autumn decay, but it felt slightly stronger here, now that she was in it. That made her lift her brows and she looked back to Rowan Spicer, who watched her curiously.

"It is a place I shall explore regardless." She paused, considering him. "Why do you live out here? It seems uncommon, given how hard it is to survive away from settlements."

Rowan Spicer blinked, then to Nova's fascination, the uncertain look he had was replaced by one that she might describe as pleased. "Oh! Well, it's actually better for my family's business."

He must have been proud of this business, given his reaction, so she found herself prompting, "How so?"

He gave her a tiny smile, teeth plucking at his bottom lip like he was very happy she asked. To her amusement, that smile grew, and he motioned for her to follow him as he started walking down the road. "My family are apothecaries, but our methodology is to acquire the ingredients ourselves when we can. My grandfather moved out here years ago, and he forages every day before he starts making potions."

Despite knowing she had other things to do, she fell into pace beside him, figuring she could observe the area while they walked. Eventually, they would part ways, then she could refocus on thoroughly searching the woods.

Rowan Spicer continued, "And when the Great Wither came, this actually made it easier for us to survive. We already knew how to forage, so we were able to identify the handful of things that still grew, including food items, and we only pay for the ingredients we can't easily source, like certain minerals."

"So you eat things besides fish?" Nova asked curiously.

In return, Rowan Spicer beamed at her. Even with the tiny smile a moment ago, she was not prepared for such an earnest expression, momentarily taken aback. He had been so nervous and unsure earlier, but now his face was warm like sunshine. Joyful. She found it rather suited him.

"Yeah! I mean, we still eat a lot of fish, but like..." He trailed off, looking around the area. "Ah! Wait here!"

He ran off the road into the pale weeds, and Nova came to a stop, tilting her head. Her keen eyesight let her see him combing through what looked like thorny plants that were a little more colorful than the grass. After a few minutes, he stood up and hopped back over to her. "Here! Blackberries!"

He held out his palm to her, and she stared at the five strange little... bumpy things in his hand. "Black... berries...?"

"Yeah, it's food!" Rowan Spicer replied, taking one of the tinier ones and putting it in his mouth. "It's sweet. Try one!"

Hesitantly, she took one of the... blackberries out of his hand, brow furrowing at its strange, slightly squishy texture. Some weird ichor leaked out of it, dark and staining her fingertip, and her expression must have been funny because Rowan Spicer began to giggle at her. "Really, I promise I'm not trying to trick you. Try it."

Not one to be defeated by a... blackberry, Nova put it in her mouth and bit down. A mixture of tastes she was vastly unfamiliar with washed over her tongue, and she made a startled noise as she swallowed. "What did I just eat?"

"Wow, I've never..." Rowan Spicer covered his mouth with his free hand, but it did nothing to hide how much his eyes were laughing at her. "I'm sorry... I don't mean to laugh... you just... you look so alarmed. Did you not like it?"

"I do not..." Nova trailed off, trying to figure out how she wanted to describe it before her gaze dropped to the remaining blackberries in his palm. She narrowed her eyes and grabbed another, putting it in her mouth. This time the flavor was... not as sharp and far more pleasant. "I do not understand. Why do they taste different?"

He blinked at her before his expression became abashed. "Oh... you probably got a sour one. Sometimes that happens. I'm sorry."

"I have never tasted this kind of 'sour,'" Nova admitted, sucking on her finger. She barely noticed that he had started walking again and she had simply fallen into pace with him. To her dismay, the purple stain on her fingertip did not disappear, and she glared at it disapprovingly.

Rowan Spicer stifled another giggle, and she leveled that same glare on him which made him squeak.

"The color fades after a bit. It's not permanent, I promise," Rowan Spicer said with an amused smile. He was red in the face again, but she did not know why. "I didn't mean to pick a sour one. I was hoping they were all sweet because that's the best flavor."

"The second one was... not as sharp," Nova admitted, trying to describe it. "Pleasant. It reminds me of a spring rain. Is that how 'sweet' tastes?"

Rowan Spicer tilted his head thoughtfully. "Sure. I guess you've never had anything sweet before, either? Have you only ever eaten fish?"

She nodded. "Yes. I have also had kelp before. It does not taste like this, though."

"Want the rest?" he offered, nodding to the last two berries in his hand.

"Do you not want them?" Nova asked. The one he described as 'sour' was not so appealing, but the second one she liked. But he was the one who found them, so he should get to choose how many he wanted.

"I can find more later. I think... I get the opportunity to eat different things more than you. So you can have them if you'd like," he replied shyly, tucking his hair behind his ear again and averting his eyes.

She did not know why he seemed so bashful again, but she took the blackberries and ate them one at a time. Unfortunately, the first one was sour, but the last one was 'sweet,' and she let the last one sit on her tongue for as long as possible, pleased at the flavor.

Finally, she looked at him, finding him watching her almost... hopefully. Like he was waiting for her approval. She was not sure what he wanted, but she realized she had not shown proper gratitude, and that must have been it.

"I thank you," she said, bowing her head. "To provide someone you do not know such an experience in this world is quite an honor. I will remember this, Rowan Spicer."

His mouth fell open, and she wondered if she had said the wrong thing because he was just gaping at her. Why were human customs so difficult to navigate? She was *trying*.

"I'm... I'm glad you liked it!" he said, and his voice was higher than it was a moment before. He swallowed, the bump in his neck bobbing, and he added, "And, you know, you helped me, so this is kind of a repayment. Not that it's the same. I don't want to pretend some berries make up for you fending off a group of thugs trying to cut off my hair."

She snorted softly, lips quirking upward as she looked ahead. "Just as that was easy for me, this was easy for you. Different strengths, so to speak. Do not downplay what you did."

Out of the corner of her eye, she saw him grin and look away. She did not look at him, instead curious about the path they were taking. It was no longer the main road, but the Viridian magic still stayed strong out here, slightly more so than the town.

That was interesting.

They fell into a pleasant silence, and Nova found herself taking in the details of the land. The faint hint of green in the tree leaves. The presence of brambles that did not look dry like tinder. Even a rare yellow flower in the hilly grasses. It was so different from the war zones, and it made her feel a longing she did not quite know what to do with.

They rounded a bend and Rowan Spicer came to a stop. Nova blinked, focusing her attention on the structure now in view. It was a small house of stone and hardwoods, built over a stream, with wide flagstone steps leading from the house to the road. It had a large wheel on its side that moved very slowly, carrying water over it from the stream. Nova had seen similar things on bigger buildings in towns, but she did not quite understand the purpose.

Smoke rose from the chimney, and it carried the scent of smoked fish, along with things she could not identify. Perhaps they were potions.

"Is this your home?" Nova asked, and Rowan Spicer nodded.

"Y-yeah. Um, it is. I'd... offer for you to come inside, but my mom probably wouldn't like that."

"I would decline anyway," Nova said, turning to him. "I have work I must do."

"Yeah... that makes sense," he said softly, rubbing the back of his neck. "I'm... actually surprised you walked me home."

Nova blinked at that. Although it was not a question, she felt like he wanted to know her reasoning, and truthfully, she was not sure. Why *did* she escort him back? The other humans were trapped in town and would not have followed them. She could argue he could not defend himself from undead, but she could not smell any nearby so he would have been fine.

She tilted her head, studying him as he regarded her with questioning eyes. Truthfully, she should not have stayed as long as she did, but when she thought about it...

He was different. He did not remind her of war or death, or even duty. He did not have hubris or arrogance like she expected from most humans. He did not smell of blood or fire, and he did not remind her of everything wrong in the world.

He was just... pleasant, small, and kind. He was something that she did not realize she was fighting for, and that knowledge was precious. The bitterness towards both dragons and humans alike had been nudged aside, if just a little, to remind her that there were those in the world worth protecting.

It felt strange to look at someone like Rowan Spicer and realize his kindness and innocence inspired her more than her own sense of duty, and yet... she found she did not mind. And she wanted to appreciate that, at least for a moment.

She could not say these things, however, without exposing what she was, and knowing he hoped for an answer, she huffed and gave him a half smile. "Why not?"

He blinked several times. "Well... I mean... not many people would."

That made her frown, reminding her once again that many humans did not deserve to benefit from her power. However, she knew that she would continue to do her duty because it meant protecting people like Rowan Spicer.

She huffed again, turning her nose up. "Then I must be better than most people, for I can easily see how your presence is rewarding."

He gaped at her, and she used his shock to take a bow and announce her departure. "I must leave now. I bid you farewell, and I thank you for your company, Rowan Spicer of Bascor."

She turned smoothly, walking down the path, and a moment later he must have figured out what he wanted to say. "Nova! W-wait!"

She turned, looking at him over her shoulder with an arched brow. He took a few steps towards her, a hand lifted questioningly. "Will, um... Do you think you'll be around here for a while?"

"I do not know," she replied truthfully, turning to face him. "Why?"

He hesitated, mouth open as he fretted over what to say. He looked so... small, but in a way that simply made her want to be his shield. She wondered about that, waiting patiently for him to respond.

"I..." He swallowed, then squared his shoulders and said firmly, "Because I really enjoyed talking with you. I'd like to do it again."

She smiled faintly. It was too bad her kind did not keep human advisors anymore. If so, she would likely invite him back with her to her home, for it would certainly give him the respect he deserved. Alas, even with the protection of the islands, it was far too dangerous for him to be a part of her world.

She wished, though. She did not have friends, but if she had to imagine what they would be like, Rowan Spicer was certainly what she pictured.

"I agree, our encounter was enriching. I cannot say what the future holds, however. I do hope fortune shines on you, Rowan Spicer. I would say out of all who I have met, you deserve it most. Take care, and may your sunsets carry the magic of the skies."

She bowed her head once more and turned, but she did not miss the way his face fell. It made her feel strange in a way she did not understand, but duty came first.

Chapter 9
No Good Choices

The moment the sirens rang in the distance, Sorrel felt like she had just fallen deep into an icy river. She looked up from her mortar and pestle, staring at the wall that blocked her vision of the road leading into town, her face contorting into one of horror.

"That's..."

"The warning bells, yes," her father finished quietly, walking over and putting a hand on her shoulder comfortingly. "Something bad is near town, dragons or undead or both."

"Rowan's out there," Sorrel whispered in disbelief.

The sirens had gone off a few times before. Usually at night, when they were safely at home, but once when Rowan was ten. They had been in town, with her delivering potions and him in school. That day she cried and cried, clutching him to her the moment she got to him. It didn't matter that the undead had never reached the city walls. It had been too close for comfort. But never had the sirens gone off when Rowan was out there by himself.

Sorrel pressed a hand to her chest, feeling her heart flutter underneath. It felt hard to breathe. "We have to— I have to find him."

Her voice was barely a whisper, but the gravity and urgency in her words still carried like a shout from the top of the hills. However, when she stood up, her father's hand on her shoulder tightened.

"Sorrel, wait—"

"Papa, *Rowan* is out there!" She whirled, staring at him with wide eyes. How could he tell her to wait when her child was out there in an undead attack?

"And what is your plan?" her father asked, an edge in his voice as the crease in his brow deepened.

"I'm going to find him!" she replied incredulously, heat creeping into her words. How could he ask such a stupid question?

"When the sirens sound, they close the gates, Sorrel. If he's inside the town, you can't get to him." He spoke calmly, too calmly, like he wasn't worried for her son. It agitated her, but there was also an edge in his words and a hardness in his eyes that made it worse. It meant he was going to fight her decisions—*like he always did*—because he didn't understand.

Rowan was her *everything*.

"What if he's not in town?" Sorrel asked, feeling panic bubble up from within. "What if he's *trapped* out there—"

"Then trust the guards to do their job, and trust the head on that boy's shoulders," Zebb said firmly, putting his other hand on her other shoulder and squeezing gently.

"I can't just sit here and—"

"How will you save him, Sorrel? Will you suddenly wield a sword, when you've never picked one up? Will you miraculously whip up a potion that kills the undead on sight? Will you shout at the dragons and tell them to leave him alone? You don't even know where he is or what's out there. You could spend hours trying to find him, only to learn he came back home the moment you left!"

"But I have to do something!" Sorrel sobbed, tears falling down her cheeks.

"That *something* is to calm down and trust Rowan to be at least a little bit smart about this!" Zebb snapped, frustration coloring his words. "You have got to stop tormenting yourself every time—"

"I should have made him stay home!" Sorrel cried, collapsing back down into her chair as she covered her face with her hands. "I should have— I should have…"

She broke down into ugly sobs, hunching over on herself as it all came tumbling down. Her father said nothing as she fell apart, drowning in fear that her child would die and knowing she had no actions she could take. Her entire life was this endless torment of knowing something was out there that wanted to kill him but not knowing what that something was, and she just knew Rowan didn't understand. He probably *hated* her for it, when all she wanted was to keep him safe!

Over and over again, her mind played out the worst-case scenarios: of him running from monsters that chased him down, of finding his mutilated body, lifeless with his face frozen in terror. The images wouldn't stop coming, and she cried harder, hands on her head as she hunched over on her stool.

Hot tears dripped onto the stone floor and her face burned as her fears consumed her. What if it was the thing that killed the archmagus all those years ago? What if Osier's killer had returned? So many dangers were out there, waiting to gobble her baby up, and it killed her to know she couldn't protect him.

She was trying so hard! He resented her for it, but he didn't understand. She wished she could make him understand. It was all for him, and yet she still felt like she could lose him at any moment, and it was *torture*.

She cried, over and over again, unable to calm down. At some point, the stool was replaced by the floor, and she cried more, feeling trapped in a way she couldn't articulate into words. She barely noticed her father disappear and return, not until he sat down beside her and began to stroke her hair.

His fingers smoothed over her crown, over and over again, steady and reliable as they waited her turmoil out. Eventually, her sobs quieted and her heart stopped pounding. Ragged heaving was replaced with shuddering breaths.

Sorrel stirred, seeing her father had grabbed a cup of water and a small cloth for her. She sat up, taking both so she could clean her face and sip the water. She wasn't sure how much time had passed, but it felt like it had been both days and mere seconds.

"I'm sorry," she whispered between sniffles, not looking at her father. She didn't want to see how he was judging her.

Her father sighed, rubbing her back with his hand. Hesitantly, Sorrel met his gaze, finding it was bereft of judgment. He just looked sad. "It's been about an hour now, I reckon. Sirens haven't gone off since, which means things are probably settling down and they'll soon lift the gates. So how about you get cleaned up and we go walk up to town and find out where—"

"*Nova, wait!*"

Sorrel's heart skipped a beat as she recognized Rowan's voice. She rushed to her feet, knocking over the stool in the process and dropping her cup as she pulled up to the small window and looked out of the dusty glass. There, at the bottom of the stairs, was her son, alive and safe! She felt utter relief wash over her. "Oh! Rowan! He's okay!"

She hurried out of the room, following after her father who was already hastily moving to the front door. He opened it, and they both spilled out onto the veranda. Rowan's back was to them, and he was staring down the path. Sorrel followed his line of sight, seeing someone in a dark travel cloak walk around the bend. Had a guard walked him home? The man was too far away for her to see the details, but the guards didn't wear cloaks, either.

"Rowan!" she called, rushing down the steps, her heart pounding in her chest. He turned to her, and she felt the tension leave her as she saw his freckled face. She pulled him into her arms, squeezing tightly and burying her face into his hair, unapologetic in her need to hold him. "Oh, I'm so glad you're okay! You must have been so scared!"

Rowan hugged her back, and she felt tears form again when she heard his voice. "I'm okay! Honest! It wasn't that bad! No one even got hurt!"

Sorrel pulled back, looking at his face. Sure enough, he seemed excited, eyes bright and a big smile on his lips. She frowned, confusion mixing in with her relief. "What— was it a false alarm?"

Rowan shook his head, hair bouncing like it could convey his excitement. "No, it was a pack of undead! But a Dragon Knight appeared and cut them down before they could even reach the city!"

Sorrel frowned, pulling back to look at him. "A Dragon Knight? Aren't those... the warriors who fight the undead at the border? Why would they be here?"

Rowan nodded, glancing back towards the road as if looking to see if the cloaked person was still there. "Yeah! I was at the gates, and suddenly there was this fog, and then she appeared in all this silver fire and cut them down using lightning and ice!"

Silver fire.

Sorrel's blood ran cold. Memories of the day of Rowan's birth, of her father saying that Avelore Amantius was dead and that a being wrapped in silver fire was seen leaving the area, hit her full force.

"Silver fire... and you're *sure* that's a Dragon Knight?" her father asked as if honing in on the same piece of information that she did.

Rowan nodded, looking at him in slight confusion. "Yeah. I mean, I saw it, and well, Silas said that's how they've always appeared when he's seen them."

Sorrel hadn't known what that silver fire could be, but ...now she knew. A Dragon Knight had killed Avelore Amantius, the archmagus who sealed Rowan's magic. And now one was here. In Ladisdale.

Blood pounded in her ears, and she barely heard her father ask, "Okay... How do you know the Dragon Knight was a 'she'?"

She watched Rowan stiffen, looking at her father, then back at her with wide eyes, and it took Sorrel a moment to realize just why that question was important, and why her son looked nervous. He was supposed to avoid talking to anyone strange or suspicious, and it was clear he hadn't done that.

Sorrel swallowed the cotton in her mouth and asked in a quiet voice, "Who was the person walking away from here, Rowan? Was that the Dragon Knight?"

At her question, the color drained from her son's face, before he quickly replied, "That was just someone who walked me home. T-that's all."

Sorrel's stomach twisted in knots, feeling every part of her body scream 'danger.' Beside her, her father ran a hand over his mouth before replying, "Didn't realize Dragon Knights walked young men home after slaying undead. What was her name, 'Nova'?"

Rowan looked like he might faint, which was answer enough, and Sorrel felt like she wasn't faring any better. Did this Dragon Knight know? Was she here to hurt Rowan?

No, this 'Nova' must not have known because she left Rowan here, unharmed. He was *safe*. But they couldn't take that risk again.

Her eyes fell to Rowan's arm, and she swallowed. "I'm... I'm glad you're home safely, but Rowan, you need to stay away from this Nova person. We don't know anything about—"

"I know she took down a bunch of undead that could have hurt people!" Rowan blurted out, brow furrowing. "A-and I know that she stopped Brewer and the others from cutting off my hair today."

"Shit, Rowan," Zebb hissed angrily. "I swear, those bastards—"

"Got scared off before they could do anything," Rowan promised, looking between them. "She didn't have to step in and help me, but she did. And then she escorted me home."

"Why you, though?" Sorrel asked, immediately realizing how it sounded when her son gave her a devastated look. "I–I mean—"

"What, I'm not allowed to have people do nice things for me because I'm 'cursed?'" Rowan asked bitterly. Sorrel felt like a knife cut into her at seeing the tears in his eyes. "Am I not good enough for a Dragon Knight to show me a little kindness?"

"That's not what I meant—"

"Then what *did* you mean, Mom? Please, tell me how you meant it!" He took a big step back, looking at her like one more wrong word would shatter him completely.

She made a pained noise, trying to figure out how to respond. That's not how she meant it, but she couldn't say what she truly meant!

She wiped at her eyes as the tears formed once again and did her best to force out an explanation that wasn't the truth but still hopefully worked. "I just meant that Dragon Knights are only known for fighting in the war, and...it seems strange that this Nova person claims to be one and just... walked you home. Did she say why? Did she try to do anything, or ask you to go with her, or—"

"No!" Rowan said, balling his fists in frustration. "She didn't tell me anything! She was just nice to me, and I figured out who she was on my own. Sometimes people are just *nice,* Mom, including people who fight in wars, and maybe you would know that if you stopped assuming everyone's just a bad person!"

Sorrel leaned back slightly, expression pained. "I'm not—"

"Yes, you are!" Rowan shouted, tears running down his cheeks. "All my life you've tried to keep me from making friends! You never want me to leave the house and you constantly act like someone's around the corner with a knife! But you won't tell me why! What is so damn scary out there, and why is it only after *me?*"

"*Please—*"

"No! No more 'pleases'! No more apologies! I know you know more about my curse than you're telling me! This is ruining my life, Mom! *You* are ruining my life!"

Zebb stepped forward, putting a hand on Rowan's shoulder. "Hey, now. That's far enough, Rowan—"

Rowan shrugged away from his grandfather's touch, glaring at him. "Yeah, of course it is. It's always 'enough' when I get angry, and not a question of why I'm angry in the first place. It's like Mom doesn't even want me to *exist.*"

Those words, wrapped in bitter defeat, shattered what was left of her fragile composure, and Sorrel covered her mouth with her hands to muffle a sob. Her son flinched at the sound but otherwise didn't look at her as he moved past them both to stomp angrily down the path toward the river.

Zebb sighed, stepping forward and pulling her into an embrace. Sorrel buried her face in his shoulder, clinging to him as she cried for the second time that day.

"He— He *hates* me, Papa!" she wailed, her words half indistinguishable from her sobbing. Despite that, her father seemed to understand, rubbing her back as he tried to get her to calm down.

"He's upset, Sorrel. He doesn't hate you. You both just need to calm down right now."

She shook her head against his shoulder, crying and uncaring of the mess she was making of his tunic. She was trying so hard, but she felt like the worst mother in the world! All she ever wanted was a child, and she wanted nothing more than to keep her child safe, but he was *miserable,* and deep down, she really couldn't blame him for hating her.

This wasn't the life she wanted to give him, but what other choice did she have? Someone out there wanted him dead, and she didn't know *who.* And now a being of silver fire, a *Dragon Knight,* had found her son, and she had to pray that they never found out the truth. But how could she get him to understand the danger he was in except to tell him?

But to tell him meant to tell him of his origins, to go against the warnings of both Osier and Avelore Amantius. Telling him might also bring him closer to harm, and she had no idea what decision was the right one. They both felt *wrong,* and that was even worse.

She cried and cried, feeling worthless and deceived. She was trying to do right by her son, but she wasn't given good choices! Osier had tricked her, and Avelore Amantius never came back. And now she lived every night fearing someone would take her baby from her, and Rowan hated her for it.

She wished so badly she could take back some kind of control and ensure his safety. She would *die* if she could guarantee he would no longer be in danger. She would do anything for Rowan, but the world wouldn't give her anything to work with!

Slowly, she calmed down, lulled by the way her father ran his fingers through her hair and shushed her like he did when she was a child. Eventually, she pulled away to look up at him, and he regarded her with a mixture of patience and sympathy.

"I don't know what to do, Papa," she admitted in a pained voice. "You heard what he said… that was a Dragon Knight that walked him home. And how he described her…"

"Silver fire. Yes, I caught it, too. You think that archmagus was killed by a Dragon Knight?"

"Do you think he *wasn't?*" Sorrel asked incredulously.

"I... don't know," Zebb admitted. "We don't have any proof—"

"We have enough proof," Sorrel replied bitterly. "And now there's a Dragon Knight here, and she's following my son, and he won't listen to me!"

Her father gave an exasperated sigh. "Of course he won't, Sorrel! You won't tell him anything. Hell, you haven't even told *me* everything. In his eyes, you're just being unreasonable! Would it really be worse to tell him the truth?"

"I can't tell him," Sorrel said firmly, wiping at her face. "I just can't. It's too dangerous, He's too young, and if he knew he might—"

"There you go with that 'too young' business. He's sixteen, Sorrel. Need I remind you that you made some weighty decisions at his age—"

"And they were the wrong ones!" she screamed, shoving her fists down at her sides. "This is where we are because of the decisions *I made!* I live every day fearing he'll be taken from me because I was young and foolish!"

Her head hurt from crying. Her heart ached with anguish. Why was it always like this? She didn't deserve this. Rowan didn't deserve this.

Her father took in a long, steadying breath, then pointedly asked, "Do you think Rowan was a wrong decision?"

Sorrel pulled back like the question itself had slapped her in the face. She pressed a hand to her mouth, feeling distraught at even such an implication. *"No!* I love him, and I would do anything for him! But he's in danger, Papa! He's in danger because of the choices I made!"

"Which choices put him in danger, Sorrel? That you chose to have him? That you let the archmagus bind his curse? You gave him a chance to live—"

"It's not a curse!" Sorrel cried, dropping to her knees. "He told me it wasn't a curse!"

Her father took a step back. She looked up at him, and through her tears, she could see him staring at her.

"What do you *mean* it's not a curse?"

She shook her head, face contorted into agony as she tried to keep the tears under control. She hadn't meant to say it, but she had, and now it was all coming down around her. "He— He told me Rowan was a gift but that we had to lie and say it was a curse because people were hunting him. He was going to come back with help. He told me to keep quiet until he returned, but then... that Dragon Knight killed him."

She broke off into a whimper, and it took her a few seconds before she continued. "I think they killed his father, too. That's why I do this, Papa. They both died, and I just know the people who killed them are out there looking for Rowan, too."

She bit back a wail, squeezing her eyes shut. On one hand, to finally say even that much was like a huge pressure releasing inside of her. On the other hand, it terrified her, like the skies themselves might smite her for uttering anything about her child's origins.

Her father was quiet for several seconds as she wrestled with her emotions, and then he crouched down and wiped the tears from her face. "My poor girl, I wish you had told me this sooner."

"I'm sorry, Papa... I was scared," Sorrel cried, leaning into his touch. "I don't want to lose my baby."

"I know, I know. But let's try to look at the facts. We know they both died, but we don't know for certain who killed them. I think it's important to be cautious, but not to our detriment. That Dragon Knight walked him home and didn't hurt him."

"That doesn't mean she's good," Sorrel replied, shaking her head. "His gift is hidden as a curse. She may not have recognized it..."

"That's true, too. But we don't know. Did the archmagus tell you what this gift was?"

She hung her head. "N-no. He told me that the more I knew, the more it could be used against me. He told me to never speak his name because the wrong people would find Rowan. He was... He was supposed to come back. He *promised* me..."

She trailed off, staring forlornly down at the ground, feeling like she had no more tears to cry. He promised her. Avelore Amantius promised he would come back. Osier was supposed to come back, too.

Why did it turn out like this?

Her father sighed deeply, looking down at the ground. "All right. I get it. But... I think you should tell Rowan. I know you want to protect him, but I don't think this is the best way. What you're doing is not a solution, Sorrel. It's just a slow death."

She squeezed her eyes shut and shook her head. "I don't have a choice. I refuse to let him die, Papa. I just want to keep him safe."

Zebb sighed, pulling her close again to hold her, resting his cheek against her head.

Neither of them noticed that Rowan had doubled back and stood behind a tree, listening.

Chapter 10
Conflictions

The rest of the day, Rowan barely talked to his family, staying largely out of the house. He didn't want to talk to them, not yet. Everything felt too raw, too painful, and too confusing.

He wasn't cursed.

He *wasn't cursed.*

Out of everything, that part hit him the hardest, more than the near-confirmation that his life was in danger, more than the possibility that Dragon Knights killed the magus who bound his... gift.

It hurt. His mother lied to him. She led the world to believe he was marked, and she let him live a life of misery because, in her mind, that was 'safer.' He questioned that, bitterly. He questioned everything else, too. Was it really a Dragon Knight that killed the magus? An *archmagus* no less?

He didn't feel like that was right. Even with Silas's cautions, even with what his mother speculated... it didn't match up to the person who walked him home and made faces at accidentally eating a sour blackberry. It didn't match up to the silvery being reaching out to him in his dream.

None of this felt right. No, it all felt wrong, and it all really hurt. He felt betrayed. He felt cheated. He felt awful.

Why didn't she just tell him? It would have made things easier. He wouldn't feel so worthless if he knew the truth. Sure, he still would have hated pretending to have a curse, but he would have understood. Instead, she let him live this life and expected him to just accept it. How was he supposed to reconcile this?

He didn't know, and it made him feel so many unpleasant emotions. His skin crawled uncomfortably that night as he lay in bed. He could hear his grandfather snoring across the bedroom, and his mother was still in the living room, the firelight of the hearth seeping in through the open doorway. It was too chilly to close the door. Her sniffles told him enough of what she was doing.

He felt bad, but he wasn't ready to talk to her. He wasn't ready to apologize, because he felt his anger wasn't unfair. She should have told him because this was about him. He felt raw. He felt tired. He felt sad, too.

Sleep eventually came, and with it, his recurring dream. The shadows grasped at him, promising him darkness and peace if he let them take him. He found himself staring at the man with green eyes, wondering if maybe the shadows had a point...

Then, the Dragon Knight came.

Silver fire cut through his despair like it cut through the darkness, and the man with green eyes melted away to be replaced by the knight wrapped in silvery flame. The Dragon Knight held out their hand, and Rowan gazed at it longingly. He wanted so badly to touch it, to take their hand and see what happened. He reached forward, fingers itching to touch the palm full of undefined promises...

He woke up.

Rowan stared at the ceiling of the bedroom. It was before dawn, although a hint of pre-dawn light was starting to crawl in from the dusty window. His heart wasn't pounding this time, but it ached nonetheless, for so many reasons.

Was his dream about Nova? It was pretty obvious that she was the Dragon Knight, but he didn't know what to do about it. Clearly, she didn't want him to know, even if she was kind of terrible at blending in.

But he didn't have the nerve to ask her. Originally, it was because he hadn't wanted to scare her off. Although she was a little standoffish and aloof, she was also... kind. She complimented him, and a part of him was still soaring from it. And, of course, she saved him and didn't judge him, and then walked him home and... He sighed, closing his eyes.

He hadn't wanted her to leave. He knew she had to, but what really stung was her non-committal response about if he could see her again. He supposed that was what he should have expected, given what she was. She probably had really important things to do, and he was lucky to have any of her time.

"Why you, though?"

He opened his eyes, staring at the ceiling again. The sting from his mother's comment had been replaced by far deeper cuts today, but it still directed him toward the real concern.

He didn't know why Nova helped him or walked him home. She hadn't done anything to indicate she thought he was special besides noting he had a very powerful curse. She could have easily hurt him or kidnapped him, or anything she wanted, but she didn't. She simply... treated him like he could be her friend. That was precious to him, and he really didn't want to let it go.

But he couldn't ignore what his mother said. She said a Dragon Knight killed that archmagus. Rowan got the impression she wasn't completely sure, but it was enough to make him uneasy. Because, for all of his anger and pain, he didn't think his mother was lying. Not at all. But he did hope she was wrong.

He was glad he didn't tell his mother about his dream changing because that would make everything worse. Maybe Silas was right about that. He needed to keep his dream to himself for now.

He sighed, glancing over at his mother's sleeping form on her bed. Her back was to him, and he wondered how long it took before she retired last night. He didn't plan to tell her he overheard her yet. Truthfully, he wanted her to talk to him first. He wanted her to trust him, to show him that she wanted to fix things. He wanted her to give him something, *anything*.

It wasn't even so much because he felt he deserved it, but rather... He just felt alone.

She didn't talk to him. He gave her the day to try.

He went foraging with his grandfather, who talked about 'safe' topics, like the cold weather and winter foraging. The temperature continued to drop, and now they were wearing their jackets as they looked for more fire root for warming draughts.

Rowan half paid attention, lost in his thoughts more often than not. His grandfather seemed to notice but didn't press the issue, although he did stop to wrap an arm around Rowan's shoulders on their way back.

Rowan waited for some talk or lecture to come, but instead, his grandfather simply held him close and quietly said, "You mean the world to me, bean."

He cried on the way back, tears silently falling down his cheeks. He was pretty sure he saw a tear or two in his grandfather's eyes as well.

There were no deliveries to make that day, so when they got back, Rowan stayed home to help with housework and brewing potions. Although he was still considered an apprentice by the Athenaeum, his mother and grandfather both trusted him with most recipes, so they paid him little mind as he worked.

But his mother still didn't talk to him. She made small comments about his work. She would ask which brew he was working on or how much was left of a particular ingredient so she could keep up with inventory, but she kept the conversation quiet and professional.

By the evening, he felt sad and dejected again, and he went to bed early so he could be alone with his thoughts. That probably was worse, to be honest, lying in the darkness of the bedroom and wishing for something different, even if he didn't know what.

Eventually sleep claimed him, and his dream met him once again.

The next day started like usual, with an early morning round of foraging, breakfast, and Rowan preparing to go into town to do his deliveries. The only difference was the heavy air between him and his mother. It was palpable, but he wasn't yet going to address it.

His mother stood quietly by the door, hands clasped together as he slipped on his sandals. Bags were under her eyes from poor sleep, and she looked pale and withdrawn. When he finished putting on his sandals, the room fell quiet, and finally, she said, "Please be careful, and... and watch out for danger."

He gave her a forced, tight-lip smile and a small nod. "Yeah. I will."

And that was all they said.

He walked silently down the road to town, with the only sounds accompanying him being the gentle clinks of the potions in his basket and his sandals crunching against the dirt.

It was a chilly morning, so he kept his pace brisk, eyes on the road as he stayed lost in his thoughts. When he got to the main road, he looked up and then blinked in confusion. The entire area was covered in a dense, swirling fog. It clung to the base of the hills and pooled in the dips in the terrain. He didn't know how far it went, but it did well to obscure his vision, swallowing the road and painting everything in pale silver.

If this had happened at any other point in his life, he would have simply ignored it and moved on. Instead, he found himself taking a deep breath...

...and smelling petrichor.

He tensed, eyes flying open at that. This was Nova's doing, and that must have meant she was in the area or had passed through here! Then he realized... if it was her, that meant she had reason to do this.

He swallowed, looking around for any sign of movement. The roads were empty for what little he could see, and the blurry shapes in the distance were daunting but unmoving. However, just as he was convinced he was alone, he heard a faint noise. He stiffened, straining his ears to try to determine the source. It sounded like someone walking on the road, and it came from the direction leading into town.

Rowan took in a nervous breath, eyes cutting in that direction. Here he was, standing in the middle of the open road, unarmed, wrapped in a magical fog, and uncertain of what was out there. Carefully, he took a step back, moving off of the road and into the withered grass. The potions in his basket clinked slightly from the actions, and he grimaced, glancing around for a place to hide. The trees here were thin and without foliage, but with the fog, they would have to be good enough. He stepped back into them, crouching down behind one of the bigger ones, and waited.

The source of the noise came into view not long after, and Rowan blinked several times as the person came into focus and he found himself staring at a familiar eyepatch and half cape. Silas moved carefully along, scanning his surroundings. Rowan swallowed when he realized Silas's one hand was resting on the hilt of a sword at his hip. Why was he out here, and why was he armed?

Silas paused when he got to where Rowan had been standing, and Rowan bit his lip, crouching down as low as possible. He didn't know why he was hiding from *Silas* of all people. Silas was probably the best person he could have run into out here! But Rowan had this feeling that he shouldn't be seen, so he held his breath and stayed quiet.

Eventually, Silas started moving again, and to Rowan's surprise, he turned down the side road that went to Rowan's house. Rowan blinked, staring after him. There wasn't much down that road these days besides his house. Silas knew Rowan lived down by the river, but to Rowan's knowledge, he'd never visited. So why would he choose that direction?

Rowan watched him go, teeth worrying at his bottom lip. This was just weird. So many strange things had happened lately, and all of them felt related, but not in any way that made sense. But it made him feel uneasy.

He took a deep breath, slowly standing back up and readjusting his potions. He'd just have to talk to Silas about this later, but for now, he needed to hurry and get to town. He walked back up to the main road, but the moment his foot touched the packed dirt, something grabbed him. He tried to shout, only to have a hand cover his mouth and stifle the noise as the person hauled him off of the road and into the trees. He thrashed, but they were strong.

...They were very strong and strangely warm, and the scent of petrichor was suddenly stronger...

He swallowed, eyes going wide as he heard Nova whisper, "Do not shout, Rowan Spicer."

He nodded shakily, heart pounding, breath shallow, and fear gripping him. His mother's words came crashing back to the forefront of his mind, and he began to shake, wondering if Nova was going to drag him off. Now he wished he hadn't hidden from Silas, and—

Behind him, Nova exhaled softly, and her grip on him loosened. He took that opportunity to yank away and whirl on her, the potions in his possession clinking noisily.

She frowned, eyes flicking to them before looking back at his face, then lifted a finger to her lips. He stared back at her fearfully. She must have realized she had scared him because she slowly lifted her hands, palms open, and bowed her head in apology.

He watched her, saying nothing, then took in a long, deep breath, trying to calm down. He exhaled shakily, fingers tightly gripping his basket. His voice was barely a whisper as he hissed, "Why did you do that?"

Nova set her jaw and glanced around, eyes skimming the fog like she could see through it. He wondered if she could, given that he knew she made it. He also wondered if she realized that he was onto her.

She was silent for a moment before she looked back at him. "Strange people are moving through here. They are shrouded in arcane, and I do not like it."

Rowan frowned, thinking back to Silas. He wasn't a magus, though, and he'd never mentioned using magic. Did she mean him? But she said 'people,' so maybe it was someone else? Or maybe she was lying.

He swallowed thickly, looking around, although he could see nothing but fog. "What kind of people?"

Nova frowned, shaking her head. "I do not know yet, for they run away quickly. You should be cautious, as people with magic who hide in the shadows should not be trusted. You did well to hide earlier from the warrior, although I do not think he is a threat. This pleases me, though. Your senses are sharp."

His lips parted as he processed what she said. Technically, she was a person with magic hiding who she was, although she hadn't actually dragged him off through the fog like he feared she would. He plucked at his lip with his teeth, considering her words, then uneasily asked, "What are you doing out here?"

She stiffened, and it was clear she wasn't prepared for him to ask her that. He swallowed, nervously clutching the strap around his shoulders that supported his delivery basket. He watched her eyes flit back and forth and uncertainty pass over her features.

"I..." She furrowed her brow, grasping for words. "Nothing."

"You're a terrible liar," Rowan whispered before he could catch himself. He watched as she flushed, pink tinting her otherwise pale face. He hadn't quite meant to say that aloud, even if it was true. He now understood that half of their previous encounter wasn't her being bad with Bascori dialect, but because she had absolutely no skill in evading truths.

"I do not know what you speak of," she denied quietly, brow furrowing as she glanced away. "I was on my way to... Ladisdale."

He should have been terrified. He *was* terrified. She was clearly lying, and something was going on here, and he knew there was some unknown danger out there looking for him, and it could be her. But if it *was* her, she didn't know he was what she was looking for, he didn't think. And if it wasn't her... it made sense to keep someone powerful nearby, right?

He debated on what to say, and despite that, it still felt like an impulsive decision as he replied, "Well, so am I. And if you're doing nothing out here, and people are being suspicious, it means we should walk to town together, right?"

She blinked several times at him, confused. His neck felt hot, half from embarrassment, half from anxiety, and he had to hope his face didn't follow. Silence passed between them, tense and somewhat awkward, and he became half aware of the white-knuckled grip he had on his basket.

Finally, she sighed, shoulders sagging. "Yes, that is— You are right. It would be... safe."

"Shall we, then?" he asked, and despite it being a whisper, his voice still cracked.

She nodded, following him back onto the main road, and they fell into pace. Rowan pretended to keep his eyes ahead, but he did his best to watch her out of the corner of his vision. Her expression was hard and wary, eyes flitting around as the fog swirled around them. He really was convinced she could see through it.

He also wondered if he should push his luck on trying to get more information out of her. Would it help, or would it put him in more danger? He wasn't sure, and he debated for several long seconds on what to do.

Rowan wasn't the bravest person, and he also didn't think he was the most foolish, but right now he must have been a terrible combination of both as he adjusted the strap on his shoulders and admitted, "I can't remember the last time I saw fog this thick. It feels unnatural."

She didn't look at him, but her eyes widened slightly as she quickly replied, "I do not understand. Fog is a very natural thing. This seems very natural to me."

Wow, she really was a terrible liar. That took some of the edge off of his anxiety, even if it didn't guarantee she wasn't dangerous. Still, her tricking him seemed pretty low on the list of worries. Not that she needed to trick him when she was as strong as she was. He just had to make sure she was on his side or believed herself to be.

He really hoped she was, though.

"I guess," he said quietly, unsure of what else to say at this point.

She glanced over at him, and then her eyes fell to the potions he was carrying. "Why do you have so many of these with you?"

He blinked, realizing what she was talking about. "Oh, these are deliveries. People request different kinds of potions, and I deliver them when they're ready."

"I see. You do this frequently, then?"

Rowan nodded, noting they were now in the farmlands at the base of the hill, which meant they'd be at the town gates soon. He still couldn't see the town's shape through the fog, though. He wondered how far her reach went with her magic.

"Yeah, I'd say I come to town about four days a week. Sometimes more if we have a lot of orders."

She hummed thoughtfully but didn't say anything else, returning her attention to the world beyond the fog. He watched her, his eyes flicking between the road and her face. Finally, he said, "I'm surprised you're still around."

She looked back at him, tilting her head slightly, something he noticed was quite common for her. "You wished for me to escort you to town, yes?"

He shook his head. "Not that. I mean, in general. Is Ladisdale any different from the rest of Southern Bascor? You said you were looking for why things were greener here."

Her brows lifted slightly. "There is... *something* different here, that I must admit. I do not know what, though."

"Like... 'different' as in people with magic moving in shadows?" Rowan asked lightly, curious if she would elaborate.

Her expression darkened. "That is... not the difference I speak of, but I think it is related." She paused, looking at him thoughtfully. "Do many people in Ladisdale use magic, Rowan Spicer?"

His lips curved up slightly at the way she said his full name. Come to think of it, she had addressed him like this the last time, too. He let it slide for now, wanting to focus on the more pressing question. "I mean, people use enchantments a lot. Like, most heat and light sources, like hearths and lamps, are enchanted, and of course, a lot of things made from natural materials are preserved with magic. But if you mean actual spellcasting... not that I know of. Anyone who does is probably associated with the Athenaeum in town."

"The what?"

"Um... the Opus Athenaeum. It's sort of a magic research institute. All of the ones in Bascor are owned by the Arcane Academy. I think Wescheca has an equivalent, but I don't remember the name?"

She stared at him blankly, either missing his prompt or knowing she didn't actually have an answer. Finally, she said, "I see."

At this point, Rowan was pretty sure Dragon Knights only had secret identities because they rarely went into town and talked to people. If danger wasn't looming over his shoulder, he would have found it both hilarious and ridiculous.

The gates finally came into view, and he sighed, feeling some tension leave his shoulders. "We made it."

"Did you think we would not?" Nova asked earnestly.

"I mean..." Rowan hesitated, eyes flicking around. The fog was thinner here but still obscuring some of the more distant buildings. "You're the one implying people are sneaking around using magic and could be dangerous."

"I did not imply. I saw," she said, and Rowan caught a touch of indignance in her tone.

He plucked his bottom lip with his teeth, knowing he was about to regret what he was going to say. "You saw people through this very natural fog?"

Her mouth fell open, a look of dismay crossing her features as she realized she was caught in her own lie. That dismay changed into frustration as she snapped her mouth shut and screwed her face up into what he would call a childish pout, and he found himself thinking it was adorable. He had a moment of appreciation before his brain caught up to him, and he felt a heat spread over his face all the way to his ears.

He thought Nova was cute.

He swallowed, furiously trying to pick apart when that happened and why it did when she muttered, "I sensed them. It is close enough."

They passed through the gates into town, her sulking and him awkwardly pushing aside the realization he found the poorly disguised Dragon Knight who *might* be hunting him 'cute.'

She came to a stop, sniffing the air, then stiffened, looking over at him awkwardly. They stared at each other, him utterly embarrassed and hoping she wouldn't ask why he was blushing, and her with a stone-faced expression that *still* somehow seemed uncomfortable. The awkwardness was almost worse than the terror he felt earlier when she grabbed him.

"I think I will go look at this... athenaeum. I thank you for accompanying me, Rowan Spicer."

"It's just Rowan," he replied, glancing down at his potions. "You don't need to say my full name."

"...Is it not a sign of respect?"

He looked up at her, finding her giving him a pensive, questioning glance like she didn't understand. He offered a half shrug. "I mean... It's very formal to call someone by their full name. I'd like to... not be so formal, I guess. And besides, you only gave me your first name."

Her expression shifted slightly in a way he didn't know how to interpret. "I... yes. I did. My other name is... hm. I cannot freely give it."

He sighed, knowing what that meant. "Because it's personal?"

He wasn't sure why he wanted to get to know her better, not when he couldn't rule out that she was actually dangerous. But it did sting just a little.

However, she shook her head. "No. It is not. Nova is my personal name. The other is... how you would say... professional. But I do not wish to tell it, for it is something I cannot explain to you."

He didn't expect that response. His lips parted slightly as he considered her words. "Oh. Okay. Well...I'd like it if you just called me Rowan. That's my personal name."

"Rowan," she echoed. "Not Rowan Spicer."

He nodded. "Correct."

"And to be clear: this is respectful, yes?"

He smiled at that, shrugging. "If I give you permission, then yes, it is. It means I want to build a friendship with you."

She looked surprised, and he didn't know if that was a good thing or a bad thing. "You wish... to call me a friend?"

The way she said that sounded incredulous like she didn't believe him. ...Or like she had no friends. He wondered if perhaps the life of a Dragon Knight was a lonely one. It was something he could relate to in some ways, and such thoughts made it much easier to ignore the potential dangers of the woman before him and focus on the potential benefits of building a connection with her instead.

He smiled at her, which was enough to answer her question. She took in a sharp breath, lips parting in a way he thought was pretty. He tried not to think too hard about that because it wasn't *really* relevant here. But he had to admit he liked her face when it was unguarded.

"I..." she trailed off, looking uncertain. "I am flattered, truly, Rowan, but I do not know if I can be your friend. I will not be here forever, and—" She hesitated, deliberating on her words before quietly admitting, "The life I live is a dangerous one, and I do not want it to bring you harm."

He stared at her, surprise on his face. He hadn't actually expected a real admission that implicated her as someone dangerous, and yet... she did it. And admitted she didn't want it to hurt him. He inhaled softly, standing awkwardly in the street. It was mostly empty, and the fog was starting to clear, scattered by a gentle breeze that hadn't been there earlier.

Was that her doing, too?

She glanced down at the ground, then looked back up at him. "I am s—"

"I think," he started softly, not letting her finish her sentence, "that I'd still like to be your friend. Maybe I won't see you again after you leave. Maybe you have a dangerous life, but... you seem worth knowing, anyway."

She swallowed, and the look of vulnerability on her face was something he did not expect to see. It took him by surprise, but then it was replaced with a resolution that made his stomach tighten.

"I cannot."

He sighed softly, disappointment on his features, and she glanced away almost shamefully.

"I wish things were different."

"Do you?" He didn't mean to sound accusatory, but it came through anyway. She picked up on it, evident by the way she looked crestfallen. More and more, he was convinced she wasn't there to bring him harm, and that's what made her rejection sting even more.

"Yes," she replied, her voice a near whisper. "You also seem worth knowing."

He gazed up at her, feeling his eyes water. Ugh, he'd been crying too much lately; the tears came too easily now. Hopefully, she wouldn't judge him for it. "Really?"

"Yes." She nodded. Her voice was soft, but it was sincere. Besides, he already knew now she couldn't lie for shit.

He bit his lip, thinking. Truthfully, this was still a rather reckless idea, given he was putting a lot of weight into his interpretation of his dream. But he just had this gut feeling she was important, and not in a way that was detrimental to him. Maybe he was wrong, and he was just desperate and lonely. Maybe he was tricking himself into seeing what he wanted to see, to prove everyone else wrong. Maybe this would have dire consequences, but it was a risk he really wanted to take anyway.

She watched him patiently, eyes on him intently as he deliberated on what to say. Finally, he replied, "I'm going to fight you on this, I think."

She pulled back slightly, her expression a mixture of doubt and confusion. "You are challenging me to a duel?"

He laughed at that, both at her shock and her interpretation of his words, feeling a tear slide down his cheek. He wiped at it with his shoulder, then smiled at her. "Not that kind of fight, silly. I'm going to fight for your friendship."

"I... I do not understand," she admitted, eyes searching his face. "How does one fight for this?"

He shrugged, still smiling. "Guess you'll have to see, won't you? Anyway, I have potions to deliver, and you have places to explore. Shall we part ways?"

While part of him didn't want to end it here, he had work to do, and he needed to collect his thoughts. He still wasn't entirely certain he wasn't making a huge mistake, but that voice was definitely subdued by every other part of him insisting he wasn't. Besides, he didn't want to go around in circles with her. It would probably have the opposite effect of what he wanted.

She opened her mouth, confused, then snapped it closed, clearly at a loss for words. "Very well. May your sunsets carry the magic of the skies, Rowan Spicer."

"Rowan," he corrected gently. "And may your future hold good friendships, Nova. I look forward to seeing you again."

She huffed softly, then turned and stalked off, her cloak swaying with each forward step. He watched her go, and just as he wondered if this would be the last time he ever saw her, he felt an unusually warm breeze rush past him, strong enough to whip his hair and make him close his eyes.

When he opened them, he saw her looking at him over her shoulder, studying him. He blinked, and then to his surprise, she offered him a faint smile and a slight bow of her head. "It shall be an interesting duel, Rowan."

Without another word, she turned away and disappeared down the street.

Chapter II
The Viridian Curse

The moon was bright, illuminating the countryside in pale light. It reflected off of the river snaking between the hills and cast strange shadows through the thin forests. Even the gray, nearly lifeless grass almost looked enchanting under the moonglow. Nova watched the world around her quietly from her perch atop a barren hill. Fog swirled just below the peak, making it appear like an island in the middle of a silvery sea.

Every night these last two weeks, Osier had returned to her in her dreams, wanting her to find and protect his legacy, and yet she had not found it. Even in the places where his magic lingered the strongest, it left her with more questions instead of answers.

Of the two locations that caught her interest, one was very clearly where he died. She found it far south of Ladisdale, deep in the hills where humans did not seem to live. The crater was half flooded by water from a nearby brook, but the evidence of that day still lingered in the combined scent of Viridian and ...arcane. She could not call it *Golden* anymore, for it was too twisted to sully the clan name like that.

She found nothing else of interest there, other than proof humans had at some point discovered the location, for they had carved signs in clay that seemed to warn others to turn away. She supposed that even human senses could feel the wrongness in the arcane magic left behind.

The other location was even stranger because she was not sure what happened there. It was a small clearing in the forests just south of Ladisdale. In fact, it was very close to Rowan Spicer's home. Thick Viridian magic was concentrated right in the center, old and stale, but stronger than anywhere else.

The glade itself looked like the rest of southern Bascor, slightly greener, with a couple of flowers that she could not name, and patches of soft moss that she found quite curious to touch. It all painted a picture that something important happened there, but it still did not give her insight into what could be Osier's legacy. It frustrated her because it did not give her answers, but it was different enough that she did not yet want to move on. Osier had been here, and she had a feeling this was the last place he went to before he died, and he did *something* in that glade. But what did he do?

What did he leave behind?

She sighed, lowering her gaze away from the moon to survey her surroundings. She sniffed the air, smelling old Viridian, her own magic, and fortunately, very little else.

This time.

She knew that humans had been following her since she left the battlefield. She noticed almost immediately once she slowed down enough for them to catch up, but it was *how* she noticed that gave her important clues into who they were.

For starters, they were magi who tried to hide their magical scent. Magic always left a scent, and those who used it regularly would always have a lingering odor, even if they were not actively using magic. Unfortunately, humans could not 'smell' magic like she could, so their attempts to mask their presence were only as effective as their own awareness. No matter how skilled, there was still a trace of arcane she could detect when they got nearby.

But this also meant they knew what she was, or they would not go to such lengths to hide the magical residue. And if that was the case, then it seemed plausible that they were followers of the lich, and they were the ones controlling the nearby undead. She did not like it, but it did not surprise her that the lich had these people hiding in human towns away from the war. After all, dragons had to come to the Reprised Shores to fulfill their roles, and how better for the lich to know when that happened than to have human spies?

Which, of course, led to her last observation: they were only trying to observe her. They had not attempted to engage or attack her, and she found it did not take much effort to lose them, although they were admittedly persistent. And when she did try to pursue, they always fled, never eager to confront her. Likely, they wanted to know what she was doing away from the war, which meant she would need to be careful. Once she found Osier's legacy, she would have to move quickly.

She only wished she knew what she was looking for.

With a sigh, she stood, dispelling the fog around her into a cool mist that scattered on the winds. It brushed against her cheeks lovingly, and she smiled slightly as she watched the traces of her magic carry on the skies. Briefly, the mist collided with the moonlight to form a rainbow above her, then it faded away into the night.

Pulling on the hood of her cloak, Nova turned her head away from the night and descended the hill. As she moved, her mind drifted to the little human who wanted to be her friend. She had never spent much time around humans. She had never wanted to, and yet, after her initial encounters with Rowan Spicer, she found herself continuing to seek him out. To observe him. To wonder. Rowan nurtured her curiosity, but he also demonstrated her naivety. She did not know what to do about that.

Truthfully, she felt rather foolish in believing she could blend in so easily. Being human, as she was learning, was more than appearances. She lacked knowledge of how humans behaved and what they were capable of, enough that even pretending she was simply from another human country did not fool everyone.

Rowan was a smart human. Nova had realized by the end of their second encounter that he knew she was not what she said she was. But he had not directly said it. No, he had used his words in clever ways to trap her into saying the wrong things, and now she was starting to understand how one could manipulate others with words. She did not know when he figured it out exactly, but it had to have been before she had grabbed him off of the road because he had been *so* fearful. She could smell it on him, but she had not understood what had changed between their first encounter and the next.

But then he had asked her to walk with him, and that request had not matched his fear. She thought that perhaps he had been afraid of something else, but what she did not know. Still, she had obliged him, telling herself he needed protection, even if walking beside him had meant she could no longer easily tell where the magi were. The arcane magic wrapped around his curse drowned the other scents.

It was no matter. Even if they had been attacked, she was confident she could have defended him.

Rowan had still smelled of fear as they had walked to Ladisdale, and yet he had continued to talk to her. He had held that basket of his so tightly, but he had *told her* he knew she was lying. And yet... he had announced his desire to be her friend, and she had found herself shocked beyond belief. There he had been, scared and knowing she was not a human, asking for her friendship.

She had almost felt it was a trick like his clever word games, but something inside of her, her *intuition,* had said it was not.

Nova's intuition was largely attuned to battle. She read the enemy's attacks and knew how to stay ahead in a fight. She understood combat and survival *intimately.* However, that was where it ended. She did not have practice in reading others outside of a battle sense, given that her life revolved around her duty. It was a shortcoming she knew she possessed, but she did not ever see a reason to correct it, for she did not have the luxury of existing as anything but the Tempest.

But for the first time, her intuition had *screamed* at her that this little human was important, and as he asked for her friendship, she felt it was genuine. Despite his fear, despite suspecting she was not human, he still offered.

And that scared her.

For the first time, something like that was dangled in front of her, and she wanted to *take* it. She wanted this concept of 'friend' with Rowan. She had this feeling that he understood loneliness like she did and that he would not care —*did not care*— who she was. Or *what* she was.

But this gracious offering of his she could not accept. He did not know what he truly asked for, being the friend of the Tempest. She had no friends, for her life was nothing but violence and death. Even in the shattered ruins of her home, she did not think of other half-dragons as friends. Her clan was her clan, and other clans were simply allies.

And yet... he claimed he would fight for it. This silly, little human with barely an understanding of what she was, declared he did not care, and he would fight... to be friends? She still did not understand. No one had ever defeated her in a duel, and truly, she should have ended the conversation there. Instead, she had given him a subtle invitation to try because she *desperately* wanted to see if he could succeed.

And he was certainly trying. Since that declaration, each time she encountered him, he engaged her in stories. First, of the plants used in potions. She had found him foraging for ingredients, and at her curiosity, he had explained each one to her and how they could be used. She did not remember most of it, but she remembered how energetic he was. He enjoyed what he did, and she envied that.

Another time, she had smelled him as he walked towards the town with his potions. She accompanied him part of the way, letting him talk about the different kinds of potions and the strange effects they had. She left once they reached town, wishing to patrol the perimeter.

He called out to her, smiling and thanking her for spending time with him. She did not think she deserved the thanks, but she had bowed her head anyway. As she left, she realized she liked his smile. It was pure and unguarded. It suited him, and she wished she could see more of it.

The rest of the time, he did not know she watched him. Sometimes when she smelled him nearby, she would observe from afar to sate her curiosity. Often, he was by himself carrying potions or foraging with the older man who lived with him. Even in these moments when he did not know she was there, she found herself wondering what a friendship with him would be like if she could have such a thing.

Could Rowan Spicer the human defeat her in a duel for her friendship? Part of her hoped so because she felt like it might change everything she knew.

She blinked, coming out of her thoughts at the smell of arcane. Her hackles rose, only for her to realize where she was, and then she felt foolish.

The little cottage was quiet, with a warm light coming out of the windows. Smoke came up through the chimney, carrying the faint scent of cooked fish and something medicinal. The arcane, of course, was Rowan's curse. Nova did not know exactly where in the building he was, but the concentration of magic promised he was inside.

She stepped forward once, then twice, and then she realized what she was doing. She stopped, staring down at her traitorous feet. This was not what she needed to be doing.

She puffed out her cheeks in annoyance and turned to walk away when she caught a whiff of something that cut through the arcane. She paused, eyes narrowing, before she turned her head sharply towards the source. The individual stayed in the shadows, beckoning her forth with a nod of their head, but Nova did not need light to see who it was. With a deep sigh, she crossed the road and stepped into the woods.

Nova came to a stop, staring at a woman with the same ice-blue eyes and pale skin, and the same kind of stormy gray cloak draped over her shoulders. But while Nova's cloak was disguised as plain fabric, the other cloak's surface swirled like an angry storm. This woman also had the illusion of pale blonde hair, braided and pinned atop her head. She stood a little taller than Nova, with a lighter build, but with a young face despite having seen more years in her life. Nova knew her well.

She was Rime the Frostweaver. A half-dragon like herself.

"Why are you here, Frostweaver?" Nova asked quietly, looking around. "You should not be here."

Rime scanned the area slowly before looking back at her. In this form, she lacked the silver scales on her forehead, but the scar under her right eye still marked her, a reminder that she was not full-dragon. "Neither should you, Nova. Why have you left the war? You slayed Somnambula and disappeared. I volunteered to find you when you did not return after several days. I feared something had happened."

Nova sighed deeply, pursing her lips. She did not quite meet Rime's gaze, expression pensive. "My dream changed."

Rime tilted her head slightly, eyes narrowing. She knew of Nova's dream, so she knew of the importance of it changing. "Because of the Dream Keeper?"

"Yes," Nova admitted. "With her magic returned to her clan, my dream became a message. Osier the Life Walker wishes for me to find his legacy in these hills."

Rime's eyes widened at the revelation. "Elder Osier? You are sure?"

Nova nodded, not missing the hope in Rime's words. "He appeared before me with flowers growing at his feet. It is like the stories you told me of how life grew where he walked. He has returned every night since my dream changed. I... I cannot ignore this, Rime."

Rime frowned, expression pensive. "Yes, I agree. A message from an elder is indeed important, but it has been many days since you left, and we are lacking your strength. Have you found something in your search?"

Nova exhaled softly, glancing off to the side. "Not... yet."

Rime's frown turned from pensive to troubled. "That is not good, Nova. I am certain you know this, but the others grow concerned about your disappearance. They feel you are not addressing your duty—"

"My *duty,*" Nova interrupted, a sharp edge to her words, "is to protect what remains of our people and to take back what has been stolen from us. For years that has been only through battle. I have slain more of the undead than any others of our clan; do not lecture me on duty."

Rime held up her hands, bowing her head. "I am not your enemy, Nova. I am telling you what I know will happen if you do not find your answer soon. We know very well that even if I tell the others of your message, it will only lend you so much time. It will come back to what *they* believe your duty is, you know this."

Nova took a step back, exhaling harshly as she recentered herself. "I apologize for my words."

"They are justified," Rime said with understanding. "Just be aware of where you aim them. I am with you, not against you."

Nova nodded again. Silence fell between them, Rime patiently waiting for Nova to continue. After a moment, Nova sighed, folding her arms across her chest. "I... think the way I carry out my duty can change."

For a moment, she thought of a little human with freckles and damaged hair, and she blinked, shaking her head. "Osier the Life Walker contacted me, and my intuition tells me that this is most important, that our survival rests on this."

Rime sighed. "I hope so, but admittedly, I do not know what kind of legacy he could have left behind, Nova. It cannot be an heir, because Viridian magic no longer truly moves. It is simply stuck in a... stasis. And if there was an heir, we would smell them. We would know. The world would recover."

"Yes, I know," Nova said softly, sadly. "I have found nothing here yet, other than old magic. Admittedly, a lot of it. I do not know why it lingers."

"There is a lot, yes, but I am impressed you can smell anything through all of this arcane. What lives in that little house, an archmagus?" Rime asked, lifting her brows. "It is quite impressive."

"It is just a human with a bound curse," Nova said softly. "Not an archmagus. A small, kind human."

Rime hissed softly, snapping her head towards the source in disbelief. "Surely you jest. The only kind of curse that needs so much magic is a dragon curse."

"It is not—" Nova's response died on her tongue, eyes going wide as she followed Rime's gaze. "No..."

Rime looked back at her, her irises almost glowing in the dark. Nova met her gaze, feeling unsettled in a way she was not certain she could put into words. She knew of dragon curses, but she had not ever seen one in her years alive. So few dragons would have a need to apply their magic in such a way, and with so few remaining...

"Are you certain?" Nova's voice was soft, hollow. She had assumed the curse was human. It had not occurred to her that the curse could be *dragon*. Was Osier's legacy a curse? Did he mark a human with Viridian magic somehow?

Was Rowan cursed by a dragon?

"I do not know what else it could be," Rime replied truthfully, interrupting Nova's troubled thoughts. "Human curses are not as powerful, for they do not have access to the vast magic pools that we do."

"But...can a human truly bind a dragon curse?" Nova asked in disbelief. She did not want to believe this possibility. But... the Viridian magic was strongest here, right by his house. And that magic wrapped around his arm was powerful.

Osier's legacy... she was supposed to protect it. How did one protect a curse?

"I think an archmagus could," Rime admitted. "I know you did not meet the advisors, but they were powerful, especially Advisor Avelore and Advisor Giselle, and they were archmagi, too."

"I... did not consider this," Nova admitted quietly, eyes wide in shock. "I do not know why Osier would curse him. I do not know why he would want me to protect a curse."

Rime shook her head. "It does not seem like Osier's doing, I agree. He was very fond of humanity. However, if this is a dragon curse, then it is an embodiment of the clan's magic. Releasing a Viridian curse would let the magic manifest, I think, even if no Viridians remain."

Rime paused, expression becoming troubled. "But...if the curse is attached to a human, then that is worrisome. You would be protecting the Viridian purpose by releasing the curse, but that would very likely harm the human, if not kill them. I... do not think Osier would do that unless he had no choice."

Nova shook her head, expression contorting into one of extreme displeasure as her eyes sought out the cottage again in the dark. "I... I do not think Rowan could survive a dragon curse. If I release it, he will die."

Rime was silent for a moment, regarding Nova curiously, like she was inspecting something new. "This... I do not recall you ever feeling like this towards humans. It is a welcomed change, but admittedly an unexpected one."

"I..." Nova did not know what to say to that, but it caught her off guard. "I do not..."

Rime tilted her head, then gently instructed, "Tell me about the human, Nova."

Nova inhaled and held onto the breath for a beat, returning her gaze to Rowan's house. She exhaled slowly, eyes on the soft firelight coming through the windows. Surprisingly, the words came easily. "He is a kind human. He is... expressive. He laughs and cries. He hides his face when he is embarrassed, and he talks quickly when he is excited. He is clever in his words, and he likes to tell me stories. I enjoy his presence. I do not want him to have Osier's curse. I want him to live."

Rime huffed through her nose, causing Nova to look over at her. There was a softness in her gaze that made Nova flush in embarrassment. "You use words to describe him that I have never heard you use for anyone before now. And with such a tone... Nova, are you smitten?"

Nova jerked, snapping her gaze up to meet Rime's. "I am not smitten!"

Rime pursed her lips, tilting her head. "It is not a bad thing to be. Even if it is for a human—"

Nova shook her head. "I am not smitten, Rime. Besides, I cannot have such things. It conflicts with my... duty."

But so did her pursuit of Osier's legacy, by definition. She just did not want to believe it.

Rime shook her head. "You can and should have those things. They make us better people, Nova. We are not just soldiers. We are the very lives we fight for."

"You may be," Nova replied with a weariness she did not realize she possessed. "I am only the Tempest. That has been made clear."

Rime growled, lip curling as she seemed to bite back the words on her tongue.

Nova sighed. "Do not be angry at me for speaking the truth."

"I am not angry at you, Nova. I am angry for you. Do not confuse the two," Rime said, stepping forward and pressing her forehead against Nova's. They stood there for a moment, eyes closed and cherishing a connection they did not often get a chance to share.

It ended very quickly, but it was still worth more than Nova could describe. "Thank you."

Rime shook her head, looking back at the house behind her. "Nova... I fear what you seek is right before you. It concerns me, especially if the human has a dragon's curse."

Nova clenched her jaw as the statement brought her mind back into focus. She did not want to believe Rowan was cursed by Osier, but it aligned with everything else. It bothered her for reasons she did not understand. Her stomach churned, and she felt like something was crawling under her skin.

She was drawn to Rowan, but she did not think it was because she was smitten with him. She had experienced that once, fleetingly, and this did not feel the same. And even if she was, it was not something she could embrace. She was a soldier; such feelings did not suit the Tempest.

"I'm going to fight for your friendship." Rowan's promise echoed between her ears, and the strange feelings it invoked unsettled her even more. If she was not smitten, then what *was* she?

A traitorous voice answered back: *lonely.*

Rime sighed, folding her arms across her chest as she looked back at Nova, expression concerned. "I must return to my watch. What will you do, Nova?"

"I must first confirm he has Osier's curse," Nova said carefully, fingernails biting into her palms as she focused on the possibilities that she had overlooked. "If we are wrong, then it will have consequences. I shall observe and determine if the curse is dragon."

"And if it is, what then?" Rime asked carefully.

"I... do not yet know," Nova admitted. "I want to protect Rowan. I do not know if I can do that if he wears a Viridian curse."

"Rowan..." Rime echoed softly, in a tone Nova could not interpret. "You are so very powerful, Nova, the strongest of our clan, but you are so very young."

"I do not know what my years have to do with this," Nova replied, frowning. "I am a prodigy."

"You are," Rime said with a smile, but the smile looked... sad. Nova did not understand, and she did not like it. However, Rime shook her head and continued, "I shall tell the others of your dream, and it will buy you time, but not much. If they grow too impatient, they may decide for you."

Nova growled, disliking the warning despite knowing it was very true.

Rime stepped back, a cold mist swirling around her. "For your sake, I hope his curse is not dragon. I shall leave now. May your sunsets carry the magic of the skies, Nova. Good night."

With that she wrapped herself in a frosty fog and threw herself into the air, taking off through the sky in a concealment of clouds and the beat of Silver wings.

Nova watched her go, full of emotions she did not know how to identify.

Chapter 12

Friends with the Sky

Morning came with a chill in the air that made Nova's breath visible in the sunrise. She stirred from her perch on a large, barren tree branch, opening her eyes as the first rays of light peeked over the hilltops.

Rest had not come easy last night, her mind plaguing her with possibilities as she mulled over the facts she had, the ones she did not, and how to bridge the gaps.

She did not want to believe Rowan had a dragon's curse, had *Osier's* curse. However, the magic wrapped around him was monstrous, indicating whatever it contained was equally powerful, and she had found no other explanation for the Viridian magic still lingering in these hills.

She did not like it. She wanted to be wrong.

She had never wanted to be wrong before, and it confused her. Why did it disquiet her so much, the idea of Rowan carrying the curse? Well, that part she knew. If he truly had a dragon curse, unleashing it would likely kill him. And without a living Viridian clan member, removing it was not an option.

But how did an archmagus know this and seal it? So many questions she asked herself as she tried to sleep through the night, and she hated that the moment she woke up, she began to repeat them again.

She sighed and sat up, stretching her back as the sky lit up above her with morning light. The brush of sunlight against her exposed skin was welcomed, replacing the atmospheric chill that had cradled her during her sleep.

Truly, she admired how the weather would shift on its own without her clan's direct aid. While dragons kept the world moving, they did not need to do so constantly. The world continued forward as long as each clan existed and fulfilled its role when needed. Of course, that meant the world chose to do what it wanted in between.

She did not mind, really. Her feet were cold, but she had quite the resilience for adverse conditions when she was not actively using magic, even if she was not invulnerable to the elements like a full-blooded dragon.

Her eyes fell on the Spicer home, visible from her perch across the tiny valley. She could see movement through one of the small windows, although even with her keen eyes, she could not determine who it was. However, after a few minutes, the door opened and Rowan stepped out.

He carried an empty basket like the one he used for his potions, but he did not walk towards town. Instead, he said something, closed the door, and turned down the path that followed the stream to the river, so Nova knew he must be going to forage.

She leaned forward, eyes following him as he moved through the naked trees. He walked quickly, likely because of the morning chill, and she frowned when she realized he did not have proper layers to keep himself warm. Just a jacket over his usual clothes and leather skin boots instead of his sandals.

She supposed most humans did not have good clothes these days. They could not easily make them from their hair, after all.

Without much flourish, she swung off of the branch and landed down on the ground, as silent as could be. Rowan was not hard to follow, not with that magic on him, so she took her time before trailing after him. She ate her breakfast, noting she was running low on food, and pulled water out of the air to quench her thirst.

Once she felt her basic needs were sufficiently addressed, she followed the scent of arcane, letting it lead her down to the river that crawled through the valley between the hills. With a hop, she pulled herself up into a tree, eyes easily finding Rowan along the waterfront some distance away, where the stream met the river.

Even with her keen vision, it took her a few minutes to realize what he was doing, as this was not his usual foraging. The shells he picked up must have been food or perhaps an unusual potion ingredient. He moved along the intersection of the two bodies of water, sifting through the bed and putting the shells in his basket.

The water was shallow, only going up to his knees. His shoes and jacket were sitting on the river bank, and he had rolled up the legs of his pants and the sleeves of his shirt so they would not be wet.

Nova frowned, though, because she could tell he was cold. He shivered as he worked, and she knew humans were not resilient against weather like she was. The shells must have been important for him to stay in the water like this, and as the minutes persisted, Nova found herself growing displeased.

He was very cold. She did not like it.

With a quiet snarl at nothing in particular, she lifted her hand and shifted the air around them. She was not sure how much he understood about what she could do, and she did not wish to simply give it all away, so she made the change in temperature soft and gradual, like the pace of the rising sun.

Slowly, steadily, she pulled the chill out of the air and pushed away the clouds, letting the morning sun shine brightly down on the riverside. It was only a subtle shift because too much of a change would be as noticeable as too fast of a change, but this made her feel better in a way she could not fully describe.

It just... did.

However, as the sun shone down on him, he stood up and lifted a hand to his eyes. Even from a distance, she could see the confusion on his face as he tilted his head up, almost like he was catching a scent. That was ridiculous. Humans could not smell magic.

She chuckled at that. Rowan was a clever human and quite observant, but she knew very well he was just that: human.

...A human who was now looking directly at her.

She blinked, staring back at him across the way. Surely he could not see her from this distance—

"Nova?"

Oh.

He stepped out of the water, putting his basket of shells down on the bank beside his shoes, and then took a step towards her. He stopped, looking at her as he flung the water from his hands in an attempt to dry off.

Knowing she had no reason to stay hidden, Nova hopped down from her perch and walked across the withered grass towards him. The wind blew gently, not of her own accord, and Rowan shuddered, turning his back to it.

She frowned, willing the wind to stop with a twitch of her fingers. At least this was weak magic. Anything stronger and it might bleed through her disguise. She did not need Rowan to see her eyes burn silver. He already knew enough.

Nova came to a stop in front of him, gaze flicking down at the basket of shells beside them. They were indeed as unimpressive up close as they were far away. She looked back at him, expression pensive. "You saw me?"

He lifted an eyebrow, making a noise that sounded... amused. "There's not exactly a lot of canopy to hide in up there. And the sunlight was reflecting off of your bracelets."

She blinked, holding up her wrist and the two silver bangles on it. Oh.

She glared at her traitorous bangles, realizing they were indeed not stealthy. Rowan watched her, biting his lip like it might prevent the smile that was forming on his face.

It did not.

She leveled her glare at him, which caused him to lose control and burst into giggles.

"I'm sorry! I just— You have really cute expressions!" He froze with that declaration, and Nova watched the color drain out of his face like the Great Wither had taken him. He was now almost as pale as she was.

Was 'cute' not what one called whelps or small children? Was he calling her young? She was pretty sure he was no older than herself, most likely younger, given the shape of his face. She tilted her head at him, pinching her brows together in confusion. "How so?"

He swallowed, and the loss of color in his face was quickly replaced by the hue of the setting sun like her question had embarrassed him. He was the one who said this. Why was asking for clarification causing such a reaction?

"I-I mean..." He trailed off, brushing his hair from his face as he looked around like he was searching for something. His lips were parted, like the words he wanted to say had fled from him, or perhaps he did not know what he wanted to say. Finally, he quietly admitted, "I dunno. I just like the faces you make."

"Oh." Nova nodded. "I think I understand. I like your face, too."

He sputtered, snapping his gaze back to her. "W-what do you mean?"

Why did he seem so confused? Was this not what they were talking about? She resisted the urge to huff and instead replied, "I mean that you are expressive, and I find it interesting. Your eyes tell many stories. I do not understand all of the stories, I do not think, but I feel as though I would like to."

He gaped at her, mouth hanging open like a fish. ...It did not suit him, and the irony was not lost on her after she just complimented his face.

She waited patiently for him to respond. Finally, he shook his head, his messy hair shivering with the notion. "S-sorry. Just... no one's ever said that? Um, t-thank you. Anyway, uh, hi! What are you doing here?"

He sounded so small again, and she frowned. Had she made a misstep again? Part of her wanted to ask, but he seemed so uncomfortable, folding his arms around himself and not meeting her gaze.

She tilted her head again, regarding him. "I came to see you."

"Oh!" He blinked at that, looking at her in a way that was both surprised and pleased. She once again found herself admiring how expressive he was, and how he looked more interesting with the pink on his cheeks behind his... what were they called, spots? No... Freckles?

But then she watched as his expression was replaced with confusion. "How did you know I was out here?"

She felt her lips pull up into a slight smile and nodded to his arm. His eyes followed her gaze, and he lifted his brows in realization. "Oh. Right. That. Right. Um... well, I'm just collecting food today. Kind of boring, really. Normally I forage with my grandpa but the weather is making his knee hurt again, so he's home brewing a numbing potion for it while I do this."

"These are shellfish, then?" Nova asked, leaning over to peek at the basket. They did not look like they could be anything besides food, after all. They were black and unimpressive. Not even shiny like the ones that the Cerulean clan wore for jewelry.

"Oh! Yeah!" Rowan said excitedly, a smile on his face. "There were quite a few safe to harvest! I pulled the biggest ones but left smaller ones to grow. They're not very fast growing, but my grandfather says it's important to not overharvest anything."

"Why?" Nova asked, watching as Rowan walked a little way down the bank of the river. Curiously, she followed him, stepping over the stones and avoiding the muddy spots.

"Because very little grows in the world already, and if you take too much of what's left, it won't grow at all," he said with a tiny smile as he looked back at her. "Not everyone abides by that, and I get it. People are hungry. But... if we're too greedy, there won't be anything left."

"I see..." Nova said softly, watching as he stopped by the water's edge. He stayed there, surveying the water, and when she followed his gaze, she realized he was staring at something a little ways into the river. It looked human-made, but she was not quite sure what it was.

"Anyway, um, excuse me a minute. I need to check this trap, and, uh..." He trailed off awkwardly before turning his back to her and pulling off his tunic. Nova tilted her head, watching him fold it and put it on a rock.

The sunlight hit his freckled skin, showing how his arms were darker than the rest of his upper body. He was slight in form, but not as underweight as she expected. She supposed his knowledge of the land meant he ate a little better than most humans. That thought pleased her. He was resourceful and clever, and she liked how that made life a little better for him.

Rowan rubbed his arms and glanced back over his shoulder at her nervously. She tilted her head at him, unsure of why he was now shy. Was he ashamed of his body? She knew humans sometimes felt that way, albeit often for reasons she did not quite understand. She was not unfamiliar with shame, but the causes were far different. She wondered, briefly, if she had somehow said or done something to make him feel shameful, but before she could ask, he looked away and stepped into the water.

Although this part of the river was shallow, it was still deeper than the place where he was hunting for the shellfish. Nova was not sure why he bothered to remove only his shirt when his pants were getting wet. She frowned, watching the water go up to his thighs as he stopped by the trap he spoke of.

He reached into the water, grabbed the trap, and pulled it up, and to Nova's surprise, it contained fish. Water poured on him as he stepped back out of the river, leaving him shivering as he put down the trap of flopping fish.

Nova frowned, noting the temperature had started to drop again now that she was no longer actively curating it. The skies were indeed fickle this season. She watched as Rowan wiped the excess water off of himself, hands swiping at the droplets clinging to his arms. Even if he managed to get the water off of his skin, his pants were still fairly wet, and that would prevent him from keeping his body heat, she knew.

He sighed, reaching for his discarded shirt. "It normally doesn't start feeling this chilly for another few weeks. Makes me wonder if we'll have another harsh winter. It's a shame though, 'cause I felt like it got warmer for a little bit when I was collecting mussels."

It took Nova longer than she wanted to admit to realize that 'muscles' were what the shellfish must be called because he did not really have muscles to speak of. However, more importantly, she knew redressing was not going to be enough. Even as he pulled on his tunic and jacket, his pants were still wet from his thighs down, and the sun would not be able to dry them quickly.

With a displeased huff, Nova untied her cloak and stalked forward, catching his attention as he pulled his hair out from his shirt. He blinked at her, mouth opening just as she stopped in front of him and swept her cloak over his shoulders. She pulled it closed, watching as he shuddered from the sudden change of temperature around him.

He sucked in a breath, eyes falling half-shut as the enchanted fabric covered him. "Ohhh... it's so warm..."

"You will get sick without it," Nova said quietly as she tied the cord so it would not fall off. "Cold is dangerous."

Rowan nodded, grabbing the edges of the cloak and hugging them close to his chest. He stayed that way for a moment, soaking in the heat before he looked up at her. Once again, she found herself lost in those big eyes that offered to tell her stories. Stories that she would gladly listen to every day if she had the luxury.

"Thank you. You're really kind to me."

Nova went still at that, arms falling to her sides. Kind? She did not think that word was correct. 'Kind' were people like Rowan, who tried to befriend strangers from other lands, and who said and did nice things for people he did not know.

She stopped, pursing her lips as she realized her description of Rowan also described how she treated Rowan. Here she was, doing things to keep him from being cold and sick, speaking fondly of him to Rime, and interacting with him...

...Because she needed to know if he had a dragon curse.

...And because she wanted to be his friend.

She scowled, feeling something uncomfortable in her gut like she had swallowed something unpalatable.

Rowan took a step back, shrinking in on himself at her obvious displeasure. "Did I... say something wrong?"

Nova stopped, looking over at him pensively. She did not like how her desires conflicted with her duty, but she did not know what to do. Her eyes fell to where his arm was, and for a brief moment, she imagined cutting it off, if only to spare him the pain and probable death from the curse unleashing. Humans could live with one arm, but would he forgive her? Would she forgive herself?

She blinked, realizing she had not responded. "...No. It is nothing."

"Oh."

His voice was tiny again. She did not like it. Nova wrinkled her nose and glanced away, trying to ignore the uneasy feelings inside of her. "I do not think 'kind' is the right word for me. You will become cold without protection. It makes sense to lend you my cloak so this does not happen, for I am not bothered by the cold. But that does not make me 'kind.'"

Rowan was silent, staring up at her with a furrowed brow. He seemed to be thinking, though she did not know what about. He was so expressive and yet... often so hard to read. After a moment, he sighed softly and stepped past her towards his basket of shells—*muscles*. She followed him, unsure of what to say.

He broke the silence first. "I dunno. I kind of disagree. I think it was kind of you to lend me your cloak."

He picked up the basket and turned to her with a smile that she thought looked pretty on him. "And it was kind of the skies to warm up for me earlier."

She swallowed, feeling a strange heat on the back of her neck like the sun was bearing down on it despite it being at the wrong angle. She needed to change the conversation, as this topic was dangerous because of how clever he was with his words. And yet she found herself saying, "You speak like the skies have feelings."

He laughed a little, face pink as he walked back to the fish trap and began to move the fish into his basket. The sound was so much better than his tiny voice a moment ago, and she relaxed slightly.

"Well," he started thoughtfully, not looking up from his task, "in my experience, they seem to. And if that's the case, I think I'd like to be their friend, too."

She snorted softly, looking up towards the scattered clouds and morning sun. "Even when the skies are cold?"

She glanced at him to see him grinning at her. "Yeah. Being a friend is accepting the bad with the good, I think."

She did not think words could cut her in such ways, both because it was an offer she wanted to accept and a reminder of why she could not.

He would not feel this way if she had to kill him.

Chapter 13
Quality Time

"You're still here, aren't you?"

Rowan's voice broke through the quiet of the morning as he rounded the bend that put his house out of view. The only sounds were the distant running of water from the brook, the soft clinks of the potions he carried, and the occasional groans of withered trees in the wind.

He came to a stop, looking around, because truthfully, he was just taking a guess. He had a feeling his Dragon Knight shadow had not truly left after he said he needed to return home.

Perhaps it was because she'd refused to let him get back in the river to reset the trap, demanding he tell her how to do it. After all, he was 'too small to stay cold and wet.'

Perhaps it was because she'd let him keep wearing her cloak and had followed him home, only taking the cloak back when his house came into view and she hadn't wanted to go further.

Perhaps it was because she hadn't said goodbye, instead choosing to nod to him and stay put as he carried forward.

Perhaps it was because he had turned back to her and said, "I'll be going to town in an hour or so. Maybe...I'll see you there?"

Perhaps it was none of those things, or maybe it was all of them. Regardless, he felt a little spark of triumph when she walked out from between the trees, silent on her feet in a way that was so unnatural. And yet, he expected it.

Nova tilted her head, an action Rowan now mentally described as 'very Nova-like.' "How did you know?"

He gave her a lopsided grin, shrugging. "Intuition?"

Her brows lifted, but she shook her head and hopped down onto the road beside him. "I understood earlier that your statement that you would be going to Ladisdale was supposed to be an invitation for me to join you. Is this correct?"

He laughed softly, starting down the path once again as she fell into pace beside him. "I mean... it was open for interpretation. If you wanted it to be a statement, that's all it was. If you wanted it to be an invitation, it was that, too."

"I see. That is clever," she said quietly, staring out onto the road. "I am not sure what I wanted it to be."

"Well...you're here, right?" Rowan asked, tilting his head forward to look at her. Her eyes flicked to him, but she didn't otherwise react.

After a moment, she sighed. "I am, yes."

"You sound disappointed." Rowan made sure to sound playful, but there was something different about her today. She seemed conflicted, and that, coupled with how she had actively sought him out, made him wonder just what was going on. What if she really was supposed to kidnap him or something?

He didn't want to think that. He wanted to believe she really wanted to be his friend and this was just new to her. And in a way, he did believe that. But he just couldn't shake the feeling that wasn't all it was.

He thought back to earlier, how she didn't hesitate to wrap him in her cloak when she saw he was cold. He also knew that the warmer temperature was her doing, too, if only because he could smell her magic in the area when it happened.

He paused, thinking back to something he saw when she took off her cloak. Tied to her belt had been a leather-wrapped hilt to a sword with a ring pommel but no blade. He hadn't remembered seeing it before when she'd given him her cloak the first time. Maybe because it was in her travel bag or because he had been too distracted by everything else. "Why do you have a sword with no blade?"

She looked over at him and blinked slowly. He felt like he could *see* her struggle to come up with an answer, and it took everything in his power to not smile. Instead, he kept an innocent expression, knowing very well she was bad at lying and that he was maybe a little bit of a jerk for using that to his advantage. But he was curious. He wanted to know about her. He wanted to be her friend.

"Because it is important to me," she finally conceded, and truly, he was proud of her for saying something that was probably true but wasn't a real explanation. He'd let her have that one, this time.

They talked a bit more, with him driving the conversation, not that he minded. He learned that her clothes were made of a type of 'silk' but she wouldn't elaborate on the details. He also learned that she was eighteen and that she didn't know her actual birthday, only that she was born during the summer.

He thought that was kind of sad.

In return, he told her that he was sixteen and that his birthday was just a couple of weeks away. She asked if birthdays were important, which made him realize she had probably never celebrated any age milestone in her life.

He went on to explain Bascori coming-of-age ceremonies, and how they were held when someone turned fifteen. Before the Great Wither, the parents would throw a big feast and invite local friends and family. People wore traditional Bascori garb dyed in the country's colors of green, gold, and black, and they would light colorful lanterns that were supposed to stay lit for a full day.

Now, since most of that wasn't really feasible anymore, most families didn't do more than keep a lantern lit through the night and be grateful for another day. He didn't elaborate on how many children never reached their coming of age due to the prolonged starvation of the Great Wither.

However, in his family's case, they surprised him with a small 'feast' of foraged foods they had gathered behind his back. Rowan recalled the modest selection of seasonal foods, from nuts and berries to a variety of mushrooms and some edible plants. His mother even traded some potions with the Fishers for some fresh salmon, and his grandfather called in a favor to have their lantern enchanted to be green for the night.

It was one of Rowan's favorite memories.

Nova was pensive after that. Rowan wondered if it was because she'd probably never had a chance to celebrate her birthday. So, he offered, "Next summer, I'll light a lantern for you to celebrate your birthday. If you're around, I'll find some berries, too."

She gave him a sidelong glance. "But we are not family."

He shrugged. "So? Friends can celebrate birthdays, too. It's pretty common across a lot of cultures, even. For some places, even the entire town celebrates!"

Nova blinked, tilting her head. "How would you know?"

Rowan grinned at her. "I read a lot."

Nova furrowed her brow at that, and Rowan predicted her next question before she could ask it. "The Athenaeum in town has a library.

A, uh, a collection of books open to the public. I used to spend a lot of time reading through the books there. I've read all of them and many of them twice. It's... it's nice to get lost in a book, I guess. Lets me escape the stress of the world a bit."

"You are a scholar then," Nova declared, rather than asked. "This explains why you are so clever!"

Rowan felt himself blush all the way to his ears. That wasn't true, but it sure felt nice to hear, especially from her. He tried not to think about why. "I— no, I'm not. Not really. I don't do research or anything, and I've only got a basic education. Not really allowed to pursue higher learning." He didn't elaborate on why. He didn't need to. "I just...pick up books and read them. Doesn't matter what kind, really. As long as it's available and in a language I can read, I'm gonna read it."

Nova blinked at him, brows lifting in disbelief. "You speak multiple tongues, too?"

"J-just Common! I mean, I can kind of read some Old Bascori, but I can't speak it. I don't know how to pronounce half of the words," Rowan clarified nervously, face still burning. The library had a sizable selection of books in Old Bascori, despite having copies of the same texts in Common. They shared the same root language, so Rowan found that reading them side by side was fun. But his vocabulary was mostly basic and *definitely* not noteworthy.

"That is still..." Nova trailed off, a look of disbelief on her face. "That is impressive. Truly. These are very scholarly traits. You should be proud."

He shyly ducked his head, grinning down at the ground, grateful his bangs were partially hiding his pink face. He wasn't trying to impress her, but he felt his skin tingling at her praise. "Thanks."

As they reached the city gates, Nova looked over at him. "So you do not go to this library anymore, no? Since you have read all of the books."

"I still do," Rowan admitted, glancing down at his potions to remind himself of which house he needed to visit first. He grimaced when he realized which household it was but pushed the thought aside. "I like to reread books, but I have other reasons, too. Usually, I play a board game with someone instead. Um, a strategy one."

A small concern that she would find it silly surfaced, and he bit down going into any further explanation, suddenly feeling unsure of himself. He knew he shouldn't though. She hadn't ever laughed at him before.

He saw Nova tilt her head out of the corner of his eye. "Why?"

He swallowed as the feeling of uncertainty grew, but hid it the best he could. So instead he shrugged and looked at her. "Why not? It's fun and a good way to get to know someone."

Nova nodded carefully as if she was thinking very hard about that. "So it is something friends do?"

His concern faded with her question, and he made a thoughtful noise as he steered them down a side street as they entered town. His eyes flicked around out of habit, but the fact that he was with Nova did a lot to temper his usual anxiety. "I mean, sure, I think so. But not just friends. You don't need to be friends with someone to play games with them, I don't think."

"Is your game mate not your friend?" Nova asked quizzically, her eyes flicking to him and then back to the road.

Rowan smiled, drumming his fingers on his delivery basket. "I'd like to think he is, but I mean, he's old enough to be my dad, and I honestly don't know if there's some unspoken rule about that."

"Why would there be?"

Rowan shrugged one shoulder, turning down the street that had his first delivery destination. He half noticed as he tightened the grip on his basket. "Because society's weird? I mean, at least Bascor's. I can't pretend other places are the same because I've never been there, but...

we have a lot of assumptions about how people should behave based on who or what they are. I kind of find a lot of them silly."

"I do not think I understand," Nova admitted, but not in a dismissive way. "Can you explain more?"

He came to a stop, and she did as well. "Well... sure, here's an easy one. My hair is not supposed to be long because I'm a man."

To his fascination and, admittedly, his amusement, Nova looked incredibly unhappy about that. "That is the most foolish thing I have heard, and I have heard many foolish things since I have been in Bascor."

Rowan laughed quietly, feeling some comfort in her indignation. "Yeah, I don't like it either, but it's true. Now, some people argue it's because, for laborers, having long hair is a hazard, and I *would* agree, but not everyone is a laborer. Even scholars are discouraged from it. So really it's just because people have weird ideas of how men should keep their hair."

Nova nodded, her expression shifting to something more pensive than outright offended. "I see. So it is a rule that does not make sense but people must still follow it. This I can understand. Perhaps... more than I would like. I do not know why these rules exist. I wonder if things would be better if they did not."

"That is the question," Rowan agreed with a tiny smile. They were both silent for a moment, then Rowan looked towards the house they were standing in front of. Right. Deliveries. "Anyway, uh, I need to deliver this, and it'll be weird if you're standing beside me. Can you maybe stay out of sight until I'm done? It shouldn't take me longer than a couple of min—"

He turned to look at Nova, only to find she was already gone. He blinked several times, then exhaled and shook his head, walking up to the house. The Naylors weren't the nicest folks, much like the Carpenters, but usually, the wife was home and she was only mildly obnoxious compared to her spouse.

But of course, as Rowan knocked, he learned he was not lucky enough to be greeted by Mistress Naylor, and instead, he found himself looking up at the tall, lanky form of Mister Naylor, with his balding head and beady eyes.

Mister Naylor sneered slightly, giving Rowan a contemptuous glare. "You're late, boy."

Rowan blinked, glancing up at the skies overhead. It wasn't even late morning yet. Was he really complaining over a few minutes past his normal start time? "Hello, Mister Naylor. Were you expecting me earlier?"

"Should've been here yesterday. We put the order in three days ago, and you said it'd be ready in two."

Oh. Of *course*, this was what it was. Rowan gave him a tight-lipped smile. "I think perhaps the details got a little switched. The potion takes two days to brew, but I also stated to Mistress Naylor that I'd not be able to deliver it earlier than today because we only deliver in the mornings."

"Are you calling my wife a liar, boy?" Mister Naylor asked, doing his best to look intimidating. It wasn't that hard, given he had well over a head of height on Rowan.

Rowan shook his head. "I've made no accusations, but I do know what I said, because I also told it to Mayor Lander, since he overheard Mistress Naylor's potion request and asked for one, too. They both got the same information."

Mister Naylor pressed his lips into a thin line, glaring at Rowan as he debated the probability of a bluff. Fortunately for Rowan, it wasn't, really, but he didn't want to have to take the extra steps to prove it.

After a moment of contemplation, Mister Naylor seemed to feel like it was too much effort to contest the story. He scowled, pulling out payment. "Should've been two."

Rowan gave another benign smile as he traded the potion for shells, even if mentally he went through several sassy retorts in his head. "Thank you for your business, sir. Have a good day."

At least he didn't slam the door in Rowan's face, even if he looked like he bit into rotten fish. Rowan turned, only to nearly run face-first into Nova. He yelped in surprise, stumbling back, but she steadied him with a hand on his shoulder. He stared up at her, giving her a wide-eyed, startled look. "Don't *do* that!"

"You did not want me to catch you?" Nova asked with such guileless honesty that for a moment Rowan forgot what he was complaining about.

"Not that," Rowan replied, exasperated. "Sneaking up on me! You made no noise!"

"Ah." Nova's brows lifted in understanding. "I did not mean to startle you. I thought you would understand I was nearby."

"Yes, but not behind me. Were you there this whole time?" he asked with mild alarm.

"No, I stayed in hiding, as you requested. I returned when he shut the door."

Honestly, Rowan had no idea where she could have been hiding that let her reappear so suddenly, and part of him was worried she'd just... jumped up on the roof or something else ridiculous. If so, he hoped no one saw her. It was bad enough that she thought she could hide in the trees this morning.

Before he could say anything, though, Nova tilted her head at him. "You are very clever with your words, Rowan. You use them like a warrior might use a sword. It is impressive."

He bit back a smile, pleased at her compliment but also feeling a little sheepish since he wasn't really doing anything impressive. She just clearly lacked social skills. With that thought, he coyly asked, "Is that so? How would you have handled that situation, then?"

Nova blinked at him. "I do not know. I cannot see myself in such a situation, but I find duels are helpful for sorting disagreements with others."

"Right," Rowan said with a roll of his eyes. "Of course. How did I not think of that?"

"It is because you are not a warrior," Nova said, completely missing his sarcasm.

Rowan blinked twice, taking a moment to process her response, then shook his head wryly and walked past her. "Okay, Nova."

"I do not understand that tone. What does it mean?"

He didn't elaborate, waving at her to follow him, a smile on his face.

The rest of Rowan's deliveries went far better than usual, all thanks to his Dragon Knight shadow. Mister Mason tried to shortchange what he owed Rowan, refusing to cooperate and getting increasingly more volatile. He stopped, though, when Nova appeared behind Rowan from around the corner, growling. That shut Mister Mason up faster than Rowan had ever seen.

Rowan was torn between being embarrassed by her *growling* and grateful that she stepped in. Growling sure didn't help her blend in, though. What *were* Dragon Knights, really?

After that, the Fishers passed him on the street, nervously requesting an order for warming draughts. Their eyes were on Nova the entire time as she leveled them with an intense gaze that was maybe a bit unnecessary, given that the Fishers were usually only snide with him. There was certainly no snideness today, at any rate.

The rest of the deliveries trended much the same way, with those who usually gave him grief feeling quite intimidated by his companion. Truthfully, it made him a little bit giddy, but he was doing his best to not let that show.

And the most interesting encounter was Tilbert. The moment he saw them both on the street, he turned an interesting shade of puce and promptly detoured down a side street and out of sight. It was the first time that had *ever* happened. Rowan shouldn't have felt so elated by that, but he really was. And when he glanced at Nova, she was smirking, eyes narrowed in Tilbert's direction.

"So a fool can learn after all," she murmured, which made Rowan grin widely.

"This has been one of the smoothest delivery runs I've ever had. Feels like I have my own personal guard," Rowan giggled, glancing down at his feet as they walked.

Nova snorted, eyes scanning the area. "It is… not what I am, but perhaps today we can pretend."

That was a strange thing for her to say, especially given that was *exactly* what she'd done the entire time they had been in town. He peered up at her curiously to find she had that distant expression again. He wondered what was plaguing her. Was it him? Was it that she knew she needed to move on?

The sudden shift in atmosphere was a loud reminder that she was a Dragon Knight and that she had a job to do. She said she was here to see why things were less bleak here, but… had she found what she was looking for? Was it time for her to go? …Was she hesitating because she wanted to be his friend? Or was it… something else?

He squished the worries aside, watching as they approached 'On Bascori Wings.' "Hey, Nova. Have you found what you're looking for yet?"

She was silent for several seconds, the only sound between them being the clap of their shoes on the cobblestone. The pensive expression she had deepened, and Rowan felt himself growing uneasy.

"Possibly," she admitted quietly. "I may have found it, but… I am unsure."

"Is it not a good thing?" Rowan asked softly. "You came here to find out why things are better in the area, right?"

He wondered how truthful she had been when she gave that answer to him. If she was, then likely she wasn't after him. But why would she need to know why things still grew here?

Nova sighed softly. "I did, yes, but... it is not what I expected to find, and now I am unsure what to do."

"Do you want to tell me about it?" Rowan asked as they came to a stop at the entrance of the courier office.

Nova looked over at him, her expression sad in a way that Rowan had never seen on her face. "No, I... cannot do that."

"You seem really sad though," Rowan said carefully. "I don't like that."

Nova glanced away, brows pinching together. "You should not care how I feel."

"Too bad. I do."

She blinked, looking back at him, and he offered her a smile. "I told you I was gonna fight for your friendship. That means I care about your feelings. I don't want you to be sad, Nova. And I want you to trust me."

She exhaled harshly, lips parting like his words caused her physical pain. "Why are you like this, Rowan?"

He frowned, giving her a frustrated look. "Don't talk like it's a bad thing."

"It is not a bad thing," Nova agreed, looking away. "Nothing you do is bad, and it frustrates me because you are too kind. Why are you so—"

She stopped, eyes going wide as her nostrils flared. Rowan watched her head snap up, and she stared off into the distance. The air around them shifted, and the scent that he described as uniquely hers reached his nose, and he realized something was wrong.

"Nova? What—"

"I must go."

And before he could question further, she took off in a sprint that few people could match, aiming for the eastern gates as a telltale fog rolled in to provide herself cover. Rowan exhaled loudly, watching her go. He would find himself drawn to someone like her, and yet... he couldn't be mad about it.

Chapter 14
Speculations

"Lovers' quarrel?"

Rowan yelped at Cengor's voice, whirling around to see him standing in the doorway of his office, arms crossed and an amused smile on his face. Rowan stared at him, heart pounding from being spooked. Cengor's words caught up to him a moment later, and he felt his face burn. "W-what?!"

Cengor shrugged, grinning as he looked off in the direction Nova took. "I don't know, you tell me. Didn't hear anything but it sure looked like an emotionally charged conversation. One of my couriers also told me he saw you come into town together as he came back from his run."

Rowan gaped at Cengor, feeling like he might melt into the cobblestone. "That's not—! We're just—!"

'—*friends*' was what he wanted to say, but she kept fighting him on it. So instead he sighed. "I don't know what we are, but we're not lovers."

"Sounds like disappointment," Cengor said with a smile, waving Rowan inside.

Rowan sputtered, following him inside the building. "That's not—*ugh*, that's not what I mean! I'm just trying to be her friend."

Cengor chuckled, turning to him. "All right, all right. Sorry then. I guess you just sorta reminded me of when I was younger, so I made some assumptions."

Rowan pursed his lips, giving Cengor a cautious glance as he placed the last of his potion deliveries on the counter. "These are going to Lord Leofard of Bouldermoor. And...how so?"

"The look in your eyes," Cengor admitted as he wrote the name and destination down on his chalkboard. "Was watching from the window, but the way you look at that Weschecan girl reminds me of how I felt when I met Giselle years ago. I would have followed her across the Shores and back."

Rowan swallowed, nervously tucking his hair behind his ear. "I mean... I think she's pretty, and I like talking to her but... really, I just want her friendship. And I guess... between you and me, I don't think she'd ever see me that way. I mean, look at me."

Cengor grunted, glancing at Rowan over his shoulder with a rather withering gaze. "There you go being down on yourself again. I think there's a lot of reasons she'd be interested in you."

"You don't know anything about her," Rowan pointed out, not unkindly, but knowing very well that Cengor had no idea that Nova was a Dragon Knight.

"I don't need to," Cengor sassed back, waving his hand. "I know *you*. You're smart, Rowan. You've turned that library upside down looking for new things to read. You're skilled, too. We both know the only reason you're still an apprentice in potion-making is that the Athenaeum won't proctor your proficiency test, and your family can't officially promote you."

Rowan ducked his head, unused to the praise, even if Cengor was preaching them as facts. Sure, he read a lot of books, but that didn't mean much if he couldn't put that knowledge to use, and well, the potion-making thing was true, but it wasn't like he was particularly gifted in it like his mother. He'd just practiced and studied a lot, and—

Cengor sighed, turning fully to face Rowan. "Honestly, Rowan, if it weren't for that damned curse on your arm, you'd be one of those people who go places. Your name would be one that would come up in conversation, *respectfully*. And between you and me, the girl being from Wescheca helps because she probably doesn't even know you're cursed, does she?"

Rowan swallowed, not meeting eye contact as he tucked his hair behind his ear. He'd never seen Cengor get so worked up on his behalf, but it was really nice. First Nova earlier during their walk, and now Cengor. Today had Rowan understandably flustered from so much praise, and he wasn't quite sure how to handle it all.

He paused, remembering Cengor's question. His eyes flicked down to his arm. "Oh, um, actually... She does. I told her."

"See?" Cengor said dramatically, adjusting his glasses with his index finger when he realized they had slipped down his nose. "She doesn't even care! Maybe she even thinks you're exciting because of it!"

Rowan flushed, shaking his head awkwardly. "Highly doubt that, Cengor. There's nothing exciting about this—"

He stopped short, realizing that wasn't necessarily true anymore, now that he knew it wasn't actually a curse. But he couldn't just *say* that... could he?

Cengor noticed the sudden shift in his demeanor and frowned. "What is it? Did something happen?"

Rowan chewed on his lip, debating on what to say. The truth is, he had no idea what was so dangerous about his 'gift', only that he was being hunted for it, possibly by Nova, and it wasn't truly a curse. Cengor was someone Rowan trusted and even considered a friend, but he was also a bit of a gossip. It was kind of a given since his job was to coordinate the delivery of goods and information, but that also meant he might let things slip even if sworn to secrecy.

Rowan sighed, looking up and giving Cengor a small smile. "Nothing."

Cengor lifted a brow. "...Sure, all right then."

The tone made Rowan cringe because it was clear Cengor didn't believe him, maybe even felt disappointed that Rowan wouldn't talk to him. Rowan warred with himself for a few seconds, then finally figured out a way to say what he wanted without telling the exact truth. "Nova showing up made me realize that this curse is more like a gift. It wasn't something she did on purpose. Just... circumstance. But I'm grateful for it."

Cengor was quiet for a moment, considering Rowan's words. "Well, that sounds personal, so I won't pry, but I'm happy for you."

Rowan shrugged a shoulder, adjusting the strap of his delivery basket. "Thanks. Me too, I think. Even if she's just passing through, I think she made my life better."

Cengor smiled warmly, in a way that made Rowan's ears burn slightly. It wasn't a teasing or unkind smile, but a *knowing* one. Rowan just knew this topic probably wasn't over with. The next time he stopped by, he was certain Cengor would ask how he and Nova were 'getting along.'

"Anyway..." Rowan continued awkwardly, glancing over his shoulder at the window before looking back at Cengor. "I should probably get going. I still want to stop by the library before I head home."

"I suppose I should get back to work as well," Cengor replied, eyeing his backroom with mock disdain. He looked back at Rowan before his brows shot up like he just remembered something. "Oh, before I forget! I have some potential leads about the career stuff we talked about. Check back with me in a couple of days, will you? I'm just waiting for confirmation."

"Oh, that's awesome. Thanks, Cengor. As always." Rowan nodded to him, turning towards the door. "I'm really grateful you're my friend."

Cengor beamed at Rowan. "Me, too! Now hurry off before the library realizes you have another woman in your life."

Rowan rolled his eyes but waved over his shoulder and left. As he crossed the small distance across the square towards the Athenaeum's library, he couldn't help but think about Cengor's teasing.

Yes, Rowan thought Nova was cute. She had a pretty face and her reactions to everything were, well, adorable, but... he couldn't even get her to be his friend. Even after all the progress of today, she got upset at the end and just shut him out before running off! That was frustrating, but even outside of that...

She was still a *Dragon Knight*. She wasn't going to stay in Bascor. And even with whatever was on his arm... he wasn't *that* special. How could he keep up with her?

And what if she really was after him? Honestly, as much as he didn't want to believe it, there was still a part of him that was uncertain. Between the story about the archmagus's death, Silas's warnings, and his own loud anxiety, Rowan still couldn't dismiss the possibility she could be dangerous.

And yet... every night the Dragon Knight chased away the shadows in his dreams. It had to be her. He just knew it. He wanted to just tell her. Tell her about his dream and find out exactly what it meant. But if he was wrong...

Rowan sighed heavily, running a hand through his messy hair as he tried to get a grip on his simmering anxiety. He just... didn't know what to do. He didn't want to make the wrong decision. But what was the right one?

With that question circling in his head, he pushed open the door to the library. The scent of musty, old books slapped him in the face, thick and cloying. He sighed again, but this time in relief because the smell was welcome. It was comforting.

He let his eyes adjust to the interior, finding Silas sitting at their usual table. Part of Rowan wasn't sure if he would be there, given he hadn't been the last few times Rowan stopped by. Come to think of it, the last time he actually played with Silas was before Nova showed up. Then the undead attack happened, and Silas had been absent since. Rowan figured it was probably related since Silas was the commanding officer of the area. It wasn't the first time their schedules didn't overlap, albeit it didn't normally go for this long.

But as Silas looked over at him with a calculating gaze, Rowan remembered he was overdue for a lecture about standing out in the open during an undead attack. He swallowed, anxiety coming back full force, albeit for different reasons this time.

Steeling himself for what might be a long, awkward game of tablut, Rowan approached. "If you're trying to intimidate me before the game starts, it's working."

Silas blinked at that, then chuckled quietly. "Wasn't my intention. I do want to talk about some things, though. It's been a while since I last saw you."

"I figured," Rowan admitted, taking a seat across from him. "Are you still mad at me?"

Silas shook his head. "I was never mad, Rowan. I was concerned for your safety."

Rowan took in a deep breath and nodded, eyes dropping to the board. "Yeah, I know. I just... I guess I expected you to yell at me."

"What would that accomplish?" Silas asked as he reached forward and adjusted a game piece on the board that wasn't quite on its square. "You understand what you did wrong already. Yelling at you now would benefit neither of us. I do, however, want to talk about your new friend."

Rowan blinked and looked up from the game board. Oh.

...*Oh.*

How much did Silas know?

Swallowing, Rowan nodded to the board. "S-sure. Uh, attackers or defenders?"

"Attackers," Silas said, smiling faintly. "I'll let you defend your pieces and your actions."

Rowan swallowed again and nervously made his first move. Silas watched him, then said, "I've yet to decide if you're reckless or calculating, so I want you to prove to me which one you think you are."

Rowan stared at Silas mutely, quietly waiting for him to elaborate. Silas considered the board, then made his move and said, "You went out and befriended a Dragon Knight, despite my warnings to be wary of them. Want to elaborate on that?"

Rowan's eyes went wide, and then he quickly looked around the library for signs of anyone else nearby. Silas shook his head, closing his one good eye. "No one else is here. I checked before you got here."

Rowan nodded shakily, rubbing his now sweating palms on his pants. "W-what makes you think she's a Dragon Knight?"

"Well, for starters, she jumped off of a ten-meter wall with you on her back and landed like it was nothing."

Rowan blanched. "You saw that? How? She covered the towers with fog—"

Silas lifted a brow as Rowan realized what he just said, covering his mouth with both hands. He then gave Rowan a wry look. "I was behind you. Neither of you two geniuses bothered to look around before she ran up the wall, and you were too busy being embarrassed by a little skin to see me walking down the alley in your direction."

Rowan was pretty sure he turned red all the way down to his toes at that. He buried his face in his hands. "It wasn't like that! I was just *shocked!*"

His voice cracked on the last word, only further adding to his embarrassment.

They sat there for a moment, Silas patient and Rowan trying to recollect himself, utterly mortified. Finally, after what felt like an eternity, Rowan pulled his hands from his face and looked up at Silas. "Is that why you've been absent? You're following her?"

Silas waved his hand noncommittally. "Partially. I've been somewhat monitoring her, but I've also been busy. Truthfully, since the attack on the town, we've increased our patrols along the main roads to ensure no undead get that close to the town again."

"What makes it different from the previous attacks?" Rowan asked, making his next move on the board as he felt his earlier embarrassment fade.

"Frequency," Silas replied. "Although we've only been attacked once, the number of attacks around the country has increased, so it's likely to happen again far sooner than we'd like. And, well, we can't rely on a Dragon Knight to always be around."

"But she has been, and that bothers you," Rowan said. It was more a statement than a question since Rowan pretty much knew the answer. Silas had already said before he didn't trust Dragon Knights and Rowan highly doubted Nova's presence had actually changed that.

Silas pursed his lips thoughtfully, leaning forward as he made his move. He sat back and nodded. "I expected her appearance to be brief, but she's stayed here in Ladisdale, and I assume the reason is because of you, given your dream. Can't say that makes me comfortable."

Rowan sighed softly, considering the layout of the board before sliding one of his pieces into a new position. "Maybe. I'm not sure, actually."

"Did you tell her about your dream?" Silas asked, moving one of his pieces in return.

Rowan shook his head. "No. Because I don't actually know why she's here. I just... I have theories."

Silas folded his arms in that awkward, one-handed way, waiting for Rowan to elaborate. Rowan chewed on his lip, eyes flicking between Silas and the board. "You're sure no one's here, right?"

"All the other doors are locked, and no one else has come through the front door. And I've learned enough over the years that the mages up in that stuffy tower don't give a shit about this library, so they no longer monitor it with magic."

"Oh. That's... actually kinda sad," Rowan admitted, making his turn. He sighed, rubbing his hands over his face. "Okay. Um. So... I, uh, I overheard mom talking to my grandpa. And apparently, I'm not... actually cursed. It's a lie to protect me."

Silas went still at that, lifting his eye to Rowan, expression unreadable. He then leaned forward and folded his good arm on the table. "Please continue."

"I don't know everything. Mom doesn't even know I overheard, but apparently, um, the archmagus who did this"—he nodded to his arm—"told her to lie and say it was a curse because I was in danger. He was supposed to come back but didn't. He died..."

Rowan hesitated, swallowing, before quietly finishing with, "Possibly at the hands of a Dragon Knight."

Silas tapped his index finger against the table before he moved his piece and captured one of Rowan's. "Let me guess: you think that's not what happened."

"I don't know for sure," Rowan admitted carefully, surveying the board now that Silas had taken his bait, "but Nova's had plenty of opportunities to hurt me and never has. Instead, it almost feels like she's watching out for me."

He ended that thought by capturing Silas's game piece, earning a hum of approval from him in return.

Silas nodded slowly, sitting back in his chair. "But she doesn't know that what you have isn't a curse."

"No," Rowan said quietly, shaking his head. "I've not told her, and well, if she knew, I'd probably figure it out. She's a terrible liar."

"You're playing a very dangerous game, Rowan," Silas warned, moving one of his pieces. "No one here could stop someone that powerful if she tries to hurt you."

"I know. But I also know if it's not her, then someone else out there is hunting me. And maybe having her as an ally might save my life." Rowan shrugged one shoulder, fingers hovering over the board as he considered his move before making it. He then sat back and folded his hands in his lap.

"Maybe," Silas agreed pensively. "I admit, I don't like you gambling with your life."

Rowan smiled sadly, eyes lowered to the board. He knew this was the point he was dreading, where Silas admonished him for his choices and told him what he needed to do: stop interacting with Nova and be more careful.

Instead, Silas ran a hand through his hair in a rather helpless, frustrated notion, then moved one of his pieces. "Convince me."

Rowan blinked, looking up from the board. "I–I'm sorry?"

Silas sat back, tipping his chin up at Rowan. "Convince me that she's an ally. Tell me about her."

Rowan's mouth moved as he stared at Silas in disbelief. Finally, he shook his head, refocusing. "Um, okay. Her name is Nova. She doesn't seem to have a surname, but she does have a professional name. She hasn't told me what it is, though."

Rowan sighed, moving a game piece forward. "She said she's here to find out why southern Bascor isn't as withered as everywhere else. I can't figure out how much truth is in that statement, but she's really bad at lying, so I feel like that's at least partially true. She also takes common turns of phrase literally, and she's really curious about things I thought most people knew or understood. It's like she's been really sheltered from society."

Rowan stared down at the board, pursing his lips. "Honestly, I don't think she has any friends. She was... really shocked when I told her I wanted to be her friend."

Silas snorted, causing Rowan to glance up and find Silas giving him a dry look. "Of course you did."

Rowan flushed, rubbing the back of his neck. However, as he opened his mouth to explain, Silas waved his hand for him to continue. "What else?"

Rowan hesitated, lips parted as he thought about anything else he could say. "She hasn't told me she's a Dragon Knight, but I think she knows that I know. She's... still kind of hiding it from me, but it's more like we're dancing around the subject. I don't think she realizes how bad she is at blending in. I mean, she stands out like a flower in a withered field, especially with those clothes and how she smells like her magic."

Silas lifted a brow. "Her magic smells?"

"Yeah, didn't you notice that after-the-rain scent of her fog?" Rowan asked, sitting back. "It's present every time she uses her magic, and she smells faintly like it after immediately using it."

Silas shook his head. "Must be losing my senses. I didn't smell a damned thing, and I'm pretty sure I walked through the thick of one of her fogs the other day."

"You did. I saw you," Rowan admitted. When Silas gave him a questioning look, Rowan elaborated, "I was on my way to deliver potions and heard you coming, but I didn't know it was you, so I hid. I watched you appear and then walk down the path to my house. Then Nova found me. She told me to be quiet because magi were sneaking about, but she also said she didn't think you were a threat."

"Interesting," Silas said, brow furrowing as he made his move. "I suspected she knew I was tailing her, but I didn't see any magi. Not that I could see a damned thing, really. Did she say anything more about them?"

Rowan shook his head. "Just that they shouldn't be trusted because they keep to the shadows."

Silas nodded slowly, reaching up to rub his chin as he thought. Rowan watched him for several seconds, before finally voicing a question clawing at the back of his mind. "Why were you walking towards my house?"

Silas blinked out of his thoughts, lifting a brow at Rowan questioningly. Rowan met his gaze briefly before shyly looking down at the board. "You've never visited before. It just seemed... odd."

"I suppose that's fair," Silas agreed, chuckling fondly. "The simple answer is that I wanted to make sure you were okay. After I saw her take off with you, I stopped by that evening to make sure you made it home. Saw you through the window. Didn't see the need to announce my presence, so I left. Decided to check back a couple of days later, and that's when you saw me."

"But I wasn't home," Rowan concluded, eyes narrowing as he made his move.

Silas nodded. "I talked briefly with Zebb. Probed a bit and found out you'd just left for town, which meant I missed you in that fog. Would have been worried, but I saw you making your deliveries when I got back."

Rowan smiled, not looking up at him. "Thanks. For checking up on me. That means a lot."

"Can't lose my game partner," Silas said mildly, glancing out the window. He studied the view for a moment, then looked back at Rowan. "Did she accept your offer of friendship?"

Rowan shook his head, eyes flicking up to Silas. "She invited me to convince her, but she seems pretty conflicted about it."

Silas hummed, then reached forward and moved his game piece. "Why do you think she's conflicted?"

Rowan sighed. "That's what I don't know. Either because I'm what she's searching for and she fears she might have to hurt me, or I'm not, and she knows she'll have to leave eventually."

He glanced down at the board, then his brows lifted as he sat up. With a soft noise of delight, Rowan grabbed his king and moved it to safety, effectively winning the match.

Silas hummed again, nodding in approval as he eyed the game he just lost. Finally, he sighed and said, "I don't like this. I am making that clear. However, you're already neck-deep in this, and I can't stop you. So instead, I'm going to give you my advice."

Rowan nodded, meeting Silas's gaze. To his surprise, the expression he saw was softer than he expected, tempered with concern. "I think that your gift is what she's looking for, even though I don't know what it is."

"What about looking for the reason southern Bascor still has things growing?" Rowan asked.

Silas gave Rowan a dubious look like he was surprised Rowan was asking the question. After a moment, he asked, "How old are you, Rowan?"

Rowan blinked in confusion. "Um, I'll be seventeen in a couple of weeks. Why?"

"How old is the Great Wither?"

Rowan swallowed, realizing where he was going with that. He hadn't really... considered the possibility because it seemed so *far-fetched*. "You think... I'm the cause of the growth here? Or at least, what's on my arm?"

"Ladisdale *is* in the center of the region," Silas said pointedly, to which Rowan fell silent.

They sat there, staring at the tablut board that showed Rowan's victory. Finally, Rowan said, "So you think she's out to hurt me."

"I think you're what she's looking for," Silas said carefully. "I just don't know what she's going to do to you when she realizes it, and that's what scares me."

The room fell silent again. Silas sighed and looked out the window to the street. "And that's the match."

Chapter 15
The Right Choice

Sometimes when Sorrel found herself on the road going into town, she would stop and stare at the world as it was and remember how it used to be. These were the hills where she grew up. Grasses used to sprawl across their crowns, with carpets of heather and clusters of shrubs. The forests nestled deep in the valleys were rich with resources and full of wildlife. Now, all that was left were memories and a faint echo of the past.

Sorrel stood on the road that led towards Ladisdale, surveying the world around her. It was like looking at a faded painting where only hints of the original color remained. A splash of green. A touch of brown. The only vibrant thing was the sky itself. This wasn't the world she wanted to raise a child in, but it was the world she got. And that was something she needed to finally come to terms with.

Since the scare about the Dragon Knight, Sorrel had spent her nights shedding tears and mulling over her thoughts. Rowan was upset with her, and their relationship was more strained now than ever. Her father advised her to sit and think for a while and try to understand what it was like to be her son.

When she asked why she couldn't get that same grace, her father reminded her that Rowan could not sympathize with her because she had hidden everything from him. He said that, to Rowan, she was unfair and irrational, and making his life worse for no good reason. And that was true. Rowan didn't understand because she didn't let him understand, too scared that knowing even a piece of the truth would result in him being ripped away from her.

"*What you're doing is not a solution, Sorrel. It's just a slow death.*"

Her father's words haunted her since he said them. Not because they were cruel, but because they were true. She may have been scared of her son being taken away or killed, but that was the quick death. Ruining her relationship with him was the slow death. He wasn't heeding her warnings. He fought her on everything. He was upset and bitter. And he was still spending time with the Dragon Knight.

Sorrel thought back to this morning, as she looked out the window to see her son return from foraging. She almost dropped the bowl she held, staring at the gray cloak on his shoulders and the smile on his face as he turned to the woman beside him. Although it was at a distance, Sorrel could see this was the same person she had seen before, except now the cloak was on her son. The woman was pale and muscular, wearing foreign clothes that bared too much skin.

The woman took back her cloak and left Rowan to return on his own with a bow of her head. Sorrel couldn't hear what Rowan said to her afterward, but when he came inside to put away the food and pick up the potions for delivery, he was in *such* a good mood. Even though he said little, there was a tiny smile on his face and a look of contentedness that Sorrel rarely recalled seeing on him. He left before she got the nerve to question him.

Sorrel spent the rest of that morning and well into the afternoon debating on what she should do, pacing in the small room where she brewed potions. She couldn't control Rowan's actions. He was going to do what he wanted, and she couldn't stop him. For years, nothing was in her control, and she was miserable for it. But... maybe that wasn't completely true. She had choices, scary though they were. And what she had been doing was only succeeding in making both of them miserable.

Movement caught her attention, and she lifted her gaze to see Rowan walking around the bend. She sighed, the tension that she wasn't aware she was holding onto leaving upon seeing him. The Dragon Knight girl was nowhere to be seen, but he seemed safe and well. She could tell he saw her the moment he came into view, not that she was trying to hide. So she stood there in the middle of the road, hands clasped together as she waited for him to reach her.

He furrowed his brow once he was close enough to speak, the clink-clink-clink of the empty bottles in his basket drowning out the sound of his shoes on the packed dirt. "Hey, Mom. Is everything okay? Is Grandpa?"

Sorrel nodded, the jerky movement indicating her nervousness. "Yes, he's napping right now. The numbing elixir has helped a lot with his pain. I just... well..." She sucked in a breath, trying to force the words out. "Would you walk with me?"

Rowan blinked several times then nodded hesitantly. "Uh... sure."

She offered him a fleeting, nervous smile that probably conveyed way more than she wanted, then began to walk. He fell into pace beside her, adjusting his basket to tuck against his hip. "What's on your mind?"

"A lot of things," Sorrel admitted quietly, folding her arms over her chest in a bout of insecurity. "I was thinking that... maybe you'd like to hear a story. About..."

She hesitated, swallowing. Her skin crawled as she fought against the urge to shut down and hide. She needed to do this. Rowan deserved this. *She deserved this.* She deserved to have a choice in what she did or said. No one had given her that in all of this, and now here she was, fearing for her son's life every day, knowing he was in danger because something was out there, and holding the pieces of her crumbling relationship with him in her hands. One of these she had control over.

"...About your birth."

The words came out easier than she expected, quiet with hardly a stutter. Rowan stumbled, catching himself from falling over in what she assumed was shock. The stunned, open-mouth expression he leveled her with once he caught his balance confirmed it, and she gave him a tiny smile in return. "Follow me. I want to show you something."

She veered off the road after a few meters, knowing the way even if there was no true path. He followed after her into the now-barren woods. She could still remember that day so easily. The heat of summer. The frustration she had at the bugs. The humidity. And, most importantly, her own feelings. It felt both too long ago and not long enough.

Sorrel turned her head slightly to look at Rowan walking behind her. He had a pensive expression on his face, eyes on the ground as he watched where he stepped. He was almost the age she was when she met Osier. She wanted him to make better choices than she did.

They reached the glade after several minutes of walking. It was larger now, given that many of the trees had rotted and died. The brook still ran through the clearing, although its path had shifted over the years. Gone were the animals and plants of before, and now all that remained were small patches of moss clinging to rocks, a few clusters of leaves on the trees, and some errant blades of wild grass...

...And a single, white spider lily, standing in defiance of the Great Wither.

Sorrel's eyes fell to gaze upon the long, thin petals that stood out against the bleak backdrop. The flower had been there every time she dared to come out here, timeless and unfading, and right in the very location Osier had hugged her. She doubted it was a coincidence.

"Mom?"

Sorrel blinked out of her thoughts and looked up to find Rowan glancing between her and the flower.

"That's a type of lily, isn't it? I recognize it from some botany books."

"Yes, it is," Sorrel said softly. "It's a spider lily. They were common garden plants before the Great Wither. Ornamental, mostly. They have no alchemic or magical properties that I know of."

"It's pretty," Rowan said fondly, crouching down to look at it. He ran his fingertip along the edge of one of the petals, admiring its texture. "I'm surprised it's growing here and looks this healthy."

"I'm not," Sorrel admitted quietly as she crouched down beside him. "Because I know what caused it."

He gave her a perplexed look, head tilting slightly in a silent request for her to continue. Sorrel sighed, moving from a crouch into a seated position and tucking her legs against her. Rowan followed her lead and sat down as well, crossing his legs and giving her his attention. The ground was dry enough, albeit cold, but that was fine.

She had a story to tell.

"Seventeen years ago I found out I couldn't have children," Sorrel said in a quivering voice as she gently touched one of the petals with a finger. "I never told you this, but I was married once. To a man in Bouldermoor. We tried for a year to have a baby. I couldn't get pregnant, and, well, he couldn't wait, I suppose. He sent me home and repealed our marriage."

Rowan stared at her with wide eyes, expression one of mute surprise. She gave him a fleeting, uncomfortable smile before she folded her hands in her lap and bowed her head.

"I was on my way home but stopped here along the way. I was upset. Angry. I wanted a place to cry. Didn't want Papa to see me yet. When I got here... everything was so... *pretty*. It looked right out of a painting. And sitting on the other side of this stream was a man I'd never seen before in my life."

Sorrel swallowed, fingers playing with the material of her skirt. "He was a beautiful man with long hair and strange clothes. We talked. He spoke in a way I found... ostentatious if I'm being honest. And yet... I sat here and bled my heart out to a stranger. Told him what happened. How I felt my life was over before it started. Then...he offered to give me a child. He said his magic would make it so."

Rowan sucked in a breath in front of her, his fingers digging into his knees. Sorrel nodded, flushing as she continued. "I... I was desperate, and I was young. Foolish, even. All I ever wanted was a child, and he offered it to me. So... I agreed."

She inhaled deeply, centering herself. "I don't think he was human, Rowan. He used magic like I've never seen or even heard of. Flowers grew up from his feet, and his eyes burned like green fire. And then he hugged me with that green fire. That's it. Just a hug. But when he pulled away, I was pregnant with you by several months. I couldn't believe it."

Her son was staring at her in utter shock, mouth hanging open and eyes wide. Sorrel found she could only bear to look at him out of the corner of her eye, feeling uncomfortable and judged, even if his reaction was reasonable and not at all harsh.

"I asked what he wanted in return, and he told me to protect you and cherish you because you would be special." Sorrel blinked back tears at that because he *was* special. "I... I know it doesn't seem that way but I've been trying to do that."

She took in a shuddered breath. "He told me to never mention his name. He said he was in danger, that he was being hunted. He left immediately afterward, and later that day, the green light that covered the sky happened. The Great Wither started after that."

Rowan exhaled harshly, lowering his gaze to the ground as he processed that, but Sorrel knew she wasn't done. With a soft sigh, she continued, "I gave birth to you two months later, a speedy pregnancy like many other women in the region. His magic... did something to all of us. When you came into this world, strange things happened. Vines and mushrooms were growing on the bed, you had a mark on your arm, and the nurse started screaming that you were cursed."

Sorrel squeezed her eyes shut, knowing this was the worst part. "An archmagus showed up then. I still don't know if it was a coincidence, but he told me you were in danger because you were special. He knew who your father was. We... agreed to hide you and let the rumor of the curse stay because your life was in danger. I'm so sorry."

Tears fell down her cheeks, because here's where she expected the outrage, the hurt, and the devastation. She would then need to explain the rest and justify why she hadn't said anything all these years.

However, Rowan sat there quietly, staring down at the ground. Sorrel sniffled and looked at him, wondering if he was in a state of shock. His brow was pinched and his lips pursed like he was thinking. Finally, he sighed and said, "S-sorry, I'm just... surprised. I didn't think you were going to tell me."

Sorrel blinked, giving her son a confused look. This wasn't what she expected at all. "You're... very calm about this."

Rowan shrugged self-consciously, eyes flicking up at her before looking back down at the ground. "I knew half of it already. Nothing really about my origins, but I knew this wasn't a curse and that it was an archmagus who bound my arm. And that he's dead, and you think it was because of a Dragon Knight, and that's why you're scared."

Sorrel stiffened, eyes going wide as she stared at him. "W-what? How? —*Oh.* You— you heard me tell..."

"Grandpa, yeah," Rowan said quietly, rubbing his arm and looking away. "I heard it all."

Sorrel swallowed, wiping at her eyes. "You... didn't say anything?"

He shook his head, still not looking at her. "At first, I was too angry to say anything. Or I guess I didn't want to say something when I was angry and hurt. Then I wanted to wait to see if you'd talk to me. Wanted to give you the chance to do it before I confronted you."

He sighed softly, shoulders slumping. "Then you didn't, and I just... assumed you weren't ever going to because you never had before."

Silence fell between them for several seconds. Finally, Sorrel whispered, "I'm sorry."

Slowly, her son looked up at her, something tired in his eyes. "About what?"

"Everything," Sorrel said painfully, closing her eyes. "I didn't... I didn't think I had a choice. I was scared to lose you. I still am. I'm still not sure I'm doing the right thing. But you're an adult now. You're making decisions. I want you to make good ones. You can't do that if you don't know."

Rowan exhaled softly, looking up at the sky through the barren treetops. "I've gone my whole life thinking the world didn't want me to exist. Woke up every morning sad or not wanting to get out of bed. Some days I wondered why I was even here and if it would be better if I wasn't."

Sorrel squeezed her eyes shut, not wanting to hear her son say those words. Rowan didn't spare her though, continuing. "I don't... know what the right answer would have been in this situation, but I don't think total silence was it, Mom. I want to be grateful you're telling me everything now but... I don't feel gratitude. I feel sad. I'm hurt."

She nodded, biting back a whimper as tears slipped down her cheeks. "I never wanted to hurt you. I just didn't think I had a choice. I want to keep you safe. Someone powerful out there is after you, and

I don't know how to protect you. I'm sorry. This isn't—this isn't what I wanted."

"I know," Rowan said shakily, his voice heavy with emotion. "I get why you're scared and why you did what you did. I do. I don't *blame* you, Mom. But that doesn't erase the hurt. It doesn't mean what you did was right."

"I don't..." Sorrel wrapped her arms around herself, gritting her teeth. "I don't think I had a right answer. I don't want you to die or be taken from me, but I also don't want you to hate me, and I feel like I can't have both."

She started crying heavily, unable to keep her composure anymore as the pain became too much to bear. She didn't even hear Rowan move until she felt him wrap an arm around her shoulders.

She leaned into him, feeling both so ashamed that her own son was comforting her and too weak to make him stop. He said nothing, hand rubbing her arm as he let her cry on him.

Eventually, sobs turned to sniffles, then sniffles turned to hiccups. It was then Rowan finally spoke. "I don't hate you, Mom. I'm hurt. I'm tired. But I don't hate you. I never have."

Sorrel wiped at her face with the edge of her skirt before pulling back to look at him. He was crying too, fresh streaks of tears on his freckled cheeks. He regarded her quietly, but she wasn't sure how to interpret his expression. She wanted very much to reach up and wipe at his tears, but she didn't think she deserved that. Not right now.

Quietly, she asked, "Can you forgive me?"

He didn't immediately reply, gaze lowering as he pondered her question. She didn't know if it was good or bad that he had to think about it, but she hoped with all her heart it was good.

"Yes," he whispered, his brow furrowing. "Forgiving you is easy. I know you never *meant* to hurt me. But getting *over* all of this... that's going to take time. You hurt me. A lot. Even if you didn't mean to, even if you felt you didn't have a better choice... you still did. I can't just pretend that didn't happen. I need time."

It was better than what she expected to hear, and she exhaled with relief, the sound stuttered and shaky. Sniffling, she nodded. "I know I can't undo what happened, but if you'll let me, I want to fix things between us. Is that okay?"

He blinked a few times, looking over at her. Finally, he forced a tiny smile. "Yeah. I'd really like that. And... I'm sorry for all the times I yelled and fought with you. I just felt trapped and unloved. N-not that you meant to cause that... it's just... how I felt."

Sorrel pressed her lips together painfully, hating the effect her reticence caused. "I love you more than I can put into words, Rowan. I promise to show you that. I swear I'll do better by you."

Rowan nodded, wiping at his eyes. "Yeah. I know. Neither of us has been our best, but we can try to fix that moving forward. Just... try to trust me a little. Please?"

She nodded, trying to get a bearing on her emotions as she whispered, "I'll try. I'm just scared."

"I know. Me, too." He looked at her, hesitating, then leaned forward and hugged her again. She whimpered, wrapping her arms around him almost desperately and feeling utter relief when he did the same.

They stayed like that, his face buried in her shoulder and her fingers digging tightly in his tunic. His hair tickled her cheek, sticking to it due to the tears on her face, but she didn't care because this moment was the closest to perfect that she had ever had.

When they finally pulled away, a full minute had passed at least. Sorrel felt a huge weight lift off of her shoulders in a way she wasn't entirely sure she could put into words. She still felt terrified about what the future held, but the one thing she didn't feel terrified about anymore was their relationship becoming damaged beyond repair.

Rowan brushed his hair back away from his face and wiped the residue from his eyes. "Is that, um, everything you wanted to talk about?"

"Well..." Sorrel shifted her position so she was better facing him and folded her hands in her lap. "No, not exactly. I want to talk to you about... the, um... Dragon Knight. I saw her walking with you this morning. It scared me. I can't help but worry she's here to hurt you or kidnap you."

Rowan sighed, looking away. "Nova's never hurt me, and she's had plenty of opportunities to try. She's really kind, Mom. I mean, I get why you're scared of her but... I don't think she's what's after me. I have a hard time believing someone who gets upset when I'm cold or who makes silly faces at sour blackberries is here to kill me."

Sorrel winced at the word 'kill', rubbing her hands over her arms. "But when the archmagus died—"

"The witnesses saw silver fire, right? But they didn't *see* that was what killed him, either," Rowan countered softly. "I don't think it was a Dragon Knight. At least... not one like Nova."

Sorrel looked at him, lingering on the firmness in his gaze. He looked determined, like he knew he had the right answer even if there was no solid proof.

"How can you be sure?" Sorrel asked softly. "I don't want to doubt your... friend. But you are my priority, Rowan. I'm so scared, and we don't know what's out there."

Rowan took in a deep breath, hands flexing on his knees like he was preparing to say something. He hesitated, then looked up at her. "Right before I met Nova, my dream changed."

Sorrel felt her whole body turn cold. She froze, staring at her son as he stared back, something fierce in his gaze. "You... the..."

He nodded. "The one you never wanted me to talk about. It never went away. I've had it every night since I was little. I just stopped talking about it because, well, all it did was make you upset."

She winced but forced herself to swallow the apology on the tip of her tongue. Instead, she whispered, "How did it change?"

Rowan pursed his lips, then admitted, "The man with green eyes is still there, but now when the shadows reach for me, someone in silver fire chases the shadows away. They reach for my hand, and then I wake up."

Sorrel stared at him in shock. Rowan looked back at her evenly. "It's Nova, Mom. Even if I can't see that it's her in the dream, I know that it is. I think she's supposed to help me. And even if she's not..."

He took a deep breath and then let it out in a long sigh. "I don't think she's here to hurt me, and I still want to be her friend."

Sorrel put a hand to her mouth, mulling over this new information. "It's been like this ever since?"

He nodded calmly, looking around. "Every night. Her light chases away the shadows. In those moments, everything around me is green and beautiful. I think it's... what the world looked like before the Great Wither."

He swallowed, then looked back at her. "And based on what you're saying, I think that's related to the person who's my father, and whatever my"—he glanced at his arm—"gift is."

They fell silent, Rowan with a distant, sad expression, eyes out of focus, and her feeling like her entire world had been turned on its head once again. How was it all related? Was this Dragon Knight, Nova, really there to save her son? Or was she there to take him away?

Sorrel's eyes fell to the spider lily beside them. Rowan followed her gaze, looking at the flower. "This is leftover from that day, isn't it?"

She nodded slowly. "Do you know what a white spider lily means?"

Rowan shook his head, looking back at her. "It has a meaning?"

"Many flowers did before the Great Wither," Sorrel admitted. "Symbolism is important in Bascori culture, especially in art. Or, well, 'was,' I guess. Regardless... several types of lilies were meant to represent different themes."

"What does this one mean?" Rowan asked in a tiny voice, as if uncertain of the answer.

Sorrel lingered with the words on her tongue, then finally said, "The good in nature and rebirth."

The silence that came after was interrupted by a branch falling off of a tree, sending them both jumping. Sorrel whirled, hand pressed to her chest as the branch landed on the ground with a thud. Rowan almost mimicked her, staring behind him in surprise.

"I think that's a sign we should head home," Sorrel whispered. "Papa will grow concerned if we're out too late."

"Y-yeah, I'm hungry anyway," Rowan said with a shaky exhale.

He climbed to his feet and held out his hands. She took them, letting him pull her to her feet, but then she stopped, staring down at his hands holding hers. They were no longer a child's hands. They were those of an adult. She knew he was an adult. He had his coming-of-age celebration almost two years ago now. And yet... It was *this* moment that made it seem real to her. Rowan was no longer her baby.

It shouldn't have scared her, but it did.

She let go of him, and he stepped back to grab his delivery basket, pulling the strap over his shoulder.

"Ready?" he asked, tilting his head at her.

She nodded, giving him a quiet 'yes.'

He offered her a tiny smile and turned, walking back the way they came. Sorrel followed after him, eyes trained on the back of his head full of messy, tangled curls.

She hoped that she had made the right choice.

Chapter 16

Who Deserves Kindness

Nova set her jaw as she twisted, her sword a whistling blade of wind as she cut through a lunging corpse. Black blood splattered in an arc as the two halves came apart, falling to the ground. She turned, walking away as frost sprawled out from her feet, covering the area and coating the thrashing wight, freezing it solid. Without looking back, she threw out a hand, letting lightning strike the frozen monster, sending its remains shattering in all directions.

Nova turned again, surveying her surroundings as the magic in her sword hissed and faded away, leaving it bladeless once more. This appearance of undead bothered her. They were not concentrated in groups but instead scattered out across the land just east of Ladisdale. Each time she found one, she picked up the scent of another, leading her to hopping through the hills the entire evening.

The wights held the usual traces of arcane magic on them, but nothing nearby indicated a source. She did not know how far away one had to be to control them, but it frustrated her that she was left with nothing.

They were not aimless, either. They knew what she was, attacking her head-on, so someone had to be controlling them. Until recently, she thought that was always the case, but her time in southern Bascor had shown her that sometimes the undead she came across barely responded to her. They moved slowly and clumsily, and they seemed unaware of her scent, instead focusing on her movement.

Additionally, the magical residue on the slower ones was weaker, which led her to believe someone had to actively control them. But how far away did they have to be? Even as she cut down the ones that tried to attack her, there was no strong scent nearby, and she did not like it.

Whoever was behind this was powerful, like a human archmagus. How did the lich get such powerful humans to follow his command? Was he using the same methods to capture dragons?

These were questions she had no answers for, but they left a strange sensation on her skin, like the energy before a storm, but wrong. She understood it to be a type of unease, and she wondered if this was another form of 'dread.' Normally, 'dread' was something she felt when she fought dragon-kind with the intent to kill, to free them from undeath.

That kind of dread lurked deep inside, clawing at her stomach like she ate something that was still alive. It would linger thereafter, unpleasant and unwanted, only fading with the fall of rain as she stood under the wet sky and wondered why this was her duty.

That kind of dread had existed ever since she took to the battlefield. It showed its face to her when she was only twelve years of age, facing down the previous Silver clan elder trapped in undeath and promising to take all of them with him.

That day, she experienced dread as she stood before her fallen kin, knowing he could not recognize her. That day, she earned her title as she ran her sword of lightning through his heart as others pinned him down, freeing him to return to their ancestors. And that day, she received her first and only timeless scar, a wound too important to fade away like the rest.

The silver line across her stomach from where his talon cut into her was an immortal reminder of her first experience with dread. It was a reminder of her duty and her pain. It was also a reminder that despite all of her power, she was still only half-dragon, for only half-dragons scarred when the wound was important to the heart.

What Nova felt right now did not feel like that dread from before. It did not leave her with the same sense of suffocation. It was not entangled with the death that shrouded her. And yet... it was still unsettling.

She did not like it.

The sun had set by the time Nova returned to Ladisdale. She knew Rowan was not in town anymore since she could not smell the strong arcane magic. That knowledge left her feeling a strange sense of longing but also reminded her of the other source of 'dread' she was contending with. One that was growing in intensity, like the pressure of a building storm.

Nova's duty was to stop the lich, primarily by killing the undead and reclaiming the dragons trapped by the lich's hand. Each second death she delivered returned the magic to its rightful place and returned the dragon's knowledge to its clan, imprinted upon the very magic they were once born from.

Everything she did was to drive back the lich, and she had done so dutifully for as long as she could wield her magic. But now... she had to exercise that duty in a way that she did not want to, and she was running out of time.

Rowan had a dragon's curse. She could not find anything to disprove that idea, and she wanted to loathe Rime for suggesting it. She did not want it to be Rowan. But it was. He was the only thing in these hills that was different. That curse on his arm was too powerful to be human, no matter how much she wanted to believe otherwise. She kept delaying, hoping to be proven wrong, but there was nothing else *here*.

The lingering Viridian magic must have been tied to his curse, and releasing it would bring back the clan's will in some way, even if it would fade over time. Rowan had to suffer for the rest of the world to live, and Nova *hated* it.

He deserved it least of all.

He was the type of human Nova wanted to protect. She wanted to keep him warm and safe, to listen to him talk and tell his stories. She wanted his laughs and smiles. She wanted his friendship.

All of these things she wanted, and she was not allowed to have them. The next time she saw him, she would have to hurt him. Because if she did not... someone else from her clan would, and they would not have the same mercy. He deserved it to be her, at least.

She hated what she had to do and refused to let anyone else do it for her.

Nova hoped she could simply remove his arm. She could cauterize the wound with lightning, and he would likely survive it. It would be agonizingly painful, and he would hate her for it, surely, for he would not understand, but... He would live. She could survive living through his hatred, as long as he lived. Perhaps the magic in the curse would create a beautiful forest that would feed him for years.

Nova sighed, staring down at her feet as she walked. She then blinked and looked up, finding she had passed through the town and was walking down the path that led to his house. She had not meant to do that, and she hated her traitorous feet for trying to lead her to him while she was lost in her thoughts.

But more importantly… she was being followed. The human following her did not have magic on him, but he masked his presence exceptionally well, so Nova knew who it was. She turned, standing alone on the path with the moon rising above her. Despite the low light, she easily saw him standing between the trees, his cape swaying softly in the breeze.

"You cannot hide from me," she called out calmly, not moving to draw her weapon. "I can see you, one-handed warrior."

She heard a snort, and then the man came into clear view. He had his hand on the hilt of his sword but did not draw it. His posture was alert, but not aggressive.

"Is that supposed to be an insult?" he asked, walking down onto the road and coming to a stop a respectful distance away.

Nova tilted her head slightly. "It is not. I acknowledge you are still a warrior despite it. It is in your movements. You have grace. You are also admittedly quiet for having no magic to conceal yourself. It is impressive."

The man chuckled in a way that Nova felt was amused, even if his posture did not relax. "Thanks; I spend a lot of time in a library."

"I do not think reading books improves stealth," Nova replied honestly. "Scholars are not equipped to be spies or assassins."

The warrior lifted a brow but said nothing, regarding her carefully. Nova waited patiently, studying him in return. He was of middle years for a human, and it was evident by his old injuries that he had seen battles. The careful way he masked his expressions made Nova suspect he was a shrewd man and skilled in hiding his thoughts as well as his presence.

He was different from Rowan in that regard. Two kinds of cleverness.

Despite that, Nova was not interested in spending all night staring down this man. She had much bigger problems to address, and the uneasy feelings inside were making her feel impatient. She pursed her lips, then asked, "Why are you following me, warrior?"

He inclined his head. "Because you seem to be very interested in Rowan Spicer, and frankly, I don't like it."

Nova stifled the urge to bristle, instead narrowing her eyes. "Why does it matter to you?"

"Because he's my friend," the man replied easily, in a way that made Nova *envious*. "I care about my friends, and when someone keeps sneaking around near his house, at night no less, I get suspicious. Especially when that someone is a Dragon Knight."

"Do not call me that," Nova snapped, turning her head away in disdain. "It is a false title given by people who do not understand. You know *nothing* of what I am."

She did not care that he knew, and she did not care that she was not denying it. She was so sick of all of this. The stupid title was only another cut to her heart, and the wounds would not *heal*.

The warrior shrugged in a way that said he was not impressed by her words nor did he care. "Yeah, and that's why I don't trust you. What do you want with Rowan?"

She growled, not even pretending to hide the way it was very clearly not human. It did not matter anyway. "He offered me friendship."

"Oh, is that all? Doesn't seem like something someone like you would care about," he replied in a somewhat derisive tone. Nova did not like it. She did not like it at all.

She bared her teeth, glaring at him, although she made no move to advance. Was this one of the things Rowan spoke of? How humans would manipulate others with their words to make them make mistakes? If so, she would not fall for it. She may not have been wise in the way of humans, but that did not mean she could not *learn*. She did not know his motive, but she did understand he was provoking her.

"You call him your friend," Nova replied through gritted teeth. "Even though you are also a warrior, you understand the importance of friendship. Am I not allowed the same?"

The man narrowed his visible eye at her, lips pursing briefly. He lingered like that for a moment, then replied, "Not if it brings harm to Rowan, no. Besides, we both know 'friendship' is not what brought you to Ladisdale. And I really have a hard time believing it's the reason you've stayed, not when your kind have only ever been seen in the war zones before now."

Nova exhaled harshly, fingers flexing under her cloak. Humans held so much weight in friendship, and yet somehow she was not good enough to be Rowan's friend. The warrior did not even believe that she saw the value in what Rowan offered her.

Never mind the warrior's words held some truth. She was not here just because of Rowan's friendship, and that truth stung. Her duty conflicted with her desires, and she loathed it, for it was a truth she did not want. It was a truth she wanted to smite with lightning. Again and again, until it finally conceded and let her have the truth she *desired*.

"I seek the source of this place's growth," Nova replied, irritation lacing her words. "It is why I came here. It is important to know the cause."

"And yet you keep coming back to Rowan," the man said smoothly, taking a step forward, hand still on the hilt of his sword. He did not seem to care about her original reason for coming, and truly, Nova admired his dedication to Rowan as his *friend*. "A young man with a curse. He's had enough people give him grief over that thing, and his life's been difficult. You don't need to add to it. Leave him alone."

"I—" Nova stopped short, swallowing her words as she worked her jaw. Any protest she could want to say she knew was untrue, and she had learned by now she was not good at lying to humans. So instead, she tried, "What do you know of his curse?"

He shook his head. "That it's just that: a curse. Some asshole with magic thought it would be a good idea to curse a baby, and unfortunately, that baby was Rowan."

Nova frowned because that was not right. He spoke like it was something so simple and careless, and that was not true. "It is not just a curse! The magic sealing it off is powerful. Whatever is underneath is too strong for it to be…random."

'Or human,' she thought, but she did not dare say it.

"Yes, well, some people have too much power and no kindness," the warrior said. "It's *just* a curse. Maybe it's a powerful one, but it sure doesn't need the interest of a—someone like you. Let him be."

Nova stiffened, staring at him with wide eyes. His words rang loudly in her ears, over and over. '*Too much power and no kindness.*'

Even if the statement had not been directed at her, it stung so much more than she would ever thought possible. Here she was, a being with immense power, a prodigy of her kind, deliberating over harming the human who offered to be her friend because he had a dragon's curse.

Where was her kindness?

Why was she not allowed to show it?

How could one fulfill their duty and still be kind?

Why could she not be more like Rowan Spicer?

She snarled, angry at the warrior for saying those words and angry at herself for letting the words hurt. They struck at her with the force of a blizzard and the cutting edge of tempered steel. With an upward thrust of her hand, the space between them exploded into a thick fog, inconsequential to her, but effectively blinding the warrior from seeing her.

"Leave me be," she snapped, voice raw and words heavy with emotions that she felt might drag her deep under the earth and never let her go. "You know nothing of what I am or what I do!"

"If I did, I don't think I'd change my stance," the warrior replied, staring straight at her despite not being able to see her now. "If you harm him, I will chase you across the Shores. You'll never know rest ever again."

"If I harm him, I shall expect no less from you," Nova replied bitterly, feeling her eyes burn with unshed tears. She turned to walk off, then hesitated and added, "Be wary of the magi who move in the shadows here. Even if you have no reason to trust me, know that you have less reason to trust them."

She did not wait for a response, walking off with her fog trailing after her like an ethereal curtain.

She hated all of this.

Nova walked. She walked, and she walked, and she walked, only to keep finding herself back at the river where Rowan hunted for his muscles.

She glared forlornly at the space where the stream met the river, with its muddy banks and smooth stones. Instead of nightfall with clouds hiding the moon, her mind supplied a cold, early morning, with a shivering little human, plucking the shells from the water and putting them in his basket.

She tried to chase the thoughts away, and all they did was turn on her, showing Rowan with his toothy smile as he clung to her cloak wrapped around him. She could easily picture his big eyes with so many emotions, and all of them out of her reach.

She could hear his laugh when she did something he found amusing. It came accompanied by pink, freckled cheeks and an energy about him that she could only describe as joy. It was not magic, but it might as well have been such.

Humans were not things she had ever felt anything but bitterness towards. They blamed dragonkind for the doings of the lich, and they praised her for the deaths on her hands. They used magic gifted to them by the wrongdoings of one, single dragon, none the wiser of the cost the rest paid for such a gift. She helped humans because they shared a mutual goal, but she felt no sympathy towards them until she came to Ladisdale.

Of course, she heard many stories, primarily from the twin clans that hid amongst humans the most. The Golden clan, dragons of knowledge and the arcane, spoke fondly of how humans were driven in their pursuit of knowledge. They always wanted to learn more and to advance, even when the odds were against them. Just a small nudge of Golden magic let humankind build wondrous things, and the clan took pride in that.

Even when the Golden magic evolved and humans rose up in the world of the arcane, the clan still felt delighted in seeing what humans could accomplish in their short lifespans.

Similarly, the Amethyst clan, of inspiration and dreams, curated stories over the centuries that told of humanity's passion. They created wonders and painted masterpieces. They wrote poems and sang stories that would span generations, all founded on the dreams the clan seeded in their minds.

The Amethyst clan boasted about being the muses of the world, and even now when dragonkind was feared and nearing extinction, the clan still knew the value they brought to humanity.

And yet... neither clan spoke of kindness. They did not talk about what made humanity worth saving. Here was a tiny, little human who represented everything Nova wanted to fight for in the world, and no one had ever told her that such a thing could be so *enchanting*.

She was not fully human, and she did not wish to be. She would never fit in anyway. But Rowan had shown her something she did not realize she was allowed to have. Compassion. Friendship. Joy.

These were gifts she had been denied her entire life. She was meant to serve and to fight. She had never been allowed friends. She had rarely tasted kindness, too estranged from others to have the opportunity. She was revered for her use of magic. She was respected for her combat prowess. But she was a soldier with a duty to reclaim what was lost.

These gifts that Rowan offered were not for soldiers. They were not for the Tempest. But she wished *with all her heart* that she could accept them.

Tears fell from her eyes, and she blinked, reaching up to touch her wet cheeks. She could not remember the last time she had cried. Emotions had no place on the battlefield, but she was not on the battlefield. At least... not a physical one. There was certainly one in her heart right now.

The tears continued to fall, each encouraging the next. She let them, not because she thought it was a liberty she was allowed to have because certainly it was not, but because they were for Rowan. That much she could give him. Overhead, the clouds wept with her, blotting out the stars as a gentle snow began to fall.

"I want to be your friend, Rowan." Her voice was barely a whisper on the cold night wind, and yet the desire behind it screamed loudly into the heavens.

Why did the kindness and friendship she wanted so badly have to die with the human offering it to her?

Tonight was the first time Nova the Tempest truly despised every part of what she was, and the tears continued to fall until the first light of dawn broke over the hills, casting her and the snow-dusted ground in pale light.

This could not be right.

Chapter 17
Nova, the Friend

"And of course, it snowed! I swear the weather hates old men like me!" Grandpa Zebb complained as he stared out the open front door, glaring at the thin layer of white dusting the ground. A moment later, he shut the door, scowling. "No wonder my knee's been killing me!"

Rowan smiled slightly from his place by the bedroom entrance, tugging at the sleeves of his tunic. "It's not that much. Barely covered the ground. I'm sure it'll be melted by the time the sun's up over the hills."

Grandpa Zebb made a sour face as he turned to Rowan. "Tell my knee that. Gotta waste another numbing potion on myself. This weather is preposterous!"

Rowan chuckled softly, walking across the room to stand in front of the hearth. He sighed, holding his hands close to the enchanted flame as he let the heat seep into his body. The bedroom was a bit chilly comparatively, being on the other side of the house. Truthfully, had he thought it would snow, he would have suggested they move their cots into the living room for the night.

Rowan offered his grandfather a faint smile. "It's okay to use a potion or two for yourself, Grandpa. We're not doing all that badly, and it's better than you suffering. Besides, it's not like you've been using the long-lasting ones."

"Yeah, those are expensive to make!" Grandpa Zebb grumbled under his breath, hobbling over to his chair while favoring the knee giving him problems. "Too damn early to be having snow."

"At least it was just a small bit," Rowan's mom said as she came in from the potion room, carrying the delivery basket. It only had four potions in it, but Rowan's eyes were drawn towards the potion kit secured around his mother's waist. It was a leather harness of sorts, with pouches for reagents and holsters for vials. They were used a lot before the Great Wither from what Rowan understood, although now his mother only used it when she gave lessons in town.

"Isn't it early for the potion crafting class?"

His mother flashed him a fleeting smile as she put the basket down by the door. "Yes, they asked to move it up due to a schedule conflict next week. They don't want to cancel since I'll be demonstrating the bubble caps."

"They better be grateful we're willing to spare some for them," Zebb said sourly. "Not like half of 'em have any skill in potion craft."

Sorrel spared her father an exasperated look. "They paid us quite a few shells and are refreshing all of our enchantments for free. It's worth it." She turned back to Rowan. "The messenger came by while you weren't here, and, well, I forgot to mention it with... everything else going on."

"Oh, that's okay," Rowan replied, walking over to the basket. "Not many potions for delivery today, though."

Sorrel nodded in agreement. "Yes, the Tanner's usual order and the rest are being delivered to Southmere's magus. We'll have a much larger delivery tomorrow, given what we have to bottle tonight. The warming draughts should be finished by nightfall, and the entire brew has already been reserved."

"Just in time for the snow, I guess," Rowan said idly, cracking the front door open to look outside. A cool wind rolled up against his face. He blinked, brows lifting as he caught a faint scent of Nova's magic.

Did she make it snow? Why?

He frowned, shutting the door thoughtfully. Beside him, his mother stared down at the potion basket, her expression pensive as she offered, "If you want, I can deliver these for you so you don't have to walk to town. I have to go anyway, and it makes no sense for both of us to go, especially with that small of an order. It's just two stops."

Rowan opened his mouth, prepared to habitually decline her offer since it felt like every other time she tried to prevent him from leaving. Then he paused and realized she had a good reason to say it this time. And it meant it would free him up to see if Nova was nearby.

He lingered on the idea, then nodded. "Actually, yeah. If you can do that, it lets me do some foraging and trap-setting while Grandpa rests."

"Don't you dare get in that water at this temperature!" Grandpa Zebb said from across the room, giving Rowan a firm glare. "We have plenty of fish right now, and it's freezing out there!"

"Okay, well, I can still go foraging," Rowan replied, rubbing the back of his neck awkwardly. Truthfully, he didn't want to get in the river right now anyway, but he didn't want to tell them that he was going to go find Nova. His mother would probably be anxious all afternoon until his return, and he honestly wasn't sure how his grandfather would react. He didn't even know if his mother had told his grandfather about their talk or his dream.

Besides, if Nova caught him in the water again she'd probably cause a heat wave out of frustration, given how she reacted last time to him being cold. Despite acting aloof and tough, she seemed to be a bit overprotective. It was kind of cute, albeit a bit ridiculous. Well, maybe. He really wasn't equipped for cold weather, to be fair.

Rowan blinked, flushing slightly as he realized he was lost in his thoughts.

"It's been a couple of weeks since we walked down the far side of the river, anyway," he added in an awkward delay, hoping no one would question it. "Thanks for doing this, Mom."

His mother gave him a timid smile, nodding. "It's just good for us to be efficient in this weather. Please do mind your grandfather's advice and stay dry, though, and don't be out too long."

"You too," Rowan replied, nodding towards the door. "I know it's always warmer in town, but the walk there isn't great."

"I'll walk fast," Sorrel promised. "I'll be leaving in about fifteen minutes or so, once the potion base I started is set and Papa behaves and takes his numbing potion."

Zebb sighed from his place in his chair. "Fine, fine. If it'll get you both to stop fretting over me. Over there treating me like a damned child."

"Treating you like we care. How terrible," Rowan replied with a grin as he pulled on his jacket. "I'll head out then, and I'll probably be back before the sun reaches high."

He saw his mother reach for him out of the corner of his eye and he turned to her to find her lingering with her hand in the air. She hesitated, before pulling back. "Just... be careful, please. You're important to me."

Rowan offered her a tiny smile before wrapping his arms around her in a hug. "I know, and I will. I promise. Trust me?"

"Okay. I'm trying." Her voice was so small as she hugged him back, clinging to him like she was scared to let him go. He still hurt from everything she hid from him, but now at least... he understood. He finally understood her. And that made things feel a lot better. He had hope again.

"I'll see you later. I love you, Mom."

She exhaled sharply, squeezing him against her once more before letting him go. "I love you, too. You are the world to me. Don't ever forget that."

Rowan smiled, blinking away the tears threatening to form. For once, he felt like things were moving in the right direction.

There wasn't enough snow on the ground for Rowan's boots to make the satisfying 'crunch' from packing it down under his weight, and Rowan almost felt like that was a shame. Certainly, he didn't want to deal with a blizzard before they were even in the winter season, but he did admittedly like that sound.

He was careful to not slip on inclines, taking his time as he followed the slowly growing scent of Nova's magic. The sky overhead was rather dismal and overcast. He wondered if that meant anything.

He found Nova by the mussel bed, facing what would normally be the sunrise between the distant hills if one could see it. Her back was to him and the hood of her cloak down, but Rowan suspected she knew he approached. Very little seemed to escape her in that regard.

Still, the fact she didn't turn to him meant she was probably deep in thought, so Rowan said nothing. He didn't try to hide his approach, but he could wait until she acknowledged him to speak, lest he interrupt her. He felt that was the most considerate approach.

He came to a stop just behind her, rubbing his hands together from the chill in the air. The jacket he had really wasn't enough for this weather, especially now that he wasn't moving. Idly, he noted there were no footprints in the snow except for his. ...Had she been out here all night?

Just as he debated on whether he should say anything, Nova spoke. "What is your favorite kind of weather, Rowan?"

He blinked at such a question, hugging his arms close against his ribs. It was a rather abrupt greeting, but he obliged her, pondering the answer. What *was* his favorite kind of weather? Sometimes he didn't mind the snow, because it covered up how abysmal the world looked, but it was awfully cold. A warm, spring rain was nice, especially when it created a rainbow, and thunderstorms were really fascinating, especially when lightning lit up the sky.

It was hard to choose just one, and he didn't know why she was asking. But when he really thought about it...

He chewed on his lip, worrying it between his teeth, then finally admitted, "I think I'd like anything as long as you made it."

It was the most direct he'd ever been about admitting he knew what she was. And yet, it wasn't like it was a secret anymore. He almost felt like it was just a game to see how long it took before either she admitted it or he simply stated it.

A loud silence, like one caused by heavy snow, fell between them. He frowned, wondering if somehow she was upset by his answer, and that worry grew when he saw her shoulders shake slightly.

He opened his mouth to ask what was wrong, but she turned to him, and his words died on his tongue. Her cheeks were wet and her eyes were red from crying. She looked so distraught, and Rowan immediately knew something was *very* wrong.

"That is... that is unfair," she said, her voice pained and raw with emotion. "Why do you make this so hard? Why are you just... so... *you?*"

Rowan hunched in on himself self-consciously, unsure of how to take that statement. This wasn't the reaction he expected, not at all. "What do you mean? Did I do something wrong?"

"*No,*" she said with such anguish that it took Rowan by surprise. "You have never done *anything* wrong. Why did it have to be you?"

Why did it have to be you?

At those words, Rowan felt his blood run cold as he realized that what he hoped wasn't true was actually taking place. As if reading his mind, Nova gave him the most heartbroken look he had ever seen, tears streaming down her pale cheeks as she drew the weapon hanging at her side.

With a sharp hiss, the hilt erupted into a blade of ice, and Rowan found himself staring down the edge of it. Light reflected off of the mirror-like surface as steam rolled up from it like winter fog atop a lake. Nova hovered there for a moment, then pointed the tip at his right arm just above where the spellcloth started, loudly signaling her intent.

She looked so sad.

Rowan's eyes flicked to the blade and then back to her, wide with shock. He swallowed, not daring to move. He was in real, sincere danger, but all he could think about was how sad she looked. She didn't want to do this but felt she had to. Why?

He licked his lips nervously, meeting her defeated gaze. "Please, Nova. Don't do this."

"I do not want to," she whispered, like admitting it would have consequences. "This is what I want least, but I have no choice."

Rowan swallowed again, feeling like if he even breathed, it might cost him. However, doing nothing wasn't going to save him here, either. Despite the fear clutching him, he knew he needed to get her to talk to him. Clearly, she didn't want to do this, and that tiny thread of hope was one he clung to desperately. "Why do you think you have to?"

"Because it is my duty." She made a pained noise, like the words hurt to say. "And my only purpose is to fulfill my duty. It is all I have ever known."

She squeezed her eyes shut, snow beginning to fall like a mirror to her tears. "This is not what I want. I am so sorry."

Rowan's eyes fell to her extended arm, the muscle flexed and poised there, and more importantly, the tiny tremor in her fingers, barely noticeable. He licked his lips again, feeling his tongue brush against chapped skin.

He debated on what to say. She didn't want to harm him, but she felt she had no choice. Was this an order? She spoke of duty, but she hadn't really given him anything telling. No explanation as to what led her to this, and it was as frustrating as it was terrifying.

Rowan blinked, eyes widening as he recognized the parallel between Nova and his mother's reticence. Why did it always come down to people not talking to him? But in this case... he hadn't talked to Nova, either. Communication wasn't a song sung alone. And perhaps... in her despair, she didn't know where to begin. But he felt like he did.

"I'm still your friend, Nova." He spoke gently, his words carrying the same confidence he had when delivering his potions to disgruntled customers. But this time the confidence wasn't faked. He *did* think of her as his friend, even as she had her sword pointed at him. And he wanted her to know that. He needed her to hear it.

"No!" she cried angrily, looking at him through tearful eyelashes. "You cannot say that! Not when I have to unseal the curse! Not when I must hurt you to do it! You might die! How am I supposed to protect a legacy when it means hurting you? Why did my dreams lead me to this?! Why do you have a dragon's curse? *Why is it you?!*"

She was almost screaming now, but it was Rowan who felt breathless at her words. The snow fell harder in response to her emotions, the storm around them picking up, but he ignored it. He ignored the cold, the wind, and the white surrounding him, his eyes trained on the woman before him. She was having dreams, too. About protecting something. His dream flashed in his mind, of the silver hand reaching for him, and he felt his heart pound.

But why did she think he was *cursed by a dragon?*

She must have gotten details wrong, and now he wished he'd just told her about his damned dream in the first place, or at least admitted he wasn't actually cursed. He knew now he was just as much at fault for them getting to this point as she was because he hid everything from her. Just like his mother had done to him.

The irony was not lost on him, and he gritted his teeth, angry at himself for being caught in the same trap. But he could make this right! Right now! He could tell her the truth!

But would she believe him? If he wasn't careful, things could go very wrong. She was distraught, warring with what she thought she had to do and what she wanted. He had one chance to make this right, for both of them.

He swallowed again, eyes flicking to her now-shaking sword, then back to her.

"Tell me about your dream, Nova." He was surprised by how calm he sounded because he felt very much like his life was in her hands. And yet... he still wanted to believe it was *safe* in her hands, and he had to wonder if that was just foolish hope.

"I..." she hiccuped, no longer the composed, aloof Dragon Knight, but a lost young woman thinking she had no good choices. He wondered, briefly, if this was similar to how his mother felt so long ago. But unlike his mother, Nova had choices. Good ones. She just needed to see it.

He needed to show her.

"I cross a sea of darkness to reach an island. It looks like what I think the world was before the Great Wither. It is beautiful and green."

Rowan nodded slowly, shifting his weight forward slightly. It wasn't a full step, but just enough for her to see it. She watched him but did not otherwise react to his advance. The blade still trembled before him, dangerously close to his arm.

"Someone waits for me on the other side. An elder of my people, long since passed. He tells me to seek his legacy in the lands where he died and protect it. That is where the dream ends."

"How long have you had this dream?" Rowan asked softly, taking another baby step. The unsteady sword glanced off of his shoulder, neatly slicing through his clothes and grazing against his skin. It stung, but he didn't do more than flinch, eyes trained on hers. They were no longer sky blue, but a beautiful, glimmering silver. He doubted she even realized.

"Since I was a whelp," Nova admitted in a whisper, not that Rowan knew what a 'whelp' was in this instance. "It was different then. I never could cross the sea, no matter how hard I tried. Then my dream changed after I returned the Dream Keeper to her place amongst her ancestors many days ago. I could cross the sea and receive the message. It has been the same since."

Rowan didn't know who the Dream Keeper was or what that meant, but his heart was pounding. The blood rushed between his ears as he carefully inched forward. The end of the blade was past his shoulder now, and Nova's gaze flitted to it and then back to him.

"Do not come closer," she whispered, giving him a wide-eyed, fearful look.

"No, I think I need to," Rowan replied, hands carefully out at his sides. "Because you need to hear about *my* dream."

"What?" She choked on the word, surprise interrupting her despair, and Rowan used that distraction to take another step toward her. He could almost touch her now, but he didn't, not yet.

"Every night since I was a child, I dream of shadows trying to take me. A man with green eyes watches me. He looks sad, but he doesn't reach to help me."

Nova swallowed, eyes going wide. Rowan wondered if the elder she spoke of was the same person he saw. He took in a nervous, shallow breath and continued, "A few days before you arrived here, my dream changed, too. Someone made of silver fire appears and chases away the shadows. I'm left standing in a beautiful, green field. The person in silver fire reaches out to me, and I wake up before I can take their hand."

Rowan smiled softly, not breaking their locked gaze. "I knew it was you the day you arrived in Ladisdale. I don't think you're here to hurt me, Nova. I think you're here to help me."

"I..." She stuttered, unable to find her words, and Rowan closed the last distance between them, gently cupping his hand over the one holding her sword.

"It's okay," Rowan coaxed softly, looking at her kindly. "Let it go. You don't need it right now."

He didn't try to pry it out of her hand, but he didn't need to. With a sob, she let it fall to the ground, where the ice shattered into a dozen pieces like broken glass. She slid down after it, dropping to her knees like she had been defeated. Rowan held onto her hand tightly, watching as she fell apart in front of him.

"I cannot do it! I cannot hurt you!" Her voice was raw with pain as she shook her head and cried. The snow fell harder, and his fingers were now numb, but he would bear her blizzard over and over again until they got to the ending they needed.

"I know," Rowan said soothingly, capturing her other hand as she reached for him. He held their hands between them, squeezing tightly. "And you don't need to, I promise. Do you know why?"

She shook her head, teeth clenched and eyes squeezed shut as tears ran down her cheeks. Snow was gathering in her hair and on her cloak, but all it did was make her look prettier. She gripped his hands tightly to the point it hurt, but there was no way he'd let go of her now.

Rowan rubbed his thumbs over her knuckles and smiled, knowing that even if she wasn't looking at him, she would be able to hear it in his voice. "Because you're *kind*, Nova! You're kind and protective, and I think that's who you're *supposed* to be."

She looked up at him, mouth open and surprise on her tear-streaked face. "You—you still think I am kind? A-after this?"

Rowan offered her his best smile, feeling his own tears break free. "Yeah! I think you're kind and strong and protective and sweet. I don't know much about who you really are, but I think I know who you're supposed to be, and that's good enough for me. I want to be your friend, Nova. I still do!"

"But—" She shook her head, blinking away her tears. "Your curse—"

"There is no curse," Rowan said softly, shaking his head and feeling snow dislodge and fall into the collar of his jacket. It was terribly cold, but he did his best to ignore it. "There never was. It was a lie."

"It was a lie? ...But the magic on your arm..." Nova's eyes fell to the cloth, searching it like it might give her answers.

Rowan nodded, though the motion was jerky as he realized he was getting incredibly cold. Still, he couldn't stop now. Gently, he tugged his hands out of hers, and before she could question it, he cupped her cheeks in his palms, fingers brushing away the frosty tears on her skin. She stared up at him with wide eyes, frozen in his touch, her own hands falling to her sides.

Rowan gazed back at her, shivering violently as he felt the heat leaving him. He forced out an explanation, fumbling over his words from the cold. "I am the child of a m-man with green fire. Maybe it's the man in my dream, I don't know. I was conceived on the day of the green light. An archmagus told my mom I was a gift, b-but because I was in danger, they hid my gift and said it was a curse. He was supposed to come back, but someone killed him."

Nova stared up at him, mouth hanging open in complete shock. Rowan shuddered, dislodging another clump of snow on his head as it fell down onto Nova's face. It was then she realized the weather, and that it was her own doing. With an animalistic snarl, she swiped her hand in a cutting motion. Rowan watched with fascination as the blizzard rapidly died, leaving behind a carpet of snow and thick clouds growing lighter by the second.

Then, the morning sun broke through the clouds, bringing with it light and warmth. Golden light spread across the glittering snow, and underneath it, Nova looked like she *shined.*

She pulled out of his grasp to stand. Before Rowan could fully register how her eyes were now glowing and mist was rolling off of her shoulders, he found himself wrapped in the heat of her cloak and pulled tightly against her. He grunted as his cheek hit her shoulder, and then he felt her pull the hood over his head.

"I am so sorry," she whispered into his ear as she held him close and slowly warmed up the area around them. "I had everything wrong."

Rowan exhaled shakily, resting his head against her shoulder and closing his eyes. He could still feel his heart pounding, and honestly, that adrenaline was probably what kept him from freezing over. "N-no, not everything."

He grimaced at how he stuttered but forced the words out anyway, hoping she could understand him. "I-if you got everything wrong, we wouldn't be here. And besides... I still d-don't know what my gift is. I just know it's not a curse. Maybe it's the legacy you speak of."

At that, Nova stiffened and pulled back, looking at him. "Do you know your father's name? Or the name of the archmagus?"

He shook his head, clutching the cloak tightly against his freezing form. "I don't. I think Mom does, but she didn't tell me. Said it was too dangerous—"

He stopped as Nova grabbed the cords of her cloak and tied them tightly, securing the fabric around his shoulders. She then retrieved her sword hilt, fastening it to the belt at her waist.

"What are you—*ack!*"

Rowan's question transformed into a tiny yelp as Nova swooped in and scooped him up in her arms, cradling him close. He felt a warmth like a summer heat wrapped around them both, cushioning them against the chilly weather. Rowan exhaled thickly, grateful for the cocoon of warmth, but before he could fully relax in Nova's hold, she took off, sprinting down the hill towards the direction of his house.

"Nova!" His protest was remarkably unimpressive, the earlier cold having zapped away a lot of his energy.

"We must know the names!" she shouted urgently as she leaped down the hill in several great strides, landing at the bottom with inhuman grace. At no point did she ever falter in her hold on him, and the warm air continued to cling to them, driving away the chill in his bones.

He then realized where she was heading. "She's— Mom's not at home! She's in the town!"

Without a word, Nova pivoted, changing direction towards the town. Despite the shift, she did not slow down, and Rowan squeezed his eyes shut as the world around him spun briefly, making his head swim. He didn't understand the sudden urgency, but at this rate, they would be in Ladisdale in mere minutes, and the entire town would know she wasn't human.

"Nova! Put me down! I can walk!"

"I do not want to walk! That is too slow!"

Rowan huffed in exasperation, but she had the most determined look in her eyes as she reached the road and started sprinting down it. "W-we can't enter town like this! People will see us!"

Nova wrinkled her nose, clearly displeased. "I will make fog—"

"No, that's worse!" Rowan hurriedly replied, wrapping his arms around her shoulders now that he could feel his hands again.

Her brow twitched. "I do not understand—"

"Nova!" Despite it all, Rowan started laughing, the tension from earlier melting away along with the chill. It was soft and barely audible, but the smile that came with it was loud, stretching across his cheeks.

Nova's eyes flicked to him, a flash of uncertainty on her features. However, when she saw his face, her lips pulled up into a tiny smile that, to his delight, grew bigger as he beamed at her. It was a radiant smile, earnest and unguarded, and utterly beautiful in what it represented.

This was the Nova he wanted. A kind, protective person, more than a Dragon Knight. More than her duty.

His friend.

Chapter 18
Unwitting Betrayal

It wasn't until they reached the edge of Ladisdale's farmlands that Rowan's feet touched the ground again. Nova came to a stop, surveyed their surroundings, and then carefully let him down. They were just outside of the view of any farmers, using the hilly terrain to their advantage as they stayed out of sight.

Rowan steadied himself, grateful they were hidden but still trying to calm his racing heart. Never mind that he had just lived one of the scariest moments of his life as he stared down the blade of Nova's sword, but she had just raced to Ladisdale in a full sprint he doubted anyone in town could match while carrying him, and while arguing they needed to hurry.

He wanted to be impressed, but he was more bewildered than anything else. Rowan turned to Nova to find her ensuring her weapon was still on her belt. Satisfied, she looked up, skimmed the area, then grabbed his wrist and started stalking up the incline towards the gates.

"Nova, wait! What's going on? Why are you in such a hurry?" Rowan protested as she dragged him along. He did his best to keep pace with her longer stride, now no longer cold but also still overwhelmed by everything that had just happened.

"Because you are in danger," Nova replied quietly, turning just enough to look at him out of the corner of her eye. "I am not the only one looking for you. And now that I know it is you who I seek, we must move quickly."

"Who else is after me?" Rowan asked, looking around as Nova dragged him along. "What do I have that's so important?"

Nova didn't immediately answer, scanning their surroundings with every bit of scrutiny, like she was just waiting for an attack from any direction. "It is not what you have, it is who you are, Rowan. If your father is who I think it was, then you are the last survivor of the Viridian clan."

"The what?" Rowan asked, picking up his pace so that he was walking beside her instead of being simply dragged along. "What's that?"

Nova shook her head as they approached the gate. "More later. The arcane magic on you makes it hard for me to pick up the scent of magi, and I do not want to risk being overheard. We must confirm the story and then get you somewhere safe. Where is your mother?"

Rowan grimaced, feeling like his tongue was burning from all the questions he had, but he refrained from pushing. "Either delivering potions or she's starting her lecture at the Opus Athenaeum. We can check Cengor's first because it's a little closer and would be faster."

When Nova tilted her head in confusion, Rowan quickly clarified, "Err, the place I walked you to yesterday before you left. Let's go there."

Nova nodded, tugging him along with urgency as they passed the town's gates. Several people stared at them as they walked by, and it took Rowan almost a whole minute to realize exactly *why*.

He still had on Nova's cloak. She was stalking through the open streets in a sleeveless, backless dress that stopped mid-thigh, in winter-like weather.

He felt his ears burn, knowing this was going to be the talk of the town for months, especially with the way she was holding his wrist and pulling him along, but he also knew she wasn't going to stop to take back her cloak right now.

Oh well, at least he was warm.

Graciously, the center square was mostly empty when they reached it, allowing them a small reprieve from the onlookers. And when they saw 'On Bascori Wings,' Rowan felt the tension between his shoulders start to give. Even if he knew he was as safe as could be next to Nova, the increased amount of attention on their way through the town streets made his skin crawl.

It didn't help that the quick pace up the hill, combined with wearing his jacket and Nova's cloak, had him breathing a little heavier than usual. Even some sweat had started to gather on his brow. Despite that, he took the lead, pulling Nova the last bit as he pushed the door open and stepped inside.

"Be right there!" Cengor called from the back room cheerfully.

Rowan frowned, noting his mother wasn't there. "It's just me, Cengor! I'll come back in a bit!"

Nova was already stepping back outside, hand still on his wrist, when Cengor came stumbling out of the backroom, adjusting his glasses. "Rowan! Oh, that's fantastic! I thought I wouldn't see you today since your mother made the delivery!"

"Yup! Sorry about that! It's been a weird day! I gotta find her though, so I'll circle back!" Rowan half-shouted as Nova practically dragged him out of the building. Ugh, Cengor was going to tease him about this later, he just knew...

However as he stepped out onto the street, Cengor followed after him excitedly. "Wait, give me just a minute, now! I finally heard back from my contacts! I have news for you about the magic careers we talked about!"

Rowan opened his mouth to respond, but Nova beat him to it, turning to look at Cengor impatiently. "We must find his mother. What you need to say can wait."

Cengor blinked rapidly, staring at her with a sort of guileless expression. "Well, no, I don't think it can, Tempest. I've been informed Rowan has an excellent skill set that absolutely must be procured, and my Lady Giselle has waited long enough. You're regrettably in the way."

Rowan's brow furrowed in confusion at the word 'tempest', but before he could really understand everything wrong with what Cengor said, the air beside him shifted.

He gasped as Nova shoved him out of the way, twisting just in time to see a brilliant golden light flash across the square and hit her in the back. The attack threw Nova into the building, sending the roof tumbling down atop her as a loud crash echoed throughout the square and dust went flying.

Rowan screamed, panic bubbling up within him at seeing Nova disappear under dust and debris. He jumped to his feet, ignoring his scrapes, only to have Cengor grab him by his arm and drag him toward the center of the square, humming as he went.

"I'm so excited we get to work together!" Cengor said happily like he hadn't even noticed his business just collapsed on top of Nova. "I actually thought we'd have to come find you ourselves, though, when your mother showed up. That would have been problematic, and Giselle wasn't keen on that. Less collateral out by your house to use to our advantage."

"Cengor, what are you doing?!" Rowan screeched, trying to pry the vice-like grip off of his arm and stumbling as Cengor dragged him along. "Let go of me!"

Cengor marched forward with strength Rowan didn't realize he possessed, cheerfully chatting as he went. "I told you! I found a great career opportunity for you! I'm excited, really. This wasn't one I originally thought would work out, but when you implied your curse was a gift, we did a bit of listening and heard your mother's story, and, well, this changes things! I'm so happy we all get to work together! It's going to be great!"

Rowan gawked at Cengor, queasy at the implications that someone he thought was a friend had betrayed him. But he also didn't *sound* right. He was too high-pitched, too happy like that was the only emotion he was capable of.

He hadn't been like this before, but Rowan couldn't afford to think about what had changed. Instead, he craned his neck to look back towards the collapsed building, ice-cold fear gripping him. There was no movement, no indicator that Nova was alive, and the entire building had *fallen on her*.

Fear that she was dead started overtaking hope that she was alive, and while he knew that he was in grave danger, all he could think about was getting to Nova. He didn't know how he could help her, but he had to do *something*. The golden light and loud explosion would pull the guards in any moment, and maybe then—

Rowan turned his head when he caught movement out of the corner of his eye, only for his breath to leave him as he saw what approached. The massive crowd of undead moved in coordinated steps, not unlike soldiers in a platoon, each swaying in unison as they ambled down the street. Black blood dripped from rotting fingers and open wounds, and bits of bone poked through the skin, some splintered and at odd angles.

And, to Rowan's horror, amongst them were fresh bodies adorned in guard uniforms; faces he *recognized,* indicating why the town's warning sirens had not gone off. Screams broke out as townsfolk drawn out by the commotion saw the undead and ran for safety. People called for help, ringing shop bells and banging pots and pans. None of the wights responded to the commotion, continuing their march forward.

Cengor turned to face the approaching undead, dragging Rowan with him and twisting his arm behind him. Rowan winced, torn between discomfort and panic, but was unable to pull his eyes away from the approaching undead army.

Were they here to kill him?

They came to a uniformed stop at the edge of the town square, then parted like a curtain, making a path for what stood behind them. Three magi in hooded black and blue robes walked forward, their leader carrying a magus's staff of dark lacquered wood and glittering gold veins.

They walked briskly towards Rowan and Cengor, leaving behind the unmoving undead platoon. Cengor let out a happy sigh as they approached. "Ah...she's *here."*

Rowan held his breath, eyes wide as he watched the magus with the staff lift a hand. With a flick of their fingers, they sent a flash of black and gold light out from their palm. Half of the wights jerked once, as if snapping to attention, and then took off, scattering across the square after the fleeing townspeople.

"No!" Rowan screamed, eyes wide at realizing his mother was out there. "Stop!"

The other two magi surrounded him, grabbing onto his arms as Cengor let him go and stepped to the side. Rowan snarled, twisting and kicking to no avail, only to have his arms grow heavy and tired. He looked down in confusion to see the hands on him glowing in golden light, and he realized they were using magic to keep him subdued.

Rowan made a frustrated, panicked noise and looked back towards Cengor. "Cengor, please! Why are you doing this?!"

"Because he knows nothing else right now," the magus with the staff replied in a feminine voice. She pulled off her hood, revealing the narrow face of a middle-aged woman with ash-blonde hair and red lips. An archmagus's golden diadem wrapped around her head, and hanging from her ears were earrings made of what looked like black scales on gold hooks.

The woman, who Rowan assumed was Giselle, reached up and cupped Cengor's cheek, dragging her fingers down his jawline in a way that seemed mocking instead of affectionate. She spoke without looking at Rowan, studying Cengor's face with a detached, calculating expression, like he was nothing more than dirt.

"Mind control is a spectrum, you see. At one end, it's just suggestions and ideas implanted into a vulnerable mind. Helpful, but the subject still has free will. At the other, it's total domination over someone mentally weaker. The psyche is usually permanently damaged, which makes them fairly useless as a spy."

She then looked at Rowan, offering him a smile that reminded him too much of the Mister Carpenters and the Tilberts of the world. The hand on Cengor's chin flexed, sharp nails biting into his skin until blood welled up around the edges.

"The ideal solution is to strike a balance between control and suggestion, allowing my pet to retain his personality and the illusion of self-control, while I get what I need. Isn't that right, Cengor?"

"Yes, Giselle," Cengor said breathlessly, his expression blissful. He didn't even seem to notice the pain.

"Of course, given how quickly the situation changed, I did have to turn it to domination to ensure his loyalty to you wouldn't override my commands. He's quite fond of you, you know. His mind won't recover from this, but that's fine. He's served his purpose."

She shrugged, letting go of Cengor's bloodied face and pushing him away. "He's not my type anyway. I prefer, hm, something a little less... human. Both literally and figuratively. Speaking of, let's have a look at my Viridian prize."

Giselle turned to Rowan, red lips pulling into a cruel smile as she grabbed his chin to inspect his face with Cengor's blood still on her fingernails. Her hand was frigid and her grip tight, making Rowan flinch under her touch. Despite himself, he glared up at her defiantly, angry tears pricking at the corners of his eyes.

"Remarkable work, really," Giselle murmured, appraising him like he was merchandise. "You look completely human. Not a trace of Viridian on you. Honestly, this makes me regret that we killed Avelore because I would *love* to know how he managed to do this and how it lasted this long without fading."

She had a glint in her eyes, her smile increasing. "He even bound your magic so well that the Great Wither stunted your growth like everyone else of this generation. You couldn't even avail of the stale Viridian magic here, you feeble thing. That's honestly hilarious."

"What are you *talking* about?" Rowan snapped, voice raw with both anger and fear. He understood some of what she was saying, and could piece together a lot of the rest: the archmagus was named Avelore, and he already knew he was 'Viridian' from what Nova said earlier, not that he knew what that meant. And if he understood Giselle correctly, 'the stale magic here' must have been what caused the Great Wither to not be as bad.

And apparently, he wasn't human.

Despite that, he still feigned ignorance. It was a long shot, but she seemed inclined to hear herself talk, and he would absolutely use that to his advantage. Because she wasn't in a hurry to run off with him, which meant she thought she had either killed or successfully incapacitated Nova.

And it also meant she hadn't noticed the faint scent of petrichor coming from the rubble, either.

Rowan didn't dare look over to confirm, but the scent of Nova's magic brought him a sort of hope that he desperately clung to. He still didn't know why he was the only one who seemed to smell Nova's magic, but if it meant he could distract this woman to buy Nova some time, then he would do it no matter what.

"None of what you're saying makes *sense*," Rowan continued, jerking his face out of her grip. He let the tears flow freely, painting his expression as panicked and confused, which wasn't hard because he definitely was. "Why are you attacking the town?! Why did you kill Nova?! What do you *want with me?!*"

He screamed the last part, proud of himself for at least spitting in her face as he did it. To his intense satisfaction, Giselle grimaced and wiped her cheek and mouth with the back of her hand.

"I forgot how much I hate teenagers," she muttered darkly. Sighing, she took a step back to be out of spitting range. "You'll be much more tolerable when you're converted. It's a shame I couldn't also convert the Tempest, but between the two of you, you're a far better prize. I'll just have to hypothesize what allegedly made her superior to other half-dragons."

Rowan blinked rapidly, mouth falling open. "H-half-dragon?"

Giselle arched a thinly sculpted eyebrow like she couldn't believe he would dare question her. "Did I stutter?"

Rowan's lips moved, no sound escaping them as he tried to furiously process that very shocking piece of information, his goal of distracting her momentarily forgotten. *Half-dragon.* But Nova was a Dragon Knight!

...And Dragon Knights wielded magic like nothing humanity could touch. It made so much sense, and yet, Rowan couldn't believe it. Nova was a half-dragon? But Giselle implied Rowan was also not human. Did that mean he was...?

Giselle's voice cut through his thoughts. "Now, enough of—"

The sound of disturbed rubble made Giselle stop and snap her head towards the remains of 'On Bascori Wings.' Rowan followed her gaze, hope welling up inside of him as mist pooled out from the pile of collapsed stone and shingles, bringing with it the rich rainstorm scent that belonged to Nova.

Giselle scowled, light sparking from the fingers wrapped around her staff. "Fuck me in *half*, how—"

Silver fire exploded from the remains of the building, sending rubble flying in all directions. One of the magi next to Rowan lifted a hand, forming a golden shield over their heads as chunks of rock bounced off of it. Rowan barely noticed, eyes transfixed on the vortex of wind and silver flames spinning where 'On Bascori Wings' used to be and the figure poised in the center.

Nova stood there, arms out and chest heaving. White-hot flames flickered around her eyes, matching the fury in her face, and blood stained her dress from several shallow gashes on her skin. However, she no longer looked human.

Now, she had a crown of silver horns wrapping around her head, with two large ones twisting up near the front. Clusters of silver scales clung to her cheeks, delicate compared to the thick, glittery plates running down her upper arms and thighs. Her hands and feet were now clawed, the silver tips glinting under the light of her fire. A great pair of leathery, storm-colored wings stretched out from behind her back, giving her a menacing appearance, and accompanying them was a long, scaled tail that flicked behind her angrily.

Nova flexed her clawed fingers and bared her fangs as the silver vortex around her surged. The skies responded above, going from overcast to a violent, churning hurricane. Lightning flashed across the sky, and rain and wind assaulted the town square in response to her presence.

Rowan squinted at the onslaught of elements, turning his head to shield his face. It was then he noticed the cloak on his shoulders had shifted from a solid gray to swirling clouds as if it were part of the very skies that Nova controlled.

On seeing Nova, one of the two magi let go of Rowan, prepared to attack, while the other kept him restrained. The energy surrounding them was palpable, making the hairs on Rowan's arms stand on end and putting a strange taste in the back of his mouth.

Giselle sneered, expression full of disdain as she turned to fully face Nova. "You really do live up to your reputation, Tempest. All that time we spent testing how to hide our magic from you, and you still somehow blocked my attack. How did you do it?"

Nova flapped her wings once before they shimmered out of sight, her tail wrapping around her waist. The whirlwind around her condensed, becoming smaller and angrier as lightning danced across her scales. Her voice thrummed like distant thunder as she replied, "I am faster than you."

With a resounding crack, Nova went from standing amongst the rubble to blurring across the square. Rowan barely saw her move, only catching the streaks of light left by the fire and lightning in her wake. She body-slammed Giselle in a burst of electricity and warm air that rushed across the plaza. Gold light flashed around Giselle's body on impact, flickering as she went tumbling across the flagstones, her staff clattering noisily in another direction.

Nova advanced, lightning spinning around her as she leaped into the air and brought her fists down, barely missing Giselle who rolled away and onto her feet with what must have been magic-enhanced reflexes. The gold light flickered around her again before disappearing, and Rowan realized it must have been a protective barrier.

Giselle waved her hands as dozens of orbs of arcane energy appeared around her, golden with a black center, humming loudly in the open space of the square. She flung them at Nova, who twisted and dodged like she was made of wind herself.

Giselle gave chase, manipulating her magic until the orbs had surrounded Nova in all directions. They rushed in and exploded on impact in a flash of brilliant golden light that lit up the entire square like the midday sun.

Nova tore through the explosion unharmed, fog swirling around her in a sphere that quickly dissipated. Giselle made more orbs, only for Nova to immediately strike them down with lightning, making them explode around Giselle before she could use them.

Giselle shouted angrily, her barrier absorbing the damage, although it seemed to be flashing slower. Golden light flickered in her hands as she prepared another spell, only to have Nova throw herself down on the ground in front of her with a frosty boom. The magic around Nova changed from the wind and lightning of summer to the snow and frost of winter as it exploded out, sending Giselle tumbling back and covering her in rime.

Rowan watched as Giselle expelled an arc of golden light, shattering the ice on her and throwing Nova back. Nova flipped and landed in a crouch, the hilt of her weapon now in her hand.

Giselle turned to her, golden smoke coming from her hands. "Interesting. You really don't fight like other half-dragons. You make me so, *so* curious. What's different about you, little Tempest?"

"Stop talking," Nova growled as the end of her sword erupted into a whip of lightning. She tensed, prepared to attack when her eyes widened and she instead flung herself to the side. A column of fire ripped through the area she had been occupying, evaporating the remaining ice with a hiss as it collided with a building at the edge of the square and set it on fire.

Rowan snapped his head in the direction of the source, wide eyes staring at what approached. A man walked out from behind the remaining undead, hand outstretched and smoking. He wore tattered robes in shades of dark red and had long, crimson hair running down his back in a messy braid. However, his skin was a dark, ashen gray, and his face was sunken in like life had left him long ago.

With each step forward, a dry heat pushed out, raising the temperature of the area by several degrees, and a strange scent like sulfur filled Rowan's nose.

Nova rolled to her feet, face full of anger. "Magma. I understand now."

At his name, flames wrapped around Magma, creating a funnel of fire that expanded, wider and wider. Just when Rowan feared the fire would keep spreading, it disappeared, leaving behind a large dragon in the middle of the square.

Rowan gasped, staring at the great, four-legged beast, with scales of vermillion and soot coating its large body. He had a pair of large horns curling out from the sides of his head, their tips lit like candles, and a long, serpentine tail with fire racing along the ridge. But most impressive was the pair of wings that rose up from his back. They were almost skeletal in appearance, with red and black flames rolling off of the spines where the membrane would normally be.

With a bellowing roar, Magma charged at Nova, the remaining undead following after him as he released a torrent of fire. The far side of the square went up in a rush of flames, but before they could expand and overtake the rest of the area, the sky opened up in a torrential downpour right over that side of the square. It was coupled with a thick fog that wrapped around the fire, sequestering it from harming anything else nearby.

Once again, Rowan found himself worried for Nova, despite knowing he was the one without any ability to protect himself. Wet wind whipped at his face and hair as he stared at the fire flickering behind the fog with lightning arcing above it. Movement drew his attention, and he saw Giselle jogging over, staff back in her hand.

Without delay, she addressed the magi still restraining Rowan. "We need to hurry. She's far stronger than I was prepared for, and we don't have much time. Give me the knife and the potion."

"You want to do the conversion here?" one of the other magi asked, tone incredulous. Rowan had a feeling that whatever 'conversion' was, it wasn't good for him. He felt a thick dread pool in his stomach as his gaze flicked between them.

"She'll catch up if we flee, and I can't mask Avelore's seal. At least this way, even if we don't win, the Viridian clan still ends," Giselle snapped, holding out her hand. "Now hurry."

Rowan's breath came out in shallow, panicked pants as he watched one of the magi hand over a bubbling, indigo potion in a thick glass vial and a black-bladed knife with an etched, golden handle.

Beside Giselle, Cengor tittered happily, completely unbothered by the chaos going on around him. "I'm so happy this is all working out. Rowan, I told you that you were special! I hate that it took this long to figure it out, but we just didn't know it was you at first! Fortunately, the Tempest didn't steal you away before we found out the truth, and I'm just so glad it's you!"

"Cengor, *please,*" Rowan pleaded, tears slipping down his cheeks as Giselle floated the potion beside her and took the knife with her free hand. His eyes flicked between his friend and Giselle, the thunder from Nova's magic vibrating through the ground around them. "Don't let them do this. You've got to be in there, somewhere."

"I'm here," Cengor replied happily, beaming at Rowan like everything was just fine. "I'm here, and you're my friend, and Giselle is—"

"Tired of your talking," Giselle muttered as she shouldered her staff and wrapped a hand around Cengor's neck. He giggled in delight at the contact as Giselle tightened her grip on the knife, brows knitting in concentration. Rowan's breath hitched as black and gold energy ignited in both of her palms.

Cengor wheezed, the color draining from his face. His eyes clouded over, and his skin shriveled up like every bit of his life force was being sucked out. At the same time, the knife in Giselle's hand began to glow a hot, wheat gold, brimming with an energy that Rowan knew belonged to his friend.

"No! Please stop! You're hurting him!" Rowan cried, tears streaming down his face as he was forced to watch Cengor die in front of him. Cengor's mouth moved slowly like he was trying to utter a word with no sound. He moved slower and slower like he was a toy winding down.

Cengor turned his head as if to look at Rowan, and Rowan felt hope leave him when that was the last thing he did. Cengor's body came to a stop, emaciated, with his face contorted in a ghastly way that Rowan would remember for the rest of his life. Rowan cried harder, sobbing uncontrollably at the loss of his friend and knowing he was next.

Giselle smiled, letting go of Cengor's withered husk as it fell to the ground beside her with a dry clatter that no human body should ever make. The volatile winds from the storm sent his body sliding across the stones like it weighed almost nothing. Rowan could do nothing but stare in horror, watching his corpse drag across the flagstones with Nova's fight against the undead as a frightening backdrop.

"Good boy," Giselle crooned, smoothing a hand over Rowan's wet hair in mock affection. "Feel that despair and let it settle in. That makes my job easier."

She reached forward, grabbing Rowan's wrist and drawing out his arm. Rowan screamed, trying to pull away as she dragged the tip of the blade along the inscribed spell cloth. The knife cut neatly through the aged fabric, sending the threads burning away in brilliant gold with a thousand hushed whispers dancing across his skin as the magic wrapped around his arm was finally freed.

What remained was a strange mark on the inside of his forearm, a spiral knot like one might see on an old tree. Rowan stared at it through his tears as green light spread along the spiral, bringing with it tiny little ferns and thin, green vines that crawled over his skin. A sweet scent touched his nose, reminding him of blackberries, and it came with a pleasant warmth that spread over his entire body.

Giselle watched him with a wild, excited look in her eyes. The dark skies and flashes of lightning cast shadows on her face, making her look even more terrifying than already she was. The knife clattered to the ground as she snatched the potion floating beside her and pulled off its seal. Then, without a moment of hesitation, she grabbed Rowan's face, forced his mouth open, and poured in the contents of the indigo solution.

Rowan coughed, trying to spit it out, but she forced his mouth closed and pinched his nose, depriving him of breath until he finally swallowed. Giselle let him go after that, as did the other magi. Rowan fell to his hands and knees, choking and coughing with Nova's cloak pooling around him, still shielding him from her storm.

The liquid left a putrid taste in his mouth that burned, and that burn spread down his throat and to his stomach as the potion took effect. It felt *wrong*. His body itched and sweat began to gather on his brow as he became disoriented, the edges of his vision blurring. A strange pressure began to build inside him, uncomfortable in a way he had never felt before. Loud whispers pushed against his ears, just like the ones in his dreams, telling him to give in, to do what Giselle wanted. Rowan shook his head, trying to push them away.

"Call all of your magic forth, Rowan Spicer. Summon it and hold it in your body, then sever your connection to your clan and end your life."

"No!" Rowan shouted, shaking his head. "Get out of my head!"

The whispers continued, urging him to obey, and Rowan lifted his head to glare defiantly at Giselle. She stared down at him, eyes narrowed and jaw set as she tried to take control of his mind. Rowan shook, the light on his arm growing brighter as the pressure inside him intensified. Just as the whispers got too loud to bear, an explosion of ice and lightning hit Giselle, sending her flying across the square and into a wall.

"Get away from him, you traitorous wretch!" Nova screamed as she chased her, leaving behind a graveyard of smoldering corpses and a sky full of ash that smelled... *cleaner* now. Nova's scales and dress were blackened in places and pink burns decorated her exposed skin, but she didn't slow down as she tackled Giselle through the wall and into the next street over.

The skies churned in response to Nova's fury, black clouds rolling violently as lightning danced across the sky. Rowan watched it through blurry eyes, distantly noting the lightning kept flashing in a pattern. The whispers were gone now, but the burn inside of him didn't relent, the intense pressure demanding to be released.

He heard someone scream his name and looked up to see his mother running toward him. He smiled weakly, relief flooding him at seeing she was alive, and then the pressure exploded out of his arm in a cyclone of viridian fire.

Chapter 19
The Tempest

"You can't go out there, did you not see the undead?!"

Sorrel bit back a scream of frustration as she pulled against the acolytes holding her back. She had been in the Athenaeum's lecture hall when the explosion went off, so loud it nearly made her drop the vial she was holding. Like everyone else in the room, she ran to the window to see what had happened. The lecture hall was on one of the upper floors, granting her a clear view of the nearby buildings and the town square a short distance away. To her alarm, she could see 'On Bascori Wings' in a pile of rubble across the square, surrounded by a cloud of dust.

Then she felt her blood run cold when she saw the familiar petite form of her son being aggressively dragged across the square by Cengor. That dread wrapped its spindly fingers around her neck, squeezing tighter and tighter as she saw a swarm of undead pour out across the square and into the streets.

The Athenaeum's two stationed magi both left the moment they realized what was happening, quickly taking to the streets to ward off the undead and help the townsfolk, but the apprentices held her back when she tried to follow.

"My son is out there!" Sorrel snapped, elbowing one of the men in the ribs. "Let go of me!"

"You don't even know if he's alive!" the apprentice snarled, though his grip on her loosened. "Going out there is suicide—"

"Then let me choose, damn you!" She yanked out of their hold, pushing through the door and down the narrow stairs, ignoring their shouts. The closer she got to the exit, the more she could hear the screams and panic over the distant rumble of thunder and magic. She didn't know what was going on out there, but she had to hope Rowan had managed to get away.

Sorrel reached the bottom of the stairs and wrenched open the door to find the street littered with body parts. Her eyes widened at the splattered black blood dotting the flagstone and lining the building walls. Some of the severed limbs twitched, giving the illusion that life was still in them.

The air was incredibly warm, like they were still in the middle of summer, and the sky churned overhead with lightning dancing between the dark clouds. Sorrel turned towards the square to see a flash of brilliant red light erupt from between the buildings. Her eyes widened as she saw the large form of a dragon barrel across the square, its entire body aflame. However, before that fire could spread, a thick fog wrapped around it, containing it as the sky directly above it opened up in heavy rain.

Something shot up into the air, brilliant and silver amidst the fire and smoke. It acted as the center of the storm, with wet wind howling around it and the storm churning overhead. Immediately, Sorrel knew who it had to be.

The Dragon Knight.

A burst of golden light and the sound of someone grunting pulled her attention back to the street. The source of undead dismemberment was pushing his way toward the square, undaunted by what lay ahead. Major Silas Baldry moved with ruthless proficiency, the long sword in his only hand glowing an intense gold along the edges. With each strike, the blade flashed and cut cleanly through whatever it struck.

There were only a few undead between Major Baldry and the square, and all of them were focused on the magic coming from his sword. Sorrel didn't wait any longer.

She dove out onto the street, jumping over chunks of flesh and dismembered limbs and ignoring the way her stomach churned at the smell of rot and decay. She did her best to not slip on the pools of black blood on the ground and pretended to not see the freshly mangled bodies of townsfolk on doorsteps and around corners. She had to focus on her goal: find Rowan.

She heard Major Baldry shout at her as she ran by him, barely avoiding the spindly fingers of a wight as it lunged for her. She ignored him, rounding the bend as the square came clearly into view. There, on the flagstone, was her son, wearing the Dragon Knight's cloak and being restrained by two magi in hooded robes. Her eyes widened as she watched a woman in a diadem—*an archmagus*—force a potion into his mouth.

Her eyes fell to his arm. The binding cloth was gone.

"Rowan! Get away from him!" Sorrel screamed, panic bubbling up in her as she dashed forward. He didn't respond to her, falling to his hands and knees as the magi around him all stepped back.

The woman archmagus ignored her, tossing the empty potion vial away and letting it roll across the flagstones. She then lifted a hand, palm facing Rowan as black and gold light ignited at her fingertips.

One of the other magi looked up at Sorrel as she approached and pointed a finger at her. Her eyes widened, expecting some kind of magical attack when something tackled her from her side. She screamed as she went down, the scent of rotten flesh overwhelming as the wight overtook her.

She threw her arms over her face to protect herself as it lunged at her, screaming in pain as she felt jagged teeth cut into her flesh. Blood dripped down onto her neck as the wight tore into her forearm, and she retaliated by beating her fist against its head, trying to get it to let her go.

Through blurred vision, she saw a flash of golden light atop her, and suddenly the wight stopped moving, its grip going slack as it collapsed on her. Its weight was gone a moment later as Major Baldry kicked the corpse to the side, its head rolling across the stones. His cloak landed on her as he shouted, "Staunch the wound, quickly!"

Sorrel fumbled for the cloth, clumsily wrapping it around her mutilated arm when the sound of Rowan's voice snapped her out of her shock.

"No! Get out of my head!"

She looked to see Rowan glaring up at the woman archmagus, his entire body shaking as the mark on his arm glowed a hot, bright green. Major Baldry was running for them, only to have both magi turn on him, ready to attack.

The sky erupted in a wave of red light like the clouds had been set on fire. Sorrel looked up to see the dragon in the air explode into ashes and cinders as a bolt of silver flames shot down toward Rowan.

The Dragon Knight knocked the archmagus away with a blast of lightning-charged ice. At the same time, a cyclone of wet wind hit the other magi, sending them flying into a wall. The wind also knocked down Major Baldry, who was trying to get to Rowan, sending him tumbling back with a shout.

"*Get away from him, you traitorous wretch!*"

The Dragon Knight's fury echoed over the square as she dragged the archmagus off, leaving Rowan alone on his hands and knees.

Sorrel pulled herself to her feet, eyes on her son. The mark on his arm was still glowing a haunting viridian, and vines had started climbing up his shoulder and down onto the flagstone. She broke out into a jog, ignoring the pain shooting up her arm and the way her vision swam slightly with each step. "Rowan!"

This time he heard her, shakily looking up at her. Relief flooded through her as he offered her a weak, pained smile...

...only for that relief to die as a blaze of viridian fire erupted out of his arm.

Rowan screamed, flames wrapping around him that looked just like the ones Osier surrounded her in all those years ago. They were followed by thick, thorny vines and large, wooden roots that shot out from his arm, racing in all directions and growing larger by the second.

Sorrel's eyes widened as she realized she couldn't dodge the oncoming danger, only for someone to tackle her out of the way. She shrieked both in surprise and pain as she tumbled roughly across the ground, although her savior took the brunt of the impact.

Major Baldry rolled to his feet, dragging her up with him as he pulled her towards the shelter of one of the nearby buildings.

"No, I have to get to Rowan!" Sorrel cried, trying to pull free. "He needs help!"

Even as she tried to pull free, she couldn't tear her eyes away from the sight. The roots had pushed through buildings and ripped into the streets, green fire dancing off of them like they were kindling in a hearth. Saplings and grass erupted between the cracks now in the roads, and moss and ivy overtook the nearby buildings. Various seeds were carried into the air, whipped up by the wind, and flowers blossomed on the remains of the undead as they decomposed before her eyes.

Rowan was no longer visible, the roots having wrapped around him like the base of a giant tree. They continued to twist and rise into the sky, taking Rowan with them, signaled by the brilliant viridian fire near the crest.

"How are you going to help him?" Major Baldry shouted frantically. "He's got roots the size of bridges tearing up the town! I thought he said he wasn't cursed!"

"It's not a curse!" Sorrel shouted, struggling against his grip. "They *did* something! I saw—" Her eyes widened. "It was a potion! They gave him a potion! I need that vial!"

Major Baldry looked down at her, staring at her like she was insane. "We'll never find it in this! It's probably already destroyed!"

"I have to *try!*" Sorrel screamed, straining against his hold. "I just need one drop, and I can save him! Let me save my son!"

She felt his arm around her loosen, and then her feet touched the ground a moment later. She stepped forward, only to have Major Baldry rush ahead of her, brandishing his sword.

"Come on then!" he shouted without looking back at her. "The roots closest to him have slowed down! I'll cut the rest!"

Sorrel let out a sob she couldn't hold back, sprinting forward into the undulating nature that moved like giant serpents across the ground. Small briars and sharp branches grabbed at her dress and the blood-soaked cape wrapped around her arm. She ignored them, moving in the direction she saw the vial roll to. Fear clawed at her, its grip tight as it tried to drag her down, but she shoved it aside with all her might, knowing this time she had a *choice*.

The tree continued to grow in size and height, forming a large canopy that overshadowed the entire square, with the center still burning like a viridian pyre. Sorrel whimpered as she glanced up at the top, knowing the fire was where her son was and not knowing if he was okay. The sky churned overhead, and the only reason Sorrel knew it was raining was because she could see it in the distance. The giant tree's foliage was so thick that the rain wasn't reaching the remains of the square.

In the distance, flashes of light and thunderous booms promised the Dragon Knight girl and the archmagus were still fighting. All of the magic in the air was palpable, leaving a strange taste on the back of her tongue and making the hairs on her skin stand on edge. There was so much chaos going on, and Sorrel still didn't even know what happened. All she knew was that the danger that she was warned about was now *here* and determined to harm her son.

"Don't look up; you're losing focus!" Major Baldry shouted, cutting through a large root blocking their way. His sword flashed with his swings, severing the wood neatly so he could kick it away for them to pass.

They hurried through, ducking under a twisting branch overhead, when Sorrel felt something crunch under her feet that wasn't rubble. She sucked in a breath, looking down at the remains of a glass vial.

"I found it!" she cried, crouching down.

Major Baldry turned, looking down. "Shit, it's in pieces!"

"I just need a drop!" Sorrel insisted, squinting as she tried to see in the low light caused by towering roots and black skies.

She tossed away the pieces that didn't have enough residue, keeping her injured arm close to her chest and doing her best to avoid getting pricked by glass shards. She knew that even a tiny amount of blood getting into a mixture could have terrible consequences. When she found the piece that had been the bottom of the vial, she exhaled in relief at seeing the droplet of dark liquid gathered on the concave surface.

"I need your help!"

Major Baldry was beside her in an instant, crouching down as the roots slowly crawled past them. Sorrel handed over the piece of glass, holding it as steady as her shaking fingers would allow. "Hold this, and don't you dare drop it."

Major Baldry let go of his sword and took the glass as Sorrel pulled out components from her potion kit. It was by some miracle that she still had a base potion that hadn't cracked, and she hastily pulled it out, along with a leather pouch containing the ground bubble cap powder.

She poured the powder into the base, trying not to think about how she had almost used it in a demonstration, and had things happened five minutes later, this wouldn't have been possible. She then nodded at Major Baldry.

"I need you to get that droplet into this potion."

Major Baldry nodded, holding the shard over the now-glowing vial in her hand. Sorrel did her best to keep it steady, praying they didn't miss.

Carefully, he shook loose the droplet, and both held their breath as it dangled on the edge of the glass before it plopped into the solution in her hands. Sorrel exhaled in relief, watching the pale blue solution turn into a deep indigo with a soft glow. "It's done!"

"How are we going to get it to Rowan? Will pouring it on this tree work?" Major Baldry asked, looking up into the sky. The tree continued to stretch out, limbs sheltering the entire hilltop, and the brilliant glow of green could still be seen through the leaves.

Sorrel froze, realizing the flaw in her plan. "N-no, it has to be ingested or injected—"

Lightning flashed overhead, followed by a thunderous boom as a form wrapped in silver fire shot across the sky towards the tree. The Dragon Knight came to a stop, hovering in the air as she stared up at the tree's canopy, her wings fanned out behind her. Sorrel looked up at her, realizing that the Dragon Knight was the only one who could get to Rowan. And once again, Sorrel was put in a position where she had to rely on someone she wasn't sure she could trust.

"I think she's supposed to help me."

Rowan's voice echoed in her mind. He seemed so *sure...*

All this time, this Dragon Knight had spent time around him but didn't harm him. Sorrel still didn't know what her role was in all of this, but Rowan dreamed about her. She made him happy. He trusted her... And Sorrel wanted to trust him.

She stood up, lifting her head to the sky as she searched for the name of the girl that Rowan wanted to be his friend. What did he call her...?

"NOVA!"

Nova turned her head, staring down at Sorrel and Major Baldry, then glanced back up the canopy, like she wasn't sure what to do.

"Nova, please! I can stop it!"

Nova snapped her gaze back down to them before folding her wings and dropping out of the sky, descending rapidly. Despite such an aggressive fall, she landed gracefully next to them in a burst of warm, wet wind that whipped Sorrel's hair out of her face. Nova was dirty and covered in wounds, although the rain had washed away a lot of the blood. Her hair and dress were soaked and in disarray, and she no longer looked human.

Sorrel stared at her, mouth hanging open as she took in Nova's appearance, from the horns and scales to the wings and tail. However, despite the shock of seeing a non-human woman in front of them, the thing that Sorrel fixated on was the look on Nova's face. Sorrel expected to see cold calculation or even righteous anger. What greeted her instead was the visage of a distraught young woman that reminded Sorrel too much of her younger self.

This was the face of someone who cared about her son, and that, coupled with the vial she held in her hand, filled Sorrel with a hope she hadn't had in years.

"How can you stop it?" Nova asked, a desperation in her voice that Sorrel intimately understood. "Tell me! We must hurry! Please!"

"He needs to drink this," Sorrel said quickly, holding up the vial, her thumb over the top to keep the contents from spilling out. "It will undo whatever that woman's potion did to him! Can you reach him?"

Nova glanced at the vial, then up at the canopy, its leaves still burning brightly in viridian fire. She turned back to Sorrel, her silver eyes burning with conviction. *"Yes."*

"Please save my son," Sorrel whispered, tears pouring down her cheeks as she offered Nova the potion. "He is everything to me."

Nova stared at her for a brief moment with an expression that Sorrel almost felt was longing, but for what she couldn't discern. Then, without a word, she unfolded her wings, tendrils of fog rising off of the spines, and carefully grabbed the vial out of her hand.

"I swear on my title, I will save him." Then with a great beat of her wings, she took off into the sky.

Nova the Tempest felt like a fool.

All her life, her enemy had been creatures without thought: mindless wights under the control of someone else and undead dragons that she suspected were much the same. She had never fought living humans before, and they were far more cunning than she could have ever imagined.

It never occurred to her they were tracking her for any reason other than to see what she was doing, but now she understood, especially after Giselle's statement. All those times when she would pick up random scents then lose them, all those times she knew they were following her but not acting, they were seeing when she could sense them and when she could not.

All so they could attack without her realizing it.

She still did, albeit far too late. An attack like Giselle's could never be fully covered, but it was nearly undetectable next to Rowan's seal. That magic was so pungent, and Nova knew it was a weakness, so she had remained vigilant anytime she was near Rowan and found her senses muddled.

She did not smell it, but she felt it in the air. The hum of energy made her hackles rise, and she reacted on pure instinct afterward, shoving Rowan away and wrapping herself in her densest clouds right before she was hit.

The impact still stunned her, especially when the damned building fell atop her, but she did not end up with a hole torn through her chest as she otherwise would have. Still, she did not laud herself for her quick thinking, because her naivety had cost her.

Advisor Giselle was supposed to be dead, just like the other advisors, hunted to extinction by the lich. But Rowan's traitorous friend had called her by name, and that face looked just like the visage in the old paintings in the Silver Spires. Nova did not know what that meant, and she did not have the luxury to think about it, not when they were after Rowan.

But Giselle was far more prepared than Nova. Nova knew magi were lurking about, but she completely missed that an undead dragon was nearby. It had not occurred to her that a Vermillion dragon was the reason for the cold weather.

Vermillion magic was the magic of heat and energy, and undeath twisted how that magic could work. This much she knew, but she did not realize that drawing in heat from around him would not leave a scent. Magma was the reason why it was so unusually cold, but it was only when he appeared that Nova realized he had been in the region this entire time.

Had Giselle covered his scent, too? It seemed likely, for Nova could not smell him until he attacked her.

For the first time in her life, Nova felt dread at the uncertainty that she could not predict what else may be coming. She could only hope Giselle bled out from the wounds that Nova left before she found a way to staunch them. Nova could not stay to confirm, not when Rowan needed her help.

She pushed on and upward, her wings carrying her into the sky towards the top of the great tree that Rowan was trapped in. She could use magic to carry her, but her body was already aching from how much magic she had channeled today. She had already used much of what she had stored up, and pulling it from the environment was difficult to sustain for a long time without consequences.

And in not knowing what waited for her in that tree, she knew it was best to reserve magic use for when it was absolutely necessary.

She did not know why they forced Rowan's magic out like this. Nova had never seen such a display of dragon magic, wild and out of control. Rowan should not have been capable of such a feat, not without decades of practice. This was like the magic of an elder dragon, and she feared what Giselle planned to do with it, and for the effect it would have on Rowan's small body.

Nova could only hope the potion she now carried was enough.

The top of the tree trunk where the canopy spread out was dome-shaped, with viridian fire licking through the cracks as the branches continued to spread. The scent of Viridian magic sat on the back of her tongue, reminding her of the sweet blackberries Rowan gave her. It suited him far more than the arcane magic that masked him all his life, and she would give her life to make sure he survived this.

Nova charged forward, her sword taking on a blade of ice as she drove it into the wood and cut down then across and back up. She kicked the chunk free, but then her eyes widened as the hole immediately began to reclose. Quickly, she wrapped herself in wind and barreled through the opening as it snapped shut behind her.

She tumbled roughly, magic-enhanced brambles and briars cutting into the skin not protected by her scales. Nova snarled at the pain, cradling the potion close with her thumb on the top to keep it from spilling out, mimicking how Rowan's mother held it.

Viridian fire was everywhere, illuminating the hollow inside the tree. It was loud and thick with the scent that Nova would forever associate with hope, with *Rowan*.

His pained cries echoed in the chamber, half drowned out by the roar of his magic. They made her heart pound, knowing he was hurting and that she had to stop it. She rolled to her feet, unsteady from all of her injuries, but still determined to save him.

"*Protect my legacy.*"

It was no longer about protecting Osier's legacy. It was about saving her *friend*.

Nova could fight through pain. She *would* fight through it to get to him. She could ignore the burns on her skin and the cuts in her flesh. She could persevere through the blurry vision from the spell Giselle slapped in her face right before Nova impaled her. She could ignore the pain from cauterizing the one wound that threatened to bleed her out, and she could force her limbs to still move.

Nova could fight through pain, but as she stumbled through the Viridian fire surrounding Rowan, she found she did not *need* to.

The flames washed over her, warm and soft against her skin. They did not burn, instead taking away her pain with each lick. Her wounds closed up as she pushed through the fire, and her vision returned with sharp clarity.

She gasped, startled at the sudden removal of pain, for she had almost forgotten Viridian magic could *heal*.

She had no time to revel over it, moving past the ring of fire to find Rowan. He was in the center, thorny vines and sharp wood tangled around him and biting into his skin. His face was streaked with thin trails of blood and tears, expression contorted into one of agony. His now unbound arm was a bloodied mess, but the mark that she now realized was his dragon mark still glowed brightly as his magic filtered through it.

If she did not stop it soon, he would die from the toll on his untrained body.

With a snarl, Nova willed the blade of her sword into the shape of an icy knife and began to cut away at the vines. Rowan opened his eyes, Viridian fire pouring from them, staring at her as she peeled away the briars holding him down. He cried out when she ripped them off, his voice raw from screaming. Nova hated that sound, grimacing as she threw the vines away and dove into the middle of his magic with him.

She pulled him close with her tail, wrapping her wings around them both to prevent the roots and brambles from grabbing him again. He collided against her chest, gasping as she jostled the many wounds on his skin.

The growth was volatile, fortified by his uncontrollable magic. Nova shielded herself with a barrier woven out of mist, providing some protection from the barbs and thorns digging into her wings as the vines constricted around them again.

"Please make it stop!" Rowan shouted, his words muddled with pain. "Please, it hurts so much!"

Nova growled and threw her sword down to cradle him so she could bring the potion to his face. "You need to drink this!"

His eyes widened in terror as he pulled back, and Nova realized he must have thought it to be the same potion as before. "No! Get it away from me!"

"It is from your mother! She said it will help you!" Nova cried as Rowan resisted. "I am here to save you! Please!"

He shook, looking up at her with the most fearful eyes, his pupils tiny pricks in the glow of Viridian green. She held that gaze, looking at him pleadingly. This time when she held the potion up, he let her, trembling as she poured the contents into his mouth.

He choked, gagging as some of it trickled down his chin, but swallowed the rest with a terrified grimace, his fingers desperately gripping her shoulders. Tears streamed down his face and never had Nova hated such a sight in all her life.

With no more need for the vial, Nova tossed it aside and wrapped both arms around him, wings still folded over them both to shelter him. She could feel the briars dragging along her body and sharp roots trying to dig through her mist, but she would endure the pain for him until the potion worked.

She felt him lean against her, his face pressed against her shoulder as he cried. "It— it hurts, it hurts! There's pressure inside! Can't keep it back!"

"Your mother said the potion would stop what they did to you!" Nova insisted, pressing her face into his hair and hoping she was right. "Please hold on!"

"Counter potions are slower," Rowan gasped, shaking his head. "I don't think I can wait that long!"

Nova gritted her teeth, trying to think of what to do. She had no idea he was *holding back* on his magic this entire time, given how powerful it already was. She did not know how long the potion would take to work, either. Her eyes fell to his arm sticking out of her mist, bloodied and angry, with viridian fire swirling around it.

So much magic being pulled through him was likely to cause permanent damage if not kill him, but letting it build up and burst was worse than letting it come out steadily, this much she knew. The only choice he had was to stop holding back. Resisting would weaken him further.

She squeezed him close, grimacing as the growing thorns managed to puncture through weaker parts of her barrier and bite into her skin. She could not protect him from his magic, but she could protect him from the growth it caused.

With that in mind, she made a decision. "I will shield you from your magic. Let it out."

Rowan pulled back to look up at her with his tear-streaked face and his mouth opened in horror. He sputtered, trying to force out the words, and the light on his arm stuttered with him as he struggled to keep it contained. "We don't know what will happen! It might kill you! Why would you do that?!"

She shook her head, meeting his gaze. "Because you are my *friend*, Rowan! And I..."

She hesitated, brow furrowing. All her life, her title was a reminder of what she was forced to be. A warrior, a soldier, a slayer of her own kind. The Tempest was what she *was* but not what she *believed,* for it was a life she never wanted.

And now, right here, she realized she could redefine that, and finally take pride in what she was.

Nova bared her fangs in her fiercest grin, pulling in Silver magic from the skies above and feeling it dance under her skin, painful but *alive*. "I am Nova the Tempest, the champion of my clan! And I will protect you, Rowan Spicer, with all of the magic of the skies! Will you trust me?"

He stared up at her, mouth moving with no sound coming out. His eyes glimmered in the darkness in an enchanting Viridian green. She found them beautiful.

"I trust you," he whispered, offering her a tiny, scared smile. Then he buried his face into her shoulder and let the magic he held back free.

Chapter 20
The Last Viridian

Sorrel stared up at the tree that held her son prisoner, clutching her wounded arm against her chest. Major Baldry stood beside her, concern etched onto his features. The roots closest to the tree had slowed to a crawl, no longer the danger they were earlier. Sorrel hoped that meant things were almost over, but she knew her counter potion was not instantaneous. The green fire still flickered out from the canopy high in the sky, a visual reminder that the threat was not yet over.

She could only hope that the Dragon Knight—*Nova*—had reached Rowan in time and that she was truly there to protect him.

Sorrel shuddered, thinking back to Nova's appearance. She didn't know what it meant that a Dragon Knight looked *dragon-like*. Allegedly, they used stolen magic from the dragons, but did that also mean she took on a dragon-like appearance? And what did the Dragon Knights have to do with her son? Who *was* Osier?

Now more than ever did she wish she had answers, and those questions circling her mind were the only things keeping her panic at bay.

"Come on, come on..." Major Baldry hissed under his breath. "Don't disappoint me, girl."

Sorrel glanced at him, then back at the tree, only for her breath to freeze in her lungs as hot green cracks raced down the trunk like streaks of lightning. A brilliant, viridescent glow wrapped around the tree, bringing rise to a fear deep in Sorrel's heart.

The light exploded, engulfing the world in *viridian* just like the day that Osier died. Specks of glittering gold and rich green fell from the skies, coating everything like a blanket of snow. With them came a rich, warm heat that washed over Sorrel, taking away the awful pain in her arm. Trees and bushes sprouted up from the roots of the giant tree, transforming the center of Ladisdale into a spring forest in full bloom like no one had seen in seventeen years.

The taste of sun-ripened fruit and floral tones touched her tongue, reminding her of that fateful day when the world lost Osier the Life Walker.

"ROWAN!"

For a brief moment, everything was *Viridian*.

The brilliant green fire roared around them, engulfing them as Nova tightened her hold on Rowan, using every part of her body to shield him from his magic. She used her scales to deflect the roots that tried to pierce him and her wings to cover him from sharp thorns and tangling briars.

She pulled mist from the environment to coil around them, letting them soothe over his skin and pull back on the growth trying to suffocate them. Despite her efforts, his magic overpowered hers, tearing through her misty barrier faster than she could keep it woven around them.

Rowan screamed into her shoulder, the sound raw and terrible to her ears. Nova held him tightly, wincing in pain as she felt the overgrowth tear into her wings and rip through the skin even with her magic reinforcing her body. She bit back a snarl, feeling blood drip down from her wings as the jungle around them attacked her.

Just as Nova prepared to weather through it, the scent of his magic changed. The sweet, floral odor from before shifted to something she could only describe as *warm*. It washed over her, and she felt the vines around them slow to a crawl and the pain in her wings began to fade.

The dome of Viridian fire around them collapsed, the roar fading away to a loud silence punctuated by Rowan's ragged gasps. Nova held still, uncertain if it was over but hoping it was.

Rowan went lax in her grip, slumping against the cradle of her arms as he tried to catch his breath. In the darkness under her wings, she could see the glow on his mark had died down to just a faint light, proof the potion had taken effect.

Nova exhaled in relief, reaching up to brush his hair from his face. The cuts on his cheeks had disappeared, leaving behind flecks of dried blood and a film of perspiration. His magic had healed him, too.

She paused at that, then flexed her wings, stretching them apart. The vines and brambles on them snapped easily, no longer strengthened by Viridian magic. With a flap, she shook them off, sending a burst of flower petals up into the air. Nova blinked as they fluttered down on top of them like a delicate snowfall.

Her gaze lifted to her wings. The growth had punctured and torn into the skin that covered them. Despite Rowan's magic healing her, those rips and tears remained, leaving the skin on her wings tattered like rags. She sighed softly at the damage. It did not surprise her, for she understood this moment was just as important as her first timeless scar, if not more so. That was fine. Her wings were still functional, and she could use magic to supplement what she lost.

Rowan made a pained noise, drawing her focus back on him. His eyes were closed and his breaths were still heavy, but she was not certain he was conscious. She turned her attention to his arm, finding her stomach tightening uneasily at its appearance. The wounds had healed, but the toll his magic had taken on his body remained behind. Scars in the appearance of roots were embedded in his skin from shoulder to wrist, and the flesh around them was puckered and angry. It looked painful, and she hated it.

His dragon mark itself was swollen and raised above his skin, looking like weathered tree bark. It still glowed faintly as magic leaked out of it. She exhaled softly, gaze fixated on the symbol. Rowan's dragon mark. Proof of his heritage. Proof the Viridian clan lived.

Now finally feeling like she could relax her muscles and calm down, Nova looked up to survey everything around them. The magic had tempered to pockets of Viridian flame that fluttered in the hollow of the tree, casting green light across the carpet of flowers now covering the hollow's floor.

The flowers were beautiful and unlike anything Nova had ever seen. They clumped together in bundles of silver and lavender, while tall stalks full of pink and violet blossoms stuck out between them. Mushrooms covered the walls of the hollow in all sorts of colors and shapes, some glowing and others not, while tall ferns unfurled below.

Movement around the flowers caught Nova's attention, and it took her several seconds to realize the tiny things zipping around were insects. They fluttered between the petals, dipping into the centers where the yellow stems were. She vaguely remembered hearing that was important, once upon a time.

Nova stood there in awe, looking around a room filled with things she had never witnessed in her life. Above her, flecks of viridian and gold light floated gently, appearing like a glittering, starry night. She watched it, then took a deep breath. The scent and taste of Rowan's magic filled her, and she lingered there, committing the sensation to memory.

It was 'sweet'. She realized she liked the concept of 'sweet' a lot. She felt like it suited Rowan Spicer.

She looked down at him to find he was somewhat awake. He gazed at her through slitted eyes that still glowed Viridian green, his face pale and damp with perspiration and his breath still labored. His hair clung to his cheeks and neck, and splotches of dried blood marred his freckled skin.

Nova belatedly realized he still had on her cloak. The magic-imbued dragon silk was visibly damaged, but it had likely warded off some of the wounds he would have otherwise taken from the overgrowth caused by his magic. Carefully, she tugged the fabric around him and covered him. It was cold this high up in the air, but at least Magma's return to his ancestors would bring the temperatures on the ground back to where they should be.

Rowan watched her with a dazed expression before he shakily lifted his fingers to touch her cheek. She went still, feeling him trace the cluster of thin scales there. He lingered for a moment, then his eyes lifted to look at her horns.

"She said... you were a half-dragon," he whispered, his voice husky and weak. "Is it true?"

Nova nodded slowly, lowering her head so he could brush her horns with his fingers. He looked exhausted, but there was a hint of awe in his gaze.

His hand fell back down into his lap. "Am I?"

Nova nodded again, her expression soft. "You are."

She nudged aside the flap of her cloak and very gently trailed her finger along the edge of the mark on his arm. "This is a dragon mark. Every dragon or half-dragon has one to represent their clan. I... am so sorry, Rowan, for I did not think sealing a dragon mark was possible. I mistakenly believed you were cursed, and you nearly died for it."

She should not have missed the importance of the location. She should have *known*. It did not matter that she had never met a Viridian dragon. It did not matter that Osier in her dreams appeared with silks that covered his arms. It did not matter that most of the Viridian paintings had been destroyed. What mattered was that she was not careful enough, and Rowan suffered for it.

He shook his head. "Not your fault. This... you didn't do this to me, Nova. You *saved me*."

She exhaled softly, feeling her eyes water. "But—"

"Saved." He offered her a weak smile. "You 'n my mom. Won't hear anything else."

Nova huffed but smiled back. "You are stubborn."

"Yup." He did not smile this time, but she could see it in his eyes anyway.

They lingered like that for a moment, and then Nova frowned. "We should return to the ground. Your mother and the one-handed warrior are surely worried about you."

Rowan sighed, closing his eyes. "Don't think I can walk."

"It does not matter if you could, for we need to fly," Nova replied, adjusting his weight in her arms. She stood, stretching her back, then grabbed her discarded weapon with her tail. She flapped her wings once more, shaking loose a few errant flower petals from earlier. Some fell onto Rowan, clinging to his hair.

He looked up at her and made a tiny sound of amusement. "You have flower petals on your horns."

She lifted a brow, not bothering to shake them loose. "I shall consider them a gift, then, since you grew them. However, you also have them in your hair, and I think that suits you."

He smiled faintly at that, resting his head against her shoulder and closing his eyes. "Okay."

Carefully, Nova stepped over the roots and foliage and made her way to the edge of the hollow. Despite her wounds being healed, she was still exhausted from her excessive magic use, and she could feel the effect on her body with each step she took.

She could only imagine how Rowan felt, and truly, she was baffled by how little damage he had for the amount of magic that was forced through him. She would have expected his entire body to be broken, but instead, the only visible injury appeared to be to his right arm. That at least made some sense, for a dragon's mark was the easiest place for a dragon to channel their magic.

She hoped the damage was not permanent.

Nova stopped at the edge of the hollow, willing just a small bit of magic into her weapon until it took the shape of a sword made of wind. She twisted, swinging her tail around and slicing through the wood, repeating the motion again and again until she had cut out a hole large enough for them to fit through.

Cool wind whipped through, and Rowan's eyes grew big as he realized they were high up in the sky. Nova dispelled her sword, wrapped her tail around Rowan, and then dove through the hole and out into the open with a great flap of her wings.

The sudden change of light made Rowan squint, turning his face into Nova's chest to block out some of the brightness. Nova paused for a moment, possibly letting her eyes adjust too, and then they were flying through the air. The wind was cold, seeping through the rips in Nova's cloak and ruffling his hair.

Despite himself, Rowan pulled back to look at the view, having never been in the sky before. It was a struggle to lift his head, but he managed to look down, unsure of what he would see. What greeted him caused his lungs to freeze as the devastating reality of what happened was laid before him.

The tree his magic trapped him in had climbed up halfway to the clouds, its trunk nearly as big as the town square. The roots had torn through buildings and ripped apart the roads. The perimeter wall was in ruins, and the roots continued down, dividing farmlands and cutting into the hillside. They continued, weaving through the valley surrounding the town before burying themselves deep under the neighboring hills.

That wasn't all. His magic had forced a lush forest to rise up through the city, surrounding the remaining buildings and sprawling out into the hillside. Trees like he'd never seen filled the roads and poked up through collapsed roofs, some flowering, others fruiting, and all painting a rich palette of color over what remained of the town.

It would have been beautiful in any other situation.

As Nova carried them closer and closer to the ground, he could hear people shouting or crying in the distance, and his panic spiraled.

He destroyed the entire town! People were probably hurt, maybe even *dead*, and it was all because of *him*. What happened to those who were nearby? The elderly? Did people like Mistress Tanner find safety? First the undead, then him—was there anything even left? Everyone had been just barely getting by. Now how would they, when he'd taken what little they had and destroyed it?

Rowan's eyes blurred as tears welled up and began to fall. "I-I destroyed the town..." The wind took his words away the moment they left his mouth, but that didn't silence the guilt that came with them.

He saw Nova shake her head out of the corner of his eye, feeling her hold on him tighten slightly. Despite the wind, her voice reached him easily. "This is not your doing, Rowan. It was forced upon you. You were not in control."

"Does that excuse it?" Rowan asked faintly, tearing his gaze away from the town they approached. He curled up against Nova as much as he could, like she might shelter him from his own guilt. He closed his eyes, cheek pressed against the fabric of her dress as the tears continued to fall.

His entire body ached in a way he never realized it could. His head pounded, and his throat was raw from screaming. His eyes burned, and everything inside felt so *broken*. It was like feeling numb, except he wasn't numb at all. It was more like everything was too much and he didn't know how to handle it.

He hadn't meant for any of this. Maybe it wasn't his fault, but it still happened because of him, and that knowledge was *crushing*.

"People got hurt because of me," he whispered, unsure if Nova could even hear him. She must have, though, because he felt a rumble deep in her chest that he realized was a growl.

"They were hurt because of Giselle," Nova said heatedly. "As were you—"

"Rowan! Nova, down here!"

Rowan jerked at his name, recognizing the panicked voice as his mother's. With what energy he had, he craned his neck to find her, heart pounding as he hoped she was okay. He felt Nova shift direction, moving rapidly through the air for a moment before she slowed down to descend into the trees. The flap of her wings sent gusts of wind in all directions, stirring the leaves as they landed.

"Rowan!"

He lifted his head, finding his mother rushing towards them, pushing past branches to get to him. She had blood all over her neck and arm, and her face was streaked with tears. Silas was right behind her, his cape missing and sword drawn, but with relief all over his face.

"Rowan! Oh, Rowan!"

A sob escaped Rowan at seeing them both alive, the relief bubbling over into a mess of emotions that came pouring out. He did his best to sit up in Nova's arms, grateful as she silently helped him. He twisted, grabbing his mother's hand as she reached him, desperate to touch her and make sure she was real.

The effort it took to move his right arm and bend his fingers drew his attention down to the state of his limb, and the sight of his arm interrupted his tumultuous emotions. He stared at the swollen, angry skin punctuated by the root-like scars running from wrist to shoulder. The dried blood and grime only added to how awful it looked.

His mother clutched his hand tightly with both of hers, her expression one of horror as she took in his haggard appearance, especially when she saw his arm. "Oh, no, no, no. Rowan, what happened?"

She looked up to his face, pale and fearful, as one of her hands let go of his to cup his cheek, thumb brushing over the skin.

"It's not as bad as it looks," Rowan lied, knowing very well that wasn't true. His fingers felt numb, and he could barely move his arm. But he could focus on that later. Right now, what mattered was that she was here. She was alive and safe.

He sucked in a shaky breath, then quietly added, "And... it would've been worse without you. Y-your potion. It worked, Mom."

She looked at him, then behind him at Nova.

Nova nodded. "You saved him, mother of Rowan. Wear that with pride."

"I..." Sorrel trailed off, squeezing Rowan's hand to her chest as tears spilled down her face. "I was so scared! I thought I would lose you!"

"Me too," Rowan admitted weakly as he slumped against Nova, too tired to keep himself up. He didn't pull his hand away, though, letting his mother cling to it as he dropped his head onto Nova's shoulder.

His eyes fell to the blood staining his mother's neck and arm. It looked dried and she wasn't acting like she was hurt, but that didn't mean she wasn't still injured. "Are you okay?"

His mother nodded, squeezing her eyes shut as she tried to reign in her emotions. "I'm fine. I'm... I'm fine. I'm just... as long as you're okay, I'm fine."

Rowan frowned, unable to determine if that meant she was still actually hurt. As if predicting what he was about to ask, Silas spoke up. "She was attacked by a wight. It got her arm. But there's no wound now. I think you healed her."

Rowan's mouth fell open, not prepared for that statement. He swallowed, then managed to stutter out, "I—how?"

Silas shook his head. "I don't know, but your magic exploded from the top of that tree and turned the skies green as far as I could see. The wounds on her arm healed, and hell, even the ache in my joints is gone now."

Silas rotated his shoulder as if to demonstrate his new range of movement, not that Rowan could tell any difference from before. "Haven't felt this good since I was in my twenties and still had two hands."

Silas paused, then admitted, "Was a bit disappointed that I didn't regrow my hand, though."

Rowan said nothing, too shocked and too tired to come up with any words. He knew all the growth was from his magic, but was there more to it? Had he really *healed* people?

Now that he thought about it, he had no open wounds anymore. His entire body still hurt, but there were no more cuts or punctures that he could see. Only the scars on his arm. He couldn't see any obvious injuries on Nova, either, although she still looked rough.

And if his magic had reached out past that tree... had he healed everyone nearby? He clung to that hope like it was a fantasy he could get lost in, even if he knew the truth was probably not so kind.

Silas nodded up towards the top of the tree, continuing, "The only time I've seen the skies turn green before was right before the Great Wither started. Lots of women in southern Bascor gave birth early. I hear that's about when you were born, too," Silas said carefully.

Although he spoke to Rowan, his eyes were trained on Nova like she had the actual answers.

Nova met Silas's gaze, silent for a moment, and Rowan could tell she was warring with herself on what to say. She glanced down at Rowan as if seeking permission or guidance. He wasn't sure which, but he appreciated the consideration.

He gave a weak nod, too tired to give a stronger signal. "You can trust them."

She nodded back, then looked at Silas and Rowan's mother. "The green magic you speak of is Viridian. It is one of the seven types of magic in this world. It is the magic of life. It is not just growth but healing and prosperity. Rebirth, and even death."

She paused, lips parted for a moment as she thought about what else to say, and then she turned her head to the side. "Look."

Everyone followed her gaze to see something scurry up a nearby tree. It stopped long enough for Rowan to see it was furry with a fluffy tail. His mouth fell open when he realized it was a squirrel—something he'd only ever seen in books.

And now that he was paying attention, he became aware of everything else. Insects buzzed in the air, appearing like little black dots between the trees. Birds chirped in the distance, recognizable because Rowan's grandfather would mimic the sounds for Rowan when he was a child.

His magic hadn't just grown a forest. It had grown an entire *ecosystem,* right here in the heart of Ladisdale. So many things that Rowan had never seen were now suddenly alive and here!

"I...did all of this?" Rowan asked in quiet wonder, stunned beyond belief.

Nova nodded, a faint smile on her lips. "The magic remembers. It is eager to return the world to what it was. It simply needs one who is connected to it, who can revive it."

Rowan's eyes flicked to his mother, who held her free hand to her chest in shock. She looked around, and then her eyes met Rowan's. "The spider lily..."

Rowan's brows lifted as he thought back to what his mother said it meant. "...The good in nature and rebirth."

His mother inhaled sharply through her nose, shuddering. "This is Rowan's gift then? To bring back life? Could he end the Great Wither?"

Nova nodded, inhaling softly like she was taking in the scent of everything around her. Likely, she was. "Yes. The Great Wither is because the Viridian magic in the world came to a stop. There was no one left to move it forward. However, it was still active in this place because Rowan was here. I think the seal could not fully sever his connection to his magic."

"And just to confirm, this explosion of magic was just because of that potion? We don't have to worry about it going off again, right?" Silas asked pointedly.

To Rowan's immense relief, Nova immediately shook her head. "No, I do not think so. That is not how dragon magic works. I do not know the purpose of that potion, but—"

"W-wait, 'dragon magic?'"

Rowan glanced at his mother, feeling his gut twist into a knot. The color was gone from her face, making her look ghastly with the dried blood on her neck. "You—"

She stopped, eyes wide as a hand came up to her lips like she was scared to voice the question. Rowan couldn't really blame her. Dragons were the cause of the war, or at least, that's what Rowan thought. After all, if Nova the 'Dragon Knight' was actually a half-dragon, then clearly they didn't have the full story.

Nova glanced at Rowan, uncertainty on her features. Rowan nodded slowly, silently giving her permission to speak. His mom deserved the truth, and, well, he needed to hear it, too.

Nova inhaled deeply, the wind around them stirring gently, rustling the leaves on the trees in a sound Rowan wanted to hear over and over again. "I am Nova the Tempest, half-dragon of the Silver clan, who reign over the magic of the skies. For many years, my clan's duty has been to fight the undead army and to free my kind trapped in undeath."

Rowan's eyes widened, several pieces falling into place.

"Call all of your magic forth, Rowan Spicer. Summon it and hold it in your body, then sever your connection to your clan and end your life."

Giselle had appeared commanding an entire platoon of undead, and she had known that Rowan was half-dragon. She hadn't just been trying to kill him. She had said as much to the other magi. What had they called it?

Conversion.

The dragons Nova fought were undead. Giselle had been trying to turn him into an undead half-dragon! But... somehow, Rowan didn't think Giselle was the sole person behind all of this. Maybe she was acting as part of a group?

Unaware of Rowan's racing thoughts, Nova continued, "An elder dragon named Osier the Life Walker contacted me in my dreams and asked me to find and protect his legacy in the land where he died."

She smiled softly at Rowan, letting the wind gently ruffle his hair. The scent of her magic lingered for a moment, comforting amidst everything else. It pulled Rowan out of his head, causing him to look up at her.

"Rowan is his legacy, the last of the Viridian clan. And... my friend."

She said the last part so pridefully that Rowan couldn't help the tiny but genuine smile that tugged at his lips. So many thoughts and worries plagued him, and he felt so raw and overwhelmed, but the one positive thing he could latch onto was that he was *right*.

Nova was never sent to harm him.

He felt his mother's fingers twitch around his hand. "You're saying... Osier was a dragon... and that means Rowan is half-*dragon?*"

Nova nodded, meeting her gaze. "I do not know how a human archmagus sealed Rowan's magic, but it is so. I have spent years tracking my own kind, but I could not tell Rowan was half-dragon, even though I spent many days around him. Whoever did it must have been powerful. Few humans would have that kind of power."

"He..." His mother hesitated, squeezing her eyes shut like she was about to say something difficult. "He knew who Osier was. He said his name carried weight, and told me to never mention it. He said we were in danger and bound Rowan's magic. He told me to pretend he was cursed..."

Nova's lips parted in realization. "It was Advisor Avelore—"

"Amantius," Sorrel finished with a whisper. "But he didn't call himself an advisor."

"No, he would have no need to. He advised dragon-kind," Nova admitted. "I never met him, but I know of his stories."

Rowan watched the way his mother's face cycled through expressions, most of them a mixture of confusion and shock as she reevaluated everything that she thought she knew.

He swallowed uneasily, feeling exposed in a way he couldn't quite articulate in his mind. The truth was now out there for all of them, even if he suspected only he really understood what Giselle tried to do to him. He didn't plan to bring it up right then, though.

But even besides all that, he worried about what his mother was thinking. He was a half-dragon. Was that better than being cursed? Worse?

Could she be okay with that?

As awful and persistent as those worrying thoughts were in his head, he lacked the energy to do more than let them hover in the echoing hollow of his mind, spiraling in place with everything else. He didn't even know how *he* felt about being half-dragon, and he probably wouldn't until later when he could be alone with his thoughts and process everything that happened.

What he did know was that the dragons hadn't turned their backs on humans. After all, it became clear to him as Giselle tried to worm her way into his head that dragons didn't become undead of their own free will.

An image of Cengor's dying face flashed in Rowan's mind and he squeezed his eyes shut, turning his face into Nova's chest as he tried to block out the memory. She said nothing, but her tail squeezed him gently. He wished he could do more than cry.

The sound of Silas sighing pulled Rowan out of his grieving thoughts. "Well, that confirms something for me, at least. But we should move while we talk. I'd like to get out of this forest. With how coordinated this attack was, I don't want to assume we're safe yet."

He turned, trying to identify their surroundings. "Don't know how easy it will be to get there, but the closest gate is this way. I'll lead and clear the path. Are you okay with carrying him?"

Nova nodded. "He fits well in my arms. It is not a concern."

Rowan said nothing, staring forlornly at the ground as he felt his mother let go of his hand.

What happened now?

He wanted to ask, but he was just too tired. He hoped someone else knew.

Chapter 21

Answers

They moved carefully down the ruined roads of Ladisdale, slowed down by the presence of overgrowth and debris. Silas led the way, followed by Rowan's mother, then Nova carrying Rowan.

Rowan watched as Silas cleared away saplings and bushes with his sword, each swing flashing in golden light and leaving behind a faint whiff of something *sharp* in odor.

He wrinkled his nose at the strange smell, brow furrowing. He understood now that his ability to smell Nova's magic was because of his dragon blood, but he still wasn't quite sure why he could now smell human magic when he never had before. Was it because the seal was now broken and his dragon side was starting to surface? Or was it just because he spent his entire life so close to such a strong source of magic that he couldn't smell it until it was gone?

He didn't have answers, but he was also more fascinated by the magic in Silas's sword. Silas had never mentioned his sword being capable of such a thing, and with the way that Nova could smell magic, surely she would have said something.

Nova seemed to have similar thoughts, tilting her head as she watched Silas. She didn't immediately say anything, instead brushing away a low-hanging branch with one of her wings. Rowan watched tiredly, observing how thin trails of mist seemed to rise up off of her wings, and how the claws at the tips of the spines hung down almost like little ornaments.

Rowan's gaze lingered on the way her wings were tattered and full of holes. He didn't recall them being like that when he first saw them. Had he overlooked that during all of the chaos?

So distracted by his thoughts, he almost missed Nova saying, "Your sword was not enchanted before, warrior. I would have sensed it."

Silas didn't look back, kicking aside a bush he uprooted. "I suppose we can graduate to real names. Call me Silas. And you're half right. It's enchanted, but it's been dormant for years. Like an empty well waiting for rainfall. All the magic thrown around today recharged it, I guess."

He sighed, then added, "Was Avelore's idea, actually. Thought it would be safer than having an always active weapon. One of those many ideas he had that was brilliantly stupid, and only worked because he was around. And then he wasn't."

"W-wait," Rowan stuttered, his voice still scratchy and lacking strength. "How are *you* involved in all of this?"

Silas spared him a roguish smile over his shoulder. "He taught me tablut."

Rowan blinked several times. Silas chuckled, turning his attention back to clearing the path. "I'll give you the long story some other time, but the important part is that he saved my life once. In return, I offered to come to his services if he ever needed it. We made a pact."

Silas held up his sword hand, twisting it until Rowan realized he was drawing attention to the ring on it, with its four-point star engraving.

"Ah!" Nova's brows lifted in surprise. "It is the symbol of the Golden clan. I am told that Advisor Avelore was an honorary member."

Silas snorted, shaking his head. "He told me it meant loyalty. Well, anyway, he said if he ever needed me, he'd contact me through this."

Silas lowered his hand, returning his attention towards clearing the path. "Then seventeen years ago, I received a partial message: 'Come to Ladisdale and protect.' At first, I thought he meant the town itself. However, when news of his death reached me, I became concerned the message was incomplete. Unfortunately, I didn't know who or what I was supposed to protect, so I decided to settle down and do my best with what I had."

Silas paused long enough to cut away another branch. "Then I met Rowan in the library, and I got the sneaking suspicion you were more than some boy with a curse. Looks like I was right."

Rowan went silent, thinking about that. Then he realized that there was a big piece to this whole story he still didn't understand. "Nova, who killed Avelore? And Osier? Was it the same person?"

Nova curled her lip in disdain, eyes narrowing. "Yes. It is one who we call a lich. He is the cause of all of this. He has killed most of our kind, corrupting them and trapping them in undeath. He then controls them to do his will. It is the reason humanity thinks we have turned on them. He also created the undead army that plagues your borders."

"And the ones we call 'Dragon Knights'... are half-dragons like you?" Silas asked as the remains of the east gate finally came into view.

Nova lowered her gaze, expression sad. "Yes. Silver half-dragons are the ones you call 'Dragon Knights,' for our magic is best suited to kill undead dragons. Humanity thinks we are dragon slayers, but they do not understand. We free our brethren from undeath and return them to our ancestors. There is no victory in our duty, not until we stop the lich."

"I see now why you dislike the moniker," Silas said. "I apologize for my ignorance."

Rowan watched Nova's brows lift in surprise before her expression softened into one that carried a lot of emotions. After a moment, she quietly said, "Thank you."

"I have a question," Sorrel interjected, carefully stepping over several large pieces of stone. "When Avelore Amantius died, the guards saw someone like yourself flying away. Silver fire. Does this... lich have one of your own working for him?"

Nova exhaled softly, hopping over the rocks with far more ease. "There are Silver dragons still trapped in his control, but I do not think that is what you saw. Before Advisor Avelore died, he sent out a signal to my clan. We did not respond fast enough, and the story I was told is that Argentum the Thundercloud, my father, arrived too late. He confirmed Advisor Avelore was dead then followed the trail of the lich. He would have used his fire to disguise his identity from nearby humans."

Rowan watched his mother nod, glancing back at him with a worried expression. He wondered if she still had worries Nova was someone she couldn't trust. If so, he didn't know what could change that at this point. Nova had fought and risked her life for him. If she wanted to bring him harm or kidnap him, she would have done so.

But he did understand his mother's fear. So many lies and half-truths, all around him.

"What about the woman?" Sorrel asked after a moment, rubbing her hands over her arms. "The archmagus. You called her a traitor."

Nova inhaled sharply, anger flashing across her features. "That was Advisor Giselle Le Du. I recognize her face from old paintings. She is supposed to be dead."

"Please tell me she's dead now," Silas muttered, cutting through some hanging vines.

"I impaled her with a lance of ice and left her pinned to the ground with it. I do not... think humans can live through that." Nova hesitated. "...Can they?"

Rowan was too tired to do more than stare at her for even asking that, and he mentally filed this moment away to revisit later. Nova needed some lessons on how humans actually were.

"Well, most certainly can't," Silas agreed, tossing away the vines. "I wager you didn't wait to find out since you had bigger problems to worry about."

Nova's face contorted into one of displeasure. "Rowan is not a problem. Why would you say that?"

Silas let out a bark of laughter, and even Rowan found a faint smile tugging at his lips.

"It's not meant literally, Nova," Rowan whispered. "I promise."

"I do not understand," Nova complained, her expression pained. "You must explain it to me later when you are rested."

He nodded, closing his eyes. He was probably the best person to help her understand these things. After all, even if he no longer qualified as a human... he still *counted* as far as knowing how to be one. And that's what mattered, right?

"Help! Is anyone there? Please!"

Rowan jerked in Nova's arms, eyes going wide at the sound of someone nearby. Ahead, Silas cursed and pivoted, trying to gauge where the cry came from. "Someone's here! Where are you?"

The voice, a woman, called from inside one of the collapsed buildings, "We're in the smokehouse! The roof fell and we can't get out!"

"Are you hurt?" Silas asked as he pushed his way towards the building, kicking clear rubble and cutting branches as he went.

"No, we're fine! We were hurt, but the injuries healed in the green light!"

Rowan sighed softly in relief. His magic really had healed everyone. It didn't make up for destroying the town, far from it, but at least people who had gotten hurt were now healed. Well, at least for everyone still alive.

His eyes fell to his mother's arm, the fabric of her dress tattered and bloodied. He swallowed, trying not to think of the possibilities of the people who didn't make it. There had been so many wights let loose on the town. And then the damage from the tree...

He jumped when Nova reached up with her tail and poked him in the shoulder. "Your face says you are thinking too loud."

"S-sorry," he whispered, watching as his mother turned to him with concern. "Just... worried about how many people could be trapped and, well... who didn't make it."

His mother pursed her lips and stepped up, brushing his hair from his face. Rowan sighed softly at the touch, eyes fluttering slightly.

"Just remember this isn't your doing," Sorrel said quietly, affectionately stroking his hair. "It was that woman's. Not yours."

Nova growled at the mention of Giselle, and Rowan nodded weakly, eyes falling to Silas as he cleared the debris in front of the door.

"I'm kicking the door open, stand back!"

Movement overhead drew Rowan's attention, and he watched as a bird landed on one of Nova's wings. It fluffed its feathers and chirped, and Rowan found himself appreciating the sight of something he'd never been able to witness before. Nova watched it as well, holding carefully still. He wondered if having such a tiny thing on her wings tickled or—

Her wings.

Rowan's eyes went wide as he looked back towards the smokehouse. "Nova, your appearance!"

He looked back at Nova just in time to see her dragon features shimmer and then disappear from view, the feeling of her tail wrapped around him disappearing with it. Now with blue eyes and no scales, she looked kind of strange to Rowan. He hadn't realized how much her true appearance really... suited her, as she might say.

It made him wonder, though. What was *his* true appearance? Would he even gain one, since he had spent all of his life with his magic sealed away? Would it 'grow in?' Would he have horns and wings and a tail? Would he need to learn to hide away those features, and would he *like* how he looked?

His racing thoughts were interrupted by Silas pulling the first person out of the smokehouse. Rowan realized it was Mistress Brewer, Tibert's mother, easily recognizable by the gaudy orange color of her tunic, which she had dyed with ochre pigments. But if she was here, then that also meant...

He watched as Tilbert followed afterward. Nova growled quietly under her breath, but Rowan shook his head, drawing her attention back to him. "He's the least of our concerns right now..."

"He is still a disgraceful human," Nova muttered with disdain. "I would like to drop him in the river for touching your hair. Especially now that I know you are half-dragon. Our hair is our pride, Rowan. He is not worthy of touching it."

Rowan blinked at that, realizing that maybe that was why he hated having his hair cut. Was that some dragon instinct that couldn't be smothered by his seal? He'd have to ask Nova more about it later. He wondered if his hair would change now, too.

Rowan looked over to see Silas help Mister Brewer out of the smokehouse, then went still when he saw Tilbert glaring at him.

"Can't even carry your own weight, Spicer?"

"You're lucky I'm here to carry yours," Silas replied wryly as he gestured to the door he cleared, causing Tilbert to scowl.

"Just drop it, Til," Mister Brewer said, clapping a hand on his son's shoulder and steering him towards the gate. "Be grateful we're alive and unharmed."

"Yeah, what in the Shores *happened?*" Tilbert asked, looking around as the group continued to the gate. "It's like nature came back to life and decided to attack the town! We're lucky we didn't get impaled by a damn tree or something."

Rowan winced, grateful no one but Nova saw the action. She growled again, but he shook his head, silently begging her to stop. They couldn't cause a scene right now, and he wanted to be as invisible as possible. If anyone saw his arm...

Nova stopped rumbling, but he could tell she was still upset, shoulders tense as she carried him towards the exit.

They made it through the gate with no one offering Tilbert an explanation, although Rowan was fairly certain the gust of wind that made Tilbert, and *only* Tilbert, trip was a certain half-dragon's doing, considering how it smelled.

He stared at Nova with an arched brow, and she pointedly did not look at him, her face comically blank. Honestly, the levity of the moment helped pull him out of his pit of thoughts, but he promised himself to have a talk with her after all this was settled. This was why she couldn't blend in.

The forest thinned rapidly once past the city's gates as if it was contained by the walls themselves. Giant roots were still everywhere, ripping through fields and tearing up the roads as far as one could see. But Rowan's magic hadn't stopped with the town.

His eyes widened at seeing the green that had overtaken the hills, lush and rich like the fields in his dream. Pops of violet interrupted the wavy emerald grass, likely some type of flower, and the meager crops in the terraced farmlands had multiplied, their bounty spilling past the fences.

Rowan exhaled in a mixture of nervousness and relief as he saw how many people were at the base of the hill. Some were looting the crops in the fields, while others congregated together in groups. He squeezed his eyes shut as he heard people crying, trying to focus on the fact that a lot of people were alive and had escaped. Maybe there were more people on the other side of the hill, too.

They hurried quickly down what remained of the road, careful to not fall down any sharp inclines. The Brewers led the way, eager to be reunited with the rest of the survivors, while Silas lingered behind to help Rowan's mom over the larger holes and uneven terrain.

Nova stayed close to Silas and his mother, carrying Rowan over the rubble and giant roots with ease. She remained alert, eyes scanning their surroundings now that they were more in the open.

Despite that, Rowan could tell she was tired, if not in pain, judging by the weariness on her face and the way she sometimes tensed as she jumped over obstacles, like the action hurt.

And yet she continued, and Rowan found himself both awed and envious. She was so strong and resilient, and he couldn't help but wonder if things would have turned out better if he had any kind of ability to defend himself like she did.

Silas always said strength manifested in many ways, but Rowan couldn't see how any of his feeble strengths helped here. What good were board game strategies and book smarts in the face of death and destruction? At best, his ability to distract Giselle had bought Nova a little time to recover, but the demolished town behind him still made it seem like his best hadn't been good enough. He sighed, letting his vision go out of focus as despair grabbed him once again.

When they reached the bottom of the hill, the Brewers ran off, leaving them alone once again. Silas turned to look at Nova. "We shouldn't let anyone get close to Rowan and see his seal is missing.

It'll draw all the wrong attention, and they'll assume the giant tree destroying the town is definitely an unleashed curse."

Rowan's mother stiffened, a hand covering her mouth in horror as she realized that was exactly what would happen. And who could blame them? Rowan certainly felt like a curse right now.

Nova frowned. "It is not just the humans here. The lich will have others like Giselle, and if they attack now it will not be good. My body is already weak from using so much magic, and now Rowan is too weak to walk. We are at a disadvantage. I have signaled to my clan to come, but given they are spread out across the Shores, it will take time for someone to arrive. We are without allies for now."

"And that tree is like a lighthouse to anyone nearby..." Silas muttered, glancing up at the forest behind them.

Sorrel lowered her hand from her face, but her expression remained worried. "Is there a place where he will be safe? Anywhere at all?"

Nova nodded. "Yes. I can take him to my homeland. It is the only safe haven for dragonkind. The lich cannot reach it."

Rowan blinked slowly, focusing on Nova's words, or more specifically, focusing on what she didn't say. "What about my family?"

Nova hesitated, glancing between him and his mother with uncertainty. "I... I do not know if I am allowed to bring humans. We have not had them among us for a long time—"

"I'm not letting you take my son from me," Sorrel said sharply, effectively cutting Nova off. The heat in her words made Rowan flinch slightly, eyeing her through the messy veil of his bangs. He didn't blame her for being upset, though. He didn't want to be separated from her or Grandpa Zebb, either.

Rowan inhaled softly. Was Grandpa Zebb okay? Now seeing how far the tree's roots had stretched, they might have reached his house. Or what if Giselle's followers had thought to grab his grandfather and hold him hostage? Rowan tensed at all the terrible possibilities, half paying attention to his mother's next words.

"So you better find a way to make it work—!"

Nova suddenly twisted, shielding Rowan with her body as she released a wall of fog around all of them. Everything lit up in a golden light that came with a deafening boom and the sharp scent of arcane magic. Rowan yelped and turned his head away, unable to block out the attack on his senses that left him feeling nauseous and disoriented in its wake.

The light faded, but Rowan found his vision still impaired when he opened his eyes. The ringing in his ears persisted, making his head scream and causing the world to spin around him.

Nova put him down a moment later, causing his panic to mount when he realized she was letting go of him. However, someone else grabbed onto him, pulling him into a tight, but shaky embrace. Through his muddled vision, he could make out the auburn color of his mother's hair, and he exhaled in relief as he leaned against her, grateful to not be left alone. The ringing in his ears quickly faded, followed by the dark spots in his vision, allowing Rowan to see what was left in the wake of the attack.

The clouds Nova created still hung around them in a gray dome, cutting off their view from outside. Silas was on one knee, shaking his head as he rid himself of the aftereffects of the attack. Nova stood beside him, seemingly the least impacted by the attack, though she had a hand pressed to her temple.

"—you okay?"

He turned his attention to his mother, who looked at him with concern. He nodded slowly, trying to focus enough to speak. "I'm okay."

She gave a breathy gasp of relief, tucking him against her as she pressed a hand to his hair. Rowan went limp in her arms, taking comfort in her needy embrace. He knew they were in danger, but he had to trust Nova and Silas to keep them safe. He was painfully aware that he had no way to defend himself or even flee. He was effectively helpless.

Silas was standing now, his right arm held out as Nova wove her magic in the air between them. Silver flames wrapped around Silas's forearm and then took the form of a shield made of clouds. They swirled around his arm like they weren't solid, but when he moved his arm, the clouds moved with it, keeping shape.

Curiously, Silas tapped his sword against the shield, the tip meeting the clouds like they were solid. But more importantly, small sparks of lightning danced across the shield's surface, promising nothing pleasant for whoever struck at him. Silas nodded in approval, then glanced in the direction the attack came from, although Nova's cloud barrier still blocked their view.

"What's our situation?"

Nova growled softly, stepping away from him as she pulled out her sword hilt and stared through her barrier. "It is Giselle. She survived the wounds I gave her. I think Rowan's magic healed her, too."

Rowan winced at that.

"Is she alone?"

"I do not know for certain," Nova admitted. "She has learned to hide the scent of magic. Not perfectly, for now that Rowan's seal is gone, I can smell her attacks when she releases them, but enough that there could be others hiding nearby."

"So they could attack us the moment you engage with her," Silas concluded. "Can you keep this dome up while you fight?"

Nova hesitated. "I... can, yes, unless she has an undead Silver dragon with her. They could dispel my magic because it is of the same origin. Or if the attacker hits my clouds with something stronger."

"I think that's a chance we'll have to take, because even with this"—Silas gestured to his new shield—"I'm not going to be able to fight off a magus of her caliber, much less a dragon. The only downside is that I can't see incoming attacks through your fog."

Nova looked up, considering the dome around them. She tilted her head, eyes narrowing in thought, and for a brief moment, Rowan felt something *shift* in her scent.

It was too quick for him to discern how, and before he could linger on it, the clouds surrounding them went from opaque grays to a filmy silver that allowed them to see outside. It was like looking out a window on a rainy day, but still better than nothing.

"Did you... just figure out how to do that right now?" Silas asked hesitantly, some measure of disbelief in his tone.

"Yes," Nova replied, matter-of-factly. "I am told it is why I am a prodigy. Magic manipulation is easy for me."

Rowan half paid attention to the exchange, instead looking past the foggy dome at their attacker. Giselle stood several meters away, one hand outstretched towards them, golden smoke still wafting up from it. Her other hand was wrapped around the neck of a body slumped against her.

...A body dressed in orange-yellow clothes.

Rowan swallowed, heart pounding as he realized it was Mistress Brewer, and that she was likely dead.

It was just like Cengor's death.

Rowan's stomach lurched, and he turned his head away, hiding his face against his mother's shoulder. She held him tightly, her own face pressed into his hair as she rocked them both back and forth.

"It'll be okay," she whispered, though Rowan wasn't sure who she was trying to convince. Things were not going to be okay for a long time.

He shook his head, clinging to her with the one arm that was still willing to cooperate with him. A moment later, Rowan caught a faint whiff of arcane just as Giselle launched another attack on the barrier.

Several small flashes pelted the clouds like a barrage of arrows, each one exploding in a small flash of light with a sharp noise. The clouds rippled around them but remained intact, silver fog swirling angrily in response to the magic peppering them.

Rowan swallowed, remembering Nova said she was weakened from using too much magic. How much longer could her shield hold out against Giselle? Was Giselle also weakened? Did humans have the same kind of fatigue? Was Nova still capable of fighting?

He glanced at Nova, at her tattered and blood-stained dress, the set of her shoulders, and the way she held her hilt tightly in her hand. He couldn't see her face from this angle, but he imagined she looked far braver than he could ever hope to be.

She turned to him, with her fake blue eyes and the scales gone from her cheeks. Her expression was distant—*guarded*—and Rowan knew that meant she was going to go back out there.

She *had* to go back out there. She had to protect him because Giselle wanted to kill him. That knowledge felt like needles under his skin, sharp and painful. Rowan felt the need to say *something*, but he wasn't sure what.

What did he want to say?

He wanted to tell her to be safe. He wanted to remind her that she was more than her duty, that she was his friend, and that she was important to him. He wanted to thank her for everything. He didn't want her to die, but he was terrified she might.

Instead, what came out was none of that and all of it at once: "Promise me you'll come back."

Her expression softened slightly, and she gave him a single, faint nod. "I promise you."

With that, she turned and walked through the clouds to face Giselle. Rowan watched her leave, tears slipping down his cheeks as he hoped she was right.

Chapter 22
Duplicity

Surprisingly, Giselle did not attack the moment Nova passed through her fog. Instead, she tossed away the body leaning against her, now dried out and mummified like the human who had betrayed Rowan.

Nova's eyes fell to the yellowish clothes, recognizing them as belonging to the woman they helped out of the building. She did not know what Giselle traded the woman's life for, but she knew it was to give herself something in return.

Assuming Rowan's magic healed her, that meant Giselle traded the woman's life for something else. Possibly a reduction of spell fatigue or a bolster in her ability to move the magic around her.

Either way, it did not bode well for Nova, especially since she had a limited understanding of humanity's use of magic. Much of that was because she spent her life fighting dragons and undead, and largely estranged from humans.

What she did know was that humans did not use magic the same way that dragons did. Dragons and half-dragons accumulated magic in their bodies over time and could use that for later use. This allowed them to manipulate and process their magic in ways that humans could not. And to recharge, a dragon or half-dragon simply needed to rest in their element.

But if their magical reservoir ran out, those of dragon blood could still forcefully draw in magic from the environment around them. However, rapidly drawing in and processing magic like this was very taxing on the body. Doing it too much at once caused great discomfort, and prolonged channeling would have detrimental effects on one's body or control. This was why Rowan was in the condition he was now, because of the way his magic had been forced through his body.

In contrast, Nova understood that humans could not store or process magic. They only *used* the Golden magic available around them. It was the equivalent of moving what was already there and active, which admittedly was a lot. Golden magic was everywhere, and the Golden clan kept it active by their mere existence. It no longer needed the same kind of curation as the other types of magic, not since its evolution.

Because of these differences, humans were not at risk of the same injuries dragon-kind could have if they overused magic. They simply had to deal with normal physical fatigue. This meant Giselle had a great advantage over Nova, given that Nova had used up her stored magic, and her body was already feeling the effects of using so much magic in a short time.

And Giselle's magic was indeed different. While it smelled like human arcane, it *looked* wrong. Arcane was golden in color. Giselle's magic was golden and black, and Nova did not know what that meant. Was this also the lich's doing? Why was it just her and not other human magi? Nova did not know, but she understood it could be important.

It was unfortunate that Nova did not finish Giselle off earlier, but when she saw Rowan's tree rise into the sky, Nova did not stay and wait. Up until now, her duty would have been to prioritize Giselle, but Nova did not regret her actions. Had she waited longer, Rowan might have died. She was proud to have defied her duty because now the Viridian clan lived. And Nova would ensure it lived past today, too.

However, Giselle was a clever human. Maybe the smartest. She knew dragonkind well, especially their weaknesses, which meant she knew Nova was worn down from channeling so much magic through her body. That was fine. Nova may have been tired, but she was resilient and no stranger to pain. She would simply have to make this quick and decisive.

If she could.

Giselle stalked towards her, black and gold light popping around her as she formed the same orbs as before. Nova narrowed her eyes, wondering why Giselle would choose an attack that Nova could effectively counter. She at least had the mind to form them away from her body so that Nova could not detonate them on top of her, but it still seemed like a poor choice.

"You're definitely strong for your age, girl, but you've never fought anything *living* and it shows." Giselle's words had an air of superiority to them like she knew she had the advantage.

Nova responded by marching forward to put distance between herself and the cloud dome. As she moved, she drew her hilt, letting her magic take the form of a whip of lightning at the end. In her other hand, she created a blade made of concentrated wind. The air around her crackled and whistled as she condensed the ambient Silver magic into the two weapons.

"Then I shall address that promptly," Nova replied crisply, eyes burning white as her true form bled through her disguise. There was no use hiding her appearance, not when that would require her to use more magic. Still, she shape-shifted her wings away, preferring to fight without them.

Nova moved first, darting over the large roots jutting up out of the ground to close in on Giselle, aiming to put distance between herself and the others.

Giselle responded swiftly, hurling her orbs through the air towards Nova. Nova wrapped herself in wind and dodged, zigzagging across the hillside as she kept ahead of the orbs. Streaks of mist trailed after her, waving like flags as she grabbed Silver magic from the atmosphere to aid her. Her body burned, but she let that pain be her focus, to remind her that she needed to be quick.

She detonated two of the orbs at a distance by striking them with her whip, the electricity lashing out like an arc across the valley. As she did, she pulled in moisture from around her, anticipating an attack from another direction.

Just as she finished wrapping herself in fog, a third orb hit her in the back. Her magic absorbed the explosion, but the impact still knocked her to the ground, causing her to tumble roughly down the slope of the hill.

Nova snarled in pain as she rolled up to her feet, mist clinging to her like a gauzy dress. Another orb crashed into her side, exploding in hot light. She braced herself and took the hit, thrusting her hand into the air as she sent several spikes of ice raining down on Giselle from above.

Giselle stopped controlling her orbs to form a shield over her head, making Nova realize that the arcane barrier Giselle had earlier was no longer active. Nova twisted, throwing the blade of wind at Giselle, then used that momentum to spin around and detonate the rest of the orbs around her with her lightning whip.

Nova made a full turn to see Giselle parry the blade of wind with an arcane blast. The impact caused the condensed air to explode out, knocking Giselle back. Her slow recovery was a clear sign that Giselle was tiring out, but Nova was not in much better condition. Her breath was labored and her body burned, and she could tell she did not have her usual reaction speed, given how few of Giselle's attacks she had dodged.

Giselle stared at her, fingers flickering with her magic as she formed a large spear that looked like black glass glowing gold. Nova crouched, ready to dodge when Giselle smiled and disappeared with a ripple.

First hiding her scent, then her location... Would she attack from the left or the right? Would she come from above or even from behind? Nova was not certain what Giselle would do. She was a deceiving human, who would do whatever it took to—

Deceiving.

Nova bolted across the grounds just as Giselle appeared by the dome with speed Nova could not achieve right now. She could hear the way that arcane magic hummed even from afar, and she knew that it had enough power to dispel her dome.

However, Giselle could not see inside the fog. She could not see how the one-handed warrior—*Silas*—was prepared to retaliate. And while Nova did not have the strength to get her body there in time, she still had the strength to get her words to him.

"The fog will let you pass. Go!"

As Giselle struck down, Silas surged up, passing through the barrier and raising his shield. The arcane lance hit the surface, detonating the lightning Nova wove through the clouds. In a burst of brilliant gold light, Giselle was thrown back, sending her crashing into one of the large roots jutting up out of the ground with enough force to make the wood crack.

Silas stumbled back against the cloud barrier, the shield on his arm melting away as the Silver magic dissipated. He grimaced, pushing himself up, hand still gripping his sword as he tried to reorient himself.

Giselle herself was far slower in getting to her feet, not resilient enough to take a blast like that without injury. Knowing that, Nova drove herself forward, ignoring the screaming of her limbs as she crossed the distance, past Silas and the barrier, and towards Giselle on her knees. Her whip changed into a sword of ice, long and thin, with every intention of piercing through Giselle's heart.

And just as she reached Giselle, the scent of arcane reached her nose, and Nova realized her mistake too late.

She twisted, feeling pain lance through her side as a flash of golden light blurred past her. The sudden change in direction, coupled with her fatigued body, sent her tumbling roughly through dirt, with stones and roots digging into her body painfully.

Nova came to a stop at the bottom of the slope, finding herself on her back and staring up at the sky. She lay there stunned, with her vision swimming and her senses dulled. She stared at the sky swirling overhead, the clouds a blur of grays, and distantly, she recognized that she needed to get up.

She grasped at the ground, realizing she had dropped her weapon. Her fingers were numb from the overuse of magic, and the fiery pain in her side promised she had taken a grievous injury.

With all the strength she could muster, Nova lifted her head, watching as Giselle shakily pushed herself to her feet. Nova realized why she no longer had her sword as she watched Giselle rip it out from her stomach and toss it aside. The blade of ice vaporized into silver mist as it hit the ground.

"Can't believe I let you impale me twice in the stomach, you stupid bitch," Giselle muttered. The winds carried the words for Nova to hear.

Despite her injury, Giselle seemed to be faring better, and in realizing that, Nova also realized she could not win this fight. Giselle was right. Nova had no experience fighting humans, and it had cost her. She played right into Giselle's attack, misreading the situation, and—

"Nova! Get up!"

Nova blinked slowly, hearing Rowan's voice. It sounded too close, and she wondered how badly her senses were muddled.

Suddenly he was beside her, replacing the clouds in the sky. She blinked, vision coming into focus to find him leaning over her, tears in his wide, frightened eyes as he weakly pressed his hands to her side. Behind him, Silas stood, back to them and sword drawn and ready to defend them, and Rowan's mother was holding Rowan by his shoulders to support him.

Why were they not behind her barrier? She blinked several times, eyes drifting towards the clouds to find they had fallen out of their dome shape, dissipating into a pool of mist that hovered above the ground. Her breath hitched, realizing she had lost control of her magic as she fell.

Nova looked back up at Rowan, to tell him to run, but the words would not form because her body was too tired. The corners of her vision were dark like night approached. But it was not night. She knew it was death instead.

Rowan stared down at his blood-stained hands, then looked up at her. Tears ran down his cheeks, but his expression was *furious*. Nova blinked, surprise cutting through some of her hazy thoughts. She had never seen Rowan like this. Why was he—

"You promised!" Rowan shouted angrily, his voice weak and cracking as he forced out the words. "You promised to come *back* to me! You can't die here! You *promised!*"

With his words, his eyes erupted in Viridian fire, and the warm and sweet scent of his magic invaded Nova's senses. She gasped as the pain in her side lessened. Her eyes fell to Rowan's arm, where his dragon mark pulsed softly in Viridian light, matching the enchanting glow wrapped around his hands.

The darkness crawling at the edges of Nova's vision retreated, like the shadows from her dream. Except this time, the light that chased them away was not her own, but Rowan's. She sucked in a deep breath, feeling a small amount of strength return as the pain in her torso faded.

Rowan stared down at his hands, shock replacing the anger on his face as he realized he had activated his magic. Behind him, his mother mimicked his expression, her arms trembling as she helped her son stay upright.

Now no longer on the brink of death and able to think, Nova grabbed Rowan's wrist. His skin was hot against her cold fingers. He must have felt it too because the action made him jump in surprise. The fire in his eyes flickered and disappeared, the rest of his magic fading with it.

Nova met Rowan's gaze as he looked at her, and she found herself strong enough to speak. "That is enough." He had already taken injury from his magic today. She did not want to add to it.

Rowan huffed, giving her a frustrated look. "I'll do it again if you get hurt!"

Somehow, she doubted he even did it on purpose, so the threat seemed unimpressive. However, she understood the real meaning of his words, and she nodded, dropping her hand back to the ground. "I promised you. I will keep my promise."

He leveled her with a fierce look that would have pulled a smile from her in any other situation. Even in moments like this, he was always so expressive. She wanted to protect that. She wanted to protect *him*. Could she still do that and keep her promise?

Truly, she did not know, but she had to try.

Nova sucked in a deep breath, fingers digging into the dirt. Water hit her face, cold and wet from the skies overhead. It was not of her own doing, but the effect it had on her was immediate. The Silver magic in each drop soothed over her skin, kissing away some of the burn from her own magic overuse as it trickled back into her empty magic pool.

And most importantly... the magic in the sky smelled *different*.

That knowledge fueled her more than anything else, and with a grunt, Nova pushed herself up onto her elbows. Rowan sat back, giving her space as Nova assessed her injury. Blood stained the ground, but the hole in her dress showed a wound closed over, pink and tender, but no longer fatal thanks to her friend.

Carefully, she rolled over to push herself onto her knees, limbs shaking. Everything else still hurt, but as the rain continued to fall and the temperature dropped, Nova felt herself filled with hope. She promised to protect Rowan. She promised to come back.

She could not do it alone, but she did not *need* to.

Nova forced herself to her feet, eyes lifting to find Silas had engaged Giselle, likely to prevent her from attacking them altogether. Despite her injuries, Giselle still had enough control over her magic to shield herself from his attacks, parrying the swings of his sword with ribbons of arcane light. Those same ribbons were wrapped around her waist to staunch her wound, but it was clear Giselle was weakened. And angry.

Silas was clever, not giving her an opening and being far less fatigued from battle than Giselle. Additionally, he did not need to get too close, it seemed, for his sword swinging through the air could project the magic it released like an extended blade. Still, Giselle had been around for over a century, and archmagi did not live that long without learning how to use their minds.

Especially not ones like Giselle Le Du.

As she countered Silas's next attack, she whipped the other ribbon around in a wide arc. As Silas turned to cut at it, the ribbon exploded into a brilliant light, effectively blinding him as he stumbled back, disoriented.

Giselle lunged for him, hand outstretched, but Nova had been waiting, slowly gathering magic in the air above. Before Giselle could grab Silas's neck and take his life, the wind grabbed him first, dragging him away from Giselle and back towards Nova.

He shouted, surprised, as Nova deposited him beside her. She took in a ragged breath from the effort, dropping down to her knees with a pained grunt.

Giselle stared at them, lips quivering as they pulled into a wide, manic smile. "Thank you for that, Tempest. You just made my job easier."

She waved her hand as two orbs formed in front of her, likely all she could manage at once. Still, they would be enough now that Nova did not have the strength left to fight.

Giselle flexed her fingers, her smile cruel and self-satisfied. "Do you wish there was someone here to save you? Does your Silver pride allow for that? Tell me, whelp."

Nova closed her eyes and took in a deep breath, appreciating the scent of first frost and winter mornings that rolled across her senses. She looked up and bared her fangs in a fierce grin. "I do not need to wish it, for it is so. And, yes, *it fills me with pride!*"

Giselle's smile slipped off of her face just as an icy fog exploded across the valley. In a rush of cold wind, Rime the Frostweaver appeared above them in her true form. Her blonde hair was now silver, the braid cradled by a crown of snow-white horns shaped like Nova's. Her stormy cloak was pulled back, revealing layers of silvery silks and thick, glittering scales, and her wings were spread behind her, pale and coated in a beautiful, delicate frost. And above her, the sky was filled with thousands of long needles of ice, ready at her command.

With a roaring battle cry, Rime threw the ice at Giselle. Giselle was not quick enough to avoid all of them, catching several in her legs as she shielded her upper body. She screamed in pain, golden light exploding around her, bright and disorienting in the reflective, icy fog.

Rime scattered her fog with an icy gust of wind, and what remained was a plume of golden smoke where Giselle stood. Rime snarled, looking around before her head snapped to the north. "She is fleeing, the cowardly wretch!"

Nova expected her to give chase, but instead, Rime descended, landing beside her with a burst of chilly wind.

"You are not pursuing her?" Nova asked as Rime folded her wings behind her and held out her hands. Nova took them, letting Rime pull her to her feet, then inhaled sharply as Rime pulled her into a tight hug. It hurt, but it was a pain Nova would gladly endure.

After a moment, Rime pulled away and looked up at the giant tree that now stood in place of the town and then at Rowan sitting with his mother. Her gaze lingered on him for a moment before she looked back at Nova. Her expression was soft as she shook her head.

"No, I am not. For everything most important is right here."

Nova turned to look back at Rowan. He sat on the ground, clinging to his mother, the grass around him growing slowly in beautiful shades of green, interspaced with feathery ferns and golden wildflowers. He still appeared human for now, but there was no denying the way the Viridian magic around him reacted, finally free to catch up after all these years. He stared up at her with wide, viridian eyes that promised to tell her stories. Stories not yet written, but stories Nova wanted to be a part of.

Nova closed the small distance between them, dropping down gracelessly in front of him. The movement caused her to grunt painfully, but she did not regret her actions, not when it put her close to her *friend*. Rowan let go of his mother, twisting so that he could reach for Nova's hands. She met him halfway, clasping his palms in hers. His hands felt so warm, like a warm, summer heat, and she never wanted to let go.

"I kept my promise," she whispered, glancing down at their hands and then back up to him.

"Yeah, but I had to yell at you, you jerk," Rowan replied, tears running down his dirty cheeks. The words were punctuated with a broken laugh, but Nova was unsure what emotions he actually felt. They all seemed contradictory, and yet... They were all very much 'Rowan.' Despite that, he still squeezed her fingers with what strength he had.

Worriedly, Nova noted his grip was non-existent in his right hand.

Silas's voice pulled her out of her thoughts. "You know, next time you're going to throw me several meters, you could give me a heads up."

Nova looked up, meeting his gaze. He had not bothered to get up, instead propping himself up with his hand, his stump arm resting on a drawn knee. "A what?"

"A warning," Rowan clarified softly, smiling at her.

Nova sighed pitifully. Why did humans do this with words? "How does 'heads up' mean 'warning?'"

"To keep your head up is to remain alert. The phrase comes from this," Rime murmured, crouching down next to Nova and Rowan. "However, as pleased as I am to see Nova has made a friend, we must not stay here."

"She's right. We have an audience," Silas muttered, nodding towards the ruins of the town. Nova followed his gaze, seeing people peeking from the fallen walls and behind the roots. "I think folks are about to realize that Dragon Knights look an awful lot like dragons."

Nova's eyes went wide as she realized the implications of being visible in her true form. She let go of Rowan's hands in surprise, reaching up to touch her horns. "That is not good—"

"It is negligible in light of everything else," Rime said as she stood, flapping her wings. "Is there a place we can retreat to discuss our next steps?"

"The Spicer house," Silas said as he stood up, sheathing his sword. "It's far enough from town that I don't think we'll be followed by citizens, but close enough to reach quickly. Zebb's probably wondering what in the Shores is happening up here anyway."

"That's assuming Papa didn't sleep through it all," Rowan's mother said wearily as she watched Silas walk off to retrieve Nova's discarded weapon. "He's one of those that feels sedated after taking a numbing potion."

"Very well. We shall go to the Spicer house," Rime said as she helped Nova to her feet. "Can you walk? I have never seen you so injured."

"Yes," Nova replied, steadying herself. "But you will need to carry Rowan. His body is overtaxed from the magic forced out of him. He cannot move well."

"Forced out…" Rime trailed off, eyes wide as she looked back at the tree. She sucked in a breath between her teeth, then shook her head. "Tell me later. Let us leave this place."

She stooped down, touching Rowan's shoulder. "My name is Rime the Frostweaver, young one, and I am going to carry you out of here, okay?"

He nodded nervously, and Rime took that as permission to scoop him up in her arms. Nova watched them, then looked away as Silas came up beside her, holding out her hilt for her to take. She nodded in thanks, securing it at her side, although her fingers fumbled with the effort.

As they started to walk away, Nova watched Rowan turn his gaze up to the ruined town on the hill, with the tree that stood like a gravestone marker for the destruction done today. He sniffled, his despair overwhelming him once more. Without a word, Rime shifted the pressure in the skies, letting the rain fall down around them but not on them, the sound covering Rowan's pain so that he could cry in peace.

Nova chose to stay in the rainfall, the water soothing to her exhausted body. The way the droplets ran down her face made it feel as though she was sharing Rowan's tears. He had not deserved any of this, and she hated she could not take the pain away.

Together, they left behind the town of Ladisdale, its fields once again abundant with crops, its walls overtaken by roots, and its people wondering how to pick up the pieces of their lives.

Nova felt for them, for her people had once done the same, and they still had not recovered over a century later.

Chapter 23
To a Better Tomorrow

"Papa!"

Rowan jerked at his mother's voice, opening his eyes to find himself staring at the *mostly* familiar sight of his house. Moss now crawled up the stone foundation and little shoots of green stuck up in the empty garden that hugged the steps. Even the trees nearby had budding leaves on the tips as if they had finally come out of an endless winter. It was not as lush as the growth around Ladisdale's perimeter, but it was still proof that his presence had reignited the Viridian magic in the area.

He blinked slowly, trying to figure out how he got home. The last thing he remembered was staring at Ladisdale, or what remained of it, and feeling the bottomless dread in his heart in knowing that so many lives had been ruined, if not lost.

Ah, that's right. Rime was carrying him. He must have fallen asleep.

Rowan looked up to see a crest of horns glinting in the midday sun and a pair of silver eyes regarding him quietly. He studied Rime's appearance, from the crescent-shaped scar under her eye to the pattern of scales on her forehead. Idly, he noted how that differed from Nova, who had small clusters of scales on each cheek. Rime's gaze also carried weight, like she had been around for a long time.

After a moment of letting him look at her, she nodded to him slightly, a faint smile on her lips. "Just rest, young one. Your mother alerts your grandfather of our arrival."

Rowan blinked again, trying to force himself awake as he distantly heard the sound of the front door opening, followed by his mother's muffled voice.

"Is he awake now?"

Rowan inhaled at the sound of Nova's voice, craning his neck to see her. Rime huffed in amusement and turned, allowing him to see Nova leaning against Silas, her arm over his shoulders as he partially supported her weight. She looked awful, her dress in blood-stained tatters and sweat clinging to her skin. Despite that, he could see a faint hint of a smile on her lips, like she was pleased to see him.

"Hi," he whispered, his voice rough and scratchy.

"Hi," she said back.

"Will you be okay?" It was all he could think to ask, given how she looked. Distantly, he knew she wouldn't be able to lie to him about it anyway.

To his relief, she nodded, eyes closing. "With rest, yes."

"Half-dragons are resilient compared to humans without dragon blood," Rime explained. "The dragon side of us grants us faster recovery and hardier bodies. Despite that, she will not be able to return to her duty for many days, I think."

Nova lifted her gaze, looking haunted at that thought. Quietly, barely audible, Rowan heard her whisper, "She will be upset. I have already neglected my duty for many days."

"Who?" Rowan asked with concern, but Nova's response was to shake her head, looking away pensively.

Rowan pursed his lips, looking up at Rime for answers to find her with a sharp expression, eyes narrowed and jaw set.

"Did you?" Rime asked pointedly, her words having an edge to them. "Or did you redefine your duty, like you told me you would?"

Nova looked up at her, lips parting in surprise.

Rime inclined her head, continuing, "You fulfilled the request of an elder dragon, Nova. You found and saved the Viridian heir, even when we thought there was none left. All of our people will rejoice for what you have done. Her anger will be drowned by their gratitude, for the Viridian clan *lives*. Today marks a victory that decades of slaying undead could not accomplish. Tell me now, do you think you neglected your duty?"

Nova inhaled deeply, gaze focusing on Rowan. "No. I do not. But she will."

"We shall see, then, if our elder agrees with her," Rime replied carefully. "Regardless, I am very proud of you, Nova. You were so lost when we last spoke, and now you are the most found that I have ever seen."

"I do not understand," Nova replied, tilting her head. "What do you mean?"

"Tell me, how did you find out that Rowan was half-dragon and not cursed?" Rime asked carefully.

Rowan stiffened, realizing Nova would have to admit how much she almost messed up. He glanced back nervously, making sure his mother wasn't in earshot, before looking back at Nova.

Nova frowned, eyes downcast. "I... went to take his arm. I thought that if I removed it, I could release the curse and he would live."

Rime lifted a brow, and Rowan noted she did not seem surprised by this. Silas looked like he bit into rotten fish, though. Fortunately, he didn't do anything like drop Nova.

"And then?" Rime asked, encouraging her to continue.

Nova lowered her head, her bangs hiding her face from view. "I could not do it. It hurt in a way I have never felt, and I could not do it. But Rowan... he was not angry with me. He told me he was still my friend."

Nova sucked in a shuddered breath, and although Rowan couldn't see her face, he wondered if she was trying not to cry. "Then Rowan told me of his dream, and I realized I had made a mistake. That I had almost hurt my friend."

"There," Rime breathed, a sense of satisfaction in her tone. *"That* is what I mean."

Nova shook her head, not looking up. "I almost hurt him, Rime."

"Yes. You have been told all your life that your only duty is to slay. And yet you did not. Your heart told you it was wrong, and you stayed your sword. Was it perfect? No. But you still did it. You redefined your duty and found your heart along the way." Rime smiled, pride etched onto her face. "I should know, I felt it in the skies."

Nova stiffened, eyes wide as she looked up at Rime. To Rowan's surprise, a pale pink blossomed across her face. "What?"

Rime smirked, lifting one delicate, frost-colored brow. "Do you think you can create a blizzard out of heartache and the *Frostweaver* would not notice? How do you think I got here so quickly if I were not already on my way when I saw your message in the sky?"

Nova looked mortified, and even Rowan felt embarrassed for her. Graciously, Rime didn't linger on it. "Remember, Nova. You chose kindness, and I think that suits you."

Nova sucked in a shaky breath, tears in her eyes. She looked at Rowan, a touch of uncertainty on her features. She lingered for a moment, a question on the tip of her tongue. Then finally, she asked, "Will you teach me how to be a good friend?"

The sincerity in her request made Rowan feel something he didn't quite have a name for. The best he could describe it was like a certain kind of dismay at the vulnerability in her words. It made him want to reassure her that she hadn't messed up like he suspected she thought she had.

There was a lot he didn't know about Nova, like why she was shackled by duty and never given a chance to be herself, but he wanted to find out. He wanted to learn who she was, and who she wanted to be. And he felt like that maybe she wanted that for him, too.

"I don't have much experience in friendship either," Rowan admitted, not breaking his gaze with her. "But I'd like to figure it out together."

She perked up, brows lifting. "Truly?"

Rowan nodded, giving her a tiny, sincere smile. "Yeah. But you have to admit I won the duel for your friendship."

She blinked, then to Rowan's surprise and delight, she laughed. It was soft, barely audible, but he heard it nonetheless. It was a beautiful sound, one that Rowan hoped to definitely hear again in the future, without restraint.

"Very well," Nova said with a tired smile. "I, Nova the Tempest, concede to you, Rowan Spicer, in a duel for my friendship."

"I never thought I would hear of the day you lost a duel," Rime said softly, amusement on her features. "To a Viridian, no less."

"I have lost, but... it does not feel like a loss," Nova admitted, glancing away with that tiny smile still on her lips.

"Huh," Rowan murmured as a particular memory came to mind. "'Sometimes losses can be victories, too.' Right, Silas?"

Silas chuckled, the corner of his eye crinkling with amusement. "Not quite how I meant that statement, but, hey, that works, too."

Two hours later, Rowan found himself in the crowded living space of his house, a lingering scent of cooked fish in the air. He managed a few bites of food earlier, but admittedly, it took a lot of effort to chew. More than once, he dozed off, only to jerk awake at every little sound. He felt so tired, but he didn't feel like he could rest, even with Rime standing guard at the front door.

His mother had dressed Nova's wounds with some salve she had saved for emergencies. Nova looked as tired as Rowan felt but seemed to have more energy to eat. She wore Rime's cloak in place of her own, covering the blood stains and rips on her dress.

His grandfather had slept through most of the afternoon due to the effects of the numbing potion. Rowan didn't find that too surprising since their house was far enough away from town that the explosions probably sounded like distant thunder.

However, Rowan's magic had touched him, too, and he said his knee felt great. Given how much destruction Rowan's magic had done, he was grateful for every bit of evidence it wasn't completely like that. He still wished things had turned out differently, though.

His grandfather had cried a fair bit as he learned what happened, especially when he saw the state of Rowan's arm. He asked Rowan if it hurt. Rowan had deflected by saying he just felt like he needed some sleep. It did hurt, though.

Now, Rowan found himself staring at his reflection in the tiny hand mirror his mother owned. Viridian eyes that glowed softly stared back at him, looking just like the ones of the man in his dream. It felt surreal, but it also felt...like he had just unlocked a part of him he could never access before.

That was the only thing that had changed, at least so far. He wondered what else would, though. Especially given what Nova and Rime looked like without their disguises.

His gaze lingered on Nova, who sat on the floor with her back against the wall, eyes closed as she tried to rest. Her tail was in her lap, and the sunlight coming through the window reflected off of her horns. Before, when she was disguised as a human, he felt like she stood out but for the wrong reasons. Now, however, with the scales running down her arms and legs, she looked like she stood out for the *right* reasons. That was the best way he could word it. She looked *right*. And as he thought about all the things he didn't like about himself, he wondered if he might someday look *right,* too.

It was too much to think heavily on, so instead he put down the mirror and returned his attention to the plate of fish in his lap. He pinched off a piece and tried to force down another bite, grimacing because he just had no appetite.

Silas walked up and sat down on the floor beside him. "Don't like my cooking? I'll have you know I've been practicing cooking fish for seventeen years."

Rowan offered a faint smile, all he could muster in response to the joke. "S'not that. Just... really exhausted."

"I know," Silas replied. "You'll be leaving here soon, I'm told. Then you can rest."

"I... haven't paid much attention to the conversation," Rowan admitted quietly, watching as his mother and grandfather flitted between the rooms, packing what they could in preparation for leaving. "Where are we going?"

"The dragons have some islands... somewhere. They claim they're only reachable by members of the dragon clans. Living ones, I'm told.

They'll take you and your family. Rime confirmed it won't be a problem."

"But we'll have to say goodbye to this place," Rowan said quietly, looking around. It wasn't that he had a great deal of attachment to his home, but it was all he ever knew. This little house held all his memories, both good and bad.

"Yeah. You will," Silas agreed, looking down at the floor. "You'll be okay, though."

Rowan sighed. He wasn't so sure he would be okay. Not because of that, but because of *everything*. Maybe he would be, but how long would that take?

At least he'd have his family with him. And Nova. And... He sucked in a breath, looking at Silas. "Wait... what about you?"

Silas lifted a brow at him. "What about me?"

"What will you do?"

Silas hummed, looking up at the ceiling. "Y'know, that's a good question. I've been trying to figure out if my pact with Avelore's complete now. I helped protect you, but how long was I supposed to do it, I wonder?"

Rowan shifted uneasily, pinching another piece of fish and putting it in his mouth. Worry that Silas only befriended him out of obligation began to seep in, adding to the swirl of unsettling emotions already weighing him down. "...I see."

Hearing the change in his tone, Silas looked over at him. "I see I was too subtle. You're misinterpreting what I'm saying."

"Huh?" Rowan looked over at him, confused.

"I'm asking you what you want me to do, Rowan. The only thing left for me here is to help those displaced by what those lich followers did. Which I'll definitely do—"

Rowan inhaled sharply, realizing where Silas was going with this.

"—but that may not be the best use of my skills. I'm thinking maybe helping some dragons win some war against a lich might be better. What do you think?"

Rowan couldn't hide the tiny smile forming on his lips as he played with the food on his plate. "You were pretty awesome out there today. I think they'd be happy to have you."

Silas chuckled, shrugging a shoulder. "I'm no half-dragon, but I have a few tricks up my sleeve. But the real question is, do you want me there?"

Rowan stared down at his food and then looked at Silas to see him regarding Rowan carefully. Rowan didn't deliberate on his answer. He knew it before Silas even asked.

"I never had a father. Can't really call someone I never met my father, and well, I have questions on how he handled things anyway," Rowan said quietly, pulling a piece of bone out of his fish. "But when I think of the word 'dad,' sometimes I see your face. And... that makes me really happy."

Silas turned his head, his eye patch and beard obscuring his face slightly. Despite that, Rowan could still see the big smile on his face. "Guess that's settled, then."

Rowan smiled too, eyes falling to the plate of half-eaten fish in his lap. Maybe he could eat a bit more. "Yeah. Maybe the dragons have a tablut board we can borrow?"

Silas laughed quietly. "Maybe they do."

"I think that's everything," Sorrel said as she put down the last bag by the door. Most of what they wanted to take were related to their craft:

potion ingredients, tools, and the like, as well as their recipe books, kept preserved all these years thanks to enchantments.

Her father nodded, folding his arms. "Then we're ready?"

Sorrel hesitated, looking at the room around her. Rowan was asleep on her father's chair, curled up under Nova's cloak. Silas had stepped outside to talk to Rime, and Nova was out there as well, having woken up from her nap.

Now with nothing else to occupy her, Sorrel found her feelings very loud in the silence of the room, pressing up against the walls of her heart and banging to be let free.

She swallowed, fisting her hand in the skirt of her dress. "Papa... will you take the bags outside? I'll... wake up Rowan."

Her father regarded her for a moment and then reached over and squeezed her shoulder affectionately. "Sure. I'll be outside. But... be easy on yourself, Sorrel. None of what happened is your fault."

She sucked in a long, deep breath, letting it out in a weary sigh. "...Thanks, Papa."

He left the room, grabbing up two of the bags as he went, and then Sorrel walked over and crouched down in front of her sleeping son. He had finally finished most of his food, the plate now on the floor. Sorrel resisted the urge to pick it up and take it to the kitchen. There wasn't a point to that now. Instead, she pushed it aside and reached up, brushing Rowan's hair out of his face.

He stirred but didn't quite wake, making a soft noise of protest. Sorrel pursed her lips, hating that she had to wake him up when she knew all he wanted was to sleep.

"Rowan? I need you to wake up, bean."

It was the first time in years she'd called him by his pet name, always feeling like she lost the privilege to be that personal as he got older and more distant. Now though...it just felt right.

He inhaled, opening his eyes to mere slits, glowing green looking at her through his eyelashes. It took him a moment to really come-to enough to speak, however. "Mom?"

She smiled slightly, watching the glow highlight the freckles on his cheeks. "Hey... I know you're tired, but we're about ready to leave. Everyone's waiting outside. Can you stand?"

He sighed again, reaching up with his good arm to rub his eyes. "Not sure. I can try?"

He started to sit up but stilled when Sorrel gently touched his wrist. "I... before we go. I have something I need to say."

Rowan blinked slowly and then nodded, sitting back against the chair. "Okay. I'm listening."

He sounded uncertain, brows pinching together as he nervously began to pick at the fraying end of his ruined tunic.

Sorrel watched him for a moment and then reached forward and squeezed his knee reassuringly. "I... know things have not been great. I wasn't the best mother, and I hid a lot from you."

He looked at her, pursing his lips pensively as he waited for her to continue.

She sighed, doing her best to remain composed. This was important. She had things she needed to say, and they were things he needed to hear. "Everything that happened today were things I never expected. I almost saw my worst nightmare come true. When that green fire came out of you, I thought I would lose you."

Rowan shook his head. "You saved me, Mom. You made that counter potion, and that's what saved me."

"I got lucky," Sorrel said quietly, lowering her gaze. "I got *incredibly* lucky, and I had help. But you still got hurt, though."

"I'm okay," Rowan insisted. "I mean... I'll be okay. We're going to be okay, Mom."

Sorrel nodded, squeezing her eyes shut as she held back tears. "I hope so. That's all I want. I want us to be okay."

She meant it more than just physically. She wanted *them* to be okay. She wanted him to know she loved him, and she wanted to be better for him. She wanted them to be safe and happy. She didn't know what it would take to get there, but she was determined to try. For the first time, everything was laid out in front of her, and she felt like she could *try*. She just didn't know how to articulate that to him.

"Is...that really all you want?"

Sorrel froze, eyes snapping open at the tiny way he positioned that question like he was terrified of the answer. She looked up at him to find him regarding her with every bit of fear in those Viridian eyes of his, and suddenly, she realized *what* he was asking.

She pushed herself up and leaned forward, wrapping her arms around his shoulders. He hiccuped, burying his face into her neck as he shook, his fears spilling out for them both to see. The words came to her easily, both what she wanted to say and what he needed to hear.

"That's really all I want," Sorrel whispered, pressing a kiss to his dirty cheek. "Because the only other thing I've ever wanted just as much was a child of my own, and he's right here, as beautiful as the day he was born."

He cried harder, his good arm reaching up to fist into her clothes, and she cried with him, clinging to him like he was her life. They were going to be okay. Sorrel Spicer promised herself that.

It took a few minutes for Rowan and his mother to both compose themselves, clinging to each other as they cried. When they finally pulled away, Rowan felt slightly better, and the smile on his mother's face indicated she felt the same.

When he tried to stand, he found he was able to, but he was wobbly on his feet, and walking unassisted was out of the question. His mother pulled his arm over her shoulder, helping him get to the door. When they got onto the veranda, Rowan stopped, staring at the sight at the bottom of the stairs. There stood his grandfather, Silas, Nova, and Rime, along with someone he'd never seen before.

The man was tall, dressed in long robes in shades of crimson and red, with dark skin like the people of Acari in the south. However, instead of having brown or black hair like Rowan had read about in his books, this man had long, brilliant red hair that was woven into many braids and wrapped around the top of his head.

Everyone looked up at Rowan, and then Rime decoupled herself from the group to help him down the stairs. Once Rowan was close enough, the newcomer clasped his hands together and bowed his head. "It is an honor to meet you, Viridian one."

Rowan blinked at him and then looked at Nova who walked up to trade places with Rime, wrapping her arm around Rowan to keep him steady. Too tired to feel shy about leaning against her, Rowan turned his attention back to the person greeting him. "Oh... thank you. Um, who are you?"

The man lifted his head and smiled slightly as he pulled back the sleeve of his robe, showing a symbol of flames on his left forearm. It glowed like ember coals, giving the appearance that it was too hot to touch. Rowan blinked at it, then his brows lifted as he realized it was a dragon mark like his own on the opposite arm.

"I am Ember the Burning Pyre, one of the surviving members of the Vermillion clan. I am here to escort you to our refuge at the request of the Frostweaver. It is my way of showing gratitude to the Tempest for freeing my brother from undeath today."

"Oh..." Rowan said sadly, realizing that Ember meant the dragon that Nova fought in the square earlier. "I'm... I'm so sorry for your loss."

"Thank you, but today it is not a loss. It is a recovery," Ember replied graciously, bowing his head again. "Now that introductions are made, I shall prepare for us to travel."

Without another word, he walked down the path towards the main road. Rowan watched him for a moment and then looked at Nova. "Hey... every clan has a mark, right?"

Nova nodded, looking down at him. "Yes. Each clan has a mark. Vermillion members always have the mark on their left arm."

Rowan pursed his lips, then curiously asked, "Where's yours?"

Somewhere behind him, he heard Rime snort. And Rowan was smart enough to realize that if Rime was amused, then the location was somewhere he was going to regret asking about. Or more specifically, he was going to regret asking *Nova* about it.

"It is on our stomachs," Nova replied honestly, fingers hooking into one of the larger rips in her dress and pulling slightly.

Despite himself, Rowan followed the movement, gaze landing on the partial view of a spiral around her navel, the silvery lines shimmering like mist. Interestingly, he could also see part of a scar across the skin just below the mark. Rowan flushed, glancing away quickly as he felt the heat spread from his face to his ears. "T-that's neat!"

He winced as his voice cracked. Then, he blushed harder when he heard Rime and Silas both start laughing. Hadn't he been through enough today? At least Nova didn't understand why—

"I think I now understand what you mean by 'cute expressions,'" Nova said, letting go of her dress and adjusting Rime's cloak back in place. "I think it is cute when your face turns pink. It is like the sunsets that I find pretty."

Rowan pressed his good hand over his face like it might hide him from his embarrassment. Nova hummed in a way that sounded amused, lightly squeezing him with her arm. "Come. I believe Ember is ready to take us home."

Rowan blinked, then glanced at Ember, who was now on the road facing them. He didn't look any different, standing there looking at them. Embarrassment somewhat forgotten, Rowan lowered his hand from his mouth and asked, "What do you mean?"

Before Nova could answer, there was a rush of heat as Ember wrapped himself in bright red flames. Rowan's eyes went wide as Ember's form grew larger and larger until a great Vermillion dragon stood on the road.

In dragon form, Ember was the same size as his brother, but without any black on his vermillion scales. He had great horns that curved out of his head, the tips flickering like candles. Flames rolled off of his wings like they were feathers, and fire raced down his tail like it was part of the spine. With a flap of his wings, Ember extinguished all of his flames, then laid down on the ground, his head resting over his forelimbs.

The transformation caused his grandfather to shout in alarm, and his mother gasped loudly. At this point, Rowan had seen too much today to be more than mildly surprised.

Nova looked back at Rowan with a faint smile. "Rime and I cannot carry all of you ourselves, and the skies are very cold. Ember can help with both of these things."

"Let us make haste. The longer we wait, the more we risk the lich's followers seeking us out again," Rime said, gesturing toward Ember to indicate everyone should go to him.

Rowan blinked and then realized what Nova meant. He sputtered. "We're—we're riding on his back?"

Okay, maybe he could still be surprised after all.

Ember rumbled softly, the sound vibrating across the ground as he flicked his tail. Rowan had no idea if that was in amusement, exasperation, or something else. Beside him, Silas shook his head. "First time for everything, I guess. Having a damn lot of 'first times' today, though."

Rowan failed to find words as Rime walked over and picked him up with ease, carrying him towards Ember since he could barely walk. The others followed them, his family with their travel bags, and Silas and Nova with their weapons. Ember waited patiently as they climbed onto his back. Rowan and Nova sat near Ember's neck, and his mother, Grandpa Zebb, and Silas sat behind his wings, each holding onto a travel bag.

Once everyone was seated, Rime created a thick pool of mist that Nova wove into several tendrils that looped around them and secured everyone in place. They were solid like ropes but soft and moist. Grandpa Zebb poked at the ones around him excitedly, like he couldn't believe they were real.

Rowan watched him and then lifted his gaze back to his house. Was he really about to leave his life behind? ...Was he ready for what lay ahead? He shuddered, anxious on top of everything else he was feeling.

He felt Nova rest a hand on his shoulder, and he turned to her, seeing her regarding him carefully. "Surely you do not tremble because it is cold?"

"Nervous," Rowan admitted, rubbing his hand over his scarred arm, feeling the bumpy and uneven skin underneath. He offered her an uncertain smile. "Maybe scared of not knowing what lies ahead."

Nova made a noise of understanding. "I cannot imagine how you feel, but I do know what it is like to be uncertain. I felt it today when I was trying to protect you. However... I felt better when I smelled Rime's magic and realized she had responded to my signal in the sky. I knew I was not alone."

Nova hesitated, then offered, "Perhaps it helps for you to know you are also not alone? You have your family and your... friend."

Rowan blinked at her and then smiled, this time more genuinely. "Yeah. It does help. I couldn't do this without them. Or without you. Thank you."

Her face lit up, clearly pleased at that, and Rowan chuckled. "See? Being a good friend isn't that hard. You're a natural, Nova."

She wasn't prepared for his compliment, her mouth falling open in surprise. It looked kind of cute with her fangs, if he had to be honest, and it was fair payback for her earlier comment about him blushing. He grinned at her and then looked away to let her collect herself as Rime took to the air and signaled for Ember to follow. With a great flap of his wings, Ember rose into the skies, the heat of his magic cushioning them all from the cold bite of the wind.

Rowan looked down at his home, watching it grow smaller and smaller. In the distance, he could see how the green faded back to gray, showing where the effects of his earlier magic ended. He twisted, seeing the ruins of Ladisdale over the treetops. The great tree grown from his magic reached for the sky and cast shadows on the nearby hills. It was haunting and beautiful at the same time, a reminder of the power he held and the lengths the lich would go to to take it from him.

With a deep breath, Rowan turned forward and closed his eyes, hoping this flight would lead him to a better tomorrow, and maybe one day, a better one for everyone else, too.

Epilogue

The Viridian Dream returned one last time.

He stood in the swirling darkness, hearing the hushed whispers heckle him from all directions. They told him they would come for him again, that he would never know peace. They would find him, and they would drown him.

Rowan shrugged away from the spindly fingers coming from the shadows, lifting his gaze to where he knew Osier the Life Walker would be. But this time, when Rowan looked up, he found not a man before him, but the silhouette of a Viridian dragon.

Through the shadows, Rowan could make out a great set of horns made of wisteria branches, their flowers dangling low to the ground. Green leaf-shaped scales glittered through the darkness, and the wings folded against his back looked to be covered in flowers. Osier's viridian eyes glowed softly, bright against the shadows pressing in around them.

They stared at each other as the shadows closed in, slowly coating Osier and wrapping themselves around Rowan's neck. They dragged

Rowan to his knees, but he refused to give in. Not because of Osier, but because of what he knew would come next.

The clouds flashed once in brilliant amethyst, and light broke out across the sky, shattering the darkness. The shadows scampered away, leaving behind lush fields and distant forests. For a brief moment, Rowan could clearly see the Viridian dragon who sired him, from the rich green of his scales to the gentle lavender of the flowers on his horns and wings. Osier the Life Walker inclined his head and then disappeared in a swirl of Viridian smoke.

Behind him stood Nova, Silver fire dancing off of her scales and a fierce, proud smile on her face. Her tattered wings were folded behind her back, and her horns looked like a regal crown upon her head. She was radiant like the sun, but not blinding, and she exuded a warmth that washed over Rowan, making his skin tingle pleasantly.

Nova stepped forward, her hand outstretched for him to take. Lightning flashed across the distant sky, with rumbling thunder that vibrated deep within him. The wind whipped at his hair playfully, warm and misty, a prelude to the approaching storm.

Rowan's gaze fell to her outstretched hand. He understood now. What Nova represented was more than just 'saving' him from darkness. She represented the truth that had been hidden from him. She allowed him to finally learn who he was and get a glimpse into who he had the *potential* to be.

Nova was the catalyst. Maybe Osier led her to Ladisdale, but it was still her actions that unraveled the threads holding Rowan down. It was still her desire to be his friend that let them find each other. She saved him in more ways than he could count, and he suspected that, in a way, he did the same for her.

Rowan sucked in a deep breath and reached for Nova's hand. This time, he didn't wake up. This time, his fingers found hers. And this time, she pulled him to his feet as the last of the shadows disappeared.

EPILOGUE

Rowan Spicer, the last of the Viridian clan, stood before Nova the Tempest, with his dragon mark on his arm glimmering in Viridian green and the wind spinning around them, laced with vibrant leaves and pale flower blossoms. He smiled up at her, his fingers curled over hers and Viridian fire in his eyes.

They both turned towards the approaching storm, its rolling clouds and silver rainfall slowly crawling over the field they stood in. Underneath the nurturing sky, a new forest was forming, its carpet thick and its trees reaching towards the heavens. Rowan wondered what kinds of things could bloom after such a storm. He wanted to find out.

Without a word, he walked forward, and Nova fell into place beside him, their fingers still interlocked. Together, they walked hand in hand through the grassy field towards the storm, leaving behind a trail of beautiful flowers and swirling mist in their wake.

It was nightfall by the time Giselle found herself past the borders of the Decaying Mountains, safe in her own territory. At this point, she had to animate her own limbs with magic, her injuries so severe that it had crippled her movements. She could no longer feel the pain, the shock making her body numb, but that was for the best. If she could feel a fraction of her injuries, she probably would collapse under it all.

Undead shambled around her as she hobbled back to the fortress. Their smell hit her like a stone wall. Normally, she filtered the putrid scent of decay with her magic, but she was too tired to do it. She vomited instead.

With an angry snarl, Giselle wiped her sleeve across her face and continued, the heat in her eyes daring *anyone* to even so much as look at her. None did, of course, all staring straight ahead as she limped by.

Giselle moved quietly through the halls of the fortress, her steps causing uneven echoes in the corridors. To think that despite all of her planning and effort, she lost both the Tempest and the Viridian whelp. She expected to have at least obtained or killed one of them, but to lose both had not been something she thought could happen.

When the Tempest left the battlefields weeks ago, Giselle had known it was for something important, *especially* when her agents reported seeing the Tempest in southern Bascor where the Viridian effects still lingered. For the first time in years, Giselle had reason to put down her research and oversee things herself because this was an opportunity she hadn't wanted to lose.

The Tempest led them right to the hidden Viridian heir, and yet... the Tempest was also the reason Giselle now returned empty-handed. Giselle had assumed the 'prodigy' rumors were simply the dragons' way of saying the Tempest excelled at using her magic.

And, oh, she did, but not in the ways Giselle expected. There was something different about Nova the Tempest, and now Giselle had many questions to ponder on what *truly* made her special. She potentially had some answers, but those would need to wait. For now, she had to report that the Viridian clan lived and that she failed to convert Osier's offspring.

She didn't even get to kill him.

The only thing that went *right* during this entire ordeal was that the Potion of Exaltation worked. The way the boy's body and magic responded to it was exactly what she wanted. Had she been able to control his mind and force him to kill himself, she was certain it would have warped the Viridian magic pool just like what happened to Golden magic one hundred and fifty years ago.

It would take a significant amount of time to make another potion, but now at least she knew it was the *right* one.

EPILOGUE

What would the world be like if all the pools of magic evolved? Would humanity evolve again? Would dragons or another race? What world could they create, if magic could be *redefined?*

She exited her thoughts as she stepped inside of an antechamber, staring through the open doorway into the much larger room. Sconces lined the walls, glowing softly with gold fire and casting shadows on the floor, but the largest source of light was coming from the throne in the center of the room.

The figure sitting on it was mostly humanoid, lithe with twisted black horns and black diamond-shaped scales going down his visible arm. His tail lay curled around him on the floor, black in color, with two ridges running down the back. His hair was white and long, pooling in his lap as were his robes, and his head was bowed as if he were asleep or lost in thought.

However, his entire right side had taken on the appearance of a blackened, petrified tree, with branches coming out of his body and roots digging under his skin. The tree was void of leaves, but had several large blue blossoms that glowed softly in Viridian light. As much as Giselle hated the sight, she still admired the tenacity of such a curse.

"I have returned," Giselle said quietly, rousing the lich from his thoughts. "The potion worked, but I failed to acquire the Viridian heir. The Silver clan has him now. The Tempest was stronger than I expected. Our losses outweigh our gains."

"Not... quite," the lich replied in a smooth lilt, lifting his head. Pinpricks of blue light glowed softly as his gaze landed on Giselle, his star-shaped pupils regarded her intently. "Breaking Avelore's seal has awakened the stagnant Viridian magic in the world."

He paused, turning his head towards his petrified hand, and Giselle's eyes widened as his fingers twitched for the first time in over a decade. "It seems that the revival of Viridian magic has begun to undo the curse that Osier the Life Walker left on me with his dying breath."

Theofanis the Visionary, the first Elder of the Golden clan, and the reason for humanity's magical evolution a hundred and fifty years ago, smiled as a petal from one of the blossoms broke loose and fluttered down to the ground, burning away in Viridian light.

"It is only a matter of time before I regain the use of magic once again, and I have had many years to think about what I wish to do with it."

Acknowledgements

I want to thank the Orb for their support, especially Thalaric, Shade, and Whod99, and to lkwritesthings for their insights. A huge thanks to my spouse who spared me no criticism when reading, and of course, to Aiole Sauce for her assistance in illustrating and promoting this book. And last but not least, thank you to everyone who heard I was writing an original series about ~~autistic, queer~~ dragons and got excited, who joined the community, and who had their favorite clan picked out before the book even launched. Your enthusiasm and support kept me going forward, and now, I have finally published my first book.

About the Author

One day, Leah Frog had an epiphany: they could take the magical ideas bouncing around in their head and put them into words so people could read them. Who knew? Anyway, Leah Frog loves to write and illustrate fantasy, especially if they can put it through a queer lens. They also love hearing from readers as much as they love frogs (which is a lot). You can check out their website, leahfrog.com for other works and links to their social media.

Content Warnings

1. The Life Walker: Death

2. The Cursed Baby: Death, famine, war

3. The Message: Violence, death, war

4. Rowan Spicer: –

5. Routines: War

6. Petrichor: Decomposition/gore, bullying/assault, language

7. The Nova: –

8. The Taste of Blackberries: –

9. No Good Choices: PTSD, panic attack, arguments

10. Conflictions: –

11. The Viridian Curse: –

12. Friends with the Sky: –

13. Quality Time: –

14. Speculations: –

15. The Right Choice: –

16. Who Deserves Kindness: –

17. Nova, the Friend: Threat of death, emotional breakdown

18. Unwitting Betrayal: Death, gore, injury, violence, language

19. The Tempest: Injury, gore, violence

20. The Last Viridian: Injury, emotional distress/trauma

21. Answers: Emotional distress/trauma, death

22. Duplicity: Death, near-death experiences, violence, injury, gore

23. To a Better Tomorrow: –

24. Epilogue: Injury, gore

Printed in Great Britain
by Amazon